Sabine Durrant has worked as a journalist for the *Independent*, the *Sunday Times*, the *Observer* and the *Guardian*. She lives in south London. *The Great Indoors* is her second novel.

Praise for *Having It and Eating It*:

'Durrant pulls off the Austen-like trick of bringing us nose to nose with a micro-class of society . . . appealing understated wit' *Guardian*

'This novel is made by the well-observed details, the conversational prose and the sharp humour, along with Durrant's particular talent for the cadences of spoken English . . . Always good fun' *Observer*

'Astute and well-written, with a marvellous twist towards the end, this is a must for all women in the throes of, or about to embark on, motherhood' *Marie Claire*

'Entertaining twist on the usual betrayed wife story, written with great pace and humour' *Sunday Mirror*

'Sabine Durrant has a lovely, wry way with words' *New Statesman*

'Sabine Durrant writes with a lovely mixture of wit and truth. An engaging and accomplished novel' Mavis Cheek

'Extremely well observed, funny and touching' Marika Cobbold

'Durrant writes about the vulnerability peculiar to women with young children with honesty and humour' Elizabeth Buchan, *Sunday Times*

By the same author

Having It and Eating It

the
great
indoors

SABINE DURRANT

timewarner
paperbacks

A *Time Warner* Paperback

First published in Great Britain as a paperback original in 2003
by Time Warner Paperbacks

Extracts from *Junk Style* by Melanie Molesworth and *The Relaxed Home*
by Atlanta Bartlett used by kind permission of Ryland Peters & Small.
Extract from *Nina Campbell's Decorating Secrets* by Nina Campbell
used by kind permission of Random House US. Extract from
Interior Transformations by Ann Grafton used by kind permission
of Jacqui Small. Copyright Ann Grafton. Every effort has been made
to contact remaining copyright holders and to clear reprint
permissions. If notified the publisher will be happy to rectify any
omission in future editions.

A CIP catalogue record for this book is
available from the British Library.

ISBN 0 7515 3350 5

Typeset in Berkeley by M Rules
Printed and bound in Great Britain by
Clays Ltd, St Ives plc

Time Warner Paperbacks
An imprint of
Time Warner Books UK
Brettenham House
Lancaster Place
London WC2E 7EN

www.TimeWarnerBooks.co.uk

'You want to have some fun?
Walk into an antique shop
and say, "What's new?"'

Henry Goodman

part one

chapter one

the drawing room

'Remember that in a social situation a sofa
never pulls its full weight.'

The Essential House Book
by Terence Conran
(Conran Octopus, 1994)

MARTHA'S SISTERS sometimes say that her furniture is her
real family. They also say she 'doesn't like' children. Martha
gets annoyed by this. 'I have nothing against children,' she
says, though secretly it is the glibness of the phrase that disturbs her, as if one could feel about children as one does
about roll-mop herrings or Japanese cinema. Because the
truth is she does quite like her nephews and her niece, and
even the occasional offspring of one or two of her friends.
The older ones at least. It is more that children don't fit into
her world: the small rented flat she has come to call home,
'her space', with its few carefully chosen objects, its soft

creamy sofa, its ash-blond seagrass, its aura of oatmeal and sand. And children have no place at all in her shop.

Martha Bone Antiques is, for the most part, like the grave: a fine and private place. In the week Martha can renovate and distress in peace, visited mainly by dealers who can be relied upon to be aloof. But the shop is also next door to a café and at weekends it is subject to a certain amount of overspill. Martha is not averse to these Pokers and Browsers – who fall in love with things and shell out for them so easily – or even their husbands, too big for themselves and awkward, like teenage boys visiting relatives at Christmas. But their children are a different matter. Martha would prefer to sit over her accounts on a Saturday, at her Swedish-style painted desk, listening to the Afternoon Play, but she has learnt that a sharp intake of breath from the corner isn't enough. Instead, at the first sight of a grumpy chocolate-rimmed face or a muddy wellington boot with ladybird spots, she jumps up, depresses the button of her Roberts radio, and discreetly (or so she likes to think) *hovers* until the small people (what a phrase is that? she thinks) make smeary faces in her eighteenth-century gilt mirrors (French) or jump on the Victorian armchairs (tastefully reupholstered in gingham or plaid) or climb up the nineteenth-century rocking horse (in, as its label is delighted to announce, its original paintwork).

'Sorry,' she says then. Her tone is light, but her grip on their clambering ankles like steel. 'Bit fragile,' she adds. She ruffles their hair. She steers them to the door, outside which their scooters and bikes lie flat and abandoned across the pavement like dead horses on a battlefield. She tries to think about the money their parents might spend. She tries not to think, 'What fresh hell is this?'

On this particular Saturday, though, the shop is childless and shut. There is a sign on the door which says 'Closed due to unexpected family circumstances'. It is a very small sign, and the woman who is peering through the window, eyes squinting in irritation as she tries to make out the exact proportions of a cherrywood cupboard, can be forgiven for missing it. It is a tag really, a brown tag. The same type of brown tag that Martha uses to price her distressed or renovated items, to draw attention, in her neat flowing script, to an artefact's attractions while drawing it away from the price. As in, if the woman could only read it from the step, 'An unusual and delightful nineteenth-century French cherrywood armoirette, £1,200'.

Martha's labels are threaded with a piece of green and brown tartan ribbon, which she then attaches to a piece of furniture, lacing it through a convenient crack in the wood, or winding it around a handle or poking it through a hole in some filigree. Without thinking, befuddled by anxiety, at three in the morning, she has slipped a piece of this ribbon through this label too. But there was nowhere on the door to tie it, so she stuck it to the glass with a piece of Sellotape. It is a charming ribbon, but it looks forlorn and useless here, as if family circumstances are somehow beyond it. 'Pretty and unusual nineteenth-century circumstances: French' are more its thing.

*

3

Martha and her stepbrother, Ian, are standing in the sitting room of their parents' house. Ian is wearing a suit, but he has taken off his shoes and is looking oddly denuded in his socks, curling and uncurling his maroon nyloned toes against the shag of a Persian rug. The lower rims of his eyes are pinker than they should be, and there are traces of dried spittle along the middle of his lower lip, a ragged line of dashes, but otherwise there is little to tell that he has been up all night. He has one of those faces that always looks as if it has been up all night: the skin along the neck translucent and papery (but bumpy like recycled paper), an extra couple of creases under the eyes. He hasn't had bad eczema for years, but he's rubbing his hands up and down against the rough edge of his jacket pocket.

Ian says, 'The thing is, with kids, you've got to go scheduled. Go, easyJet, all that: thing of the past I'm afraid.'

Martha says, 'I went Go once. From Stansted.'

'That's the problem,' says Ian. 'Stansted. You really want Gatwick.'

It is 10 o'clock in the morning, seven hours since Ian rang Martha to tell her of his father's death, and they have gone beyond the immediacy of the situation. Martha wonders if they ever actually inhabited it. When she got his phone call, she had been flooded not only with shock and concern, but with a kind of panic that, as he had rung *her*, something special was expected of her, that there was something in the situation that only she could respond to. She had got to the hospital within twenty minutes of his call and saw him through a swing door, sitting in his suit in a plastic bucket chair. His pale, gingery head was bowed and moving in a rhythmic way. She thought he was saying something, or sobbing maybe, but when she had passed through the doors, she realised he was rolling his lower lip between his thumb and finger, back and forth, as if he was . . . *humming*.

She said, 'Ian,' putting her arms out. She expected a moment then when she would sit down next to him. But he jumped up, greeted her as if she was a colleague convening at a sales conference. 'Excellent,' he said. 'That was very quick.' He looked at his watch. 'You've made very good time.'

'I'm so sorry, Ian.' She put her hand on his shoulder.

He tapped it rather patronisingly. 'Well. Yes. Anyway. Shall we?'

In Martha's Volvo Estate, he sat with his knees to his chin. She had moved the seat forward the day before to make room for a Welsh dresser. She kept saying, 'Ian you can move the seat back. There's a thing under the seat you pull.' But he said, 'No. No. I'm perfectly happy here, thank you.'

He had been in a restaurant in Croydon with some clients when his mobile rang. After his father's first heart attack, they'd thought . . . but anyway. Ian had left the car at the office and had a drink or two. 'Not more than that. Only two. But you can't be too careful. You can't risk it, can you? Obviously driving is very important in my job and a suspension would be out of the question. I did get a couple of points on my licence back in . . . um, when was it? Ninety-eight? Ninety-seven? It was enough to put the wind up me. The restaurant called me a mini-cab. Left! Left!'

'What?'

'Go left here! You don't want to go down Garratt Lane.

The congestion where it meets the Wandsworth one-way system is . . . murder.'

'Ian,' Martha said gently. 'It's four o'clock in the morning.'

'West Hill's just as bad. It's a bottleneck. Why they don't add an extra lane, I do not know.'

She drove to his father's house in Wimbledon, the house Graham had lived in with her mother before she died – the house that Martha herself had lived in as a child. 'Ah, the parental home,' Ian said as she pulled up outside number 10 Chestnut Drive (though, in fact, he had never lived here at all). It was looking manky, the house. The Virginia creeper, which her mother would prune hard twice a year, was sagging and bearded after five years of neglect, hanging off under its own weight in patches. The paintwork on the windows was peeling and the curtains in the bay window, pulled closed, were sagging in the middle.

In the hallway, Ian and Martha stood for a moment. It smelt murkily of cat's piss and old dust and unaired clothes. Ian took off his shoes. Martha was reminded of Ian's wife, who put plastic coverings over the furniture when she vacuumed, who sang, 'Feet!' when anyone came to the door. She said, 'Is Julia . . .?' Ian, still bending, said, 'She's going to wait until the twins are awake. It seemed unnecessary to, you know, disrupt their routine.'

Over the banisters, Graham's coat was hanging, discarded and empty. When Ian was lining his shoes under the radiator, Martha picked it up and quickly hung it on a peg. The pockets felt heavy with change. Ian turned round. 'Right,' he said. There was scurf in his pale eyebrows. His lips were drained of colour. For a moment, he froze, as if lost. Martha felt a surge of compassion. Now is when I should take control, she thought. But, in that moment, she froze too. Why had they come? To check that the house, abandoned so fast, was OK? To thank the neighbours for their quick action? To feed the cat? Or was it something more elemental? Maybe Ian needed to see the house's emptiness for itself. Maybe only then would his father's death sink in.

She said, 'Would you like a bath?' with an idea in her head of a stripping down, an immersion, some kind of rebirth.

Ian looked at her, and then stared, as if he'd noticed her for the first time. He said, 'Are you in your pyjamas?'

Martha looked down. A band of pale skin flashed between pink fabric and her trainers. A thread of ribbon trailed out of the V of an old jumper. She crossed her arms, suddenly self-conscious. 'I was in a hurry,' she said.

'Oh. Well, would *you* like a bath? I could check the water's on. You look a little . . .'

'No. No. I'm fine.'

'OK then. Well, I suppose I'd better get organised.'

He started going down the stairs to the basement kitchen, muttering about 'Arrangements'. Martha followed. Catching a sight of herself in the fish-eye mirror on the way down, she was the one who looked grief-struck, her face hollowed out, her features sharp, shadows looming under her eyes, her short brown hair sticking out at the back.

In the kitchen, the scene of so many family meals in Martha's past, Ian fiddled with his Filofax, making lists. Martha put the kettle on. The same old plastic kettle. Ian said, 'We'll need to get moving with the house.' She said,

'Tea. Strong tea with sugar.' He said, 'Coffee if there is any. White.'

She opened the fridge, but there wasn't any milk. Just three opened jars of Coffee Mate. The sugar pot was empty but a pile of sugar sachets sat in a saucer by the sink. The cupboard above gaped open to reveal several tins of Kit-e-Kat (cod and salmon flavour) and six Fray Bentos pies (steak and kidney flavour). Her stepfather appeared to have become increasingly eccentric in his kitchen organisation. Anything used regularly, mugs, plates, pans, utensils, had come out of the shelving and on to the melamine top, so the room looked like something that had been turned inside out: the galley of a ship after a storm. It struck Martha that it's only when people retire, and have the time for it, that they become obsessed with time-saving devices, most hung up on convenience. Maybe you start thinking that if you eke time out, don't fritter it away on tasks like cooking, or spreading hard butter, then somehow it will last longer.

She didn't feel she ought to share this thought with Ian. He took a couple of sips of his sweet Coffee Mated drink, put the mug back down on the table, and said, 'Right. Let's get moving.' Then he had sat on the stairs outside the kitchen, in the gloom, winding the spiral wire of the old-fashioned phone around his fingers, to ring relatives, his sister in Vancouver, his uncle in Borehamwood and, at 8 a.m. when it was 'decent', Martha's own two sisters. Stepsiblings of the bereaved. Stepdaughters of the deceased. Involved and yet not involved, like Martha herself, family by virtue of accident and death and divorce.

8

Martha said she could ring them. But Ian had replied that he wanted to do it. 'It is after all my . . .'

'. . . father who has died,' Martha finished for him.

He gave her an odd look.

'Place,' he said.

But that was ages ago. And here they are, still waiting.

'A,' Ian is saying, 'you can check in at Victoria if you want. Luggage and everything. B, there's long-wait carparks. You get straight on the bus and into the terminal. It's very fast, very efficient.'

Martha says, 'So, that's good.'

'Although, even with scheduled, there's no provision against air traffic control.'

'No, of course not.'

'Or weather.'

'No.'

'You can leave home in the morning and there's clear skies all over Gatwick, but what you can't see is that ridge of low pressure over Alicante. Fog. Electrical storms.'

'No, that's true.'

'I mean, take this summer . . .'

For the first time this morning, Martha feels a wave of exhaustion. She feels sorry for Ian, for losing his father. But also for being so *awful*. It strikes her how unfortunate it is that the aspect of his personality that most reveals his insecurity – this forced pomposity, this laboured smugness – is so alienating. She thinks back to the day her mother died. He doesn't know what he's doing, she thinks.

But, God, she wishes Julia would get here. Or her sisters. Because they will be so much better at comforting than she is. Geraldine, her elder sister, will clutch Ian to her bosom; she will assume a certain type of grief from him and, not noticing behaviour to the contrary, will receive it. Eliza, her younger sister, will simply match him with her efficiency. But Martha herself is no good at relationships. Sometimes, unexpectedly left alone in a room with a good friend, she finds herself lost for words. So how on earth is she supposed to cope here? Here she is, tongue-tied, letting Ian get away with his painful social chit-chat, reciting platitudes as if he is the first person ever to have thought of them. His hands are going chaff-chaff against his pockets. But he's telling her about the holiday he 'and the family' have just had with someone called Mark Warner in Kos. (This Mark appears to have been remarkably long-suffering, entertaining Milo and Rebecca for long stretches while Ian and Julia water-skiied. Mark didn't seem to have any children of his own.) Ian is saying, in a tone that would be hectoring if the subject matter wasn't so bland, 'Look, it was expensive but you can't put a price on memories you make for the children, can you?'

One thing Martha does have against children is the sentimentality they can bring out in their parents. She says sharply, 'Do ten-month-olds have memories?'

Ian says, 'Absolutely. Of course they do. And you've got to fill them with golden moments. Golden, golden moments. In my opinion, holidays are just the one single most important thing. Holidays full of golden moments. After all, when I look back, when *one* looks back, what does one remember about one's childhood?'

Martha says lightly, 'Divorce?'

'Holidays. That's what one remembers. Cornwall, before my mother died. Susie and me, father and mother. Constantine Bay, just along the coast from Padstow. Dad would take us fishing and we'd muck around in rock pools and um . . . you know, where's that picture? The day we went fishing for mackerel? It's here . . . isn't it . . . Or has it been moved?'

He has started fiddling with the photographs on the mantelpiece, but they are mainly of grandchildren now, or of Graham with Martha's mother, holding hands in front of a pretty view on one of the many jaunts they took after Graham retired from his job 'in concrete'. Happiness second time round for them both. Ian stops looking. His hands hang down. There is no sign of Graham's first family here. Ian says, 'Perhaps it's upstairs.'

Martha says, 'I'll go and look.' She feels a strong need to leave the room, to splash water on her face, maybe even to scream silently at her own reflection. But Ian says, 'No. No. I'll go.'

'It might be in the . . . in the desk in the bedroom? I know Mum used to keep a load of photos in there. Ones she wanted to reframe and . . .'

'O-K,' Ian says. 'To the master bedroom,' he adds as he leaves.

Martha sits down on the sofa. The cushions sigh behind her. She has fixed the curtain hooks on the rail and drawn back the heavy floral drapes, but it is still dreary in here. The chairs are upholstered in brown corduroy and the wood-chip paper on the wall looks pocked in little shadows like cellulite. Graham's Parker Knoll (how horrified she and her sisters were when this arrived; how irritated by their mother's impervious willingness to accept it) is matted with cat hair. It is a house that has never been styled, never been 'done'. It has been lived in by people who grew up in the war, who made the most of what they had, of what was there. Martha's generation puts its faith in things, in possessions, in interior design. You strip out the old floorboards and replace them with new, you pile skips with perfectly decent baths in 'the wrong colour', you redecorate, you replace, you stamp on your personality. Martha believes, though she might not say as much, that a person's house reflects their soul. Before her, on the mantelpiece, is a small, chipped statue of the Virgin Mary. Without even knowing she is doing so, Martha studies this with a critical eye. An interesting piece of kitsch, or too damaged to be worth attention? Martha's mother lived by her religion and so does Martha, only her god is a household god, the god of small, desirable things.

She picks up one of the magazines on the coffee table in front of her. They are free magazines – the sort that plop through the door, advertising houses – but they are laid out as carefully as if they were art books. Her mother used to put them straight in the bin, but it isn't her mother's home any more. It is a collection of rooms, of stuff, papers and letters and albums and paintings and books and furniture, stuff to be sorted, stuff to be chucked, stuff to be allocated, divided up, chosen, rejected, selected. Geraldine, she knows, has always had her eye on the Chesterfield. Eliza will want 'The Boy', a late-nineteenth-century portrait, left to their mother by an aunt. Above the fireplace, it stands out in this room, not least because, oddly, the artist has paid as much attention to the flowered fabric on the chair as to the face of the child sitting in it. It is, Martha estimates, worth several thousand, though of course it is the sentimental value that Eliza will talk about. There is a Penwork Tea Caddy (chinoiserie, brass lion feet, Regency penwork) which is even more valuable, but she suspects her sisters don't know this and will find the tug on their heart strings subsequently diminished. It was bad enough sorting out the jewellery, what will it be like with a whole house?

When Ian first left the room, Martha heard a clattering and a creaking of boards overhead. But that has stopped and it is all quiet up there now. After a few minutes, she calls up, 'Ian? You OK?' Still silence, but she waits a little while longer before going upstairs to look for him. And then, turning the corner onto the landing, she sees him sitting through the doorway of the bedroom, on the big cast-iron bed with something in his lap, and she says, 'Did you find it?' But he raises his head then and she sees that the object he's holding isn't a picture at all but a jumper, a tatty green lambswool V-neck, the one Graham used to wear for gardening. And then she sees his face. It's knotted up and twisted and he's just looking at her and there are tears pouring down it. 'Oh no,' she says, and she goes to him then and, finally, holds his heaving shoulders while he weeps.

*

13

'I am not having the cat.'

'Matty. Be reasonable.' Eliza rubs her chin with the heel of her hand. 'It's the least you can do. Ger – Matty is now saying she won't have the cat.'

Martha is kneeling on the floor by the fridge, with rubber gloves on, her face glowing white in the artificial light, handing items of food up to Eliza, who is supposed to be separating them into piles. Eliza is sitting on a stool, her long, slim legs crossed at a jaunty angle so that she looks like an office worker waiting at the bar for an early evening drink, rather than someone involved in clearing out a kitchen.

Geraldine has come in with her arms full of sheets – a jumble of horrible brown and navy polyester. She is on her way to the washing machine. She pauses, her tilted bulk swaying, and says, 'Oh Matt.'

Martha's thighs are aching, the knees of her cotton pyjama bottoms grey with dirt. Reaching into the back of the fridge, she says, 'I'm not "now saying" I won't have the cat. At no point have I said I *would* have the cat.'

'Matt-ski . . .' Eliza's tone is wheedling, coaxing. Her mouth is pouted, one of the exaggerated facial expressions she uses to hide her detachment. She has got her face on, her plummy lipstick one shade lighter than her lip pencil. She sees Martha looking at her and straightens her mouth. In an ordinary voice, says, 'Come on. Someone's got to.' She pauses over a jar of tartare sauce. Her polished nails scratch at the label. 'October Eighty-seven. Shit. No wonder he was under the weather.'

'Eliza!' Geraldine has started stuffing the washing into

14

the machine. When she bends you can see the white elastic stitching in the fabric of her blue leggings; the seams stretching. Straightening up, she releases an 'ouf' of breath – not an indication of real pain or discomfort, but an imitation groan like the one their mother used to give, a sign that Geraldine feels hard done by. She is larger and softer than Eliza, slack muscled, round shouldered. If Martha's sisters were lights, Eliza would be an anglepoise, elegant and angular, Geraldine one of those lamps made from Chinese ginger jars, with a circular base and a top heavy shade. She has the same curly hair as Eliza, but hers is flyaway across the crown. Today, with the low sun in the window behind, she looks as if she's wearing a halo.

Martha says, 'Can't a neighbour have it?' Eliza grimaces at the jar of tartare sauce. 'The *cat*,' Martha adds.

Geraldine is setting the machine's controls. 'No, they won't. They're away a lot. And Graham wasn't on speakers with the other side over that fence business.' She clamps her hands to her waist. 'Look, *I'd* take him if it wasn't for the dogs.'

Eliza says, 'And you know *I* can't because of Gabriel's asthma.'

'And Ian can't because Julia couldn't have hairs in the house, it would give her a nervous breakdown. Not to mention Ian and his eczema.' The washing machine has started its preliminary gurgling, and Geraldine is on the way to the door again. There is some sudden shouting upstairs, a high-pitched scream and a man's voice yelling, 'STOP FIGHTING YOU TWO.' She says, 'Look, fine, whatever. We'll have him put down.'

Martha knows this is her cue. But she doesn't say anything. She has started soaping the inside of the fridge now with a J-cloth. Geraldine hovers for a moment, fiddling with the crucifix around her neck. Then she raises her chin (they all have 'the Bone chin', but Geraldine more than the others) and barrels up the stairs towards the noise. Now she's gone, Eliza yawns and says, 'Oh fuck it, let's chuck the whole lot.'

Martha sits back on her haunches. There's a hole in one of the rubber gloves and the fingers on that hand are clammy. 'That's probably best in the long run.'

It is the middle of the afternoon now and her sisters have picked up the house and shaken it. ('It's important to keep Ian occupied,' Geraldine had said, though Martha suspected it was more to do with establishing territory – a different kind of occupation.) Geraldine had been the first to get there, Patrick and Anna tearing past Martha at the door. 'Into the garden!' Geraldine screeched before seeing Ian nursing a whiskey on the sofa. She knelt at his feet. 'Are you feeling just shattered?' she'd said. 'Has it come as a terrible, terrible shock?' (Geraldine's questions often include the answers: a way of ensuring that the world comes out as she expects.) Greg, her husband, had followed her in, his hand steering Ivor, their middle one, by the back of the head. 'Sorry about the invasion,' he said. Greg is a bulky man. The jowls on his face move as he walks. When he planted a kiss on her cheek, Martha smelt a very faint, not unattractive smell of sweat.

Greg, after pumping Ian's hand up and down and clapping him around the shoulder, had taken the children and their dogs – hysterical dachshunds, their whole bodies wagging – into the garden, so Martha and Geraldine were sitting alone with Ian when Eliza arrived. Geraldine got up to let her in and Martha heard her say, 'Usual funeral garb, I see.' There followed an unnatural silence in which Martha imagined her sisters wincing and suppressing laughter. She had smiled at Ian, who surprised her by raising his eyes to the ceiling. They heard Geraldine say in a different voice, 'Anyway, Eliza, leather trews. Honestly. With a babsy.'

'You just sponge them down,' said Eliza. 'You should get some. They're very practical. Practical as hell.'

Martha found, disconcertingly, that she and Ian were still sharing a look. The three sisters used to flit around in relation to each other, shifting in and out of closeness. But since the birth of Gabriel, references have been made to weekend lunches or children's teas that have taken place without Martha. It's not that she minds not having been at them; it's more that she feels uneasy that they have taken place without her even knowing. In that moment, when she and Ian smiled at each other, her sisters in the hall, she felt as if she had broken ranks. And maybe this did have to do with Ian ringing her first, or maybe it is something else, something that has crept up on her gradually, a feeling of being an outsider among her siblings.

Now Eliza has finished tagging up the bin bags and is standing on a chair beginning an assault on the top cupboards. She says, 'I suppose Ian rang you because you were closest to the hospital.' She has a tower of Fray Bentos pies under her chin. She adds with her lower jaw at a funny angle, 'Ugh. Imagine living off these!'

17

Martha is emptying her bucket into the sink. She glances up. She hadn't thought of that, which is probably why Eliza, who likes to make a virtue of her 'openness', had reminded her. But of course, Eliza is right. It was convenience that led Ian to ring her first, nothing else. She feels foolish and grubby and tired. Her eyes are at midriff level. Eliza's stomach, between her black leather trousers and T-shirt, which wrinkles up as she stretches, is flat and brown.

'You're very slim again, Eliza,' she says. 'How do you keep so slim?'

'You know me, I live on my nerves. Apart from that? Exercise and stress. Oh, and running after an eighteen-month-old!'

'Of course.' Martha puts the bucket in the cupboard under the sink. And then adds, 'Also, no children *chez moi*. He wouldn't have wanted to ring you because of Gabriel. No one likes to wake a baby.'

'Oh, I shouldn't think it was that at all,' says Eliza, but not really listening. She has got down from the chair and, after looking round the room aimlessly, has chucked the pies on the counter. 'Oh fuck it,' she says, looking at the chaos. 'I suppose we are being useful?'

Martha snaps off the gloves and sits down on a chair. 'You've got to do something,' she says.

Eliza sits down too. 'God,' she says. 'I didn't know he was going to die. I wasn't really expecting it, do you know what I mean?'

'Yes,' Martha says. 'Sort of.'

There is a pause. The house has been full of noise – shouts and the clattering of feet on stairs – but is quiet for a

18

moment. Eliza spins the thick silver ring on the middle finger of her right hand a few times, then says, 'I rang Daddy before I came. He was very sorry to hear.'

'How is he?'

'Fine, I think.' The silver ring slips on to a different finger. 'I should phone him. He hasn't rung me for ages.'

Silence. Martha thinks Eliza is going to say, 'Well, you could ring him,' but she doesn't.

'How's the shop?'

'Ticking over. The City?' Eliza doesn't actually work in the City, though she calls it 'the financial sector'. She is a financial PR, which always sounds to Martha like a contradiction in terms.

'Oh, you know. The usual. Long hours . . .'

'Difficult. What with Gabriel and everything.'

Eliza is nodding, slowly. 'Yeah. Thank God for Denis.'

'Thank God for Denis.' Eliza's husband isn't really called Denis. His real name is Tom. But he has been known as Denis since Geraldine compared his patience in the face of his wife's daily imperiousness to that of Denis Thatcher. Martha adds, 'How's Voltaire?' She is never sure if one is supposed to mention Denis's Ph.D. or not.

Eliza rolls her eyes.

'Ah.' Martha takes this to mean the Ph.D. is not going well, but, the only member of her family who didn't go to university, she doesn't feel in a position to comment further. 'Jolly good.'

'He's taken Gabriel to the Science Museum. Apparently, there's a touch and feel bit downstairs. He loves it.' Pause. 'Gabriel quite likes it too.'

19

Martha smiles.

Eliza says, 'Everything all right? Your end?'

'Yeah.' Martha looks at her watch. 'Look, about the cat? Just because I'm . . . you know. Don't think you two can just push me around. My life isn't yours to be . . . whatever . . . just because I'm on my own, just because I haven't . . .'

'I know,' Eliza says. She dabs at a spot of rust on her top, licking her finger and rubbing. She doesn't look at Martha. 'But it's only for a night or two.'

'It's the principle. It's all part of you and Geraldine trying to find something useful for Martha to do. But you know I am busy. I have things to do. Just because I don't have kids doesn't mean I'm free to . . . Anyway, I don't want him cluttering up my flat.'

'Well, whatever.' Eliza gets up and opens the door to the glory hole. Martha stays at the table for a bit in case she comes back. But Eliza, poking behind the Hoover, has started whistling in a bored way. Martha feels her own face fix. She says, 'Anyway,' and leaves the room. Halfway up the stairs, she meets Julia, Ian's wife, coming down with a waste-paper basket in each hand. Julia is wearing camel trousers and a white shirt. She has a straight blonde fringe that is like a line across her forehead. She wrinkles up her nose. 'Goodness gracious, the stuff everywhere! How can people live like this?' Julia has a thing about dust-mites.

Martha says, 'Ssssh,' though she doesn't know where Ian is. He could be anywhere. They are all over the place, the lot of them, children and dogs and bereaved relatives, in and out of rooms, somehow licensed now to take the house over as never before. Not even at Christmas. She can hear Geraldine shout to Greg in the garden from a top window. Patrick and Ivor, two dark heads, two enormous pairs of trainers, are sprawled on the rug in the sitting room, fiddling with their Game Boys. Anna, the youngest, is playing with a doll on the stairs, reprimanding it for something. She looks up when she sees Martha. She still has the round, flushed cheeks of a baby, her mouth always part open, her hair silky fine. She cocks her head and says, 'Auntie Matt?'

'Yes?' Martha sits on the bottom step. She likes to think she talks to children as equals. (Geraldine, she's noticed, says 'ye-es?' to her children, giving the word two syllables as if to demonstrate patience, or, if distracted, 'What?', to demonstrate the opposite.) She enjoys the thought that there is a role an aunt can play that is barred to a closer relative, answers she can give.

'How bad is shark repellent bat spray?'

Martha says, 'Umm.'

Patrick, eight, yells, 'I've told you. Bad enough to kill you.'

Julia comes back up the stairs then with a black bin bag in her arms. She says, 'Martha. All this in here: it was at the back of the ironing cupboard. It seems to be yours. Just letters and old . . . things.' She is shaking her head; her fringe sways. 'Shall I just chuck it?'

Martha hesitates. Her bag of mementoes. She had forgotten all about it. Letters, papers, rubbish really.

Anna says, 'Kill you like you're really dead?'

Julia says, 'It's just clutter. Clutter is the enemy of a clear mind. There was an article in *Good Housekeeping* the other day. Chuck, chuck, chuck: the three rules of a well-organised life.'

'Kill you like Graham is dead?'

Martha says, 'Actually, I'll keep it.'

Geraldine is coming down with more sheets. She is just in time to hear this. She gives Martha a pointed look over the linen.

Martha says, 'The letters, not the cat.'

Later, at the end of the day, Ian and the sisters have a cup of tea in the sitting room before going their separate ways. 'A restorative cup,' Martha imagines her mother saying, pouring it from the big silver teapot that was brought out for family occasions. Family occasions! If their mother could see them, what would she make of this: her children and stepchild more united in parental death than they ever were in parental marriage? Already grown up when Graham and Hilly got together, the children eyed each other from separate corners like in-laws; the arty, attractive, talented Bones v the Leaches with their bad clothes and patchy skin – the generations reversed. Martha thinks families at the best of times are Things To Be Avoided. And 'extended families' – people tied on by circumstance alone – were the most hellish of them all.

No one fancies Coffee Mate, so the tea is black. No teapot, either, or cups, just mugs. Julia has gone to collect the twins from her mother's so Geraldine is sitting next to Ian, the chief mourner, on the Chesterfield. She is holding his hand and talking again about 'the end'. She shakes her head and says she'd thought Graham was so much better, and Ian, who is in his shirtsleeves, with the tears coming easily now, says how busy he'd been at work and how last weekend he hadn't made it up and that if the Quinces next door hadn't had his mobile number from the last time, then . . . Geraldine squeezes his hand, puts her other hand on top and says, 'You were there. That's what counts.'

Eliza has decided against the cat-haired Parker Knoll, and is sitting in a hard frame chair with a tapestry seat. The cat, who turned up a few hours ago, has also decided against the Parker Knoll and is on Eliza's knee. She is stroking it, with firm, rhythmic strokes from the top of its head to the base of its tail. It is purring, arching its body into her hand so that its back goes up like a wave. It is also dribbling on to her leather-clad leg, which she doesn't seem to have noticed. She says, after a while, 'I suppose we'd better start sorting through some of the things.' Her eyes flit to 'The Boy' above the fireplace. 'Working out who's getting what. Furniture . . . things like that.'

Geraldine's spare hand grips the corner of the Chesterfield. 'Eliza!'

'And then there's the crematorium. We need to get on to them. Shall I do that? Ian, would you like me to do that?'

Martha, from her cross-legged position on the floor, sees what's coming. 'Eliza, um . . . Ian—'

Ian interrupts. 'I think my father would have preferred a burial. I've already discussed it with my sister. There is, as you know, the double plot in Putney Vale Cemetery where my mother's buried.'

The cat leaps off Eliza's lap. Geraldine, who is still clasping Ian's hand, looks away out of the window, her lower lip twisted. She is wearing a white T-shirt and you can see the indentations of her bra across her back. Martha feels a tug of tenderness towards her. Their mother's ashes were scattered, at her request, at Pen Ponds in Richmond Park. She and Graham had met at Pen Ponds. It was their place. Perhaps she imagined the same for Graham. But such were the messy unforetold complications of the second marriage. Naturally, Ian would choose to lay his father with his mother; the bones of his mother, Martha found herself thinking, not the mother of the Bones.

There is a silence filled only by the sound of the children shouting in the garden. Martha says, 'You think there is a certain amount of tragedy in the world, that it gets meted out equally somehow. But it isn't, is it? I mean it's so unfair that Graham should have lost two wives, and Ian, you know, that you've lost both parents. I'm so sorry. We're lucky to have one parent left.' She looks at her sisters. The cat has jumped on to the sofa now, kneading the cushion next to Ian, who bends to stroke him with his spare hand. He is nodding, but there are tears falling into the fur.

Geraldine recovers. She turns back to him and says, 'The most important thing, Ian, is that he knew you were happy. That was what mattered to him, he knew that you and your sister were both settled. You must hold on to that. I remember talking to Mummy when she was very ill and she said, you know, thank God you're all happy and in stable relationships, you've got Greg and Eliza's got Denis and Martha's got David . . .' She stops. There is a moment of silence in which Martha thinks she can hear the atoms clashing in her ears. Geraldine adds quickly, 'and of course the antique shop.'

24

Ian, unaware of what has just been said, looks up. 'Yes, I know. And he was a terrific father. I respected him. Loved and respected him. You can't ask for more than that.'

Martha doesn't look up to see if her sisters are exchanging glances. She hopes they aren't, but knows that they are.

It is past 8 p.m. when Martha finally returns to the shop. She parks the Volvo outside, in a loading bay, unlocks the front door and then gets her bag of mementoes from the boot. The door has swung to when she gets back so she has to push it with her foot, as a result of which the label on the door announcing the unexpected circumstances helicopters to the floor like a seed coming down from a sycamore tree.

She has left a lamp on in the back of the shop, on a table in the section that is mocked up to look like a child's bedroom. There is a sleighbed here, and a painted cupboard with gingham panels in the doors, and a little chest of drawers and the rocking horse in its original paintwork. The Victorian sprig quilt on the bed looks so soft and inviting, the scene so peaceful in the low glow of the small light, she sits for a moment on the bed and rubs her eyes. She thinks about lying back, curling up in the quilt, going to sleep here. But after a few minutes she gets up, unlocks another door in the side wall and heaves the bin bag up the flight of stairs behind it and into her flat. Almost to her surprise, it is just as she left it. Her space, her haven: still and serene and ordered. Everything as it should be, everything as it was. She plumps up the new linen cushions, fashioned from French

25

antique sheets, on her Howard sofa, straightens the kilim, and stuffs the bag of letters out of sight under the kitchen table. And then she goes back down the stairs and back to the car to collect the cat.

chapter two

the master bedroom

'It never answers to purchase very cheap bedding, for
the latter is apt to prove only too dear in the long
run. A cheap mattress is not only uncomfortable, but
it is an actual menace to the health.'

The Women's Book,
edited by Florence B. Jack
(T.C. & E.C. Jack, 1911)

FOR THE second day in a row, Martha is woken by the phone
ringing.

'Oh good, you're up,' Geraldine says.

Martha reaches out to nudge the alarm clock into view. It
says 9.35 a.m. 'Um,' she says.

'What, don't tell me you're still in bed? It's almost ten,
Matty. I've already been to Mass. Sorry, but lucky for some.'

Martha doesn't say anything. She can hear Geraldine's
house in her ear, the hollering of small children and the
racket of dogs and the zap and crackle of the television.
She imagines Geraldine standing by the fridge, with all those

27

hideous alphabet magnets on it, the sink next to her piled with dishes, the table still scattered with wet Krispies and spilt milk from breakfast.

Geraldine says, affronted, 'Do you want to call me back?'

Martha yawns, putting the receiver against her chin to muffle the sound. 'Can I just wake up a bit?'

'OK,' says Geraldine stiffly, hanging up.

Martha lays her head back into the pillow. The room seems unnaturally dark and quiet, as if someone is holding up a blanket against the window. She can see the shape of her chest of drawers, but none of the objects on it. She likes to tidy them in her mind – moving the lamp a couple of inches to the left, regrouping the jug and the pot that holds her earrings, and the little pile of antiquarian books, positioning them just right, both in relation to the chest of drawers and to each other. Things in groups of three are always best. But this morning it is too dim to make out the decorative touches so she gets up to pull the curtains apart and sees that there is indeed a blanket outside – a blanket of fog. Next door's garden is white and ghostly, swathed as if in smoke. Even from here she can smell the sharp tang of it. She pulls up the sash and breathes in the air, which is damp and heavy like churned up earth. But as she does, there's a flurry of fabric next to her and a brush of warmth against her hand and she has to slam the window shut before the cat jumps out.

'Oh fuck,' Martha says. 'You, I'd forgotten about.'

The cat stares at her and then, losing its balance, leaps off the sill and stalks off as if it had been going to do that all along. The night before, it had padded around her flat, its body slunk low to the floor, nostrils quivering, investigating every corner for rats or demons. In the end, Martha shut it in the kitchen, with some food, and an attractive dusky pink and sage plaid Welsh blanket which had once adorned the end of her bed but which she has since put aside to sell on. The cat dabbed at it, as if trying to get glue off its pad, and then, when a claw entangled in a thread (and broke it: damn it), shot back as if electrocuted.

It is tabby and white, this cat, with balding patches between its ears and a saggy underbelly. It is large, over-weight probably, but its fur is thin. There are cats that Martha knows she could warm to – there's one she has read about that looks like a leopard and will join you in the bath. And there are snub-nosed Persians and sleek grey Burmese. Even a black cat, one with pea-green eyes like the succession of moggies they had as children, could be an asset, curled in a ball on the end of the sofa, with a red collar to match the threads in the curtains . . . But this one? This one brings nothing to the party. It is, for one thing, a double-moulter. Its black hairs will show up on pale things, its white hairs on dark. It will scratch at the furniture. No question: she will take it to Battersea Dogs Home as soon as she is dressed. 'You're the boss,' she says to herself as she steps into the shower. She closes her eyes and puts her head back, feeling the water needle her face, stream through her hair. Free and unencumbered. 'I'm the boss,' she says loudly to nobody in particular. Or maybe to the cat. Or maybe, across London, to her sisters.

Martha's life is shot through (as in shrapnel, rather than Shantung silk) with a sense that she needs to justify the way she leads it. She knows that to be thirty-eight and single is one thing, but to be thirty-eight, single and *childless*, another altogether. Her sisters, she imagines, are irritated by her apparent contentment, baffled at how she can possibly not long for marriage and childbirth – the twin sacraments of their lives. Nobody believes in a happily childless woman of thirty-eight, just as nobody beyond childhood believes in the wicked fairy. But Martha simply says that family life is not one that has ever suited her.

There was a brief moment a few years ago when she felt otherwise. There were glimmers and possibilities then. The Martha that went out with David – who seems like a different person to her now – did envisage children, but they were artistically arranged, with pudgy bare feet, pretty gingham hats and attractive colour-co-ordinated fishing nets, on a Cornish beach. And when the relationship with David went wrong, when the storm came, she ran for the car with a rug over her head and drove away without them. Everyone, she thinks, has a moment when they come closest to having children. Her moment has been and gone. And it's true that a year or so ago she felt a twinge of sadness when she realised this fact. But not now. When Eliza had Gabriel, she caught the occasional awkward look, as if Eliza was anxious that her baby son might be a source of pain to Martha. Martha wanted to laugh. She didn't long for Gabriel, funny little squawking thing in his oversize nappy. She didn't long for him at all. Once you've decided you're not going to have your own, why would you want someone else's?

Martha showers, filling her flat with the scent of Green Tea and Pomegranate, dresses quickly and slowly makes her bed, smoothing the seagull-white Durham quilt under the top pillows, laying the dove-grey pashmina throw at the perfect angle across it. She casts her eye over the sitting room. It looks cosy and serene this morning, with the gloom outside, the curtains pulled and side lights on, a cream cube against the hoary September day. She plumps up the linen cushions on the sofa. They don't need it – they haven't been sat on since she plumped them up last night – but the act of doing it satisfies her; it makes her feel as if the day is going to be fine. She considers them, running her hands over the slubbed texture – how delicate their scalloped edges; how perfect the whole ensemble – and goes into the kitchen. It smells intense and meaty. She doesn't like to inspect the make-shift litter tray behind the door, but she had left some Kit-e-Kat in a Spode saucer and all that is left of it now is a rim of brown dried-on smears. She holds the saucer at arm's length and runs it under the tap, her nose wrinkled.

After this, she needs a cup of coffee, but when she sniffs the carton, the milk has that artichoke smell of milk on the turn. Recently, since the introduction of late-night opening, she has developed a routine whereby she shops on Saturday nights. She has the supermarket all to herself then. But last night she had been too tired. So she grabs her purse, goes down the stairs and into the street.

Right out of the shop is the café, which is just opening up, and beyond that, before the row becomes residential, Sustainable Forests, the second-hand bookshop, which is closed on Sundays. But Martha turns left to where on weekdays a half-hearted market straggles – a couple of vege-table stalls, a man selling knock-off CDs, a barrow of ready mixed flowers. She passes the tatty estate agent which specialises in long-term lets, the chemist and the gift shop, and reaches the end of the street, then turns right into Balham High Road. The supermarkets aren't yet open, so she crosses over by McDonald's and turns down a smaller road to the corner shop. Here she buys some milk, a paper, a sliced brown loaf that looks as if it's at least trying to be healthy, some flabby-looking bacon in a packet, and a carton of orange juice with the legend 'no bits'. (She used to find this an odd boast, until Geraldine explained, in one of those insights open only to parents, that whereas an adult might consider bits an addition, to children they're an insult.) The woman behind the counter smiles at her, and then Martha, who needs things to be framed to be able to see them properly, who needs distance even from herself, thinks: here I am, a single woman in control of her life, buying Sunday breakfast, with the papers, with time to read them, in a place that knows me. There was a programme on television recently in which one of the characters told another to 'spin' their life, and the idea has stuck with Martha and become something of a habit.

The fog is lifting a little now. The air feels warmer and there's a patch of insipid blue above Martha's head, the clouds around the edges like smoke. It's not yet autumn after all, but one of those interim days with warmth still in the air. Back on Balham High Road, a family is trying to cross. One of the children is in a pushchair and the other is being made to hold on to the father's hand, but he's pulling on it, his legs scraping across the ground, wailing. For a stomach-clenching moment, Martha thinks the man is

David. There's something about the size of him, the set of his shoulders, the hair. But of course, she knows it can't be, and when she passes, weaving in front of them between cars, she sees that this man is much younger. And David couldn't have done all this so quickly. Not so soon. But the thought deflates her, and the thin red and white plastic bag spins round in a tangle, cutting into her hand as she walks, more quickly, towards the flat.

She can hear the phone ringing as she climbs the stairs. She answers it, an apology already forming, but it isn't Geraldine. It's Ian.

'Hel-lo,' he says, in a dull sing-song.

Martha puts the plastic bag on the table and sits down. 'How are you, Ian? I was going to ring. Are you all right?'

'Under the circumstances. Quite beneficial that it's Sunday. I don't think I'd be much of an asset at the office today.'

'No, of course not. I mean, it's only twenty-four hours. You must be just . . .'

'Right. Yes. Well, I was just ringing to thank you. It was kind of you yesterday, to pick me up from the hospital. Much appreciated. And for everyone's help during the day. Obviously, what with one thing and another, there's rather a lot to do, arrangements to make, etcetera.'

'Honestly. It was nothing. I, we, were glad to. We've got to sort the house out some time. It's our responsibility too.'

'But also taking Kitten. I really appreciate it. I know once Hilly died, you know, my father –' There's a pause, after which Ian's voice sounds less pompous – 'really loved that cat.'

Martha scours the kitchen with her eyes. The cat isn't there. She moves, with the phone under her chin, to the sitting room and it isn't there either. Or in the bedroom. She says, 'Well . . .'

'He's all I've got left of him.'

Martha is looking under the sofa. And behind the curtains. 'You don't think you and Julia . . .'

'Not with the eczema.'

'No, of course not.'

She is looking in the bathroom now, behind the shower curtain. In the space under the bath. Ian is saying, 'So I've been to the hospital, sorted things out there. And I've found a funeral home in Merton that's quite reasonable. Copewell & Paine they're called.'

Martha straightens up, and bangs her head. 'Really?' she says. 'Are they really called Copewell & Paine?'

There's a pause and then Ian shouts a laugh. 'Do you think they're having me on? Actually I rang a few. To get quotes.' He laughs, more hysterically. 'There I was talking about types of wood and linings – would I like red crushed velvet? I don't know – and my father's just there in the hospital.'

'Oh God,' Martha says. 'Not crushed velvet.'

'Anyway, the church has an opening on Friday.' He hoots again. 'Huh! An opening! Can you believe it? I don't know. And I wondered . . . well, I know what good taste you've got. Julia is always saying you have impeccable taste. "Martha and her good eye," she says. "Martha and her perfect little flat." Could you be in charge of the flowers? I wouldn't know where to start. Something simple, obviously. What do you think? Just one big garland saying Dad or Grandad, or would Father be more dignified?'

'Or just a wreath?' Martha says, back in the kitchen now. 'Of course.' Maybe the cat has gone downstairs. Maybe it even got out when she went to the shop, to tear into the road, to be run over: all that's left of Ian's father squashed in the gutter. She says, 'Ian, I had better go. Can I ring you later?'

The cat (Kitten – *that's* what it's called: it had just strayed into Hilly and Graham's garden one day so had never seemed more than temporary) has got into the shop, but no further. It is curled up on the sleighbed, like a hedgehog, its grey mouth stretched in a sleeping rictus. Martha feels a thud of relief when she sees him there. But as she gets closer she notices the ugly nest of hairs his coat has rubbed on to the Victorian sprig eiderdown. 'Hey, Kitten,' she says, giving him a poke. He untucks his head and looks at her, but there is a moment before he realises that she's serious. He stares at her accusingly before unfurling and flopping off the bed. 'Go on,' she says, nudging him with her leg. He skittles across the floor to the flat door. But once beyond it, he lollops ahead of her slowly and regularly, pausing on each step as if the stairs have already become routine. So casual is he, you might think he feels even more at home here than she does.

Across south London, down the A3, Geraldine is sitting on the stairs of her large Victorian house in Kingston with her coat on. The front door is wide open and Greg is scrunching in and out to the car. He has collected the dogs and tied the bikes to the roof and he is rounding up the children now, switching off the video, confiscating Game Boys, chucking cushions in a haphazard manner back on to sofas, and Lego into boxes. He shouts, 'This. House. Is. A. Tip,' but it's like a celebration when he says it.

He passes Geraldine again. Despite his size, he is all energy. He spends the week at a desk job in a newspaper, moving articles about war in foreign places around a page, and at weekends it's as if he wants to see some action of his own. 'Come on, Ger,' he says. 'Old girl.' This designation used to be a joke but it's part of the language between them now. In turn, sometimes Geraldine calls Greg 'Dad', and she has noticed that he dwindles a little bit each time she does, so that even though she's being ironic, the irony eats away at her sense of him as anything other. A husband or a news editor or, God forbid, after all this time, a lover.

She says, 'All right, I'm coming. I just want to give her another minute or two.'

Greg chucks the car keys into the air and catches them. He says, 'Why don't you ring *her*?'

But Geraldine's always ringing *her*. She resents her for the number of times she rings her. The whole point is that Geraldine is the protective, not the needy one. She wants *her* to ring *her*. She says, 'It's just she said she'd ring back. It's over an hour now.'

Greg throws his keys into the air again, but this time, just before he catches them, he mimes lobbing them with an invisible tennis racket on to the drive. 'More than,' he says as he does so. 'More than an hour, not over an hour.' He has an unfussy attitude towards his own family – mother gaga in a nursing home, brother in Nuneaton, Christmas, birthdays, duty visits, duty calls – but firm ideas about language. It exasperates him how Geraldine messes around with it. Never hungry or tired, she is 'starving wharving' or 'knacker-acker-ooed'. 'Fancy a coff?' she'll ask him, shortening or lengthening perfectly decent words as if she can't leave them alone. Sisters, language, children: she never leaves anything alone. He puts the keys back into his pocket. 'Maybe she's forgotten.'

Which is, of course, what Geraldine worries about. Martha forgetting. Martha forgetting to do this, or that. Martha forgetting to look after the cat. Martha, all on her own in that grotty area, ironing her antique linen bedsheets into crisp white envelopes, forgetting to look after herself.

She says, 'I'll ring Eliza. Is that all right? Have I got time to quickly ring Eliza?'

Greg says, 'Quickly to ring.' He goes back into the play-room where she hears him shout, 'Telly *off*.' There are noises of horseplay with Patrick, squeals from Anna, but Ivor sidles out into the hall, one hand rubbing his neck from behind, a nervous habit recently adopted. The skin beneath his lower lip is reddened and raw. Geraldine has started dialling, but she puts her spare arm round her middle son. She kisses his head. She is not going to ask what's wrong now. Sometimes having children is like having your nerve ends exposed. She holds him tight while she talks to Eliza.

'Listen,' she says. 'That thing I said. Was it awful? Did you see Matt's face? About David and her being settled? God, I'm stupid.'

Eliza says, 'Oooh. There we go. Higher? Higher? Oooooh.'

Eliza must be in the garden, which has so much tasteful wooden equipment Geraldine refers to it as The Princess Diana Playground (her way of telling Eliza she thinks Gabriel is spoilt).

'Yes, well,' Eliza says, her voice closer to the receiver. 'It was a classic. But fuck it, Ger. She jilted him. Wedding date set. Apartment waiting for her in Geneva. Anyway, it's two years now. We can't be treading on eggshells for ever.'

'I know. I feel I can't say anything right around her. But I only want her to be happy.'

'She's OK.'

'But don't you think she's odd when David is mentioned? It's as if she won't allow herself to admit she regrets it. More fool her. He's got someone else now. She's called Maddy and she works at the auction house too. Oriental Miniatures. Legs up to her armpits, according to Greg.'

'Well, there you go.'

'I know . . . it's just . . . it's just . . .' Geraldine swallows.

'There's no need to get upset about it.'

'Oh, I know. It's not that really. It's Graham dying. It brings it all back. Mummy's death. It's like a full stop or something. I can't really believe it. And then no ashes . . .'

Geraldine's throat feels tight. She is awash suddenly and hugs Ivor a little closer. Ivor pulls away and says, 'I want to watch telly.'

Eliza sounds distracted. 'Yes. But, you know, life goes on. Have you spoken to Ian?'

'No, but I must. There'll be solicitors and the will. The house is just divided, isn't it? Us three, Ian, Susie. Mind you,

I don't know how much it will fetch. It's in a terrible state. Are we just going to let Ian take charge of it all, just because he's a man?'

'He is in the business.'

'Quantity surveying?'

'Etcetera. Etcetera.' Eliza imitates Ian via Yul Brynner in *The King and I*. Geraldine laughs more than the impression deserves to keep Eliza on her side.

Eliza says, 'There are one or two things . . . not that I mind what I get, but some odds and ends do have, well, sentimental value.'

An image of 'The Boy' comes into Geraldine's mind. She knows Eliza wants it and has always wanted it, and that somehow always wanting is her claim to having it, but she feels a twist of resentment. She thinks about the Chesterfield and Mummy's little lacquered desk and the mahogany three-legged table.

Eliza says, 'Can't imagine Ian or Susie caring much about the art, do you? They can share the Parker Knoll.'

Geraldine laughs. Ivor is sitting on the step between her legs now, his head at eye level, and she has started combing through his hair with her spare hand, checking for nits while she's got him. 'Yes,' she says. 'I know. Goodness, I must ring Daddy. He'd want to know. Not that it affects him, but . . .'

'It's all right. I've rung him.'

'Oh really?' Geraldine is surprised and also put out. It's normally her role to think of things like that.

'Briefly. Yesterday. Didn't I tell you? He was looking after the girls so he had his hands full. Eloise had a meeting in Marseilles.'

'How was he?'

'Fine. He said he's coming over soon to get something for the boat.'

'Oh.' Geraldine rests her chin on Ivor's head. 'Right.' She wonders who he will stay with. Last time he stayed with Eliza ('Closer to town,' he said). She says, 'He probably should stay with me this time because of the baby.'

There is the sound of wailing the other end. Eliza says, 'We'll sort it. I don't know. I'd better go. Cheer up. And don't worry about Martha. She can look after herself.'

'Can she?' Geraldine wonders.

Greg comes back into the hall, raising his eyebrows. Geraldine dials before he can say anything. Patrick and Anna hurtle past him into the drive as he stands there, looking at her, rubbing the bit of his head where the hair is thinning. She's so soft on everyone. The women at work, with their bobbed hair and boots, have such *edges*. Geraldine next to them seems frayed and fuzzy. When she was working, when she had the orchestra and her cello to think about, she was more self-possessed, more purposeful. She should spend more time on herself. That coat, so threadbare. She'll be too warm in it now the sun's broken through. And he wishes she wouldn't let Ivor drip over her so much. It's not surprising he's so clingy. 'Come on, chap,' he says in a hearty whisper, jabbing playfully at the child's jumper with an outstretched finger. 'Let's wait for Mum in the car, eh?'

Geraldine watches them go, Ivor's face sheepish, half-pleased. There is a triangle of shirt hanging out of the back of his trousers. She resists pulling him back to tuck it in, to wrap him in her arms again. Trousers, like life, never seem to fit Ivor.

Martha answers on the second ring. 'I was just about to phone you.' She sounds irritated.

Geraldine says, 'So you're up now, are you?' She means it as a joke, but it doesn't come out that way.

'I'm up. I had to get breakfast and then Ian rang.'

'Ian rang?'

'Yes. He wanted to ask me about flowers.'

'Flowers?'

'For the funeral.'

'The funeral, of course. Of course. Did he mention anything else?'

'Like what?'

Geraldine can see Greg gesticulating at her from the car. He is pretending to pull out his hair. What's left of it. 'Like furniture,' she says. 'Odds and ends. Pictures. That sort of thing.'

'Have you spoken to Eliza?'

'Just briefly.'

Martha says, 'Isn't it a bit early for all this? Shouldn't one at least wait until he's buried.'

'It's just that if we're going to be fair about all this . . .' Geraldine trails off.

Martha says, 'Oh right.'

The conversation is not going the way Geraldine intended. Martha can be unbelievably prickly and secretive she finds. And not just about David, either. When their mother died, Geraldine knows her own grief seemed excessive to some people, Greg for one, but she finds tears come easily and that the depletion she feels afterwards calms her. Eliza's anger was another form of release. But Martha had been so closed: *impenetrable*. There was one occasion when

41

Geraldine had caught her crying. It was several months after their mother had died, and they were shopping together in Bentalls, a department store in Kingston, chatting about normal things, and an assistant had squirted them, as they passed, with perfume, and after a while Geraldine had noticed Martha had gone quiet and become very interested in a rack of hosiery. When she turned, her face was pale and Geraldine was sure she had been crying, but Martha had rubbed her cheeks roughly and said she was fine. In the car home, she'd just said, 'Mum's perfume. Ô de Lancôme.' Geraldine had tried to hug her when they parted later, but Martha just mumbled something about how she'd got it all wrong. Geraldine, who hadn't liked to say anything but had thought it was Trésor, had said, 'No, they probably don't bother spraying you with old ones.'

Now she says, 'Matt, I wasn't ringing about that. I was ringing to see if you were OK, and that Kitten's settling in.'

'Kitten is fine.'

'Don't forget, you mustn't let him out. Not until he feels at home. Don't forget to butter his paws.'

'Geraldine. I am not keeping Kitten. I'm going to go down to Battersea Dogs Home this afternoon. They take cats and I'm sure they'll find it a good home.'

Geraldine feels a smart of panic. 'You can't do that.'

'It's better than having him put down, which is what you were suggesting yesterday.'

'No it's not. They'll put him down there anyway. He'll just have a miserable life in a cage for a few weeks before they do that. Staring out behind a glass wall at the people trooping past. I mean, who's going to choose him when there are kittens and . . .'

'Attractive cats.'

Geraldine laughs, despite herself. 'Martha,' she says pleadingly.

'Or dogs for that matter. I've never really got that. Do you think people go all the way to Battersea Dogs Home planning on a Dobermann or a red setter and then when they get there, they think, "Oh actually, that ginger tom's rather sweet. Maybe we need a cat instead."'

This time Geraldine just says, 'Martha?'

'Oh God.'

Geraldine knows Martha has given in by the tone of her voice.

'All right. OK. God, I'm so bullied. I won't take it to Battersea Dogs Home, but I'm not keeping it. I'm not going to be a mad single woman with a cat. I'll put a note up in the shop window. OK? Will that do? I'll find a nice home that way. It'll take longer, but I'll keep it until then.'

Geraldine can see Greg getting out of the car, striding up to the front door to get her. 'Yes, yes, I'm coming, I'm coming,' she says. 'Thank you, Matty.' By now Greg is standing in front of her and she can see his shoulders rising and falling. His breathing is ragged and there is a rash of sweat on his brow. After they make love he seems to collapse on top of her, cave in, as if it's taken it all out of him. He really should get his cholesterol checked. And the odd appearance at Mass wouldn't go astray either. She can see Father Anthony beginning to wonder. Sometimes she thinks there are so many people to worry about, she's going to go under.

*

That afternoon, as Eliza and Denis follow Gabriel around the garden with the video camera, and as Geraldine and Greg and Patrick and Ivor and Anna cycle sweatily around Richmond Park, and while Ian and Julia and the twins mourn quietly over a pub lunch in Camberley, Martha meets her best friends Keith and Karen in a café overlooking Wandsworth Common.

Keith and Karen have a small baby which they carry, discreetly, in a papoose. It is navy blue with a tartan lining, this papoose – or 'sling', Karen calls it – and the baby is so tiny it looks like another fold in the fabric, only its wine-coloured face visible, scrunched against Keith's T-shirt, below hair so dark and primeval it still looks wet from the birth canal.

'How old is she now?' asks Martha, peering, as she puts an espresso for her and two decaff lattes for them down on the table. 'How many weeks?'

Keith says, 'Two,' at the same time as Karen says, 'Three,' and they laugh. Keith and Karen are Martha's kind of parents.

Martha sits down between them. 'And are its eyes open yet?' It's her favourite new-born baby joke. Keith bends his head. He has had his hair cut scalp-short, to camouflage his balding crown, and he looks younger. He says, 'Oh yes. Won't be long before she's out in the world on her own. It's just a matter of weaning her and getting enough strength into those legs. As soon as she can manage the catflap she'll be out of here. Did you know, by the way, that mother cats eat their kittens' excrement?'

'No!' says Martha. She laughs fondly. Keith is a biology

teacher and his dropping of arcane pieces of knowledge into the conversation is one of the things she loves most about him. She raises her eyebrows at Karen, who smiles back. It is the first time she has met them out of their house since their baby was born. And it is a relief to her to find things between them unaltered. Other friends – and, God, Geraldine certainly – came out of pregnancy like changed beings, going in butterflies but coming out caterpillars, bulky and ponderous. And they all started carrying these big fabric bags decorated with pictures of nursery animals. But here are Karen and Keith, with just this papoose and a small black backpack between them, seeming to indicate that it is just a matter of choice, not circumstance.

Karen has her elbow on the table and she's leaning her cheek on her hand. Her freckly face is pale; there are shadows under her orange-flecked eyes, and her hair, which when it catches the light is the colour of toffee, is looking faded, as if the redness has been spun out of it. But she has lipstick on, which turns her mouth the same hue as her freckles. She says, 'Sounds like your cat is past the child-rearing stage.'

'It's not "mine".' Martha shields her eyes with her hand and makes her voice sound anguished. 'And it's male anyway.' She takes her hand down. 'You don't think a little furry friend for the baby? A kitten for Kit?'

This time when Keith and Karen speak at the same time, they say the same thing. 'No.'

Martha sighs. 'Thought not. Oh well, I've put a note up now and hopefully pet lovers will be flocking to my door.'

45

Keith says, 'Must be odd, a stepfather dying. I mean, how do you feel? Grief-struck? You weren't that close to him. Relieved? You don't have to worry about him? Guilty? At not having to think about not being fond of him, for not dashing round with casseroles, for thinking, oh well, you're not related, let your own kids look after you?'

Martha doesn't answer. She looks at Keith closely. He nods, 'Yeah. I can see it's tricky.'

Karen, who has detached the baby from Keith's chest, is breastfeeding, her little finger coaxing the baby's mouth on to her nipple. She says, 'He loved your mum, though. That's important, isn't it?'

Keith says, 'Of course he did. Yes.'

Martha says, 'Hm.'

Sometimes she wonders whether they would be disappointed in her if they knew her as well as they thought they did. She has known Karen, off and on, since school, and met Keith on a train when she was travelling in India. She introduced them. And since then it is as if she has become part of their relationship. They have opinions about her life, her family, they talk around her and about her. They joke about her sisters. It's true that when she first got together with David, and was setting up the shop, they drifted apart a little. In fact, in the six years that she and David were an item, the years of dinner parties and concert recitals, when she was absorbed in David's world, they did fall out of her life for a bit. But they were still there when she broke it off and, unlike her sisters, demanding reasons, took her in without need for explanation, neatly bundling any resentment they might have felt at her neglect into ammunition against him – 'your jeweller'. For a while after that, they tried to match her up with people they knew, like an awkward daughter to be found a home for. But nowadays they don't bother. They are a threesome, a unit. Martha finds it infinitely comfortable. Only occasionally does she worry that they notice, behind the jokes and the banter, how little she opens up herself.

'You are clever,' she adds. 'Where would I be without you? Without both of you?' She leans forward as Karen passes the sated baby back to her father. 'And where would you be without me?' she says to this tiny scrunch of life. 'Nowhere, that's where.'

By the time they finish their coffee, the baby has started stirring and Keith, after trying to bounce it up and down a bit, suggests they go for a walk across the Common. It's quite warm when they come out of the café, and there are lots of families with childrens and buggies and bikes striding around in a haphazard Sunday manner. It is one of those autumn days that could be mistaken for spring. The mist has lifted, but it is still smoky at the top of the trees. The leaves haven't yet turned, but the trees look not quite right, a little too green, as if they're about to.

Keith, Martha and Karen strike off diagonally across the grass towards the pond, not very fast because Karen is walking in a slow, lopsided way. Martha slips her arm into hers to hurry her along and says, 'We should go out soon, shouldn't we, you and me? Leave Keith at home with the baby. Or how about a shopping trip?' Karen gives a wan smile. Martha realises they've talked about nothing but herself all day. She racks her brain for the right sort of question.

After a few paces, she says, 'So, are you getting any sleep? Is she sleeping through the night yet?' Keith makes a spluttering noise, even though he's a bit ahead, and Karen says shortly, 'No.'

'Oh God. Are you knackered?'

'Not yet. Not really. I'm sure I will be, but it's still weird and . . . it is quite nice at night. Quiet, everyone else asleep, just me and the baby.'

'And Keith.'

'Well no, actually. He is sleeping on the sofa.'

'Too right I am,' says Keith from up ahead.

Martha looks at Karen to see if she's serious. She looks from one to the other, from Karen wobbling along next to her, to Keith, also walking with unnaturally small steps, his dark shaved head bent forward, in front. She's sure this can't be right, that parents shouldn't sleep apart. Something must have gone wrong between them. She tries to catch Karen's eye, but she is just smiling normally. They fall into step with Keith, who has stopped to rearrange the straps, and Martha puts her arm through his, too, and they are linked together the three of them, with Martha in the middle, but she has this odd feeling that something is awry, that they know something she doesn't. For the first time ever in their friendship, she feels left out.

After that things don't go quite as they should. The three of them have developed a habit of going to the cinema in the early evenings on Sundays. Today, Karen is insistent that the baby shouldn't change anything. Kit will just sleep, she says, 'It'll be dark and babies don't mind loud noises. They're used to the womb. Think of the digestive system – do you think even Jean-Claude Van Damme can throw up anything noisier than that?' But when they get there, they find babies do change things after all. Their choice, a new British thriller, 'exploring the interplay between sex and drugs in a Glasgow tenement', is an 18 certificate. 'We can't let children into that,' says the boot-faced woman at the desk. 'She's three weeks old,' says Keith. 'Exactly,' says the woman, turning to the next customer.

Martha is about to suggest a meal, when she notices again how out of focus Karen's movements seem, and says, trying out the idea, that perhaps they should call it a night. Karen and Keith both look quite grateful. They kiss her and she watches the two of them amble arm in arm down the street towards the Tube. They haven't gone far when Keith stops and Karen bends over him, fiddling again with the blasted sling thing. And Martha corrects herself: not the two of them – there are three of them now.

When Martha gets home, earlier than she was expecting, in that dusty trough of mid-evening, no lights blink on the answer phone – her sisters have clearly given up on her – and the cat is uncomfortably asleep under the kitchen table. It is half on the black bin bag and appears to have had a go at it first; there are papers, scruffed, scratched, over the floor. Martha bends to collect them: a couple of yellowing party invitations, a bus ticket, a ski pass, the invitation to Geraldine's wedding, a box of matches with a phone number scrawled across the lid. She gathers them up and picks up the bin bag to poke them in.

She sees David's writing on an envelope and her stomach lurches. Under it is a Valentine (a black and white postcard of a couple kissing: David was always big on the romantic gesture). Why has she kept all this stuff? What use does it have? She stuffs the debris in but as she does so, she sees something else. An old red and white plastic bag from The Notting Hill Record and Tape Exchange, letters from an earlier life. She burrows her hand into this and pulls out a letter from Colin Cooper, the boyfriend before David. She doesn't read it: it will be earnest, she knows. After that comes a crumpled piece of lined A4. Blue school ink. Doodles. 'Don't walk away in silence' scrawled across the top of the page, like an epigraph. She laughs out loud this time. Her first love. Nick Martin. The Nick Years: 1980–84.

It has been a long time since she thought about Nick or Colin. It is as if her memory of herself as a romantic being stopped with David. What era is this now? she wonders. The Post-David Era? Or has time frozen? She tuts at herself and stuffs everything back in the bag.

She goes through to the sitting room where the table lamps are still on from the morning and now bounce light against the dark windows. She puts on a CD and pulls the curtains closed. Then she stands in the doorway. Maybe the linen cushions on the sofa are too bland, or perhaps the dove-grey throw isn't as attractive as she thought against the pure white Durham, but there seems to be something unfinished about the place tonight, something not quite right.

In the morning she hangs the following sign in the shop window:

KITTEN

Attractive and unusual tabby seeking new home on death of owner. Enquire within.

chapter three

the work space

'Anyone who works at home without the luxury of a
dedicated workroom or office knows how difficult it
can be to combine working and living space.'

Good Housekeeping: Complete Home Book
by Linda Gray
(HarperCollins, 2001)

SOMEBODY is a little in love with Martha. His name is Jason
and he is an expert in furniture restoration. The next day,
Monday, is his day for checking in.

'Helllooooo,' he calls through the letter-box. 'Wakey,
wakey, rise and shine.'

He rings the bell and after a minute or two sees the flat
door open and Martha come round it towards the front of
the shop, smiling at him. For a moment, the sight of her, as
every Monday, stops his heart. It's not that she's beautiful,
because she isn't. Her hair isn't *full* like the girls down the
golf club. It's flat and brown, a cap of hair like on a Russian

doll, only her features are sharp not rounded. She's in jeans as usual, and her feet are bare. They are knobbly feet. No nail varnish. She gets to the shop door and reaches up to unbolt the top lock. Her eyes are puffy and she looks anxious. She often does. Anxious or cross. Maybe it is this that draws him to her, brings out his protective instinct: isn't that what they say? She is wearing a man's blue shirt, but there is a button missing halfway down and, as she stretches, he has to will his eyes away from the slight gape in the material. She smiles at him through the glass, and then he remembers that of course it isn't the anxiousness that draws him to her, but this. The mouth, pulled in at the corners, even as she widens it, as if she's self-conscious of the slightly crooked teeth behind, or annoyed with herself for giving in to anything so gentle.

She opens the door. 'Hello. You're early.'

Jason has turned away to face the street. The market stalls are setting up. He sighs and sees his own breath warming the air. He adjusts the belt on his jeans, and turns back. 'Early bird, me.'

She steps out, waves to the stall-holder unloading the vegetables. 'Golly. Nice day. I hadn't realised.'

'Not bad. Not bad.' Jason looks up at the sky which is a dark blue. But it's the kind of dark blue that can merge subtly into dark grey clouds and there are some of them collecting at the end of the road. 'For September,' he adds.

'Are you in the loading bay? Have you got the *buffet deux corps*?'

'Of course I have the *buffet deux corps*. When have I ever let you down?'

'Oh good,' says Martha. 'You OK?'

'Diamond,' he says. 'You?'

'Swell,' she says out of the corner of her mouth in an American accent. Then, 'When we've got that in, have you got time to look at a little three-legged fruitwood table?'

'*Naturellement*, I've always got time for a little three-legged fruitwood table. I've always got time for you,' he says. He mimes the theatrical doffing of a feather hat. 'Your will, my fair lady, is my command.' Then he turns to walk back to open the door of his van and, scrunching his face up, says, 'Wanker' to himself under his breath. He can never talk normally when he's with her. 'Fuck,' he adds, catching his fingers. 'Fuck and fuck.'

Martha comes out after him and helps him manipulate the *buffet* into the shop. They stand together, inspecting the new door catch and the new back legs, and after a bit she says, 'Beautiful, Jason. Very good job,' and smiles at him again.

He clears his throat. 'Right. Where do you want me?' And they go down to the basement, where he drops down on to his haunches and, for a while, loses himself in the knots of the fruitwood, smoothing it over with his hands, judging for himself how easy it will be to glue or clamp a new joint. Then, the two of them haul it up the stairs and, after wrapping it in the big grey horsehair blankets Jason carries around with him, lift it gently into the van. Martha wipes her hands on her jeans. 'Quick coffee?'

Jason says, 'Love to. Better not. Things to do, people to see.'

Martha leans forward and it looks as if she's going to kiss

him and he flinches, but she's only flicking some of the dust from the basement stairs off the shoulder of his T-shirt. Sometimes he thinks she knows how he feels and is teasing him. 'God, sorry,' she says. 'It's filthy down there.'

'Don't worry. It's just dirt.'

She puts her hands in her pockets. 'Well, if you're sure about the coffee.'

'Okey dokey, chokey lokey,' he says, backing away and getting into the van. 'Catch ya later.'

'See you,' she says, and waves him off, still looking at him with that awkward smile. He glances back in his mirror just before he pulls out into Balham High Road and she's still standing there, with the early sun on her face and that tower of mottled dark lilac clouds she hasn't yet noticed behind.

When she has seen his van negotiate the bump at the end of the road, Martha turns and goes back into the shop, spinning the OPEN/CLOSED sign to OPEN. Bugger, she thinks, I never asked him if he wanted a cat.

April arrives at 11 a.m. in a flurry of apologies. 'Sorryimlate, sorryimlate, sorryimlate, Tube,' she says, flinging some item of clothing with a fluffy edging over the back of the rocking horse. 'Overslept. Alarm clock, bla bla. Tube, bla bla. You know. Nightmare.' April is taking a year out from a degree in furniture and product design at Manchester (failed coursework, serious overdraft) and is helping Martha out while she considers what to do next.

Martha says sardonically, 'Ah, the cavalry.'

April was one of only two applicants who answered an ad Martha placed in the window earlier in the summer. The other was a sensible, early middle-aged Balham woman in search of an 'outside interest' with which to fill the hours when her children were at school. She would have been fine, diligent, a sensible choice who, on quiet days, would have genned up on *Miller's Antique Guide*. April was none of those things, and didn't. When she first came in, she told Martha that she wanted to transform the way people looked at their homes, not simply as somewhere to sleep and eat, but as a temple to their inner selves. Martha asked her where she lived and she said, 'A squat in Colliers Wood,' and then the two of them laughed for a good full minute. So Martha employed her, giving the too-short and too-tight T-shirt and the hooded sweat-jacket the benefit of the doubt. It hasn't taken her long to realise that April isn't a great deal of help but, none the less, Martha enjoys having her around. She is a lesson in how to be. On the plump side, doughy even, her face still freckled with adolescent acne, she dresses and flashes herself about with the careless confidence of youth.

April is clapping the tips of her fingers together, looking around the shop, like a new arrival checking out a party. She is wearing very low-slung, very flared trousers made out of what looks like tent material, which don't exactly draw attention away from the roll or two across her stomach and which, more to the point, will trip her on the basement stairs. Her eyebrows are plucked into a thin, high arch. 'So. What's happening?' she says, pulling her pale curtain of hair back and tucking it into the neck of her top. 'It's Monday. Why're we open?'

'Oh.' Martha tells her about Graham's death and having to close the shop on Saturday. April's face loosens in sympathy. 'Ohhhnoo. Ohhh. Poor you. Ooh.' Martha says, 'Well not really. Poor other people. Poor Ian, his son.' April says, 'Oh-aw. Bless.'

'So anyway,' continues Martha, 'I thought we might as well open today. Could you get to work on that pine corner cupboard downstairs? The off-white eggshell, the glaze and the paintbrushes are in the storeroom.'

April says, 'Cool.'

'Good.'

'Jason been?'

'Yup. Been. Gone.' April's habit of talking is contagious.

'Moonsick?'

'Don't be ridiculous.' April has this thing about Jason fancying Martha. 'Honestly.'

Martha gets up, flicks April's fluffy thing over her arm, and hangs it on a hook on the inside of the flat door. To be twenty . . . Martha was with her teenage sweetheart Nick Martin when she was twenty. He was off at university but he'd come down at weekends to visit her. You'd hear that Ducati he had vrooming down the main road towards her turning, hours before he actually got there. God, when she was twenty, she thought life would carry on as it was for ever.

She says, closing the door, 'Anyway, I'm off radar. Late thirties and moonsick do not go together.'

'Oh,' says April. 'Don't be dippy.'

'I mean it.' Martha suspects April is just teasing her anyway. A woman of thirty-eight must look over the hill to her. A spinster of the parish. 'There's more to my life than men. Now get on.'

April still stands in the middle of the shop, unconcerned. She says, 'I went to see that new thriller set in the Glasgow ganglands last night. Have you seen it?'

Martha says shortly, 'No.'

'It's brilliant. You've got to.'

Martha says, 'Yes. So I've heard. Cupboard?'

April says, 'Oh. How about coffee? What would you say to a cup of coffee?'

In her head, Martha says, 'Hello cup of coffee,' but it isn't her voice, it's Nick Martin's voice. She says, 'Oh, OK.'

April goes next door to the café and Martha stays sitting where she is. Since she saw Nick Martin's letter, he keeps coming into her head. For a moment he's fleshed out, at seventeen, in the shop in front of her, the cocky young boy in the jeans and leather jacket, a packet of cigarettes in his top pocket. Rothmans. Roth Man, he used to call himself. She tries to adjust her image of him, to add on twenty years, but she can't do it. Nick Martin. God. He was so different to David. What would David, with his taxi accounts and his matching luggage, have made of him? She stops this thought in its tracks. She shakes her head, straightens her back, swivels her legs round until they're under her desk. 'Right,' she says.

First she rings Darling Buds in Tooting and orders a large wreath of plain white lilies for Graham's coffin. Then she phones Ian, who is at home, to tell him she's done so and to discuss the arrangements further – service in Wimbledon at 12 p.m., interment at Putney Vale 1 p.m., drinks and snacks at 'the parental house' 1.30 p.m. And then she leaves a message on Geraldine's answer phone, passing those details on.

Also at Ian's request, she rings Eliza at work. Eliza says, 'Oh Lord. Friday.'

'Is that a problem?'

'Um. No. I suppose not. Very selfish, I know, but I was hoping for Saturday.'

'Well . . .'

'No, no, I know. It was only that there's a meeting. But forget it. Friday's fine. I'll be there. I'll probably bring Gabriel, if that's all right. People like to see small children on these occasions, don't they? It reminds them that life goes on. And Gabriel is such a poppet. He has a knack for cheering people up.'

Martha says, 'I expect the twins will be there. Geraldine's might be at school. Or maybe not. I'm not sure.'

'It'll be dull for him if they're not. Maybe I'll leave him. No, no, I'll bring him.'

Martha says, 'Whatever.' She smiles at April who is dancing back into the shop with the takeaway cappuccinos. She rounds her eyes as she takes one from her, and mouths, 'Thanks.'

Eliza is saying something about Geraldine. Martha, who is peeling off her foamy lid, says, 'Sorry, missed that. What did you say?' Eliza tells her about a series of phone conversations she has had with their oldest sister, culminating in one earlier today in which Geraldine broke down in tears. 'Typical, isn't it?' Eliza says. 'Everything comes down to her. My stepfather, my tragedy.' Traditionally, when one of the sisters is cross with another, she rings the third to tell them – a kind of sibling bagatelle. Martha realises this is her cue to begin a lengthy and unsparing examination of

59

Geraldine's character, but a woman in high-heeled boots has come into the shop with a pert expression on her face. April is leaning against the door to the cellar taking noisy sips from her coffee. You can tell from the woman's stance that this irritates her, that she had been expecting more formal attention. So Martha says, 'Oh, poor old Geraldine. She does get upset by things,' which stems Eliza's flow and makes her say, with matching, if slightly disappointed, sympathy, 'Yeah, I know.' The woman in high-heeled boots has gone straight to the armoirette and has called April over with some searching questions. 'Is it French? Has it been stripped? What are these darker marks? What exactly is an "armoirette"?' April is answering with a defensive certainty that would not inspire Martha with confidence: 'Absolutely. Definitely not. They are the marks of extreme age. This is a very interesting piece, smaller than your average armoire.'

'Martha?'

'Sorry, Eliza. I'd better go.'

She puts the phone down and is about to go to April's aid when it rings. She vacillates for a second, thinks it might be Ian and picks up. It's Geraldine. Geraldine says, 'I've had a very upsetting conversation with Eliza. I mean, why is she always so—'

Martha cuts her off too. 'I'm a bit busy here, Ger. Can I ring you back?'

Geraldine says, 'Oh. All right. But listen: has anyone rung Philip, Mum's godfather? I know he'll be so upset not to be invited. And what about their bridge friends? The Howards? The ones who moved to Petworth.'

60

Martha says, 'That's a good idea, Ger. Why don't you ring them?'

'Yes, OK.'

'Anything else?'

'I can't believe we're having the do at the house. It's practically falling down. And we have to start clearing it, sorting who has what . . . I'd be perfectly happy to have it in Kingston.'

'I think Ian would like it to be at the house.'

Geraldine sighs. Her tone goes flat. 'I just am beginning to feel . . . what would Mummy want?' There is a catch in her voice.

Martha says gently, 'Mum's not here, Ger. Really, it's only what Ian wants that matters. And his sister, of course.'

'Is Susie coming?'

'God, I'm not sure. I expect so. Though Vancouver is a long way. I don't know. I forgot to ask. Cheer up, Ger. Look, I'd better . . .'

The woman in the heels opens the door to the armoire, closes it and opens it again, testing the lock. Then she starts poking around inside, feeling the weight of the shelves. April is standing by a little too proprietorially. She is holding her coffee cup at an angle and it might be about to spill. Martha says, 'I've really got to go now, Ger.'

Geraldine says, 'OK. See you on Friday. Speak to you before then. Oh and . . .' She speeds up and this last bit comes out in a rush. 'Greg played squash with David and told him Graham had died and David wants to come to the funeral. I thought I'd better mention it to you first.' She laughs nervously. 'So it doesn't come as too much of a shock.'

'*How* much?' the woman in heeled boots is saying.

'Martha?' says Geraldine. 'Are you still there?'

'I've got to go.'

April is holding on to the price label by the ribbon, for security, for protection, and is smiling tightly. '*How* much?' the woman repeats. Martha feels an urge to grab the label, tear it up and stamp on it. But she says, 'Can I help you?'

'I was just telling your assistant. I tried to come on Saturday, but you were closed.'

'Yes. I'm sorry. My—' Martha doesn't mean to say what she says next. She means to say 'stepfather'. But she is feeling so tense suddenly, so defensive, she says 'My father died on Saturday.' April turns her head a few degrees like a startled bird. Martha has put her hand over her own mouth as if to stop herself saying anything more. For an instant, she imagines her father falling backwards over the side of his yacht, sinking to the bottom like a stone. Or collapsing, hand pressed to his chest, in the middle of sex with one of his students. April says, 'But . . .' and then Martha, coming to her senses, says, 'Sorry. That came out wrong,' and she is about to backtrack, but the woman in boots has put her hand on her arm and is saying, 'No, no, don't apologise. Please. God. Awful. I'm so sorry.' She has stepped away from the armoire. There is nothing imperious about her now. She just looks kind. 'God, and here I am barging in and demanding service, and trying to haggle.'

Martha says, 'No, no, actually—' But April interrupts, 'He had been ill off and on,' she says, her eyes on Martha's. 'But no matter how prepared one is, it still comes as a terrible shock.'

She puts her arm around Martha's shoulder and holds her against her bare midriff protectively – or warningly.

The woman in boots says, 'How awful. I am sorry. The death of a parent . . .' She stares at Martha for a bit and it almost looks as if her eyes are beginning to fill. Then she opens her bag and gets out her cheque book. 'Look, I love this cupboard. It's just what I've been looking for. I'm often passing, and what with parking . . . I don't often . . . but from now on I'm going to tell all my friends about you . . . Here –' She holds the cheque out, but before Martha can do anything about it, or say anything more, there is a clang and the door opens again.

All three of them turn to see a tall, thin man, with straggly brown hair and a lopsided face that seems to be all bones. He is probably in his thirties, but to April's mind he looks much older. He is stooping to get in the door. Martha notices his eyes – one is green and the other is different, bluer. The woman in the heels notices his clothes. Nothing matches. He is wearing a thin paisley shirt, with orange swirls on it, a tan corduroy jacket with too-short sleeves, and blue trousers that may, because of the fabric, have once belonged in a suit. And the kind of shoes her godchildren wear – like plimsolls only they come up over the ankles. They have stars on the side, which would be no good for tennis. And these ones are red.

The man looks from one to the other of them. He is carrying a small brown leather suitcase which he puts down on the floor. He says shyly in a voice which is deep and serious, slightly faltering: 'Sorry. Am I . . . am I interrupting?'

There is a pause. He is not what any of them would

63

expect to see in Martha's shop. He is too nervous to be a dealer, too . . . untidy to be a customer. There is a moment as the three women struggle to register him. And in that moment the woman in boots takes control. She says, 'No, not at all. I'm going.' Turning back to Martha, she says, 'I'll send my builder with his van.' She presses the cheque into Martha's hand and then cups it with her own. 'Take care,' she says. On the way out of the door, she says quietly to the newcomer, 'Poor girl. Her father died on Saturday.' The tall man says, 'Oh,' and rests his eyes on Martha again. The shop door clangs as the boot woman leaves. Martha stands there with the cheque balled in her palm.

April, breathing out, says, 'Sorry. Can I be of any assistance?'

The man, stooping slightly, sways his head to one side to avoid a wrought-iron chandelier. He looks panicked, ducks more energetically than he needs to as if about to be bombarded by low-flying objects.

'Are you looking for anything in particular?' April adds.

The man moves to the left and straightens. His Adam's apple protrudes when he talks. He says doubtfully, 'A kitten?'

April looks at Martha and then back to the man and says, 'A what?'

'A kitten. Is this the right . . . er . . .?'

Martha comes to and clamps her hands together. 'Kitten, of course,' she says.

April looks at her, nonplussed. The man jerks his head back fractionally. Martha realises two things then: firstly, that April doesn't know about the cat; secondly, that, in the

64

light of her father's supposed death, the man might expect her to sound more subdued. With effortful diffidence, she adds, 'Kitten, yes. Gosh, you're quick. I've only just put the note up.'

The man has made a couple of tentative steps into the shop. 'I was passing and . . . um . . . Was it your father's, then?' He's moving his weight from foot to foot. He's put his fists deep into his jacket pockets. 'The note said death of owner . . . um . . .'

Martha closes the cupboard and locks it. She darts April a look. 'That's right.'

'So . . . it must have been . . . was it very sudden?'

Martha looks down at her shoes. She semi-winces, gritting her teeth and half-closing one eye. 'He had been ill off and on . . .' she begins.

The man says, 'He can't have been expecting it. If he'd just taken on a cat, I mean.'

Martha draws a pattern on the floor with her toe. She says slowly, 'Ah. He hadn't exactly just taken it on. The cat's quite . . .'

'Oh?'

'No. Kitten has been around a while. You see, he's been called Kitten ever since he was a kitten.' Martha turns and widens her eyes at April, who shrugs and, heading for the cellar steps, says brightly, 'Cool. Well, I'd better get on with that chest of drawers.'

Martha turns back to the man. 'But it's definitely a kitten you're looking for?'

The man has taken something out of his pocket, something round and soft, a ball, a squishy ball, which he's rolling

65

around in one hand. He says, 'I've . . . er . . . promised my daughter a thing, er kitten. It's her, um, thing, birthday. Problem is, the pet shop says it's not really the right time of thing. And we don't want a pedigree or anything. Just a moggy. Is it . . . is it still available?' He smiles for the first time and it's a nice gentle smile, though his teeth are stained.

'Yes. It's definitely still available. But it's . . .'

The man is looking at her hopefully.

'It's tabby.'

He puts his head on one side as if considering it. 'Tabby. Now you've thrown me.' She thinks she has put him off but then she realises he's joking, which is surprising because, along with the nerviness, there is something unusually formal about him. 'Tabby's probably fine,' he says.

She tries again. 'But it is a slightly older kitten? Not in the first flush of . . . kittenhood. Though there are lots of advantages to that. Very nice nature. Speyed. Inoculated. Save on bills?'

He smiles again, but more absent-mindedly, then looks at his watch. It is a Casio digital watch with a scratched face. The thin black strap makes his wrist look delicate. There are dark hairs on the bones. 'Well it's, er, can my daughter see it? Could I bring her back after school? She's at Kelmscott, just round the corner.'

'We're open till five.'

The man bends to pick up his suitcase. The leather bows out at the sides as if it is very full. There is a corner of purple fabric sticking out of one edge. He says, 'Five would be OK. Can we come then? We have a thing to do first. Um. That would be very kind.' He turns. 'It's here somewhere is it? Hiding?'

Martha laughs. 'It's upstairs.'

He smiles again. 'I see. Well, see you later. Five-ish. And, um . . .' He makes as if to take a step closer to her and then falters. 'Sorry about your father.'

'Thank you,' she says.

After he's gone, she screams with exaggerated embarrassment down to the basement. 'Aaaargh.' April comes to the foot of the stairs. '*So* sorry about your dad,' she says solemnly, and then snorts with laughter. 'Sold to the woman in the boots,' she whinnies. Martha remembers the money then and guiltily unfolds the cheque in her hand.

At lunchtime, Martha sets off in her Volvo for the auction viewings in Chelsea. But she doesn't find anything worth bidding for. She is later than usual and she doesn't even meet anyone she knows. Usually, there's somebody – some fellow misfit: Melissa, a shop-owner from Notting Hill, and her yapping dog; or Bill and Steve, two dealers from Brighton. But today there are only unknown faces, and even though she's tempted by a one-armed nineteenth-century marble angel, it is hugely overpriced and nothing else grabs her. At any rate, not with her mother's house swirling around in her mind – all those bits and pieces, furniture other people will grab, furniture no one will want but will assume can be left to her to take care of.

It's quiet in the shop in the afternoon. There are a couple more coffee/snack runs, interspersed with a bored, at-a-loose-end visit from Nell, the woman who runs Sustainable

Forests, the second-hand bookshop. She throws herself on a daybed. 'God, business is slow,' she moans, fiddling idly with the edging on an antique cushion. 'Not here!' sings April. 'But you have to know your sales technique.' Martha shoots her an admonitory look. Nell says, 'Rent's going up. Have you heard?' Martha says she hasn't. Nell says, 'Well be warned. That's all.'

At 4 p.m., Martha sends April home. At 5 p.m., she opens the door, looks up the street a few times, and then turns the OPEN sign to CLOSED. She is still pottering about in the shop ten minutes later, straightening the patchwork cushions on the two-seater, watering the miniature terracotta pots of ivy that decorate the wine-table, testing out some of her new stock of 'Room Colognes' ('Lavender In The Wind' is particularly aromatic), thinking to herself how happy she can be alone in her shop, with her beautiful things, when the letter-box clatters and, turning, she sees two noses pressed low against the door, with a darker shape behind them. Ah, the odd man, she thinks, and his daughter. No, not daughter, his *children*.

She goes to let them in and indeed there he is again, still with his little suitcase, his hair more lanky than before, the buttons of his corduroy jacket done up wrong, and next to him, *below* him, two small children, a boy and a girl.

'Hello,' she says.

The two children stare at her. The girl is older than the boy. She's got very straight hair with a severe short fringe, and big dark brown eyes that gaze at Martha suspiciously. She's wearing a duffel-coat and tights in a multitude of stripes, but a thin summer dress, as if all her seasons are muddled. The boy is wearing tracksuit bottoms and a jacket with a teddy bear on the pocket. Both of them are carrying tiny plastic bags the size of paperback books, which appear to be decorated with pirates.

The man says, 'Say hello.' There is something odd about his complexion.

'Hello,' the girl says dully. The boy still stares.

Martha says, 'Come in. Come in.' The three of them troop up the steps into the shop, but stop just inside. Martha bends down and, smiling, says, 'And what's your name?'

'Hazel.'

'And yours?' Her voice is going up at the ends in what she hopes is a jolly manner. He hadn't said two children. He'd said one. Well, just so long as they don't touch anything.

The boy still doesn't answer, but the girl says, 'He's called Stanley, but we call him Stan. Except for my nan who says his name makes her toes crawl. She calls him Michael which is his middle name. My middle name is Twig.'

The man, the girl's father, says, 'No it's not.'

'Yes it is. Hazel Twig.'

'It's Elizabeth. Your middle name is Elizabeth.'

'But you call me Hazel Twig.'

'Yes, but that's my name for you. Your real name is Elizabeth. And flesh crawl. Not toes crawl. Your grandmother says Stanley makes her flesh crawl.'

The girl closes her eyes. 'OK. Flesh crawl.'

Martha gives a nervous laugh. They are talking to each other as if she is not here. She says, 'Right. OK. Let's go up, shall we?'

She turns and is about to open the door to the flat when she hears the girl say, 'Yes please,' and she realises that she

69

has come up quickly behind her and has slipped her spare hand into hers. It feels warm and sticky. She looks down at it. The nails are bitten and there are traces of pink nail varnish across the middle of them. She says, 'So how old are you, Hazel Twig?' and Hazel says, 'I'm six and three quarters and Stan's four. Nan says that's a difficult age, but Dad says he should try being forty.' Martha looks over the child's head to catch the man's eye, but he's not directly behind them like she thinks he is. He's further back in the shop, about to lift the little boy on to the rocking horse. Her grip on the door knob tightens. Before she can stop herself, she says shrilly, 'Ooh, careful. Fragile!' The boy looks up at her, as does the man. The boy's mouth turns just a fraction at the corner. His eyes are big and brown like his sister's. Their mother must have brown eyes. The man says, 'Sorry,' and begins to put him down on the floor. Martha releases the door knob. She says quickly, 'It's OK. Just be, er . . . be gentle.'

She can hear the horse's hiccuping rock, each creak agonising to her nerves, as she and Hazel carry on up the stairs. But then Hazel stops. 'Why doesn't the light have a shade on it? Why's it just a bulb?' And Martha begins to explain about not being able to find one that's quite right, that overhead light-shades are a very tricky area, that she never buys anything unless it's perfect and the perfect overhead light-shade has so far evaded her, and then she says, 'Look, about this cat, Hazel. He's a really, really lovely cat. But he's not a kitten. I mean, he's kitten-like, he's just not a tiny kitten like on boxes of chocolates, you know?'

Hazel says, 'Oh.'

'And if it's a kitten that you want, then perhaps we should

go downstairs and tell your daddy now that he's not quite what you're looking for. Not your favourite kind of cat. In fact I should have told your daddy this earlier, but there was a bit of a misunderstanding.'

'What's a misunderstanding?'

'It's either a lie or a mistake, depending on your view-point.'

'Oh.' Hazel sits down on the stair. 'How inconvenient,' she says.

Martha laughs. She leans against the wall. 'What does inconvenient mean?' she says.

Hazel opens the plastic bag in her hand and brings out a packet of sweets, a tube of pastel-coloured sherbets in a twist of Cellophane. 'I don't really know,' she says. 'Nan says it about Saturdays. The purple ones are my favourite. What are yours?'

Martha sits down next to her and studies them carefully. 'Er . . . white,' she says. 'The white ones are nice.'

'And the orange ones.'

'Yes, I like the orange ones, too. Maybe not as much as the white ones, but they're still nice. You sure you can . . . oh, thanks. You've got a lot of sweets in there, Hazel.'

Hazel sighs. 'Yeah.'

She puts her hand into the plastic bag again and brings out a blue and white packet, and a yellow tube Martha recognises from her own childhood. 'Sherbet Fountain, Milky Way Stars,' Hazel recites. She wrinkles her nose. 'Milky Way Stars are always a bit stale.'

'Maybe you should choose something different next time then?'

'I didn't choose them.' She shakes her head, putting out both her hands, palm-up, as if explaining something to an idiot. 'It's a party bag.'

'What's a party bag?'

'From a party.'

Martha says, 'Oh. I see. Like a going home present. Was it fun?'

The girl says, 'Not really. The usual.'

There's a pause. The girl looks very serious. They can hear muffled giggles from downstairs. Martha thinks what kind of a child is this, so blasé, and says, 'Listen, shall we go and look at the cat? Or would you rather not bother?'

The girl sighs again. She says in a sing-song voice, 'No, let's go.'

So they do. They carry on up the stairs and into Martha's flat and together they look in the kitchen ('Not there,' sings Hazel), and the sitting room ('Not there') and finally the bedroom, where on the end of the duvet, on top of Martha's beautiful, delicate, dove-grey pashmina, they find Kitten.

When he opens one eye and sees them, Kitten behaves like a cat that has got used to its habitat. He stretches out, his mottled stomach rippling, the tips of his paws and his claws reaching out away from them as he stretches, lengthening his body into a crescent. He tucks his head upside down, revealing to them his throat. Then he twirls over on to the other side, as if he is no longer interested. The girl says, 'Oh,' and goes up to him cautiously. 'He-llo,' she says. 'Hell-o.' She strokes the top of his head with straightened fingers.

Martha resists the temptation to shoo the cat off the shawl. Instead she says quietly, 'He won't bite.'

72

The girl turns, looking irritated. 'I know. I'm just letting him get used to me.'

Martha says, 'Oh right.' And she stands and watches as this girl, this Hazel Twig, massages the cat under his chin and buries her face in his fur. 'Do you know,' the girl says after a bit, 'his feet smell just like feet. Like our feet – they have that sort of feety smell.'

Martha laughs. 'You'd think they'd smell of fur.'

'Yeah.' The girl bends to sniff some more. 'But they don't. They smell of feet.' She burrows her nose into his out-stretched stomach. She stays there a bit, making a cooing, chortling sound, and then she stands up and says, shrugging, 'I did sort of want a kitten.'

Martha feels a wave of unhappiness come over her. This cat and this little mite, whose mother doesn't dress her properly. She says, 'I know. I know. It's just the cat is called Kitten. I think that's where we went wrong.'

'Daddy said it was going to be a kitten.'

'I know. It was a misunderstanding.'

'A mistake?'

Martha nods her head and then shakes it. 'More of a lie.'

The girl thinks for a bit and then says, 'Why are there price labels on everything?'

'Sorry?'

'All your stuff. It's got tags on it.'

'Well, it's a shop.'

'Up here, I mean. Why has all your furniture, like your blanket, got prices on it?'

'Well, some of it's from the shop and some of it's going to go back to the shop.'

'Why?'

'Because that's my job. I keep things. I sell things. I . . .'

Hazel says, 'I wouldn't sell my things. Like my Barbie duvet cover. It's mine. I wouldn't want to sell it.'

'Yes. Well, you don't have a shop.'

Frown. 'Oh. I think I'll go and find my daddy now.'

They meet the man and the boy coming up. The boy is grinning, though he stops when he sees Martha, and the same wary look comes over his face. The man says to the girl, 'Find the kitten?'

Martha can feel Hazel looking at her. And then Hazel says, 'It's a cat. He's nice. His tummy is soft. He gave me a kiss on the nose. And his feet smell like feet.'

Martha says pleadingly – she's not quite sure if she's addressing the girl or her father – 'He needs a good home.'

The man still doesn't look at her. He says to the girl, 'Do you want to go back now and think about it? We can ring the lady later.'

Hazel doesn't say anything. She is still holding her bag of sweets. The boy starts swinging on the banisters. He's leaving marks with his trainers on the wall. The naked bulb hanging from the ceiling sways. Martha thinks the girl wants a kitten: she should have a kitten. She's about to say this when Hazel says it for her. 'No.'

Martha says swiftly, 'No, I didn't think so.' They should all leave her now and she won't have to think about them any more, or worry why their clothes don't match. She gives a quick smile at the father. His hair is long in some places and short in others. There are smile lines at the sides of his eyes, a neat fan, but also deep grooves between his eyebrows, hacked at random. And those odd eyes. Martha makes a small movement with her hands which is meant to urge them down the stairs and out of her shop and off to wherever it is they belong. It's too crowded all of a sudden. It's only a small stairwell after all. The man nods awkwardly. He makes an abrupt exhalation sound, like a train coming to a halt, and turns as if to go. But the girl hasn't moved. She says, with more panic now, 'No.' The man, who is holding the boy's hand, turns his head up to her. 'No,' she says again. She has sat down on the stairs with her little plastic bag of sweets on her lap. 'I know I said I wanted a kitten,' she says. 'But, Dad, would it be all right if I had this cat instead?'

The man is looking up at his daughter. He widens his eyes, which causes the grooves between them to disappear, and opens his arms theatrically. His wedding ring spangles in the air. The little boy starts laughing, and the girl has jumped up and is laughing, too. Martha feels something well inside. It isn't tears, she knows that. It's more like indigestion. Heartburn maybe. She takes a deep breath. 'Well. Whatever,' she says.

They don't take the cat that night. There are things to get. Food and a basket ('And toys!' the little girl cries. 'Pretend mice, and balls with bells in them'), and both children have school all week so it would be better, their father says, if they waited to collect him until the weekend. He has come up to inspect the new cat and, as he says this, he is rubbing his finger under his tabby chin. 'Kitten,' he says, smelling his feet, and the name comes out like an endearment.

Martha says fine to everything. She is feeling sheepish now. The woman who rejected the nice cat. She tells them to come before she opens. On Saturdays, she says, we open at 10 a.m. We can get very busy. The woman with a lot of commitments. Then she waves them out and watches as they go up the street, the tall, awkward man still holding the boy's hand, the girl skipping ahead, a gypsy in her stripy tights and summer frock. But it's not summer. It's autumn. Though it's hard to tell today; bright one minute, stormy the next. And there's something odd about the light. She can't see the sun from here but it must be slanting through a cloud, sneaking low across a garden, because it's hitting the side of the building at the end of the road, striking it orange as the girl and the man and the boy walk past. And she stands for a moment wondering how an ordinary wall can look so magnificent.

chapter four

the kitchen

'Given a chance, unusual exotic food packaging can
make a decorative statement.'

The Relaxed Home: Creating Comfortable Homes
with a Romantic Feel
by Atlanta Bartlett
(Ryland Peters & Small, 2000)

MARTHA had planned a trip to the north of England this
week. There is a big trade fair every month on a disused air-
strip at Newark that attracts traders from all over Europe.
Usually Martha heads up there in a hired Luton van, and
buys so much furniture, both at the fair and from local dealers, she has to secure the doors closed with string. But
Graham's death means she won't go this time. She is not
very sorry (it is odd, she reflects, how her first reaction to
any cancelled activity is usually relief), though she is disappointed to have missed out on one of the dealers. A few
months ago, after a day of frenzied rummaging and haggling,

she had found herself studying the finer details of some of his choicest pieces at close range. His kitchen table (zinc-topped, possibly nineteenth-century French *chocolatier*) had come under particularly close scrutiny. She had enjoyed herself – contrary to her sisters' belief, she does find some men attractive – but she hasn't gone back. This time she was tempted. Not least because he is also a very good source of pine sleighbeds (very popular with the under-fives in the Balham area).

With the Newark trip off, she has unexpected time on her hands and she wakes on Tuesday, her head full of lists. There is the house, all that furniture to be divided up and shifted, with the attendant arguments no doubt. And the funeral. She could ring Ian and Julia and see if she can help. But as she lies there, a strange lassitude comes over her. Her resolve dissolves. She doesn't leap out of bed, but flexes her legs across into the smooth, cool, unslept in reaches of the other side. The movement disturbs Kitten, who appears to have joined her in the night. He stands up, stretches and collapses back down in a new position against one of her feet. Martha is about to kick him off, when she thinks about Hazel smelling his paws.

She twists and buries her face in the pillow next to her. It smells of fresh ironing and violets – Eau Du Lit, in fact, which she buys in a bottle. That's one of the advantages of sleeping alone. No matter how clean a person is – and David *was* clean, a monument to sandalwood and limes – there's no escaping the stale smell of morning breath.

She thinks about all the people she has shared a bed with. When their parents had overnight guests, Eliza would be put in Geraldine's bed and she and Geraldine used to double up, only they'd sleep – if they ever did get to sleep – top to toe like shoes in a shoebox. Only shoes don't scratch and tickle you. And now Geraldine lets her children sleep in the bed with her and Greg. And Karen too, by the sound of it. What must that be like? Jostling for space. A small foot in your ribcage.

She used to sneak Nick into her room after the disgrace of her A levels, when everyone had given up on her. When their father left, the house grew lax. Geraldine was at the Royal College and was always bringing musicians home. Their mother started seeing Graham. It was as if sex had somehow been let out of a box. She remembers the discovery of sex, the nights when she and Nick would curl around each other's bodies, hot, smooth, languid, sweaty.

She remembers making love to Nick. But not to Colin, the boy – no, *man* – she left him for. Obviously, they *did*. But maybe that wasn't what the relationship was about for her. Colin's bed was in the middle of the room – beached – with books and papers all around it. He taught English literature at a crammer in London, was always writing to Susan Sontag, and at the time she thought of herself as embarking upon a voyage of intellectual discovery. 'Honestly,' she says now to the cat.

With a sudden movement, she gets up and goes into the kitchen. The bin bag of letters is where she left it in the corner. She hauls it back into the bedroom and up on to the bed, and sits cross-legged on top of the duvet in her pyjamas in front of it. At first, she doesn't know what she is looking for. She has a vague thought that she might divide the contents into piles. But once she starts going through it, after she has cast aside a torn-out page from *Brides* magazine, a dress she had once imagined wearing next to David at the altar, the task begins to overwhelm her. In the last eight years, she hasn't given a thought to her youth, as if the Big Relationship with David swept it away and closed it off. David and she were measured, mature. They spent the week apart and weekends doing grown up things together. But now, flicking through all these letters and bus tickets, postcards and scraps of notes passed in class, she has a sense of the texture of other, more rough-hewn affairs. A ticket for an Ian Dury concert brings back not the music but the bus ride home from it, Nick and her in the back of the bus, the velvet seat rough beneath her knees. And the hot chips they bought on the way home from the kebab shop on the corner. Vinegar and salt and sex.

She is gazing at the wall in front of her, at the nineteenth-century French candle sconce which is askew, she now notices. But then she turns back to the bag. There are scraps from Nick, but from Colin there are reams, proper self-conscious love letters, full of quotations from Dostoevsky and Donne, and flickers of jealousy concealed in pages of character analysis – *her* character. (She spent her days lurching between mortification about her own behaviour and longing for his approval.) Next to him, in that chain of insidious comparisons that link one affair to another, Nick had seemed immature and frivolous. She met Colin at Camden market: he stood there watching her in the drizzle in the grey overcoat that had belonged to his father – 'dead man's coat' he called it (still full of bitter, unresolved grief). She worked on a stall selling Peruvian hats. Her family told people she had 'dropped out'. Colin was clever and serious – and twenty-nine! – and made her feel like someone worth bothering with. She went travelling in India and he wrote to her every day. The letters piled up at rest-houses from Bombay to Cochin. At Heathrow, when she got back, he was waiting with flowers and a copy of *The Literary Essays of Ezra Pound*. 'For you,' he said.

She left him in the end. Leaving is what Martha does. Colin found solace with someone he met at the London Library. A Ph.D. student. She makes a noise, a muffled laugh, at the back of her throat, which makes the cat open his eyes. He is stretched out on his back now, up close to her ribs. She wonders what happened to Colin. Did he marry the Ph.D. student? Did he fulfil his ambition for Oxbridge tenure? Did Susan Sontag ever write back?

As for Nick. She hasn't seen him since their last stilted cup of coffee on 'neutral ground'. Decisions when you are young, she thinks, are as light as dandelion seeds. Only later do you see how each one, made on a whim, has taken root somewhere. She thinks of herself as headstrong, as knowing her own mind. But if she hadn't met Colin, maybe she would never have left Nick, never have met David. And without David encouraging her, informing her taste, would she ever have started her own shop? Would antiques still be her life, or something altogether different?

She is about to close the bag up when she sees something else. She pulls it out. It is a small vinyl address book with a picture of Snoopy on the front. She opens it. The writing inside is childish, some letters sloped one way, some another, which pulls her up short for a moment (it was *so long ago*), but under M she finds an entry for Nick – for his parents. She remembers their house – a big, solid family house, full of Moroccan rugs and faded velvet sofas, a house you wouldn't leave in a hurry. She stares at the number. She hears her heart in her ears.

A paw stretches out. The cat is purring – a motorbike pur, an idling Ducati. And it occurs to her what an extraordinary position it is in, hammocked like that in the crook of her arm, like a person in a deckchair. And it strikes her that maybe he isn't such a commonplace cat. Maybe actually he is quite exceptional.

Karen is breastfeeding when Martha drops in on her later that morning. She is still in her nightie and sits nursing the baby in the kitchen armchair, plump and A-line, like an angel on top of the Christmas tree.

Keith and Karen's house is in a state of flux. There are swabs of different coloured paint on the walls with pencil marks underneath saying things like 'String' and 'Dead Salmon'. The floorboards have been sanded, but the skirting boards are scuffed. Martha thinks the house has potential. Keith calls it 'a work in progress'. Karen, who campaigns for the homeless, says they are lucky to have a roof over their head at all.

The kitchen is in a particular mess today. Bouquets of flowers are stuffed in inappropriate vases and New Baby cards litter up the dresser. A plastic basket is piled high with dry, creased clothes; something towelling is soaking in the sink and the dirty dishes are cramped for space on the side. The baby, such a small thing in itself, seems to have created an enormous amount of displacement, the contents of the house splattered like bathwater after a hippopotamus has got in. There are clothes everywhere. The computer is on the table; piled up haphazardly are the biology books and dictionaries, all the paraphernalia Keith needs for the textbook he was supposed to have finished this summer. Karen's files and journals are stuffed on top of the recipe books, next to the new Jamie Oliver which Martha gave them as a New Baby present. (She thought it made a change from Babygros and talc – and it won't be long before they start inviting her to supper again.)

Martha fusses around, making tea. She feels tender towards her friend and this tiny baby, so vulnerable somehow in the middle of this chaos. She is chastened, too. She had been so self-absorbed on Sunday and yet here is all this evidence, all this upheaval.

She says, 'I think I like Pickled Herring best: what about you?'

'What?'

'On the walls.'

Karen looks vague. 'Oh God, I don't know,' she says, and starts telling her about the midwife who's just been to visit and the indignity of having her stitches inspected. 'She poked around and then she said thoughtfully, "Hm, three layers, I see."'

'Three layers?' says Martha, not wanting an answer. 'Poor you.' She lays Karen's tea down gently at her side and hovers at her shoulder, trying to look more closely at the baby's wrinkled face. 'She's very noisy, isn't she? She's really slurping it in.'

Karen rearranges the baby and with her spare hand carefully moves the mug to the other side of the table out of range of the baby's foot. 'She's got the knack now. Can you pass me that muslin?'

Martha straightens up.

'That white thing on the back of that chair.'

'Oh right.'

Martha passes her the muslin and sits down next to her. She watches as Karen wraps it around the baby's chest and then manoeuvres her into a sort of sagging sitting position. One of Karen's hands cups the baby's tiny boneless chin, the other taps her gently on the back as if in congratulation. Karen sees her looking and says, 'Wind.'

Martha says doubtfully, 'I know.'

'Did you have *nothing* to do with your sisters' children when they were babies?'

Martha says, 'Yes I did. Of course I did. Though when Geraldine's were born, I was so busy starting up the shop. And Eliza . . . well, you know Eliza, she's quite controlling.'

'I know Eliza. How's Denis?'

'Fine.'

'And the Ph.D.?'

'Don't ask.'

Karen is carefully wrapping Kit in a small white sheet on her knee. She says, 'The proverbial pram in the hall. He won't get anything done if he thinks he can work at home with a toddler in the next room. I was watching a programme about

Vermeer when I was feeding last night. His contemporaries, on average, produced something like fifty paintings a year. Vermeer created two or – at the most – three. The theory was he was just meticulous, but I reckon it was because he had eleven children and worked at home.'

Martha says, 'Eliza thinks one of them should be around. And she won't sacrifice her career for his.'

'No. Well, it's hard. Particularly if you're Type A like Eliza. Did you read about that new study on birth order? Your position in the family dictates how you turn out more than anything else, more than class or race. So that youngest children, who tend to be mavericks, are most adept at getting their own way. And eldest children –' she smiles down at her baby – 'tend to be the most motivated. High achievers.'

'Oh right.' Martha widens her eyes at the baby, too. 'I suppose that could be Geraldine. She got her scholarship to the Royal College of Music. Not that she's done much with it since she married. Oh, and Keith, too,' she adds. 'He's done all right. Head of Department. What else?'

'Eldest children also tend to have more broken marriages.'

'I have to say, I've never thought Geraldine and Greg were particularly well matched. What about middle children?'

'I think it said middle children had the lowest need for intellectual achievement, that they competed in areas not attempted by the eldest. That they had the greatest feeling of not belonging.'

'Oh. And what about their relationships? Do they tend to break too?'

'I don't know.' Karen lays the baby, who is now asleep,

into the Moses basket. Carefully, she tucks a white cellular blanket around her. 'It didn't say anything about middle children's relationships.'

'Maybe,' Martha says, 'because they don't have any.'

Karen looks up and studies her. She says, 'Are you lonely?'

'No.' Martha starts fiddling with the objects on the kitchen table in front of her. She puts a camera neatly on top of a packet of photographs, lines Karen's wallet up next to that. She says, 'Not at all. Anyway, I was just telling April, I'm off radar. It's all been and gone for me. I don't think you age gradually. I think it rushes up on you. There's a house in scaffolding near the shop and I walked by it the other day and thought, "That's interesting: builders don't wolf-whistle any more." But then I happened to pass a few hours later with April and all hell broke loose, a concerto of whistles, and I felt such an idiot.'

Karen laughs and stretches out in her chair. They both look at the baby, its fingers up to its wizened face.

Martha says, 'I'm fine.'

There's a silence. Martha gives a noise, like a short hum, an accelerated sigh, to break it. And then, after another pause, she tells Karen about the bag of mementoes. She makes it sound like an adventure, like a piece of magic that has happened to her. She has been 'whisked' into her past, she says. These old letters just 'fell into her lap'. She hadn't thought about her old lovers for years, they had lain in her head, collapsed like marionettes, but now it's as if life has been breathed into them and they have 'got up and danced'. She gets up herself when she says this and, if she doesn't dance, she paces around the room. 'I know it sounds mad,' she says. 'And I know it sounds melodramatic, but I just have this feeling that somewhere in those letters there's a message for me, an answer.'

'Like what was wrong with David?'

Martha starts. 'No,' she says. 'Not David. Before David. That's the point. Like Nick Martin.'

'Nick Martin. That's going back.'

'I've been trying to look him up.'

Karen sits there in her nightie, looking bemused. 'Are you sure that's a good idea?'

Martha pokes the clammy towel in the sink. 'I had a number but it was unobtainable.'

Behind her, Karen says, 'He was nice. Slightly wild on that motorbike of his . . . Are you chasing your youth?'

The water in the sink is cold and grey. 'No, I'm not.'

'Well . . .' Karen's voice is pointedly cheerful now, coaxing Martha to turn round. 'My theory is you're only ever two phone calls away from anyone you've ever known. Who do you see that might see him?'

Martha turns round. 'No one. All the people we used to hang out with have dispersed.'

Karen gets the ironing board out and starts sorting through the basket of crumpled washing, but then she pauses. 'Friends Reunited,' she says. 'The website where you can track down people at your school? Let's try that.'

So she leaves the ironing and the two of them ease past the sleeping baby to the computer, and for a good half hour they discover that Penny Hatch is a practice nurse in Kent, Samantha Toay has four boys and is run off her feet, and

Helen Cohen imports olives with the husband she met on safari. Their contemporaries at St Hillier's School for Girls are, it seems, alive and well and keen to hear from anyone who knows them! At St Hillier's School for Boys, there are fewer entries for their year. There is no mention, or sign, of Nick Martin. 'Figures,' says Karen. 'He was never a conformist.'

Martha leaves a bulletin by her name saying, 'Antique dealer. Keen to track down old friends – particularly anyone in touch with Nick Martin.' Karen writes, 'Charity consultant. Married. New baby. Exhausted.' And leaves a photo of Kit.

They laugh a lot while they are doing this, but when they have logged off, mindful of the last part of her bulletin, Martha tells Karen to go up to bed for a bit and says she'll look after the baby. Karen resists, but says finally that maybe she wouldn't mind a quick nap, and to wake her immediately if Kit stirs. 'Oh God, she won't stir, will she?' Martha narrows her eyes and pretends to look panicked. 'I mean, will she?'

After Karen has gone up, Martha sits and looks at the baby closely for a while. She rocks the Moses basket back and forth gently with the ends of her fingers. The wicker feels scratchy, but there is padding inside. The baby makes small, soft snuffling noises – at one point her hands shoot back in the air as if something has startled her, but she doesn't wake, doesn't stir. And after a while, Martha stands up and gets to work on the kitchen. She rearranges the flowers, attacks the stove with a scouring brush, washes the dishes and mops the floor. She puts the army of cereal packets away in the cupboard. A bottle of olive oil with a pretty label and a slim frosted-glass bottle of balsamic vinegar are stored away here, and these she takes down and positions, decoratively, by the stove. Finally, when all is clean and tidy, she plugs in the iron and starts on the basket of washing. She is humming slightly as she does this, spreading out the tiny scrunched Babygros and folding them, watching the steam rise, hot and white, from the sheets. And before long there are neat, colour-co-ordinated piles across the scrubbed kitchen table.

'Oh, Matt. I wasn't expecting you. I was expecting the machine.'

'Geraldine.'

'Ah. Yes. Um.'

'So why ring if you thought I was out?'

'I was just going to leave a message.'

'Well you can leave it with me instead.'

'Oh. Yes. Of course. Are you sure you've got a minute? Or am I disturbing you?'

Geraldine is at her most twittery. Martha has just walked into her flat. She is feeling positive, full of action. She has been to the electrician. She has tidied Karen's kitchen. She has *helped out*. And she has started a campaign to rediscover her past, to redecorate her life. She is determined not to be irritated. She says, 'No. No. It's fine. I've just popped up to make a cup of tea. April's in the shop. Fire away.'

'Ah. Well. I was ringing about Friday. It just struck me

that maybe we should all – you, me and Eliza – visit Pen Ponds on the way to Wimbledon. At elevenish? There would be plenty of time. We could take some flowers and leave them on the bridge there, or scatter the petals in the water. I thought that might be nice. Or we could take something of Graham's . . . some personal item. If you think that is a good idea, should we go in one car, us three, or in separate cars? I don't know. What do you think? Also, shall I take the children out of school? I mean he was their stepgrandfather, but it wasn't like they knew him terribly well. Um . . .'

Martha says, 'It's a good thing you got me. You'd have filled the answer phone up for the whole day.'

'Oh, I'm sorry.'

'I'm joking.'

'Oh. So what do you think?'

Martha takes in a deep breath but lets it out quietly so it won't sound like a sigh. 'OK. Pen Ponds good idea. Item of Graham's? Um. Can't think of anything. Copy of *Concrete News*, shredded? That's a joke. I'll think. Separate cars best. Kids? I don't know. Let them come? It's up to you. Anything else?'

'No. That's it. Are you sure about separate cars? It wouldn't be nicer if we went together? Us three?'

'No, I think separate cars are a good idea. Because we'll be going straight on to the tea and buns won't we and I don't know how long . . .' Martha breaks off. The dislocation is her way of letting Geraldine know how she feels about David being there. 'How long I'm going to stay.'

Geraldine says hastily, 'No, no, of course. No, I understand. Eliza and I will go together.'

Martha is about to put the phone down when she feels Kitten weaving in and out of her legs, hoping for food. 'Oh, I almost forgot. Are you still there? One piece of good news. I've found a home for Kitten.'

'Really?'

'Yes. A nice man saw my ad, wanted a cat, liked Kitten, there you go. Signed, sealed and delivered. Actually not delivered, they're coming on Saturday. But the whole thing was much easier than I thought. Isn't that good?'

Geraldine says, 'Oh, what a relief. Where do they live, nearby?'

Martha has put down some cat biscuits and has begun absent-mindedly to tidy up the kitchen. But at this she pauses, a carton of milk in her hand, the fridge door open. 'That's a good point. I forgot to ask that.' She laughs. 'Must be quite near because the kid goes to Kelmscott Primary.'

Geraldine says, 'You don't know where they live?'

'No.' Martha replaces the milk and swings the door shut. 'I forgot to ask.'

'Oh Martha.'

'What do you mean, Oh Martha?'

'Well, you can't just let Kitten go without checking out where they live. You've got to do a house check.'

'Geraldine, I am not doing a house check. For a second-hand cat.'

There is a long silence. Finally Martha adds, 'I mean for a cat. Honestly. Ger.'

The phone in her ear fizzes. She can't even hear Geraldine breathe. Martha says, 'A cat, Ger. It's not a person. It's not Graham. It's not Mum. It's a cat.'

There is a further beat. Then Geraldine says quietly, 'Give me their number. I'll do it myself.'

Martha sits down at the table. 'I don't have their number,' she says.

'You don't have their number?'

Martha says, 'No.'

'You don't have their number. You don't know where they live. They could be anybody. For all you know they don't even have a garden. You're just going to let them waltz off with him. If they do, that is. They might not even come back.'

Martha has an image of the little girl with her face in Kitten's fur. And then another of her dancing down the street. 'They'll waltz,' she says.

Geraldine's voice sounds a long way away. 'Well, people don't always do what they say they're going to do.'

Martha smooths the tablecloth with her hands. It's linen. The pattern is called Gypsy Print – roses, sprigged together but loosely so, as if someone had picked them but then dropped them, still bunched, to the floor. 'Look, Ger, don't get upset. I'm sorry. They were nice. They seemed to like the cat. But you're right. I'll see what I can do. Maybe I should have asked a few more questions. Found out about a garden. Met the wife. I'll look into it, OK?'

Geraldine says, 'You haven't met the wife?'

'No. I haven't. I'm sorry. I've been hopeless.'

'It's just . . .'

The cat is on the counter, staring out of the window. There is the staccato squeak of bluetits in the tree outside. The cat is making odd chirrupy noises deep in its throat.

The roses on the tablecloth in front of her don't look as if they've been dropped, but scattered, abandoned. They wouldn't last a minute out of water. 'I know. I know,' Martha says. 'It's not just a second-hand cat.'

After she puts the phone down, Geraldine leans at the kitchen sink, looking out at the last roses in her garden. She pruned the Gloire de Dijon sharply this year and there are six or seven creamy pink blooms on the wall just by the window. But the leaves of the sycamore have begun falling on to the lawn, which is damp even though it's past lunchtime, and the beds are ragged. The Himalayan honey-suckle at the back has gone mad and the mint has self-seeded in a rash. She should get out there; she should be getting on top of things now Anna is at nursery. She puts her forehead against the glass. Once she travelled the world with a national orchestra. Now she can't even keep a house together. Her head is buzzing with things to organise, but the day seems to slip away.

She turns to the back door and reaches to unlock it while shoving her feet into a pair of suede loafers she keeps by the mat. The dogs hear her coming and start barking up at her, rubbing their wet noses in smears against the glass. It's a jolly good thing Martha hasn't found herself with a dog to look after. How would she cope with that? She opens the door and bends down to wrestle affectionately with them. Montgomery licks her face and she rubs his silk-purse ears. 'There you go,' she says, in her breathy doggy-voice. Dogs are so uncomplicated, there are no edges with them, no treading round their feelings all the time.

She straightens up. All this pretending Martha doesn't know anything about cats, as if they hadn't grown up with a succession of them: trips to the vet and annual jabs and small hand-made tombs in the garden. The callousness with which she just blithely announced she knew nothing about these people she's just giving poor old Kitten to. She hasn't even met the wife. And fancy deciding to go to Pen Ponds in her own car. Now she will have to go on her own with Eliza and there will be awkwardness because of 'The Boy'. Geraldine hadn't meant to bring this home. But she found herself earlier today slipping it off the wall and loading it in the car. She wants other people to consider her feelings for once. Martha, at least.

A phrase of her mother's arrives in her head. This happens more and more these days, which she finds peculiar. You would think they would have flown in and landed straight after her death, but for a long while there was silence. Only now – maybe as she reaches the age her mother was when she figured most strongly in her life – does she keep finding herself echoing the familiar intonations. The other day when she was telling Patrick and Ivor she couldn't understand why they didn't put away their toys, she'd added, as she was walking out, 'I. Just. Don't.' And the side of her that was only putting on a display of being cross, thought, 'That's Mummy talking.' Sometimes in the mirror, she sees her mother's face looking back at her, too: the furrows between the eyes, as if she's frowning into the sun even when it's cloudy, the lines pressing down from the nose to the mouth, little pockets on either side of her chin. When she coughs, it's the ceh-ceh-ceh her mother used to make, and it's the same when she sneezes. She goes to the sink to wash her hands and turns them over to look at her nails – thickening and yellowing, splitting at the corners. Her mother's hands.

She wonders if Martha feels the same. Does she sneeze their mother's sneezes? Not that she could ask her.

'She is the limit,' she tells the dogs.

April is in a bad mood. She is reading *Hello!*, but not idly or conversationally, not calling out the good bits. She's snapping the pages over, one after another. Snap. Snap. She has pulled the zip of her top up to her chin. Martha has bought April coffee. And a doughnut (April has a new thing about the café doughnuts). She hasn't drawn attention to the still unfinished cupboard in the basement. There are emotional dramas in April's life, a man up in Manchester, that she doesn't ask about, that she treads around.

At 3 p.m., after getting back from taking a pair of metal beds to the sandblaster in Mitcham, Martha waits a few minutes and then asks April (who really *could* be getting on with some painting) if she minds her 'disappearing off' again for a few minutes. April doesn't look up. 'Go ahead,' she says, still flicking. Martha wonders if it's something she's done. But she doesn't ask. When she gets into the street, it is chillier than it felt earlier, so she has to go back through the shop to get a jumper. April is on the phone herself then – laughing and giggling – and Martha feels awful for a moment, awkward and resentful, and left out, and she wishes she had said something after all.

Now she is walking down Kelmscott Road towards the school. The street is always heavily parked, but as she walks along it today, she notices the occasional woman in the driver's seat, reading the papers or just sitting. Some of the cars have babies sleeping in them, too. It is beginning to spit and, closer to the gates, there are groups of people in huddles, clutching their jackets around their necks, heads bowed, chatting.

Martha stops on the outer reaches and puts her hands in her pockets. Nobody seems to notice her. She's not sure that she's in the right place. She wonders if they have different gates for different age groups. She looks at her watch. It's ten past three. More people arrive: a couple of women with pushchairs, the occasional man. She moves over so that she's against the wall, slightly apart from the others, her eyes scanning for the children's father, though it has occurred to her that maybe their mother collects them – that woman over there perhaps, her henna'ed hair piled up in a bun secured by big black artistic knitting needles, her eyes heavy with kohl? Or that slight creature, with the short blonde spikes and the sheepskin gilet? An image of the man comes into her head. He would have to be married, she thinks, to one of the interesting ones.

A door beyond the gate is opening and a wash of small boys and girls pours into the space between. She cranes her neck, looking now for Hazel and her brother. Children are being plucked from the mêlée, parents and carers swooping like seagulls, bearing them off like morsels from the waves.

Small children with big bags, tired faces and waving arms, disappearing into cars and up the street. No sign of Hazel or Stan. The crowd is thinning when suddenly a car pulls up next to her, double-parking, and tooting, and the teacher at the door peers in and waves and calls something behind her into the building. And then out trot Hazel and Stan with another child, a girl that Martha doesn't know. Hazel is holding her brother's hand, but she's talking to the other girl, her head bobbing self-consciously from side to side, her hair poking in tufts from two plaits. She's wearing her duffel-coat, but the buttons are done up out of synch. Today, her tights are purple with stars. The little boy's face looks pinched and tired. He is trailing slightly behind.

The children's father has got out of the car and walked round it to meet them. He has bent down on the pavement, his arms wide open, and the little boy runs into them. The two girls follow. Hazel's mouth is at an angle, as if she's stopping herself from grinning. She sidles up, allows herself to be hugged and then pulls back and says something to the other girl, who giggles. But the man is all smiles as he opens the back door, extends an arm in greeting to the teacher, and steers the children into the car. It is one of those tinny Japanese cars that you wouldn't want to trust on a motorway. It is lime green, with a scratch along one side. The boot is full to the roof with boxes. The man is so tall and thin, when he bends it's like a coat-hanger being twisted out of shape. He is still smiling, but as he straightens up, Martha sees him glance at his watch and a blast of worry hit his face.

She has held back until they were bundled into the car. She hasn't wanted to get in the way and further complicate the negotiation between road and pavement and school bag and car door, but now, as she starts forward, she sees another car has come up behind, its engine idling loudly, and she panics. She runs forward and taps on the passenger window. The man, who has hurried into the driver's seat, looks startled, frowning properly now. She says through the window, 'Sorry. Um . . .'

He leans across and opens the door. Then he looks over his shoulder at the build-up behind. There are several cars now. 'Yes?' he says. 'Yes?'

'Sorry,' she says again. 'It's about the cat. Have you got a sec?'

The man looks over his shoulder again. A car three down has started tooting. 'Er . . . not really,' he says. He hurls his leather suitcase off the passenger seat and onto the floor. 'Um . . . Get in?' It's not a command so much as a question.

So Martha does. She slams the door and, before anyone says anything, he drives off. They are both looking for somewhere for him to pull in again, but the road is lined bumper to bumper. Martha says, 'Sorry, sorry,' again, but the man says 'Hang on, don't worry. Ummmmm. Hang on. Ummmm.' This ummm fills the space between them so that Martha doesn't say anything, even though she realises she's the one who needs to explain. She's got her legs squished over to one side in the way of the gear-stick because the rest of the space is taken up with dented plastic Coke bottles and newspapers and a carrier bag stuffed with clothes. The ash-tray is open and full.

He says again, 'Ummm . . .' Hazel in the back says, rather peremptorily, showing off Martha thinks, 'What about the cat? What is it?' And then to her friend, 'She's got the cat I'm having.'

Martha has twisted round to face the children. She says, 'Oh no. Kitten's fine. I just want a quick word with your dad.'

The man says, 'Er. Gosh. Bit crowded down here, isn't it. Hang on. Just turn a sec . . . OK. Sorry. Yes.' He rounds into a road where there is a free strip of single yellow line at the end, and comes to a halt. He turns to face Martha for the first time. 'Goodness. Sorry. Didn't mean to er . . .'

'Kidnap me,' Martha finishes for him, and then feels embarrassed. So now she puts on her most businesslike of tones. 'I'm the one who should be apologising. Leaping out at you like that.'

'Not at all,' the man says. Martha notices again how his eyes are slightly different colours, one a shadow of the other, like the sea when there's a rock underneath it. He is freshly shaven. His jacket is brushed with wet sparkles from the rain.

Hazel from behind says, 'Dad, you're going to be late. Again.'

'I'm so sorry,' Martha says. 'It's just I wanted a very quick chat about . . . I was talking to my sister about finding a home for the cat, a good home,' she corrects herself, 'but she mentioned a garden and I realised I hadn't asked about that and—'

'We've got a garden,' Hazel says, boasting now.

The other girl says, 'So have we. And a climbing frame and a sandpit.'

The man says, 'Er, we have got a garden. If that's it. Er. Is that it?'

Martha feels suffocatingly hot suddenly in her extra jumper. She has closed her fingers around the door handle, about to push. 'Yes,' she says. 'So. Good, I'm glad about that. Um. Just one small thing . . .'

'We've got to hurry,' Hazel says again. 'It said three thirty.'

'Yes, er, I know,' her father says.

Martha speaks very quickly now. 'So would it be all right if I just popped round and checked? A house check, I think is what they call it.'

The man frowns.

Martha says, 'I wouldn't. It's just my sister . . . she's quite . . .'

'A house check?' he says.

'Yes. A house check.'

'You want to check the house?' he says. 'Yes. Of course.' He looks at his watch. 'I'm terribly sorry. We're a bit busy now. I've got a thing.'

'No. No. I realise. No hurry.'

'You want to check the house. Um. When?'

'Any time really. Um.'

The man says, 'Ummm.'

'Unless I delivered the cat. Would that be the thing to do?'

His eyes flick into the rear mirror and then at her. 'But what if we failed the . . . thing and you had to take the cat away?'

'Oh.'

Hazel says, 'Dad. We're going to be late.'

'Tomorrow?' he says. 'Oh no, damn. Thing. Look, Friday morning, how's that? Tenish? Would that be all right?'

100

Martha, hot and red and awkward, says that would be fine, even though she knows it isn't, that there's Graham's funeral and now Geraldine's Richmond Park ceremony. But she lets him give her their address, and finally she can get out of the car. She bends in to say goodbye.

'Hope you're not late,' she adds, 'for um . . . whatever.'

'Kids' party,' he says.

'Oh,' she says. 'Another one! Have fun then, kids.'

The man, whose name she *still* doesn't know, smiles. Hazel looks at her. 'We won't,' she mouths – grumpy little thing – as they drive off.

Martha has to walk past the school on the way home. It's empty now and the gate is closed. All the parents, and the children, have gone. She is troubled by her encounter. And also curious. The boy still silent, and the girl too big for her boots. And the man? You want to close your hand over his shoulder through his jacket to check the bones are there.

Martha turns the corner into her road, the end with houses rather than shops, her hands in the pockets of her jeans, her head slightly bowed against the drizzle which is more pervasive now.

She is shivering slightly. And for some reason – a link from the man's wet jacket – a dark blue cashmere jumper wet with rain like glitter comes into her head, and for a moment she can physically feel it against her cheek. She stops. She is adept at keeping David's body at bay. Oh, she can cope with the thought of him. If Karen had pushed the point earlier, she could have answered easily. She left him because, after her mother died, she felt stifled, because the list of pluses in his favour became overwhelming, because

101

one day she'd been eating fish and chips and he wouldn't kiss her. She left him because, probably, she made a mistake. She's used to this now. The idea of him is fine, but occasionally a memory of his physical presence squeezes her. Oh God, Friday. She will see David on Friday. Panic leaps inside her.

She is standing there, hot behind the eyes, when she happens to glance to her right, through the window of the house next to her. The paper lantern in the middle of the ceiling is on, throwing a blank white glow over the whole room. It must be rented, a bedsit, because the decor, swirly carpet and flocked wallpaper, is at odds with the details in the room: the batik rug chucked over the armchair; the Che Guevara poster; the windfall of CDs scattered across the floor. There is a Pot Noodle on the mantelpiece. But it's not all this that has caught her attention, but the man – no, the *boy* – with the scruffy T-shirt and the grubby hair who is hurled, headphoned, in a haphazard heap on the sofa. It's not Nick Martin, she knows that, but it's *like* him, and for a moment she imagines herself sitting on the floor next to him, in the layered cotton skirt she used to wear, those big dangly silver earrings she'd brought back from India, his spare hand in her hair . . . It was long then, and blonde, dabbed with those ridiculous highlights that made her look like Rod Stewart. She puts her hand up and touches it. No highlights now – short and brown and tidy. When *did* she become so neat?

She looks back into the room and realises that she wouldn't have been wearing those Indian earrings. She broke up with Nick *before* she went to India. But, as she stands there looking in, the light flickers, as if the wind is playing across the wires, and after that the electric bulb seems to shine brighter for a few moments, as if it's been given a second chance.

chapter five

the lavatory

'In a multi-purpose bathroom, try to place the loo in
a corner. It hides it a little and provides a sense of
security when sat upon.'

Home Front Bathrooms: Inspirational
Makeovers and Practical Projects
by Kevin McCloud
(BBC Books, 1998)

This is a message from Sasha Doughty email:
sashadoughty@hotmail.com who is contacting you through
http://www.friendsreunited.co.uk

The message is as follows:-

Hi there! Remember me! I'm one of the saddies who keeps an
eye on new entries. Only kidding!!! But I saw your name and
bells began ringing!!! What are you up to? I live in Wiltshire
now. I'm married and have two children, Flora, 8, and Tim, 5.
Still see Jane Pritchet. Remember her? She's a midwife. And
Amy Blanche: she's in catering. Rather her than me! It's all I
can do to keep my house and family together! What about

*you? I haven't seen Nick Martin since A levels – sorreee – but
it would be great to meet up and chat about old times. Love
Sasha. (You might remember me as Susan. I changed my name
back in 1990.)*

*This is a message from Simon Fletcher email:
simon.fletcher@virgin.net who is contacting you through
http://www.friendsreunited.co.uk*

The message is as follows:-

*Well hello. We lost touch. The number you gave me that time
we bumped into each other at that motorway service station
turned out to be unobtainable. I would love to find out what
you were up to. As for me, I fly big shiny jets out of Heathrow.
No jokes about engine-size please.*

Pip, pip

Si (Fletcher)

P.S. I still have your chewing gum

NUMBER 10 Chestnut Drive – 'the parental home' – is looking dismal when Martha turns up to meet Ian's wife Julia and
the estate agent late the following afternoon. On the step is
a shelf of wind-huddled leaves and, inside, the house is cold
and damp, as if humans protected houses from the elements
rather than the other way round. To Martha, closing the
door behind her, it feels like a husk. She is reminded of a
wildlife programme she once watched in which a large crustacean struggled out of its shell; one minute the shell *was* the

crustacean, the next it lay there detached, next to a piece of old seaweed, lifeless.

In the sitting room there are spaces where pieces of furniture have been taken away. All that remains of the rosewood bookcase is a bright square on the carpet. The Chesterfield has left a yawning hole, rimmed with dust. A large yellowing rectangle marks the spot above the fireplace where 'The Boy' hung. Martha doesn't mind. One of the advantages of working with objects is a certain sentimental detachment. Chests of drawers come and go. She has seen faces of customers screwed with frustration, with personal betrayal, on discovering that a particular kitchen table is sold, as if that table was unique, as if there was one kitchen table in the world for them. They believe in love at first sight, in the ideal match, while she recognises that there'll be another along at Kempton in a few weeks. She feels none of Geraldine's urgency, none of her panicked desire for owner-ship, as if what you got, what you went home with, was a reflection of your standing within the family, as if they were still twelve and everything had to be fair. Maybe she'd think differently if there was anything really special to be nabbed. But to be honest, nothing, Penwork Tea Caddy aside, is worth much anyway.

The door was on the latch so she knows someone is here. She calls a greeting down the stairs and a 'Helloooo' comes back up. Julia is in the kitchen. 'There you are,' Julia says, turning at the sink. She's wearing black rubber gloves, with pink flowers at the arm holes. She seems to have had her hair restreaked since Saturday. 'Shoes off. I've just done the floor.'

She comes across to kiss Martha on both cheeks with her dripping rubber hands held away at an angle. Martha says, 'You look nice.' Julia's white jeans have gold buttons instead of a fly. 'Does Mummy look nice?' Julia says – Martha's cue to notice Milo and Rebecca who are still in their car-seats on the kitchen table.

'Hello, there,' Martha says casually, as if greeting a couple of adults. Their legs waggle, causing the car-seats to rock. They are dressed in identical yellow Babygros, but Martha thinks again how different their faces are. She's noticed with twins – though people never seem to admit it – how one, and here it's Rebecca, often looks unfinished next to the other, rougher, almost lopsided. Martha bends to kiss the top of Rebecca's head.

'Yes, well,' Julia says. 'You just never know with estate agents, do you?'

'Know what?' Martha worked in an estate agency once – Chester & Jones it was called – in one of her many 'inbetween' stages, after India, before Alfie's and her launch into antiques.

'Whether it makes a difference, making an effort. I know it's the house they're valuing, but none the less, looking smart might tip the balance, do you know what I mean? It just might imbue the place with a sense of quality. God knows –' she runs her finger along a radiator – 'it needs it.'

Martha feels she may need imbuing herself. 'Would you like me to change?' She is wearing her usual shifting-furniture gear: jeans, a man's shirt and plimsolls.

'No. No. I tell you what. I'll do the honours. You'll be . . . *useful* as you are.' Julia takes off her gloves and rummages in her handbag. 'I've made a list.'

'Oh good.' Martha smiles. She and her sisters always enjoy Julia's lists.

'Right. Lounge. One, hoovering. Two, dusting. Three, curtain. It keeps coming away at the top: any idea how we can fix that? Four, toilets, upstairs and down. Funny smell. And then, Food . . .' She continues but more to herself. 'A, order sandwiches. I've done that and I'll nip to M&S on Friday morning. B, booze. Ian's popping into Oddbins on the way home from Heathrow . . .'

'Heathrow?'

'Yes. Ian's sister gets in this afternoon.'

'I didn't realise.'

'Yes. Not that I noticed her dashing across the world to visit her father when he was ill. Now, of course, it's grieving daughter.' Julia is applying handcream to her fingers, massaging it into her cuticles. 'Typical Susie.'

'Really?' Martha racks her brain for the inside story on Ian's wife and sister. She vaguely remembers something about a birthday present and an inadequate thank you note.

'Spoilt, of course,' says Julia.

There is a loud banging on the door. The estate agent is middle-aged with thinning mahogany-coloured hair, and stands with his legs wide apart and a clipboard under his arm. He's wearing beetle-black shoes with rounded toes that look indestructible. Julia apologises for the state of the house and then gives him the tour. 'Shall I give you the tour?' she says, her fingers touching his sleeve.

Martha is left in charge of the lavatories. The estate agent comes in while she's squirting mucus green Mr Muscle into the bowl in the downstairs cloakroom and says, 'Very much an asset.' On her way up to the upstairs bathroom she passes them coming down and Julia gives a tinkling laugh and says, 'Oh absolutely, absolutely.' The man's voice is gravelly. He says, 'Obviously in a state of some disrepair. But original features. Extensive garden. Obviously I *will* need to return *to* the office *for* confirmation, but I would expect *at* this juncture to invite offers in the region of . . .' He names a price which seems realistic to Martha, but Julia says coolly, 'Oh really?' and he says again, more nervously this time, 'Obviously I will need to return to the office for confirmation.'

After he has gone, Julia shouts up, 'Used to be a policeman,' before going down to the kitchen and leaving Martha to laugh about this on her own. 'Hello, hello,' she says to the bathroom plug. 'Open up, open up.' She wonders whether if he goes for a viewing and the vendor doesn't open the door quickly enough, he says, 'Stand back,' and knocks it down.

When she has had enough of scrubbing the lavatory rim and has begun to feel resentful at her sisters for not being there to wield the loo brush, she goes into her mother's room and sits on the bed. Things have altered up here over the years – when her father moved out, her mother prettified the bedlinen; when Graham moved in, space was made for the Corby trouser press, and loose coins reappeared on the bedside table; when her mother died, all her little things vanished, her 'effects' divided between the girls. (Martha retreated from the battle for the jewellery and settled for the art deco dressing table set, turquoise shell, circa 1930.) But the counterpane has never changed. It is gold with squiggly lines running down it in tufted fabric. As a little girl, she used to run her fingers down the grooves, imagining they were rivers or the paths in quiz book mazes. She remembers lying on this counterpane in a towel waiting for her mother to finish bathing Eliza. Her mother would be exasperated when she came in. She would say, 'Haven't you got your nightie on yet?' and her hands would shove it roughly over Martha's head. Sometimes all three girls would mess around on the bed and the phone would ring and it would be Neville, their father, and when their mother talked, her voice was scraggy with irritation.

She gets up and goes into Geraldine's and her own old bedroom. It is a guest room now, the poster-strewn cupboards painted lemon, the bunks replaced by twin beds with padded floral headboards. Martha used to lie on the bottom bunk, listening to her parents through the wall. She had a terrible feeling inside her, scared and horrified, and yet hungry for it. When their voices got loud she would feel herself cringe down, but if they quietened, she would strain her ears to hear them. It was an obsession to hear every detail. She would go and sit on the lavatory if it helped. Not hearing was worse than hearing.

She used to think, 'Why does she shout at him all the time? Why isn't she nice?'

From the bedroom window, you can see across the street and down the adjoining road. Once, when she was about thirteen, Martha was coming home from tennis practice and saw her father sitting in the car. They were several yards from the house and she started smiling and walking towards him, wondering why he had parked so far away. It was only when she got closer that she saw he had a girl with him. She knew the girl a bit. She had just left the sixth form at her school. It can't have been long after that that he left.

110

She goes downstairs, past 'the study' which used to be Eliza's room, through the hall and down to the kitchen, her head full of pop music and shouting and slammed doors. Julia is here folding paper napkins into water-lilies. It is like seeing a stranger in the house, a stranger doing origami.

Julia sighs when Martha comes in and, folding a final water-lily, extends the sigh into a shudder. 'I'll be glad when this is all over.'

Martha sits down on the edge of a chair. 'How many are you expecting?'

'Oh, fifty odd. But I don't mean that. I mean, the house. The finances. The clearing up.'

'You're very kind to do so much. I'm sure Geraldine and Eliza intend to.'

'Ian's very busy with the accountant. Your sisters both said they'd come back at the weekend, but I want to get on. I can't bear it all sitting here. We have to put "it" behind us and get on with the rest of our lives.'

Martha rocks one of the babies, though they are both asleep now. She supposes that 'it' means her stepfather's death. 'I guess one does,' she says.

'I mean, I know one has to grieve, but at some point you have to let go. I don't think Ian has even recovered from the death of his mother yet. He never got over Graham marrying Hilly so quickly.' She looks up from the paper plates she's been counting. 'Do you think I'm being hard-hearted?'

'No. I don't know. People are different. Some people take longer to get over things. Other people find it easy to move on, to be more dispassionate.'

111

'You and I are similar in that way – when Hilly . . . you were much more sensible than the others. You seemed to get it out of your system much more efficiently.'

'Did I?'

'And it's not really as if Ian and his father were that close.'

'No. Poor old Graham.'

Julia looks up. 'What do you mean?'

Martha feels a pinch of sadness. No one seems to be thinking about him this week. She says, 'Not having been close could make it worse for Ian, not better.'

'Well. Anyway, I'll be glad when the house is sold. All this old stuff. Eliza was here this morning going on about that gloomy picture over the fireplace. Apparently Geraldine went off with it yesterday. So now Eliza's taken the Chesterfield and is coming round later for that chest in the window. God knows why she wants it. Gothic. I've never been one for dark wood. Like you, I much prefer paler wood, painted and varnished. All those scrummy white Scandinavian cupboards that we both love. You are I are the same that way. I like to think we share the same good taste. I'm thinking of having the house Feng Shui'ed by the way. Do you know anyone good?'

Martha stops rocking the baby. 'Not really,' she says. She wouldn't admit it out loud, but Martha thinks her taste and Julia's are poles apart. She believes in an objective standard of good taste: that she has it and Julia doesn't. She agrees that Scandinavian cupboards can be scrummy, but *only if they are genuinely old*. She thinks the ones Julia buys from Ikea are vile.

Julia says, 'And I've just had Geraldine on the phone in tears.'

'Oh God.' Geraldine and Eliza have both left messages on her answer phone. Martha makes a mental note to ring neither of them back.

'So there's big trouble brewing there. And then there's all this other rubbish. Ian came home with a box of his father's school papers. I mean, what is the point? All yellowy round the edges. And there were these horrible little things in some of the workbooks.'

'Things?'

'Yes. Like tiny, tiny insects. You might think they were flecks of dirt. But I saw one of them move. Ugh.' She pauses. 'So the workbooks went straight in the bin.'

Martha thinks how nice to be Julia, to live so fair and square in the present. Julia has an amazing ability – not a weakness really, but a strength, a bullishness – to banish anything disagreeable from the scented pot-pourri of her own life. For most people, Martha has heard, IVF is a 'rollercoaster' of emotion – raised and dashed hopes, messy hormones. But Julia's experience has been as scrubbed as her kitchen floor: the squeaky clean rub of disappointment and then the lovely, lovely news. And it's not just doctors or death. Julia is the one person who isn't always banging on to Martha about David – in fact she hasn't mentioned him since they split up. It's as if he simply ceased to exist the instant he left her frame of reference. But is Martha like that, too? Is that how people see her?

'Silverfish,' she says.

'What fish?'

'Those insects. They like damp places. They have tiny jaws on the side of their heads. They eat the starch in old books.'

Julia shudders.

'Did he have a chance to read them before they were binned?'

'What?'

'The school papers.'

'God knows.'

'It might have been interesting. He might have found out more about his father, about what made him tick.'

'I think he knows. Local planning regulations. Complaints thereof. All those wrangles with the council and property developers, his one-man crusade against out-of-town supermarkets. All those legal cases. Finances in a complete mess. Oh, and concrete. That's what he poured his energies into.'

Martha smiles at the joke, even if it was unintentional. But she feels sorry for Ian, and implicated somehow, and explains to Julia about going through her own box of papers and a little about Friends Reunited. It has its rewards, she tells her. So far she's had one message from a person she hardly remembers, who's changed her name anyway, and one from a teenage mistake she has spent the previous twenty years trying to avoid. She thinks all this might make Julia laugh.

'Oh God. I haven't time for things like that,' Julia says, lining up her water-lilies on a tray. 'I've got enough to be getting on with as it is.'

For Martha, the world is suddenly full of ghosts. When, on Wednesday night, she meets a fellow dealer for a drink in

Kentish Town, the Tube takes her through Camden and she sees herself, age twenty, wending down the platform to the escalator – a day selling South American hats ahead of her. The mini-cab that takes her home drives down Lisson Grove and she catches a flash of green skirt disappearing round the turning towards Alfie's Antiques Market. (In a hurry a year later, with her own stall to open.) Then up Oxford Street – past a bus stop where she sees an arm covered in bracelets and the corner of a (dead man's) tweed coat – to Hyde Park and the Serpentine Gallery, where a woman in a black scarf is waiting for her auctioneer boyfriend, clapping her hands together to keep warm. The ghosts are indiscriminate. These are not important moments she remembers, though they are *specific*: a definite occasion when she was hurrying to open up at Alfie's for example, not just any old day. But why that one? Are they moments in which she was outside of herself even then, thinking detached thoughts about her life ('Here I am, a woman on a mission, opening up my own stall at Alfie's')? Or are they random? Either way, she feels a sense of immediacy, as if she has opened something up and now her life is happening on two planes at once, as if she could drive around London for ever, witnessing different occasions in her past.

It happens when she's not expecting it. On Thursday, she has an early morning appointment at a house in a tree-lined avenue in Clapham Old Town. The house is owned by an elderly Polish couple who have painted the woodwork around their windows red. Their neighbours have smart black arrow-headed railings and chequerboard tiles leading up to the front door. The Collofs have a white picket fence and a sign saying 'Beware the Dog'. This time it's spoons. Once a month, they find something in a box or under the bed, or in the attic, that they think might make their fortune. On previous occasions it has been wooden shoe-horns and damask antimacassars. Martha should say no – she should say no before she even leaves the shop – but she visits them none the less. April, who was with her the first time, would kill her if she knew how much she bought. None of it is worth selling, so it stays in boxes at the back of Martha's car. It is not pity – the Collofs are too dignified for that, too contemptuous of Martha's cheques as it is. ('Ach,' Mr Collof always says, jabbing at the Yellow Pages, 'the man from the other shop will offer more.') It is something else to do with the light rustling of Mr Collof's large bulbous thumbs, dry and cracked, as he rubs the dust off an old leather tie-box, clumsy and yet reverent, the way Mrs Collof wipes her hands on her apron before taking it from him, that touches her. For them, these objects are worthy of reverence because of their age, the life they've seen, not because of their value.

So, anyway, here she is today, standing at the door, listening to their ancient barrelled Jack Russell (a genuine antique) scratching in circles on the other side, when, like the blurring in a timelapse photograph, like a hologram, she sees herself at twenty-three, outside a similar door with Eric Butcher. Eric Butcher! She hasn't thought about him for years. How could she have forgotten him? When she was at Chester & Jones, bored out of her mind, he was her lifeline. They would mess around and play practical jokes on each other, snort at the vendors' decor, moan about the bosses. And then she left, and he didn't. There was the odd drink, slightly awkward as they no longer shared a job. Then nothing. And now here he is standing next to her.

Inside, there are more memories. A sniff of air freshener in the downstairs loo which reminds her, acutely, of staying at her grandmother's house. The taste of the Collofs' coffee – a caramelly, sweet taste she now knows is chicory – which pulls her back to Nick's mother's kitchen. And when she spins the silver cutlery in her hands, so worn in parts it's purple, for a moment she expects to see the lamp her parents used to hang above the kitchen table – a gas lantern converted to electric – spinning in miniature in the round pockets of the spoons.

Martha's old Snoopy address book – the one with the sloped childish writing – is still in her bag. After she has buried the plastic-wrapped cutlery under the back seat of the car, she returns to her shop, opens up, and settles down with the address book at her desk. Several of the first numbers she tries are unobtainable. She doesn't mind too much – she is starting wide, like you might do with carpet shampoo on a stain. She's still at the Bs when she finds a number for Eric Butcher. His mother answers. She sounds surprised when Martha explains who she is. She tells her Eric has his own place now, and his own estate agency, too. 'You must be very proud of him,' Martha hears herself say (in an answer-within-the-question Geraldine sort of way). 'Well, yes,' Eric's

117

mother says warily. 'We are.' Then she adds, 'And Cherie is a lovely girl, too.'

Martha hangs up with two phone numbers for Eric (for *married* Eric, for Eric and Cherie), but she doesn't ring them yet. It's like detective work, she thinks. Collect your evidence first. In the Ds she finds an old address for Susan/Sasha Doughty. She is in the mood to ring anyone. Just for the sake of it. She dials the number Susan/Sasha left in the email. Susan/Sasha was just sorting out the laundry when she heard the phone ring and almost didn't answer. 'And what a coincidence that I did!' she says. 'After all these years.'

'White wash or coloureds?' Martha asks, as if they'd spoken to each other just the day before.

Susan/Sasha pauses. She says, 'Delicates,' with a nervous laugh.

Later, Susan/Sasha says she's old as the hills now, but Martha can't tell that from her voice, which is unchanged. There are all these years between them, but they talk about Miss Spencer, their English teacher in Upper Three, who told the class one morning that the night before, on finishing *Anna Karenin*, she had called off her own engagement. 'There is more love out there,' she had told the group of thirteen-year-olds. 'Greater passion to search for. Settling is not for me.' Susan/Sasha had bumped into Miss Spencer at Reading Station only a few years before. 'And?' Martha asks. 'Still searching,' says Susan/Sasha.

There was a big craze in their school to go around talking like a character from *Abigail's Party*. 'Little top up, Ange?' they'd say, proffering a can of Coke and a plastic cup. Susan was the only person Martha knew who talked Mike Leigh for real. Martha isn't sure why she has rung her, or why she has embarked upon this archaeology at all, but it surprises her how the years smooth certain judgements out so that she feels she can see this partial friend with a clarity and a warmth that wasn't available to her at the time. Is there comfort in that, Martha wonders, or not?

Before they hang up, they promise to meet up soon. (It has, after all, been far too long.) Susan/Sasha is to be up in London at the end of the month to pick up some curtain material from Peter Jones. Lunch is planned at the third floor restaurant: 'They do a good quiche there. Well, they do if you're a goat's cheese person which I am, are you?'

Martha says she is a goat's cheese person. 'Though not if it's too strong,' she says.

'Oh it's not. It's really quite smooth. And baked, you know. Or half baked. Really quite mild.'

'Good,' Martha says. 'I look forward to it,' she adds and, to her surprise, finds she means it.

Susan/Sasha has supplied her with the phone number of Tracey Richards, another girl in their class, who had gone out with a boy called Mark Leonard, who used to hang out with Nick. 'I don't know if he still sees Nick or if she still sees Mark,' Susan/Sasha said, 'but she's in PR so she might.'

Martha rings Tracey Richards straight away. Tracey Richards is in PR so she answers. She says, 'Oh. Hello. Martha. Um. Eliza's sister, right?' She says Eliza, whom she bumps into at industry dos, is a 'wonderful woman. A really wonderful woman.' Susan/Sasha is an 'absolute honeypot'. As for Mark Leonard, God, going back, she's not sure, but she'll do a bit of phoning around and see what she comes up with. 'Tra-la,' she says, hanging up.

After this, Martha turns to directory enquiries. She rings the politics department at Manchester University, and Nick's former hall of residence, but neither can help. 'He's one of our lost persons,' the registrar says, after looking him up on the computer. 'We'd be delighted to have him for our data-base if you track him down.'

It has started raining outside the shop now. Martha puts some lights on and plugs in the electric radiator to take the edge off the chill. She opens the door and looks up and down the water-washed street. There is only one veg stall today, the holder lurking beneath his tarpaulin. A group of women huddle in the doorway of the chemist. A teenager runs past, pushing a buggy. No sign of April. No sign of any customers. She returns to her desk. 'Who now?' she thinks, in the manner of one choosing their third chocolate from a box of soft centres. She flicks through her address book. Back to front. She flicks again. Front to back. A name jumps out at her. Oh she can't, she thinks. She can't ring Colin. Why would she even want to? She turns back to the beginning. Oh to hell with it. He won't still be teaching spoilt teenagers at the crammer anyway. He's one person who will have moved on. To serious academia, to dinner in gowns, and seminars with Susan Sontag.

She dials.

A brusque woman's voice answers. 'Oxford and Cambridge College of Advanced Studies.'

Martha begins, 'Hello. I was just wondering . . . I'm trying to track down an old friend who used to work there a long time ago. Goodness, almost fifteen years now. And I just wondered whether there was any chance anybody there remembered them, or had any clue at all where they work now.'

'Name?' the voice says.

'Oh.' Martha is tapping the address book on the table. 'Martha,' she says. 'Bone.'

'I'm sorry,' the woman says, 'I've never heard of anyone working here with that name. Hang on, I'll just ask . . .' There is a muffled noise and while Martha is saying, 'No. No. Sorry. Hello? No. That's me. Hello?', she can hear the woman calling something on the other side. Then she comes back on the line and says, 'Sorry. No one of that name here.'

'Actually. Sorry. I'm Martha Bone. It's someone else I'm trying to track down. Someone with the name of Colin? Colin Cooper.'

There's a pause. The woman says, 'Hang on,' and this time the line makes that white-noise dead sound. Martha is about to ring off when the white noise ends in a 'blip' and a man's voice says, 'Hello. Colin Cooper.'

It takes a second for this to register, a second in which the muscles in Martha's face seize up. She drops the phone back on to the receiver. Agh! Still there. Colin Cooper. On the phone! Agh! Behind the safety of the dialling tone, she starts to breathe again. So he hasn't moved on. And then she realises something alarming. She gave her name. It's one thing to chase the past, quite another to think it might turn round and chase you.

This is a message from Jane Pritchet email: jane.pritchet@easynet.co.uk who is contacting you through http://www.friendsreunited.co.uk

The message is as follows:-

Dear Martha

Hello! Sasha told me you were on Friends Reunited and I thought I'd email you and say Hi. So, hi! How are you? Sasha says you've got your own shop, which is fab. Well done you. Hope it's going well.

Some of the girls and I thought it would be fun to arrange a reunion. What do you say? Did you know I'd married Phil Dunston? Well, I did. So I see some of the old crowd. We were thinking some time before Christmas.

Anyway, get in touch (if you want!)

Love Jane

This is a message from Simon Fletcher email: simon.fletcher@virgin.net who is contacting you through http://www.friendsreunited.co.uk

The message is as follows:-

Hi Martha. Did you get my email? Thought I'd try again just in case it went astray.

My phone number in case you didn't get it is 07779 532410.

Si.

chapter six

the hall, stairs and landing

'A hall is pivotal, not only because it provides the
first impression of your house, but also because it
sets the tone for what is to come.'

Nina Campbell's Decorating Secrets
by Nina Campbell
(Clarkson Potter, 2000)

THE CAT and Martha oversleep. For the cat, this is all in a
day's work, but Martha wakes at 9.30 a.m. on Friday morning
in a state. The funeral. Richmond Park. The bloody home
visit. The moment she left the man's car on Tuesday she
knew she would have to get out of it. But events – Julia and
the house, the Collofs, her own dreamy absorption in the
contents of the Snoopy address book, an irate customer
claiming to have discovered woodworm in a set of ladderback chairs – took over and she hasn't. It is her fault
probably for not having secured a phone number for the

cat family. But, throwing water on her face, she suppresses this and blames Geraldine instead. She blames her for suggesting the home visit in the first place, for organising this loopy ceremony at Pen Ponds, but also, more importantly, for never giving Martha leeway to *get out* of anything. Being a few minutes late wouldn't matter if she hadn't long been diagnosed by her sister as 'perennially late'. In her good moods, Geraldine even calls her 'The late Martha Bone'. There are few things more irritating than fulfilling one's family's prophecies for one – for being *reduced* like that.

She dresses quickly in a dark purple shirt she hasn't had time to iron and her smartest pair of black jeans, decides against coffee and thunders down into the shop. Here she is delayed by a flashing light on the answering machine: April (clever tactic not to have rung upstairs where she would actually have to *talk* to her employer) to say she's feeling a bit sick and will be in after the doctor's. Martha gives a sigh which turns into a groan when she notices the white envelope on the doormat. It is from the landlord and, tearing it open, she sees Nell from the bookshop was right: he is suggesting a thirty per cent increase in the rent 'due to the area being on the up'. She thrusts the letter on to her desk, where she will worry about it later, and slams out of the shop. She doesn't even leave a note.

The cat family live in a crossword puzzle of identical streets full of identical late Victorian terraced houses known as 'The Nightingale Triangle'. Martha has been in one or two of these houses before and they vary only in being laid out either to the left or the right of the staircase and in their owners' varying attitudes towards period detail. The house opposite the cat house is nice. It has linen curtains in the window and the original cast-iron railings are painted not black but an authentic blue-grey. (Martha considers the hacking down of London railings for ammunition a particularly dark moment in the history of the Second World War.) Number 35, where she is heading, also has its railings, only they are chipped and gap-toothed. The lid is off the bin and the foxes must have been in to investigate because there are chicken bones on the flower bed. But there is a window box in the bay housing a lonely heather and, as she climbs the steps, she notes favourably that the door still has its original decorative glass panels – even if the door itself is painted a decidedly inauthentic shade of mauve.

She rings the bell, which doesn't seem to work, and there isn't a knocker, so she does that rather awkward slapping thing with the letter-box until she senses the light thud of someone approaching and sees the going-on-forever shape of him fractured through the coloured panes. 'Hello,' he says cautiously when he opens the door. He is in jeans and a loose-necked grey sweater which sits at an angle across his collarbone, drawing attention to the pallor of his skin and the dark hairs on the knuckle in his throat. He is also wearing glasses, with thick, black rectangular rims, which are the ugliest glasses Martha has ever seen. On his feet – sockless – are some sort of Turkish slippers. He hasn't opened the door any further and is still looking at her enquiringly, his brow furrowed above the black hook of his specs. 'Hello,' she says. Then, as he still looks at her, 'Cat?'

'Indeed.' He's holding the door with one hand, but he draws it back now. 'The Home Visit,' he says, and the way he says it makes her realise that he hadn't forgotten, that it was just awkwardness that held him up, not confusion. 'Hello Martha,' he adds.

'I'm sorry. God.' Martha speaks quickly, head on one side, to indicate that she is in a hurry. 'And I don't know your name.'

'Oh. Fred. It's Fred. Fred.' He puts out his hand and she shakes it. She has to step in to do so and he backs against the radiator to make room, his head almost disappearing into a bundle of coats that is hanging there. His handshake is firm, the fingers bony. And then she's in – and she almost wishes she wasn't, it is so crammed in here. The walls are crimson from the dado rail up, but purple beneath, which makes Martha feel even more oppressed, and there is junk everywhere. Bikes and scooters and plastic bags and a strange black box and what looks like a load of fishing rods. On the stairs there is the little leather suitcase and a trail of shoes and clothes. Higher up, on the landing, she can see more fabric devastation. Dirty washing on its way up? Clean washing on its way down? 'Uh,' she says, when there's a crack under her feet. She's trodden on something. She picks the pieces up. There are bits of jagged plastic in her hand. 'I'm terribly sorry.' She holds them out to the man. He says, 'Thunderbird Two. Don't worry. It's just the er . . . thing . . . middle bit.' He takes the pieces from her and looks at them in his hand. 'I'll . . . er . . . Anyway. Sitting room?'

He goes through a door and she follows. She has never been in such a hideously decorated room: that's all she can think when she goes in. The walls are fleshy pink, and they clash horribly with everything else – with the cheap marine blue sofa and the reproduction winged armchairs (factory 'tapestry-style'), and the orangey-fake pine coffee table. And it's not just that, it's the stuff everywhere: piles of tatty cushions and toys, and, on the shelves and surfaces, not just books, but countless bits of *tat* – pieces of pottery, loose playing cards, batteries, ornaments made by children out of loo rolls, a calendar with a cotton wool snowman on it, his head hanging down at an angle, brown with dust. Martha wants to put her arm out and sweep the whole lot into a refuse sack. Instead she makes a noise, meant to express surprise and interest, if not exactly approval. The man has negotiated a path through the furnishings and is carefully laying the remains of Thunderbird Two on the mantelpiece, alongside a pile of foreign money and some dried-up leaves. The fireplace is the original marble, Martha can tell, because someone has begun stripping the white gloss paint off it, though they obviously gave up after the right-hand leg. Now it looks streaky and bubbly, like the funnel on a rusty liner. In the grate are the scuzzy remains of a fire, the coal dissolved into pink dust, shards of charred wood and snippets of burnt paper. Martha is very particular about her own fireplace. When not in use, she brushes it meticulously and fills it with fir cones. She buys them from the Conran Shop where they come ready infused with the scent of orange and cloves.

'So this is the, er, sitting room,' the man says. 'It's a bit . . .' He sweeps something up off the sofa – a packet of children's crayons – and some pieces of paper off the floor, placing them haphazardly on top of a monstrous television in the corner. He adjusts the glasses on his nose and, squeezing past the piano, turns to go out of the door again. Martha follows, noticing for the first time the picture on the wall behind her – a large oil of purple horses galloping through white spume. The paint, which is thick and spiked, seems to rear out at her as she passes.

'And this is the kitchen,' he is saying ahead of her. Behind him she feels like someone from the council come to investigate a bad smell. She should have a clipboard. Or a collecting tin.

The kitchen is not as bad as she expected – 'Farmhouse-style', her estate agent friend Eric Butcher would have called it. There is a big old oak table which she wouldn't mind having a closer look at, but the chairs are peculiar. They are made of see-through plastic string on an aluminium frame, which would be interestingly modern if the plastic strings weren't thick with gunk. There is a big clock above the door with the numbers playfully (irritatingly) muddled, and more books on a shelf by the oven and children's paintings plastered everywhere and photographs stuck all over the fridge and piles of newspapers on the table and a jug with dying tulips in it, but the room looks clean. Cleanish anyway. There are brown splatters behind the oven, maroon streaks in the sink where the water has run down from the taps. And the walls are . . .

'Burnt umber,' she says.

He looks at her.

'The walls, I mean.'

'Oh,' he says. 'Er . . . orange, I think.'

He studies her from behind his glasses. 'Um,' he says.

128

There's a fraction of a pause and then he continues with, 'We did take the liberty of . . .' He crosses the room and bends down to indicate a catflap in the base panel of the back door. He opens it once or twice to show her it works. Martha goes over and says with enthusiasm, 'Excellent.'

'We bought it yesterday and, um, I got a man to put it in this morning, so you'd see it. Hazel was very keen that it should be here when you came. She was worried . . . I'm not very good with that sort of, um, thing, but the man next door . . . he is.' He lets the flap flip shut. It clatters once, then silence.

'It seems fine.' Martha looks out through the glass at the top of the door. 'Very impressive.' The garden, small and overgrown with a lawn as threadbare as the rugs in the sitting room, is dominated by a large phallic leylandii. Martha thinks leylandii should be universally scythed to the ground.

Remembering Graham, who agreed, she looks at her watch. 'Well, I think you've passed,' she says.

Fred has crossed the room and is at the kitchen door. 'But you haven't even seen upstairs yet.'

'I'm sure it's fine.'

'What about his sleeping quarters?'

'His sleeping quarters?'

'We've bought a, um, basket. Hazel wanted him on her bed and I wanted him downstairs, so we've, er, compromised. A basket under the radiator in her room.'

'I think,' Martha says, 'that he would like that very much.'

'Good,' the man, Fred, says. 'Er. Very good.'

Martha smiles at him across the kitchen. 'I think Kitten will be very happy here.'

129

He doesn't smile back, just stares at her from behind those black glasses. 'They are . . . *we are* . . . very excited about having him.'

While Martha is wondering if this corrected 'we' means him and the children or him and his wife, or whether he's a widower (all this chaos), Fred says, 'If you don't want to see upstairs, would you, er, would you like a coffee?'

Martha looks at her watch. Twenty past ten. She should get going. The traffic across to the park can be unpredictable. She mustn't be late for Geraldine. She says, 'I really ought to get going. I've got this funeral to go to.'

He puts his hands to his glasses. 'Oh. I am so sorry. Your father. Of course. Today. Goodness.'

Martha thinks, 'Oh God.' Then she says, 'Actually . . .' She is about to explain how she came to be pretending, that day in the shop, that her father had died, when in fact it was her stepfather. But a mixture of embarrassment and apathy stops her. Instead she says, 'OK, well maybe a quick one.'

He nods and fiddles around with a coffee pot on the stove. 'By the way, I meant to say . . . I'm very sorry about that.'

'Thank you.' So now it is too late anyway.

He says, 'Excuse me.' He's trying to get past her to the fridge. She moves out of the way – there's a sudden stench of garlic and miscellaneous left-overs – and when the door swings she sees the photographs stuck on it with magnets. There are pictures of Hazel and her brother in swimming costumes – laughing, tongues sticking out, sand in their hair – and pictures of them with other children, eating lollies on a bench. There's one photograph of Fred on his own in some sort of fancy dress costume, and another of him with a woman. She has blonde shoulder-length hair and a pretty, open face. She is wearing a halter-neck top and she's grinning, one of those open, unself-conscious grins in which the gums show. 'Is this your wife?' Martha asks.

The man is returning the packet of coffee to the fridge. He says, 'Yes.'

'She's very pretty.'

He pauses, looks at the photograph as if to consult it, and says 'Yes' again. He moves to clear some space at the table. 'Do sit down.'

Martha sidles gingerly into one of the plastic-spaghetti chairs. The strings bend beneath her bottom. She doesn't like to lean back, not trusting it to support her whole weight, not wanting to get her black trousers sticky. On the table in front of her, next to a packet of cigarettes, are more of those miniature plastic bags with pictures on the outside. Party bags, she now knows. While Fred pours the coffee, she picks one up. It is decorated with a slightly off, too bright illustration of Winnie the Pooh. Inside are sweets and a packet of outsize neon-coloured jacks. She says, 'Do your children spend their entire lives at birthday parties?'

The man puts some tiny pearl-blue cups and a packet of biscuits on the table and sits down opposite her. He says, 'Er, ye-es.'

'They must have an awful lot of friends.'

'No. No. Didn't I . . .?'

'When I was little –' she has taken a sip of her coffee, dark and syrupy – 'I'll never forget the feeling of *not* being invited. The invitations would be on some of the desks in

131

the morning and you'd see this paper trail across the classroom and you'd walk towards your desk and then when there wasn't one . . .' She breaks off and taps her fingers on the table. She glances up and laughs.

He is looking at her with an impenetrable expression on his face. He passes her the packet of biscuits. They are Italian ones with almonds. She takes one and dips it in her coffee. It is heavenly, half-melting, half-rocky, so that her mouth can't quite close. Fred has crossed his legs. In his jeans, they look like the lanky legs of a teenager. 'So why weren't you?'

'Why weren't I what?' says Martha, through a mouthful of biscuit.

'To the parties. Why weren't you invited?'

She swallows. 'Well. I'm sure I was. Perhaps there was only one time when I wasn't and it's that that sticks in my mind. You know, like when there's a big family outing to the circus, a huge treat – acrobats and clowns, gas balloons, a car ride in the dark – and all you remember afterwards is not being allowed candyfloss.'

'Memory is a funny thing.'

'Yes, and I'm going through a nostalgic phase at the moment. Keep remembering things like that. Perhaps it's sorting out the parental home.'

Martha is surprised at how much she is talking. There is something about his stillness, about his expression. She looks down at the table, suddenly self-conscious, tracing the grooves in the wood with her finger. She has forgotten about being in a hurry now. Fred cups his hands over the cigarette packet and taps it up and down on the table. He says, 'And your father? Were you, er, close to him?'

'Oh.' She looks up. 'Yes . . . no . . . not really. I adored him when I was little. Don't all little girls? Love their Dad, I mean. But he and my mother separated when I was thirteen. She had their marriage dissolved, so we all had to pretend it never happened. We stopped calling him Dad, or I did, and he became Neville. He ran off with a friend of mine.'

She waits for his sympathy.

But he just says, 'A friend of yours?'

'Well she had been at my school. Several years ahead.'

'So . . . not really a friend?'

Martha pauses before answering. She has believed her own elaboration of this story for so long it takes a moment to adjust. 'No, not really,' she says. 'You're right. Anyway, it didn't last. He met a French woman, an architect, called Eloise, and moved to France, near Grasse. Had two little girls. A second family. Second time round. Incredibly charming, my father, talks to everyone as if he's known them all their life. Very endearing, unless of course you have known him all your life in which case it's galling not to be treated differently. Everyone's best friend.'

'I'm sure he was.' Fred's voice is low and gentle.

Martha sits tight and waits for the moment to pass. Finally, Fred says, 'The reason my children are always at parties is that I'm a magician.'

She's not quite sure if she heard right. 'Sorry?'

'I'm a magician.' He pokes his glasses back up his nose again. He has picked up the Winnie the Pooh bag and is dropping it from one hand into the other, as if weighing it. 'That's why they go to a lot of parties. They come with me when I work.'

133

'A what?'

'A magician. A children's entertainer.'

'You're not.'

'I am.'

'What a strange thing to be. Is that . . .? Are you . . .?' Martha breaks off. She is about to ask him if that's all he does but realises just in time that to a serious magician that might sound rude.

'I'm Mr Magic.'

'Mr Magic!'

'Simple but does the trick. They know what they're getting.'

'God.' Martha leans back against the plastic spaghetti supports and studies him. It strikes her for the first time that his diffidence, his fumbling over language, is maybe not shyness but a form of exhibitionism, a pose that he has chosen.

'I do some corporate things, but mainly it's tea time things. Saturdays. Sundays.'

'A magician. Have you always?'

'No. Only quite recently.' He clears his throat again. 'I was an accountant. In the, er, City. But I was made, er, redundant two years ago. Gardening leave, as they say, initially . . .' He looks up at the sparse patch of grass outside the kitchen and shrugs. 'I'd always done a bit of magic on the side, since school. Mr Magic was supposed to be a stop-gap but it's become, well, rather more established, and I can fit it around Hazel and Stan. I'm quite good, you know.' He had been doing his deep-voice mumbling thing, but when he says this, his voice rises and, with a twitch at the corners of his mouth, he looks at her straight on. 'Kids like me. The mums

134

like me. I'm really very popular on the age four to eight party network.'

Martha laughs. She looks across to the fridge. 'And what about Mrs Magic? Is she part of the act?'

He looks down again. He says, 'No. Actually no.' He breathes in through a grimace and fondles his cigarettes. 'Ah. Yuh. No, Mrs Magic isn't. She's not with us at the moment. She's um travelling, finding herself.'

There is a detached note in his voice which makes Martha think she can add, 'Oh, done a disappearing act, has she?' but she regrets her words the moment they are out there. 'Sorry,' she says. 'That was a silly thing to say.' He smiles slightly as if it doesn't really matter. He says he loves Lucy, his wife, and that he misses her and the children do, too. But that you can't make people stay with you if they don't want to. Martha is taken aback, not by what he says but by the fact that he says it at all. The words seem to come out so simply.

He says, 'I'm lucky. Some people, when their wives leave them, they lose their children too.'

The topsy-turvy clock on the wall behind him says ten to eleven (actually it says half past four) and Martha knows she has to go. She can hear it ticking now she thinks about it – reminding her with every new second of her lateness. And maybe it is the rhythm of that, or the comforting honeyed strength of the coffee inside her, or maybe it is simply the fact that she has moulded the strings now with the warmth of her back, but the spaghetti chair seems unfathomably comfortable all of a sudden. And when she gets up to go, it is a wrench to leave.

135

chapter seven

the garden

'Leave small posies of flowers in unexpected places
for your guests: a few sprigs of lavender tied
with ribbon on the pillow pinned to a note
saying "sweet dreams".'

Spirit of the Home: How To Make Your Home A Sanctuary
by Jane Alexander
(Thorsons, 1998)

WHEN Martha turns her Volvo into the carpark above Pen
Ponds at ten past eleven, Geraldine is standing by the gate,
a bunch of roses held stiffly in one hand and an object
Martha can't quite make out clenched in the other. The
carpark is almost empty this early, but Geraldine still waves
wildly, beckoning her in and pointing to her own car in the
far corner as if ensuring Martha doesn't get lost in the crowd.

Eliza is here too, though she is away over on the other
side of the lot on the grass verge beyond Geraldine's car.
Her head is down and she's scuffing the leaves with her feet.
For a minute, as Martha bumps the car over the uneven

ground towards her, she thinks Eliza is crying – or sulking. But when she gets closer she realises she is talking into a mobile phone.

Geraldine strikes across the gravelly mud towards her. 'At last!' she calls. 'I was about to send out a search party.'

Eliza has turned, snapping her phone shut. It's one of those minuscule silver ones which remind Martha, incongruously, of the leather and brass alarm clock their mother used to have which would fold up, with a clunk, for travelling. Eliza says, 'Oh don't be ridiculous, Ger. She's only five minutes late.'

'Ten, actually. I was just anxious she wasn't coming.'

Eliza puts the phone back in her briefcase. 'I don't know why you thought that.'

'Well you know what she's like. And she didn't seem that keen in the first place.'

Martha says benignly, 'I'm here,' because they seem to have forgotten this. She moves over to Geraldine, who is wearing a long black velvet skirt over wellies, and gives her a kiss on the cheek. They are not a kissing family, but it seems appropriate today. Geraldine's skin, pale and powdery under what Martha now realises with surprise is foundation, smells of warm apricots. Geraldine looks pleased. She gives a sort of half nod and is about to say something, but then looks away instead.

Martha says, 'I had to do a cat check. Remember? Check the house. And the garden? Well, it's OK. They have one. And then traffic on the A3. Accident, I think.' She kisses Eliza, too – she finds herself instinctively moving up a social gear and doing both cheeks for her.

Eliza says, 'There's always an accident.'

Geraldine says, 'Well I don't know why you had to do the house check today.'

'You asked her to do the house check.'

'Anyway: accident or no accident, we'd better get on.'

They start walking across the carpark. There is what Martha's mother would have called 'an atmosphere'.

Geraldine says, 'I don't remember a café.'

'It's not really a café,' Eliza says. 'More of a van.'

The van-café is humming as they pass it and there's a smell of hot dogs and plastic in the air. The man who runs it is sheltering in a car. It is exposed up here and the wind is sharp. Martha says, 'Anyone fancy a tea?'

Eliza gives her a warning look. 'Maybe later,' she says.

They pass the van and set off down the path towards the pond. It is a sullen day – the sky is slate and dirty cream in horizontal layers, whipped in places into darker peaks. Some deer graze over on one side, and a seagull flies low across the scrubland, wings flashing oyster-white against the grey. They seem miles from London and yet, in the silence, you can hear it on the wind – the boom of a jet heading for Heathrow; the squeal of a police siren, bouncing off distant roads and roofs and landing in these trees. An Alsatian noses past them, followed by a middle-aged man in a mauve anorak. A woman, also in a mauve anorak, tramps up the hill some way behind him. The air smells of curry powder and fennel: bracken, Martha supposes.

She says, 'You haven't brought the dogs, then?'

'No.' Geraldine looks unfamiliar in her foundation. And

she's behaving all stiffly, as if it has made her feel different, too. 'Of course not.'

'Oh.' There is a pause. The three of them are walking alongside each other on the path, only Martha is in the middle, in the dip where rainwater collects, and she keeps having to leap over the puddles. She is lolloping to keep up. Eliza and Geraldine are both walking crisply. Geraldine has the grimly self-conscious expression of The Organiser. The high heels of Eliza's leather boots catch in the mud every other step but she must have decided, for the sake of short-term expediency, not to notice. 'Of course not,' Martha adds. 'Stupid of me, sorry.'

'I couldn't think what of Graham's to bring,' Geraldine says, just ahead. 'He wasn't the sort of man that one associated with anything in particular. Nothing stood out, do you know what I mean?'

Eliza says, 'Concrete, of course.' Beat. 'But that would be hard to disperse.'

'I wondered about a book, or, you know, an atlas? Because he liked travelling, and they did a lot of that together . . . But you can't really scatter a book.'

Martha is still a little behind. The leaves on the path are skipping low to the ground like tumbleweed. She catches her sisters up. 'You could pull out the pages and hurl them to the wind.'

Geraldine says, 'Yes, but that would be littering, wouldn't it?'

Eliza says, 'You can't be too careful where sentimental value is concerned. It would be a shame to destroy something that somebody else loved.'

Geraldine says, 'Anyway, in the end I thought of this.' She holds out the small bottle in her hand. 'His aftershave. Eau Sauvage. It's easy to pour, it'll disperse easily. I thought it would do, don't you?'

Martha is trying not to laugh. She knows she should be feeling sombre. (Sometimes she thinks she is a very ordinary person surrounded by mad people, and sometimes she wonders if she isn't the mad one.) She says, 'What if it poisons the ducks?'

The woman who was plodding up the hill towards them passes. Her head is down and you can hear the pant of her breathing. There is something resigned in the heavy roundness of her shoulders. Martha turns her head and sees that the woman's companion – husband? – in his matching anorak, has already reached the carpark. But he's not looking this way. Martha thinks, why hasn't he waited? Why aren't they walking together?

Geraldine says, 'Obviously it's not *actually* Graham's aftershave. I didn't have time to go over to the house and rummage through the bathroom cabinets.'

Eliza says, 'Oh no?'

'But I know it's the one he used – certainly recently anyway, we gave him some for Christmas only last year – and Greg happened to have some.'

This time Martha does laugh. Eliza and Geraldine both look at her. 'Sorry,' she says, turning the laugh into a cough.

They reach the pond. Or rather ponds. From a distance it looks like one, but close up you see there are two: a pair of murky pools, a breeze rippling over them, edged with reeds with a bank wide enough for a path between. There's a tree here too, its bark thick and gnarled like a picture of a tree in a fairy tale. A flurry of ducks is paddling in the shallows, and a couple of swans glide towards the shore, hopeful for bread.

It was summer when they came here, five years before, to scatter their mother's ashes. It was a Saturday and sunny, and the place was alive with dogs and children. The swans were bread-sated and superior, away from the bustle by the other bank. But the ducks were still busy and bobbing and the water glinting, spangled with chips of light. And even though Martha and her sisters had been sad, unbearably sad, furious with loss, still in the filthy thick of it, that day they had laughed a lot. Geraldine had stopped in her tracks, stricken suddenly with what they were doing. 'Do you think we need a permit?' she had said, and Eliza had roared as if that was the funniest thing she had ever heard. And they stood together on the path between the ponds, creasing up with secret laughter as they tried to disperse their mother's ashes, forgetting the other walkers and the wind, which had blown all gusty, scattering pearly dust across their feet, and Greg, Denis and David waiting, solemnly, for them up at the carpark.

But today it is as if Martha is inhabiting a different story to her sisters. What has happened to their sense of humour? she thinks. She feels a tug of irritation, but then sees that Geraldine, despite the wellies, has picked up some mud on the back of her skirt, and the irritation lets her go. 'Where do you think, then?' she says cheerfully.

Geraldine says, 'Ummm. Well, obviously it'll have to be over there.' She points to the tree in the middle of the path between the ponds where they had stood last time.

Martha says, 'OK,' snapping her fingers in a 'let's get this show on the road' kind of way, and the three of them walk across the sandy earth and hover together under the branches.

Geraldine says, 'Shall I . . . or would you . . .?'

Eliza shrugs. 'No, no, you.' Martha just nods and puts her hands in her pockets to indicate that she too will stand down to let the eldest do the honours.

Geraldine unscrews the lid of the Eau Sauvage and shakes the bottle over the water. Some of it lands on the bank by her feet and Martha's nostrils flood with the intense perfume-stench of peppery nutmeg. She hasn't thought about Graham properly for ages, not even in this week after his death, in fact she hasn't thought about him at all, but for a moment she has him in her head, not as an idea, a concept (The Stepfather, The Man Who Brought Her Mother Happiness, Mr Corby Trouser Press, The Deceased), but as a person: Graham in his best suit and smart sideburns neatly kissing his bride in front of his children outside the church, two pursed lips meeting like birds pecking on dry earth. Before Sunday lunch, in the garden, poking about with his stick as he talked to whomever he could find to listen about whatever local planning application had most recently excited his indignation. And then, at their mother's funeral, an old man with skin dry like paper, wet eyed.

She looks at Eliza and then at Geraldine to see if they are glaring at each other. But they aren't. And for a few moments the three of them stand there quietly, looking down, as Eau Sauvage mingles with the tame water at their feet.

*

There is time after all, between the Richmond Park ceremony and the church ceremony, to join the brothers-in-law and the children in a café in Wimbledon Village. There are nine of them – five adults, four kids – and, once in, they fill a great slice of the restaurant, scraping two tables together and clattering across more chairs. Martha can see respectable groups of twos and threes looking up from their papers or their conversations as Eliza trills, 'Oh, but make that a skinny one,' as Geraldine hoots back, 'Aren't you skinny enough already?' Ordinarily, she would cringe, but she doesn't mind so much today.

Denis, shambolic as ever, shoulders hunched, raises his arm to greet Martha, like a policeman stopping traffic. 'All right?' he says, plonking himself down next to her and swinging Gabriel on to his lap. Martha is very fond of Denis. (The fact that he loves Eliza makes her like her sister more.) Today he is in an Oxfam tweed coat and black trousers with an overwashed shine to the knees. Gabriel is wearing an immaculate blue duffel-coat with wooden toggles.

'Yup,' she says.

Denis musses the front of his hair. 'I hear you've adopted the cat.'

'I have not—' she begins, but Eliza has brought a highchair over and there is soothing and negotiation to be done as Gabriel goes rigid when they try to put him in it, kicking his laced-up feet in her direction, so she turns to Ivor on the other side. Geraldine has cut her children's hair for the occasion. Anna, across the table on her father's knee, looks sweetly tomboyish in her short bob, and Patrick, with his high pink cheeks and his mole-dark widow's peak, like a miniature marine. But Ivor's trim has given his six-year-old face, which has just begun its lengthening, thinning process, a pinched, raw look. The skin above his ears is white and exposed. He is wearing dark green corduroy trousers which match his older brother's, only his are a little too large and are rolled up at the ankles. He is chewing the sleeve of his shirt.

'How's school?' she asks.

He doesn't hear her, or if he does he doesn't look up. The highchair has been abandoned, Gabriel is back on Denis's knee and everyone is talking loudly. The trip to Richmond Park has become, for Eliza, the subject of anecdote now. The brief armistice between her and Geraldine is over and she is hurling jokes, sheltering behind everyone else's laughter. 'And then we couldn't even remember where we'd scattered Mum's ashes!'

Geraldine, injured, shouts, 'Eliza, how would I have forgotten that?'

While this is going on, Martha watches Greg catch Ivor's eye and frown, making a flipping gesture with his hand. Ivor stops chewing his sleeve and puts his arm down on the table. He keeps his eyes low.

'It's OK,' he says.

'Working hard?'

'Yup.'

'And then Geraldine got aftershave all over her hands . . .'

Martha bends towards him and whispers, 'Good to be bunking off for the day, though, isn't it?'

Ivor looks at her. The skin below his lip is chapped and he keeps running over it with his tongue.

Geraldine arrives at the table with some mugs. 'I did not! Hot chocolate! Cup of Darjeeling!' She puts the mugs down and goes back to the counter.

Eliza says, 'And Martha kept going on about how much the dogs would be enjoying it!'

Ivor has said something. She has to ask him to repeat it. 'Do you like Harry Potter?' he says.

'I haven't read it yet,' Martha answers. 'Have you?'

'Everyone at school has.'

'That doesn't mean you have to.'

'No, but they say you're a Slytherin if you don't.'

'Oh dear.'

'Patrick's a Gryffindor.'

'Is he?' She doesn't have to say any more because Geraldine, who has just conducted a hissed conversation with Greg involving several frowns and darting looks in Martha's direction, is at her shoulder. 'Just to warn you,' she hisses, 'Greg told David to meet us here. Sorry. Tactless idiot. I wish he'd told me he was going to do that. He doesn't seem to get it. Ivor! Stop licking your mouth.'

Ivor stops but rubs it with his hand instead. Martha says quietly, 'Oh Geraldine.'

'I know. I know. He is the limit.' Geraldine says this with some bitterness. 'Would it be awful? Is it too much for you to bear?'

'Here?'

'Apparently.'

They are talking under their breath, but Eliza has noticed something is up and is looking at them from across the table. Geraldine shakes her head at her almost imperceptibly.

145

Martha takes a gulp of her tea. It's still so hot she can feel it scalding her on the way down. She gets up and pushes her chair back. 'I'll meet you at the church. I need to check on the flowers anyway.'

'Oh, please don't.'

'No, I am. I will.'

She is easing her way behind Denis, her things in her arms. 'I'm just going to go and check on the flowers.' Everyone stares at her. Greg is looking uncomfortable, Geraldine anguished, Eliza confused. Ivor is still staring at the table and, without thinking, she hears herself say, 'Do you want to come?' To her surprise, he wrinkles off his chair and scrambles over to her. 'OK,' he says. She is aware of the whole café watching as they leave. Once outside, suddenly, she wants to run – to scream, to hide – but here's Ivor at her side, hovering, plodding. She wonders why on earth she asked him to come. He is not what she needs right now. She says, 'Actually, why don't you go back inside?' But he says he doesn't want to so she sets off at a pace that she knows is a little too fast, in the hope that he will change his mind. He half-runs to keep up. Clumsy, awkward, charmless little thing. She quickens. He starts to run properly and trips. He doesn't actually fall over, it is really more of a stumble, but he gasps and any colour there is drains from his face. Martha stops. She takes his hand. 'Sorry,' she says.

They walk slowly together down the high street and, just before they turn off, they pass a shop selling gifts and toys – one of those places designed for the panicked purchasing of last-minute, thought-free presents. In the window, next to a pile of slogan-embroidered cushions ('Home Sweet Home';

'I'd Rather Be Fishing'), there's a collection of Harry Potter merchandise. Martha, on impulse, pulls Ivor through the door and to the counter where she asks the assistant to point out 'the most sought-after Harry Potter item'. The assistant ums and ahs and finally says, 'The Harry Potter wand is very popular.'

'I'll have one of those then please,' Martha says, thinking what a day it's been for magic wands. To Ivor, she says, 'I met a magician today.'

Ivor says, 'Uh?'

'Mr Magic. Ever heard of him?'

Again Ivor just says, 'Uh?'

'Maybe his fame hasn't reached Kingston yet.'

While the assistant wraps the wand and Martha pays, Ivor continues to stand by her, unresponsive. Outside the shop, she puts the parcel in his hand. He looks blank. Martha feels that maybe she has done the wrong thing, but she says grimly, 'I just don't think a Slytherin would have one of these. Do you?' And he grins and says that maybe a Slytherin wouldn't.

He adds, 'You didn't buy batteries. It's no good without them.'

The church is further out of Wimbledon Village than Martha remembers, and when they get there she finds she is not in time to check the flowers after all. The rough patch of grass that is used as a carpark is three-quarters full and the short private lane is crammed with vehicles on both sides. In the

147

small churchyard, where squirrels dart up yew trees and down ancient mossy tombs, you can just pick up the groaning yawn of the organ. A brace of elderly women in feathered hats have just gone in and two young undertakers in suits are having a cigarette, leaning against the far side of a black sedan. She hasn't been to many funerals, but it always surprises her that it's all in a day's work for them. She wonders whether they go out and get drunk every night to drown other people's sorrows.

She smiles as she passes and one of the young men nods before chucking his cigarette on the ground and twisting it out with his foot. She and Ivor go through the big open oak door into the church. It smells of polish and sap, like the inside of a wooden box. For a moment she wavers, wondering which side to sit on before remembering that it's weddings that like a nice divide, your side versus mine; funerals are egalitarian, democratic, pacifist. She slips her hand through Ivor's arm and guides him up the aisle to a pew on the right. Julia is in the front with the twins. Next to her is a thin, tanned woman with long blonde hair and a spikey fringe whom Martha realises (though she is much changed) is Susie, Graham's daughter from Vancouver. Across the aisle there are other people with faces formed from the same mould as Ian and Susie's – the sloping chin, the hawk nose: relatives of Graham's first wife. They are all perched on the other side. So there are divisions in funerals after all, Martha thinks. At least when a second marriage is involved.

She and Ivor are sitting under stained glass windows of Saint George and Saint Francis. There are needlepoint cushions at their feet – clover leaves entwined around a prayer. The vicar is fiddling about at the altar, and there is a general creaking of pew, but otherwise it's subdued. The couple who had moved in next door to Graham, the ones who travel a lot, sidle in next to her. The pew gate rattles shut. The music seems to get louder, more formed, and through it she hears murmuring and the clopping of heels and there is her family at the door of the vestry, Gabriel on his mother's hip, Patrick and Anna pressed against their mother's legs, Geraldine crossing herself, and behind them all, the unmistakable figure of David.

Quickly she turns her head to face the pulpit, lowers her face to study her order of service. He was wearing a dark coat over a dark suit and a white shirt, and glasses – little round glasses. Ivor is tugging at her sleeve. 'They're here,' he says loudly. She lowers her head. She hasn't seen those glasses before. 'I know,' she says.

The first time she saw him was in this church. She and Eliza had been wearing oyster taffeta which had clumped over Martha's thighs like fabric cellulite, and they'd been clutching posies. June. A June wedding with a cruel June wind chilling their bare shoulders. They were waiting for Geraldine in the porch, and Eliza, peering, told Martha the best man had made it after all. 'So much for being stuck in Geneva,' she said.

Martha hadn't been interested. She'd said, 'Sssh.'

'Sssh,' someone says now. The congregation comes to its feet and turns to the back of the church as the pallbearers – Ian at the front, in blue, with the undertakers alongside him – walk the lily-laden coffin to the front. Martha watches.

149

Ian looks like a celebrity with his bodyguards. How heavy a man in a coffin is, she thinks. You imagine all those young men, six of them to one frail old fellow, would trip down the aisle, but here they come, unbalanced, awkward, heaving and slow.

They reach the front, the coffin is laid down and Ian turns, with a poignant crooked smile, to join his wife in the front row. He shakes out his shoulder before he sits down.

They stand to sing 'Jerusalem', and Martha tries to concentrate, to renew the intensity of her emotions in the park. She fails. It was later, after the wedding service, when she met David properly. She was standing at the opening to the marquee that filled most of their mother's garden when he came up behind her and said, 'Ah, the naughty little sister, I presume,' and she said no, that people always thought that because she was shorter than the other two, but actually, she was 'the naughty middle sister'.

He had put out his hand. 'David Ford.'

She had put out her hand too, suddenly conscious of the bunching drag of taffeta across her thighs. 'Martha Bone.'

They had talked a little about his job at the auction house. He told her he was in jewellery which made her laugh. She imagined him running his hands around a beautiful woman's neck, clicking the diamond pendants off her ears and slipping them into his pocket. He said there was a lot of that, that he was nifty at fingering sapphire-encrusted cufflinks too, but that his main interest was Elizabethan. 1559–1603. 'Personally, I don't go for flashy and shiny,' he said. 'I go for ornate and rare.'

He asked her about her stall at Alfie's, and after a while,

when she was tired of the formality of their conversation, she teased him about the to-ing and fro-ing that had gone on before the wedding, the would-he-make-it-or-wouldn't-he? She said, 'So is it really possible to "get stuck" in Geneva?' and he laughed, with his eye on her, as if he wasn't used to having his movements questioned, and later, when she went off to dance with Denis, she felt his gaze following her as if she'd caught his interest.

'Bring me my bow of burning blerghgh.' The woman from next door has stopped singing and is blowing her nose. She rolls her eyes at Martha. It's true, Martha thinks, that funerals conform to a strange pattern: the closely bereaved stiff-backed and stoic and the people on the outskirts dissolving or, like her, not even able to engage, their minds elsewhere. Loss itself doesn't happen here. None of them, not even Geraldine, cried during their mother's cremation. And yet there was some third cousin twice removed gulping uncontrollably five rows from the back. Loss catches up with you at unexpected moments, in a supermarket queue, walking through the perfume hall of a department store.

They sit again. Susie goes up to the lectern to read a poem that she wrote when she was a little girl about her father. 'Oh Dad/When I am sad/You're there/On the stair/Mother, father, both.' And the trite sentimentality, and for a moment the image of Graham as a young widowed dad, makes her own throat catch. She knows this feeling, high and acute, imagined emotion, romanticised, is no better than detachment. It is the thought of other people's grief that has got to her, not grief itself. And she is doubly contemptuous of herself, because all the time she is also aware of thinking something trivial and frivolous and nothing to do with Graham's death at all. She's wondering where exactly David is sitting and whether he can see her.

Martha is first out of the church, first to the burial ground. She prepared her tactics during Communion. No hanging around, no chance to be collared.

Putney Vale Cemetery is large and impressive. It stretches up a hill and is edged on two sides by the brambled wilderness of Wimbledon Common. But a third side is banked by the rush and scream of the A3, and the high formal gates, which once led into it from the dual carriageway, have been closed off. Now you have to enter via a sliproad behind the hypermarket, which feels oddly undignified, like meeting death through the back door.

Martha parks before the entrance, outside a newsagent, and enters the cemetery on foot. Further in, it is wild and Victorian. You can get lost among the broken angels. But down this end, in the modern part, where the rows are ruler-straight, the highway roars in your ears and you imagine that, if you strain, you can pick up the beep of the supermarket checkout through the fence. A couple of cars roll past her on the cemetery road and she steps off on to the grass. The ground is sodden and clay sticks to her shoes. She passes the row of most recent graves – no headstones and the earth still heaped high and round, like duvets over sleeping forms, the mounds of chrysanthemums like extra blankets – and plods on towards older rows with headstones, in white and black and pink, heart-shaped, book-shaped, plank-shaped, where there are tidy miniature leylandiis and fabric violets in pots. She stops to read a dedication, self-conscious with cars purring past behind her, aware of herself as a woman in mourning looking at a dedication. Most of the deceased are memorialised as Beloved Fathers and Mothers, Much Missed Sons and Precious Daughters. She feels a stab of self-pity. What would she be? Martha Bone: Quite Good Antique Dealer. Sister, at a push.

Then, a hundred yards ahead, she sees where she is supposed to be. One of the graves in an established row has been opened and standing there already is the priest from the church and Graham's globetrotting neighbours. The black funeral car arrives and more cars pull up as she tramps across, rather ungainly as the ground is even more boggy here. And then coming up behind her and pulling in just ahead she sees Eliza and Denis's car and behind them Geraldine and Greg's. They're parking and they're all clambering out and she sees the children and her sisters and then, coming out behind them, David.

There is no getting away from it now. She walks towards them. A woman in mourning who has been looking at dedications heading towards her ex. But then a hand grabs at her shoulder. It belongs to an old man, with bags under his eyes like reflections, thick dark eyebrows and spindly hair: Walter, Graham's brother from Borehamwood. He leans on her as if his balance is a little dodgy, and says, 'Are you the second wife?' His voice creaks. Martha smiles. Geraldine and David have joined the graveside now. 'No. She's dead,' she says. 'I'm her daughter.'

Walter looks up at the sky. 'Both dead,' he says with some surprise. 'The other one, years ago, wasn't it? Poor bugger. Never thought I'd outlive him. I'm not what you might call sparking on all eight cylinders.'

'You look all right to me,' Martha says.

'I'm inbetween and out,' he says, patting his pockets. 'Up and down like a fi-fo-fum. Now where the bloody hell did I put my tobacco?'

Martha takes his arm – his jacket smells of damp and smoke – and together they hobble to the graveside. Walter says, 'Bloody things, funerals.' They stand behind Ian and Julia. She organises it so that other heads hide her from David. Walter whistles when he breathes. He has shaved, but has missed a whole tranche of whiskers below one side of his nose. He leans with both hands on his stick.

The priest begins – his words almost get lost in this wide space, with the traffic in the distance. Ian is standing with his arms behind his back. She watches his fingers scratching inside his cupped palms.

Walter says loudly, 'Bugger this. I hope nobody's going to put me in a box in the ground.'

Martha whispers, 'I'll remember that for the future.'

But now the priest is shuffling back and Ian has thrown – ungainly, thudding – the lilies into the grave, and people have started turning away, doubtful as to what to do next, and Ian is crying and has stepped back in the direction of Martha, so she is, once again, the first thing he turns to – only literally not metaphorically this time – and she puts her arms around him and hugs him, and then Julia and then Susie too. She looks up to check on Walter, who's still

154

standing by her, but when she raises her head she realises Walter has wandered off towards his car and that the person next to her is David.

Susie has released herself and is being hugged by Julia. Martha scans for somebody else to embrace, but there isn't anyone close enough. She has nowhere to go.

David says, 'Hello.'

He looks trim in his narrow black coat, both terribly familiar and strange. His hair is much shorter, more fashionable than it was two years ago, and Martha finds herself feeling strangely betrayed by this. His face is close shaven, but she can still make out the line where the stubble grows. His Sunday beard. The creases in his cheeks when he moves his face, as if the skin only just fits. The darkened gum above the single front-capped tooth. The way his eyebrows fan out at the far corners. She knows if she breathes in she'll smell limes.

The A3 roars in the air between them. 'Hello,' she says back. There's a lull and then the screech of a motorbike, and for the few moments after that she feels she can pick out the sound of each vehicle that passes as if all her nerve endings have been sensitised.

Geraldine, who is putting her two sons into the car with her back to all this, is not having a good funeral. She is irritated with her sisters – Eliza is proving herself bitchy and grasping; Martha, once again, superior. Her children are driving her mad. And now – typical – she sees she's got mud all over her new skirt. 'Is it too much to ask for you to behave yourselves for two minutes?' she says as she straps the boys in. (All she had wanted, for her mother's sake, was for Graham's in-laws from his first marriage to think, 'What nice children.')

She pulls her car door shut and slots her own seatbelt round her. 'We'll have something to eat in a moment,' she says over her shoulder. She says it like a reprimand because they've done nothing but fight since they got there. That piece of Harry Potter plastic rubbish is the main problem. She snaps the wand away in the glove compartment. Honestly, you'd think Martha would know: buy one for all three or none at all.

'Nwwwwwwww,' says Patrick. 'But I'm starving.'

'Won't be long,' she says. 'You can wait a few more minutes. We'll get going as soon as your father . . .'

She can see him through the window. He is standing in the middle of the road, chatting away to a woman she doesn't recognise. She has got blonde hair and is wearing a slim dog-tooth coat. He has got Anna by the hand, except that she's bored – and overtired – and she has put both her hands in his and is swinging, like a one-sided attempt at that game Geraldine and Martha used to play when they were little, crossing arms and spinning round against each other's gravity until you were so dizzy you fell over. But Anna isn't getting up any speed. She looks more like a pendulum and as Geraldine watches she sags down, her dress riding up, until she's almost on the ground. Greg doesn't seem to notice. He carries on chatting, regardless of his bungee-jumping arm.

They are lucky that he is here at all. Last night from the bath he had asked her, cajoling, if there was a 'three-line whip'. It's one of the expressions he grew up with and had

156

never grown out of, along with OC, as in, 'OK, old girl, you're OC picnic; I'm OC bikes.' The first time he used this, she thought he was saying '*eau si*'. And as what he'd actually said was 'You OC contraception?', she'd imagined he was referring to some new sophisticated French barrier method. Later when she learnt he meant Officer in Charge, she wondered if she would have slept with him at all if she'd known. Military jargon in relation to love-making seemed rather dubious to her; not quite – to use another of his catch-phrases – 'the thing'.

Anyway, last night she'd told him it *was* a three-line whip. She had been sifting though the bathroom cabinet looking for Christian Dior at the time, or she would have asked him how he thought he could possibly *not* turn up – a family occasion after all. But Greg's head was buried under the water, floating, disembodied, in a mesh of soapy bubbles. Then he rose, shaking a spaniel head, squeezing his nose with his thumb and forefinger, and said, 'OK. But I'll have to go in at the weekend to make up.'

Geraldine had sighed and said fine, but because she hadn't articulated the feelings this aroused in her – a faint perplexity at the idea of herself and her relatives as something separate from Greg – she felt disgruntled. It wasn't as if he was doing her a favour. It hadn't exactly been a treat for her either, for God's sake, having to sit stiff-backed in the church while their mother was edited out of Graham's life.

'Get off,' Ivor says in the back.

'*Get off*,' Patrick says, imitating him, twisting his voice into a taunt.

'Just stop it. Both of you.' Geraldine turns and removes

Patrick's ankles from Ivor's knees. 'Stop irritating Ivor,' she says. 'Leave him alone, will you? Just for one minute.'

Ivor looks at her. He should be grateful, but his face has that sheeted look. She says, 'And you – Stop. Sucking. Your. Sleeve.'

She turns back and leans her head against the window. It feels cold against her cheek, like a turned pillow. A car has come up behind Greg and the woman on the graveyard road and they jump apart. Greg waves goodbye and then strides towards the car. He thrusts Anna, giggling now, into the back and gets into the driver's seat. Before he opened the door, the car had felt still and self-contained, like an aeroplane. But he brings new stirred air with him and outside noises.

Geraldine says, 'OK?'

'Yup. Let's go. God, terribly nice woman, that neighbour of Graham's. Camilla Quince. You remember her?'

Geraldine says, 'Oh yes. Away a lot.'

'That's the one.'

He is making a three-point-turn, with lots of jerky, urgent yankings of the wheel, as if he had got in thinking he was Starsky. He says, 'Three children, fund manager: wonderful woman.' He has his eye on the rear window and has started driving off when he adds, 'Looks after herself, too, by the looks of it.' And then, his voice stretching out with mock intrigue, 'A-hoh. Nothing to worry about there, then.'

Geraldine scrabbles to see behind her. People are drifting towards cars; many have already left. She sees the woman in the dog-tooth (what does he mean, looks after herself?) sidle into a Spider sports car with a man in a Nehru jacket. 'What are you talking about?'

'Very cosy,' he says, in the same voice. 'I don't think you needed to get in such a flap about the café after all.'

And it is only then that Geraldine tears her eyes away from the dog-tooth – this wonderful Camilla Quince – and sees Martha and David walking alongside each other towards Martha's car. They are a little bit apart – you could fit a third person between them, a small one anyway, a child maybe, if you tried – and they're both looking at the ground.

'Oh, God. Oh . . . I . . . We . . .'

'I think he's all right for a lift if that's what you're worried about.'

'Oh, but . . .' Geraldine has pulled down her window and is straining to look behind. 'Do you? You don't think we ought to check?'

Greg is turning out of the graveyard now, swooping behind Asda. 'No,' he says. 'I don't.'

'Oh.' Geraldine turns again but they have gone from view. 'Oh, but stop, can't you? Go back.' She had meant to orchestrate the meeting, to chaperone Martha, and then subtly drift away. But the children had distracted her. She hadn't meant it to be like this.

'Too late.'

Geraldine slumps forward.

'What?'

'Well do you think they are all right?'

'Of course they are all right.'

She groans. Greg says, 'They'll be fine.'

'I know, but . . .'

'What?'

'Is he still with Maddy Long Legs?'

159

But Greg has turned his attention to his wing-mirror now. He waves at the Spider as it overtakes them in the outside lane. He says, 'We don't have to stay long, do we? I might be able to make afternoon conference if I try.'

They drive the rest of the way in silence and when they get to the house, there are cars everywhere so they have to park quite a long way down the road. The front door is ajar and there are people in the porch. Geraldine keeps a bright smile on her face as she hangs up their things on the hall pegs (other coats are being taken upstairs, but she doesn't care). My house, she is chanting in her head, full of strangers. She looks out the front door again to see if Martha is coming. The kids, who seem to have left their hunger in the car, tear into the garden. Greg strides ahead of her into the sitting room and is accosted by a former colleague of Graham's who reads Greg's newspaper and has a few points of issue to raise about the leader articles relating to Northern Ireland. Greg looks uncomfortable and his eyes flail frantically in Geraldine's direction, but she hasn't forgiven him for the car yet, and anyway he is too close to Eliza, whom she has decided to avoid. Instead she crosses to where Julia is standing, an infant car-seat hooked over her arm like a supermarket basket. Ian is serving drinks, another car-seat at his feet, and Julia is greeting guests like a hostess at a cocktail party.

Geraldine hadn't expected so many people, so many faces she doesn't know, or to feel so sidelined. In the front window the table is laden with shop-bought sandwiches (prawn and mayonnaise; turkey and cranberry) dolled up on doilies. If only somebody had asked her, she could have made their mother's Coronation Chicken at a fraction of the cost. Ridiculously over-elaborate napkins, too. Julia notices her looking and Geraldine says, 'Magnificent spread!'

Julia whispers, 'M&S.'

Geraldine says, 'I'd never have guessed.'

'Ah! So *you* must be the second wife.' Geraldine swivels and there is Graham's brother, Walter, wiping his mouth with a large red handkerchief. His knuckles are round and purple; his hand movements as he puts a whole sandwich triangle in his mouth exaggerated, as if he's not convinced he won't miss.

'Sorry?' she says.

'Second wife, are you? First one died, know that. Tragic.' Walter shakes his head. There are beads of froth at the corners of his mouth, which he wipes again.

She says, 'His second wife died too, didn't you know that?'

He looks at her. 'It seems I did,' he says. His eyes look faded and milky. He says, 'Losing your memory is said to be one of the hardships of old age. Sometimes I find it makes life easier. Wh-oops—'

He has lost his balance, an arm flailing towards her, and Geraldine is about to steer him to the sofa when he is taken over by Ian, the solicitous nephew. She wonders about hauling the kids in from the garden and getting them to eat something, but through the window she can see them mucking about with Denis. Greg is talking again with Mrs Quince and doesn't catch her eye. Nobody needs her. Everyone is chatting and laughing. Standing by the sandwiches, she looks out of the front window. Where are Martha and David? She tries to breathe slowly. People start

161

helping themselves to food – hungry work, grieving – and she passes them their plates. Plates with special clips at the side for fixing your drink. The noise level rises. Still no Martha and David. There are peals of laughter deep in the room, the funeral becoming raucous, as if the pressure of keeping sombre has become too much, as if life has started bouncing back before the earth has even settled. Where are they? What are they up to?

And then, just as she feels she can bear the suspense no longer, she glimpses Martha's car drive past the gate, and she is about to get closer to the window to look beyond the hedge, to see them parking, to watch them approach the house without them noticing her, *to see what's happening*, when someone gets between her and her view.

It is Susie, Ian's sister, and she's saying, 'So, Geraldine. A lot of water under the bridge since we last saw each other.'

Geraldine, craning, says, 'Yes. Absolutely.'

'Must be ten years. So,' Susie, who has hair down to her bottom and holes in the tops of her ears, is leaning over the table to study the sandwiches, lifting the bread to see what's inside, 'life treating you well?' She plucks a slice of ham, puts it on her plate and returns the empty bread to the platter. As Susie straightens, Geraldine sees Martha coming up the steps. But there's no sign of David. Is he with her? Has he come up ahead? 'Life's OK,' she says.

Susie is not moving away. She has folded her piece of ham into neat quarters and is eating it with little bites. 'So – three kids, is it?'

'Yes. Three. You haven't . . .?'

'No. Not yet. We're waiting, my boyfriend and I. We want

162

to get as much out of life as we can first, you know? Really enjoy each other.' Martha has just come into the room. She is pink in the cheeks. Her eyes look bright. Geraldine tries to catch her attention, but fails. Susie is saying, 'I mean, kids are one thing, but a good relationship is something else.'

Geraldine is about to say something sharp like, 'Well don't leave it too long,' or 'Eggs don't last for ever,' when she pulls herself together. She says, 'Of course,' and she means it sympathetically – Susie, the orphan now. But, as she looks at her kindly, *charitably*, she feels an unexpected pang of envy. Susie, only a few years younger than her, was the one they'd all laughed at, gawky and grey and suburban. She wore hairclips and brown cords and ill-fitting polo necks. And now look at her! It is not just the tan, or the hair, or the clear complexion (not smothered like Geraldine's in 'Almost Nude', which is making her skin sweaty and the back of her neck feel dirty), but something more than that, something *free*. Geraldine used to imagine herself so radiantly fortunate: a golden person, with her looks, her music scholarship, her marriage, shimmering with good luck. Like that Camilla Quince over there. And now? Well, now she is blustered about, blistered with worry – her children, Ivor's problems at school, her husband, her sisters, Eliza and her bloody picture, *Martha and David*.

She sits down abruptly. 'Yes,' she says. 'Good idea. You wait for as long as you can.' And maybe she says it with just a little too much conviction because, before she knows it, Susie has launched into an account of this fantastic exercise regime that Geraldine must try, and how much more energy Susie herself has felt since she stopped 'combining', and how the one lesson she has learnt since she moved to Vancouver is the importance of quality of life. And then Susie says something Geraldine doesn't quite catch. 'Sorry,' she asks, leaning towards her. 'I need *what*?'

But when Susie repeats it, one of those strange lulls falls upon the gathering, so that her voice is louder than it need be. 'More time for yourself!' she says. And there is a short while before the noise level rises around them again, as if the whole room needed a minute to get used to the suggestion.

part two

chapter eight

the baby's room

'As most parents secretly admit to themselves,
decorating a child's bedroom is an excuse to design
the room that they longed for themselves as a child.'

Interior Transformations
by Byann Grafton
(Jacqui Small, 2001)

'AND THEN?'

'And then I dropped him at the station. And then, like a
dog slinking home after an illicit and fruitless rabbit-chasing
session, I went on to the tea and buns. That was strange. The
house full of people – glasses clinking, mouths chomping.
People coming and going, up and down stairs, in and out of
the loo. And you had this strange feeling that someone was
missing but you couldn't quite remember who. Poor Ian got
drunk, and . . .'

'And what?'

'And then I went home.'

167

'Martha.'

'Sorry. Then I went home. And then, a few days later, he rang.'

'Oh.'

'I know. Pass me the roller.'

Martha and Karen are in Kit's bedroom. Or rather they are in Karen's study, trying to turn it into Kit's bedroom. Martha is at the top of a ladder, painting the ceiling. Karen is below, cross-legged, sticking masking tape to the rim of the floor. Karen's hair is dusted with silvery-blue flecks of paint. Martha, who is more experienced in these matters, is wearing a plastic floral showercap. It still smells of the packet it came in, and scratches slightly at the back of her neck.

'This one?'

'That's the one. So he rang. We met up. We talked.'

'He conquered.' Karen's tone is too flippant for Martha's comfort. Karen's head is dipped away from her so she can't see her expression, but she wonders if she is being mocked.

'No . . .'

'Who conquered?' Keith comes gingerly into the room, his shoulders negotiating the obstruction of sheet-covered furniture. He is holding the baby in one arm, her legs hanging down on each side of his wrists, her head in his elbow – like a pelt, Martha thinks. Daddy's gone to get a rabbit skin to wrap his little baby in.

Karen says, 'You know.'

'Ah.'

Martha's roller drips a gloop on to her foot. She tears off a piece of kitchen paper from the roll on the step and, as she bends to rub the paint off, she catches Karen and Keith

168

exchanging a glance. 'What are you looking at each other for?' she says.

Keith doesn't say anything and Karen only laughs. 'We're silently casting aspersions on your decorating skills,' she says. 'Oh she who never drips.'

'Oh, were we? I thought we were silently casting aspersions on the showercap,' says Keith. 'Purple pansies, my favourite.' Martha considers her friends for a moment, then, without expression, pretends to flick paint at them. The moment passes.

'And how many times have you seen him?' Karen asks after a while. She has started painting the woodwork, though she is thrusting the brush so carelessly dabs of eggshell are hitting the wall.

'Um. Twice. Once or twice. And then again tonight.' Martha runs her roller along the tray, listening to the paint crackle. 'I'd have seen him more but I've been so busy.' She shakes the roller above the tray and stretches for the corner. 'My social life over the last fortnight has gone mad!'

Keith is leaning against a ghosted filing cabinet. 'And have you slept with him yet?'

'Keith!' Karen reproves him, but she has her eye on Martha as if she wants to know the answer too.

'Only asking.'

Martha smiles doubtfully. She would have told them, if she hadn't recorded that shared glance, if she wasn't experiencing a slight sense of unease. She suspects they never really liked David (the four of them once spent a weekend in Kent and it had been socially sticky). Earlier they had asked a lot about Nick and why she had given up tracking him down. She told them he appeared to have vanished off the face of the earth. 'My lost love,' she said. They made jokes about her past flashing before their eyes. 'Like a drowning man,' Keith said. 'Only he's got his memories muddled up with someone else's.' She laughed with them, made a gesture as if sinking to the bottom of a lake, turning herself into a soap opera for their amusement. But she wishes they would take her seriously.

She has finished the ceiling so she gets down from the steps and takes over from Karen on the woodwork. It is her idea, the colour scheme, and she is pleased with it. Powder Blue and Old White. She thinks it would be nice to be a child and to look up at this. The two shades together are classic: calm and comforting, the beige-white a perfect balance to the cool turquoise. She has seen the same blue with a creamier white and it doesn't work nearly so well. (She is glad, too, needless to say, that this whole redecoration project indicates that they are finally getting that baby out of their bedroom.) Keith is still hovering so she asks him again if he likes it, and he says that actually he's disappointed they weren't going with his spring-lamb frieze idea. 'Or what about that nice Teletubby paper they had in B&Q?' he mutters on his way out of the door. 'Or some nice little girl pink?'

'I think it's lovely,' says Karen. She is sitting on the floor again, leaning back against the stepladder, feeding the baby now. 'Your taste in household decor cannot be surpassed.'

It doesn't take long to finish the first coat. It's a tiny space after all. Hardly room to swing a cat. 'Talking of which?' asks Karen.

170

'Very happy. Very settled. The kids love him. He sleeps on Hazel's bed.'

'That's the mother?'

'No, it's the little girl. So all's well . . .' She trails off.

'. . . that ends well,' finishes Karen, though actually Martha hadn't been going to say that.

She has time for a quick cup of coffee before she leaves. They go down to the kitchen, where Keith is reading the Saturday papers, and Martha tries to persuade Karen to come to the school reunion. Further emails have arrived on this subject, both from Jane Pritchet, the midwife, and Susan/Sasha, the name-changer. Karen isn't really listening. The baby is crying in an irritable sort of way and Karen keeps coming in and out of the room, fussing about new nappies and lost bottles of 'colic drops'. 'Give her here then,' Keith says at one point, throwing the papers onto the table with an angry rustle. Karen says, 'There!' and thrusts the crying bundle into his hands. Then she leaves the room.

When she comes back in, Martha says loudly (over the bleating), 'So what about this school reunion? Are you going to come with me?' and Karen says, 'No.'

'Oh. Go on. Be a sport!'

'Why would I want to go to a reunion and see lots of sad people that weren't my friends then and certainly aren't now?'

'You wouldn't catch me at one,' says Keith. 'I spend quite enough time at school already.'

'Curiosity?' says Martha. 'To see how they've turned out? To see what they look like? It's just natural interest, isn't it?'

'Not really. It's a bit odd if you ask me.' Karen is rummaging through the paperwork detritus on the table. 'For one thing, even if you saw someone you used to like, your whole conversation would be threaded through with the fact that *you haven't bothered to keep in touch.* The friendship *has* failed. Why bother digging it up? Where is the fucking Infacol?'

Martha wheedles and cajoles. She runs through all the people who might be there. 'For me?' she says finally.

Karen makes a noise at the back of her throat. She takes the baby off Keith again and says she is going to try putting her down. At the door she turns and says, 'What about Eliza or Geraldine?'

'Wrong year. Eliza wouldn't anyway, not if you paid her a million pounds. She'd think she was far too cool. And Geraldine, who by the way is on no speaks with Eliza and is still hanging on to the picture . . . well, she's too busy. God, haven't I told you about Geraldine? She's undergone some sort of spiritual conversion. She won't eat meat and bread at the same time. She's bought loads of new clothes. She's joined a gym!'

'A gym!' exclaims Keith, rather as one might exclaim, 'A closed order of Franciscan monks!'

There is no opportunity to tell him any more because he follows Karen out of the room then and, as Martha calls up the stairs to tell them, she has to fly! Sometimes, these days, she finds herself gasping for air, as if there is a leak at the bottom of her lungs. It seems that by becoming a busy person, a person not only with a shop to run but – hallelujah! – a social life, she has become different in other ways, too. She

172

has hardly deliberated about Geraldine, while two weeks ago she was riddled with irritation every time she rang. Now she doesn't know why she wasted so much energy. Or on her father and his neglect. Or Eliza's aloof indifference. Or this ridiculous ongoing row between them about possessions. She was on her way to becoming one of those mad old women who sit at street corners, shaking their sticks at people, muttering furiously under their breath, eaten up with rancour and bitterness. No longer! Now she's the kind of single woman you read about in magazines, kicking off her shoes at the end of the day, chucking clothes all over the bed in the search for the ideal outfit, the perfect little black dress, tinkling back glasses of Chardonnay before heading out for a night of irresponsible fun! All she needs is a couple of flatmates and a little job in publishing! Or the City!

It began with David.

'Hello,' he said at Graham's graveside. 'You don't have any tissues in your car, do you? I seem, well, rather to have plastered my shoes in mud.'

'Oh, your poor Churches.' Martha was glad for an excuse to look down at the ground. David's stiff black leather brogues were creamed with clay. 'I might have some in the glove compartment.'

They walked back together to her car and he sat next to her on the passenger seat, scraping the dirt off, knocking the soles against the door until little circles of soil fell out of the decorative puncture holes on to the floor. They talked first about important things – his job, Graham's death, her worries about the rent rise, the durability of leather stitching. Martha kept darting looks at his face: the slanting eyes, the long lashes, the loose mouth. She watched his Adam's apple move up and down as he talked. David's social manner is polished, his conversation the verbal equivalent of a French courtier doffing a wide-brimmed feather hat (which was the bit of him her mother liked). But Martha has always seen the muscle twitching in his cheek, and known, through the layers of further education and auction house training, how hard he worked at it, how important it has always been for him to be liked. When she thinks back to their time together, it is moments of embarrassment that tug at her the strongest: the aitches he dropped in conversation with taxi drivers; the overenthusiastic laughs at other people's anecdotes (banging the table so that sometimes even the joke-teller would look at him askance); the way he would, if feeling awkward, hold his hands flat between his knees and twitch his legs.

She knows, too, that with his clothes off he talks differently. At orgasm he cries out, high.

'How's your new girlfriend?' she asked boldly. 'Maddy, is it? Very attractive . . . long legs, I believe.'

Head bowed, he paid attention to a coin-sized area of leather on the side of his shoe. 'Hm. Fine.' Pause. (A pause Martha is later to interpret as 'telling'.) 'I think.'

A little while later, as she rabbited on about this or that friend of his ('So Quentin? Is he still in Old Masters?'), he turned and looked at her with the kind of look that is working hard to draw attention to itself as a look. 'What?' she said.

'Nothing.' He smiled, flicking his thumbnail against his teeth, so that in the quiet car it rang out like a gong. He narrowed his eyes; the new gentle swellings underneath them crinkled. There followed a short silence. 'It's just good to see you, that's all.'

The story is that Martha left David, but you could argue that it didn't happen that way. He was the one who wanted her to get married, have his children, follow him to Geneva, give up the shop, to change. Everyone thought she had been so intransigent. But you could say he was the one who had offered the stark choice. He was the one who had moved away.

'You back then?' she said, thinking all this. 'For good, I mean.'

He put his shoes back on, pulling the laces so tight the leather creaked as if in pain. 'For now,' he said.

She had taken him to the station. He had a departmental strategy meeting to get back for.

'Diamonds and pearls?' she said.

'Important clocks.'

'Time waits for no man,' she said.

Getting out, he asked if he could ring her and she had nodded without giving herself permission first. His cheek when he kissed her goodbye smelt not of limes, but strangely new, of nutmeg.

When she got back from the funeral, she found a yellow Post-It stuck by April on the flat door. 'Someone calling himself Colin rang. Please ring him back.' Upstairs, there was a message from her former schoolmate Tracey Richards, the one in PR. The cat wound around her ankles as she sat on the sofa, listening. Tracey had 'good news and bad news'. She hadn't tracked down Nick. Someone she talked to thought he had got a job in local government. Which local government he couldn't say. The good news was that Tracey was involved in the launch of a famous dress designer's new range of houseware and 'needed numbers'. Saturday night, she said: 'you're in the business – please come.'

Martha had gone. She told herself she needed cheering up now rent rises and bankruptcy were staring her in the face. The new range of houseware was being exhibited on the top floor of a major department store in central London. There was champagne and clever canapés: pancake rolls made to resemble cushions; carrots hollowed out like vases with sprigs of parsley as flowers. The famous dress designer wore an outfit fashioned out of her new range of sheets. Martha felt carefree, but also anonymous. This wasn't her normal environment; she could be anything she wanted. Tracey Richards, bulging and smiling in tight black Lycra (the famous dress designer's old range), was delighted she came – absolutely delighted, *thrilled* – and said she hadn't changed a bit, *not one iota*. Martha chomped on a case of filo pastry folded into a miniature photograph album and believed her.

That was the Saturday after the funeral. Since then there has been a Monday and a Thursday and a Friday and another Saturday and a further whole week of assorted dates involving her past. She met David on three of these occasions (one drink, one Sunday afternoon walk, one dinner, no sex), but she has also twice gone out with Tracey 'and the girls' (one winebar, one meal in a Conran restaurant the size of an airfield). 'The girls' were three other women in their thirties who Tracey hung out with at weekends. All three worked in fashion or retail. All three were single. They all lived in north London. None of them had ever met anyone who lived in Balham before. They said, don't you need a passport to go south of the river? But they were good fun. They talked a lot about 'hunting down men' (they dressed to kill), but Martha got the impression their lives were pretty settled as they were. She wondered how you got to hunt like that in a pack of your own.

She has become fussy in her nostalgia now. 'Sasha' rang to finalise their Peter Jones quiche arrangement and Martha found herself backing down (trade fair in Sussex). One day the phone went and when she picked it up, a voice said, 'Want to take a Butcher's?' and she said, 'Sorry, I think you've got the wrong number.'

'It's Eric!' the voice said. 'Eric Butcher. You know, Chester & Jones. You know, "Want to take a Butcher's"? You used to say it all the time. Mum said you'd rung.'

'Oh of course,' she said, and they talked for a while about his new agency ('Anytime you need a house in Shepperton; you know the man to call') and his wife and the baby they were expecting, but she couldn't wait to get off the line. She couldn't think why she had ever rung him; she felt embarrassed she had ever been interested in speaking to him at all.

On the other hand, she did finally email Simon Fletcher – the boy, the emailer, she briefly went out with when she was fourteen. Partly it was curiosity, partly it was that she liked the joke about the chewing gum. They had met up the week before for tapas and a movie. He *had* changed. Mainly through hair loss. They talked about the pros and cons of working 'out of Heathrow'. He complained about the privatisation of air traffic control. He said, 'When you're cruising at thirty thousand feet, you want to know you're coming safely down, do you hear what I'm saying?' Martha said she did. She thought about him pogo-ing at a bus stop in torn jeans. She said she had heard the long-term carparks at Gatwick were good. He fell asleep during the film, his head back and his mouth open. She looked at him sideways on, wondering how she'd ever kissed him. He was like a stranger to her, and yet here was this twenty-five-year-old connection between them.

Most of his memories were completely different to hers. He asked her if she still hung out with Danielle Lawrence, a name that meant nothing to her. 'But you were inseparable,' he said. 'Peas in a pod.' He said, 'I bumped into Mike Philby the other day? Do you remember him?' She said, 'Er, y-es.' She had stopped dating Simon after she kissed Mike Philby at the school disco. Simon rang her to say he could never trust her again and he was going out with Phoebe from the pub. Now he said, 'Why do you say it like that?' and she realised he didn't remember the incident, the break-up, at all. 'Nice bloke, Mike,' he added. 'Scrum half.'

Later, when they said goodbye, he shook her hand. Pumped it up and down. He said he had been feeling nos-talgic recently too, though when it came down to it, you can fly all over the world but it's still good to come home. 'Super girl, my wife,' he said. 'You don't know what you're missing not having kids.' Martha wondered at his lack of tact, and realised that he wasn't seeing her at all. He was only seeing his own life bouncing off her. For him the whole experience was simply an exercise in self-justification. He said he hoped she'd enjoyed the evening and that they'd be seeing her again soon. Then he walked off to his car, cruising at 30,000 feet back to his life.

She has also – amazingly – spoken to Colin. On more than one occasion. The night of the funeral she had stared at April's note for a long time before plucking up the courage, but in the end it had been easy. She had dialled his old number and he had answered. Colin was still living in the same flat. He was still working at the same crammer. She could hear Neil Young still playing in the background. She said, 'Is your bed still in the middle of the floor?' and he said, 'No. It's by the wall.' It was the only time in their phone conversation that he sounded surprised. Martha's own voice came out high in one squeak of startled exclamation. They arranged to meet – an early drink one night in Victoria after he 'knocked off' ('knocked off'? she thought; does a glittering academic 'knock off'?), but he rang again nearer the time to cancel. He was feeling 'a little under the weather' and fancied an early night.

She had told Karen about all of this, but had the feeling that she wasn't engaging her attention. Karen laughed indulgently and didn't ask the right follow-up questions, as if all these were just one-off experiences, as if they were things that just skated across the surface of Martha's life, as if they were all a joke. Martha thinks Colin, dark-night-of-the-soul Colin, fancying an early night *is* funny. It is just that there are other things at work inside her, too. She feels that by seeing Colin, by tracking down Nick, by meeting up with all these others, she is undergoing some sort of liberation, giving herself the chance to reset the dial, to find a resolution. Recently, she has become overwhelmed by the feeling of herself as fixed and rigid. Geraldine said the other day, moaning into the mirror at her crow's feet, that at a certain age you get the face you deserve, but Martha wonders whether she has the attitudes too – as if how she responds to people and events has become leaden, set in stone. She doesn't know how it has come about, but thinks it might be just little things, things that happen along the way that change you without you realising. One day when she was about sixteen, she went sailing with her father and got horribly sunburnt on her shoulders. It was one afternoon without sunblock, a few hours only, and the soreness was gone after a few days. And she didn't notice at first, but a few weeks later she realised that the sunburn had left freckles and that the freckles had never gone away, and were still there now. And maybe it's like that with your personality. Maybe something happens, something minor, but it sets your reactions, your 'personality' in motion. You decide one night to go to a party instead of doing homework and the next day at school you feel a bit lost and a month later someone tells your parents you're 'not university material'. Or maybe you're about to confide in a friend or a sister, but they say something that holds you back – something they might not even mean – but it stops you and you're a little more loath to confide the next time, and before you know it you're keeping everything in. Or you get into the habit of leaving people before they leave you, and you never properly explain why. You become 'secretive' Martha; Martha with a closed sign around her neck.

When Martha was a child, her mother was always telling them not to pull that face or the wind might change and they'd be stuck with it. They didn't believe her then, but she was right. One day the wind does change, and what you're stuck with isn't a face but a person.

She doesn't say any of this to Karen or Keith today. She doesn't tell them how important seeing David or Colin or Nick is to her, how she thinks one of them might have the key to unlocking everything that has felt locked. Keith sees her out. Karen only hangs her head over the banisters to say goodbye. Martha, to conceal the fact that she minds (she wants them both, her pseudo parents, at either side of the door, cheering her out into the world), calls up, 'Tonight's the night then. Take two. Let's see if Colin's little bug has cleared up.'

'Oh?' Keith raises his eyebrows. 'I thought you were seeing David?'

'That's tomorrow. Quick drink with Colin tonight; dinner with David tomorrow. A weekend of double-dating.'

'Well, aren't you the wild one,' says Karen from upstairs. 'Think of us tomorrow, having sausages in front of *The West Wing*.'

Martha feels a little itch of anxiety in her temples. Has she somehow been inconsiderate to her friends? 'Oh . . .'

'That's all right, M.' Karen's face looks different upside down, the skin sagging. 'I'm not really in the Sunday night cinema sort of frame of mind at the moment. It'll be easier when we've got some babysitters in place.'

'Oh good. Actually, I'm not double-dating, am I? Double-dating is one couple going out with another couple. And what I've got is two dates in succession. Succession-dating!'

'I think it's called two-timing,' says Keith.

'I'm not two-timing. I'm not one-timing. I'm not *timing* anyone. Friends. Old times' sake!'

'Good.' The paint flickers in Karen's red hair and Martha wonders whether it's only because she's upside down that she seems to nod so forcefully.

chapter nine

the bathroom

'It is crucial to incorporate items in the bathroom
that will counteract the draining effect of the
plumbing on the room's energy.'

The Feng Shui House Book: A New Approach to Interior Design
by Gina Lazenby and William Spear
(Conran Octopus, 1998)

THE PUB where Martha meets Colin Cooper, her Older Man, has changed in fifteen years. It used to be the sort of place office workers might pass through for a quick pint, or quick grope, before braving the commute home. It wouldn't have thought twice about its image then. It had probably had the same plush red wallpaper, haphazard bar stools and grubby carpet for years.

But Martha isn't the only one to have discovered nostalgia, and the Three Crowns has become more 'period' in its outlook. Scrubbed refectory tables are lined with simple benches. The floor has been sanded. 'The Rake', his progress artfully framed in maple, gazes down from the walls. The Space Invader consoles have gone. Colonial-style fans whirr overhead.

She doesn't spot him at first. There are only a few drinkers here because it's Saturday and this part of London tends to drain away at weekends. But then she sees someone at one end of a table, studying the crossword, and she realises she hadn't noticed him because this man seems so small, so ordinary.

'Oh,' he says when he sees her. 'Hello stranger.' He fumbles his paper to one side and stands up. They don't kiss. They nod at each other a few times. His face, which she has remembered as Byronic, scoured with intellect, looks weaselly. He has lost weight, there are caverns in his cheeks, and peels of dandruff are scattered on his shoulders. The dead man's coat has gone. He is wearing a sports jacket, pale blue with white cuffs. The muscles in his neck are slack.

'Colin,' she says. 'Gosh. Well.'

'What are you having?' he says.

But she insists. She goes to the bar to buy another Guinness for him and a gin and tonic for herself, and because the pub is so empty she feels she has to turn and nod at him again while she is waiting. The room gapes between them.

When she sits down, she joggles a bit of his drink and there is a race to mop it up before it spills over the edge and on to his trousers. 'Oops, oh dear, oh dear,' he says. 'Got it. Don't worry. Don't worry at all.'

'Clumsy old me,' she says.

'Yes. Interesting.' He taps the newspaper with the end of the pen, clicks the nib a few times in his hand. 'It's almost as if it was on purpose? As if you were trying to sabotage this meeting. What's that about?'

It is a rhetorical question. He isn't even looking at her. But Martha says, 'It's just the table. It's got uneven legs. It's all joddery, that's all.'

'Hm. Hm.'

'Well. If I was clumsy, it's only because I'm tired. I've had a busy day. You know I run my own business now?'

'I see,' he says.

It turns out he himself is doing very well at Oxford and Cambridge College of Advanced Studies. He has been promoted three times and is now Director of Studies. 'Brilliant,' Martha says. The Duke of Somebody had sent their son last year – failed his A levels at two different schools, and passed this summer with flying colours. Colin had received a letter only that morning from the Duke, thanking him for everything he had done. 'Three of my personal students,' he says, 'have got places at Oxford to read English.'

Martha says, 'You must be very proud.'

He seems to have shrugged off his contempt for the crammer. 'Slogging facts into stupid rich kids,' is how he used to put it. Now it's all Dukes. He used to be scathing about the ancient universities, too. (Elitist, over-rated.) Apart from his contradictory ambition for tenure at one of them. She doesn't feel she can ask him about that now. Or his Ph.D., or his poetry, or how the correspondence with Susan Sontag panned out. So instead she enquires after his mother (still in Epsom), and his sister (married now, with two children), and another teacher he used to like (moved to Australia, lost touch).

'And no wife?' she says girlishly, her eyebrows arched in what she hopes is a light and unthreatening manner.

'Nope,' he says.

'Me neither,' she laughs. 'Well, husband, I mean.'

And then he says, 'Modern society encounters such difficulties with sexuality. The expectation is that everybody should conform.'

Martha says, 'Yes, I know.'

'At its best monogamy may be the wish to find someone to die with. At its worst it is a cure for the terrors of aliveness.'

'Gosh.' Martha laughs. 'That's clever. Is it yours or someone else's?'

He continues as if she hadn't spoken. 'They are easily confused.'

'I'll have to ask Geraldine,' she says.

He looks at her. 'Geraldine?'

'My sister.'

'Your sister?'

'You know, Geraldine?'

Colin shrugs. And Martha realises that he doesn't remember Geraldine, and that therefore, in the narrative of his life, Martha herself had played but a walk-on part. You have to bother to remember things about people (his mother, his sister, his friend), and he hadn't.

She drains her drink. She looks at her watch. 'Goodness,' she says. 'Well, it's been lovely. After all this time. I'm glad we . . . Let's not leave it so long next time.'

'Yes.' He stands up and proffers his hand again. 'No. Well, I'm glad you're looking so well. I haven't asked you: how are the scarves, the Peruvian scarves, was it?'

'Oh.' Martha laughs. 'They were never mine. Hats anyway. That was just a thing, don't you remember? Just a passing thing. I went to India and came back – you met me at the airport, do you remember? With Ezra Pound? And after that I worked for a bit as an estate agent and then I took over that stall at Alfie's? I gave up being flakey and got a proper job. You used to pick me up and we'd walk through Marylebone to Oxford Street to get the bus to your flat? You know, after I got a proper job?'

'Oh yes.' He looks vague. 'I must admit I'd forgotten that. Well,' he shakes her hand again, 'it was a long time ago.'

'Yes, it was,' she says. She bends across the table to kiss him goodbye. His cheek is warm. The texture of it – the scrape of it – is so familiar she feels a surprising lurch of longing, and pity for both of them.

She rests her cheek there for a fraction of an instant longer than necessary. Was he just as pompous and self-absorbed then, only she didn't notice? Or has he changed? Have his humours, like her own, become more fully drawn out? Or is he a perfectly nice man and it is simply her presence that is making him behave like this? For her part, she feels a carica-ture of the person she used to be in his company – all ingénue exclamations and desperate attempts to prove herself worthy ('My own business', 'Proper job'). And perhaps her presence does the same to him, only in his case it is age and wisdom he perceives the need to impart (diminishing her along the way). Is what you are, or how you are perceived to be, simply dic-tated by whoever you are close to at the time?

She pulls away. 'Goodbye, stranger,' she says.

*

Martha spends Sunday in the shop. She notices Nell from Sustainable Forests is in too, and at lunchtime they share a stuffed baguette in the café and moan about the rent rise. Nell says she'll have to sell – or diversify. Overpriced photo-albums and vases are what people spend their money on, she says, not second-hand books.

There wasn't much point Martha opening up. People wander in in dribs and drabs. A newly married couple (her guess from the clenched hands and the sparkling ring) buy a dented aluminium watering can ('A charming, original gardener's friend, £40'). Martha sorts out the desk drawers and makes some calls and tidies up the cellar. She finishes distressing a dresser that April started on and hasn't finished. With each efficient stroke, she asks herself what April has been doing all week. April's usual pattern of behaviour is a lurch from lethargy to animation. She can spend hours doing nothing but text on her mobile, or fiddle with her hair, and then, suddenly, she will lunge into action, attacking and finishing some arduous task in a matter of minutes. This last week, though, she has slouched in, hungover, every morning and just *sagged* around. Her attitude has gone to pot, too. She groans when asked to do any painting. She says the Barley White Eggshell makes her feel sick. Maybe Martha should have a word. With things as they are, she can't afford to carry dead weight.

She rings Ian to find out if there is any news about the house. He says, 'Only the battle of the dustpan and brush, but you've heard about that?' Eliza and Geraldine are engaged in a bitter competition to see who can spirit the largest proportion of Chestnut Drive into their own house. Martha, though curious as to who will inadvertently end up with the Penwork Tea Caddy, is having nothing to do with it. She says that she meant outside interest. Ian says, no offers yet. 'It would be unwise to get your hopes up, income-wise,' he adds. 'I don't know how much there is going to be to go round.'

'Oh,' Martha says. 'I'll have to diversify instead.'

At random, she tries four N. Martins in the phone book. Two answering machines ('Nigel isn't here right now'; 'Please leave a message for Ned after the beep'), one Nicola, one number unobtainable.

She has arranged to see David in a restaurant near his flat in Kensington. He suggested they meet at his first, but she wanted neutral ground. She got the train and then the bus. The number 11: her time chariot, her DeLorean, her Tardis.

The restaurant is perfect. A perfect choice by him. If you were writing a guidebook to restaurants in which to meet your ex, you would give this one four stars.

It has: 1) ambient lighting; 2) discreet service; 3) delicious food – or so it sounds on the menu. (She'll have the antipasti followed by the radicchio risotto.) And 4) one full wall of plate-glass windows so there is plenty to look at if conversation flails – cars, buses, passers-by.

And here he is himself, walking briskly along the plate-glass window to the door. He is frowning in that I'm-late-but-don't-be-annoyed-because-I'm aware-of-it way that is very familiar to her. He has always had a thing about punctuality. Martha's mindless disregard for clocks used to drive him mad. He was a stickler for smartness too, but this suit seems excessive. Even with no tie and the buttons of the plain white shirt underneath undone. David has a lot of plain white shirts. They are lined up in his cupboard, synchronised, like chorus dancers, swaying their arms in perfect time. At times, alone in his flat while he played squash or worked out (activities he would pursue with a sort of sheepish determination, as if he felt they were things that were expected of him), she would trail her fingernails along the shirts as you might scrape a stick along a fence. But she has the odd sensation now, seeing him wend his way across the room, still separate from her, but getting closer all the time, of wanting to bury her face in their clean starched whiteness.

'Sorry. God.' He has arrived at the table, shaking his head in irritation. 'The traffic coming down from the Cotswolds was murder.' He kisses her on both cheeks and then looks at her direct. No glasses today. He rounds his mouth. 'Hello.' It comes out like a coo, like baby language, like the old days.

Martha notices that his shirt isn't plain white, but has textured stripes like expensive bedlinen. She wonders what he was doing in the Cotswolds, in his suit, and whether she can ask. 'Hello,' she replies.

'God, but I'm hungry,' he says, switching to the present. Sitting down, he plunges straight into the menu, running his eyes over it with his head nodding from side to side as if he just needed familiarising with the details, and then casts it aside. 'Ravenous. Brazed oxtail, I think. With Thai-style fish soup to start. So how are you? How's the shop? What happened to that set of ladderback chairs? Did you get a buyer for all eight?'

Once they recover from the order in which they arrived (David, as if still on the move, is for a while overly animated; Martha, the seated one, destined at first to feel static, almost sullen, forcing her face to respond), conversation comes easily between them. The thing about David and Martha is *they have so much in common.* Geraldine once said that if she didn't know better, she'd think David was gay. (Greg disputed this hotly. He had played rugby with him at Cambridge, after all.) But he is one of those men who is interested in areas of life commonly considered 'feminine'. They talk through their starters about furniture and fittings, linen and lino, corbels, bangles and semi-precious beads. Martha had bumped into a former colleague of David's at an auction in Crystal Palace, who had set up a business on his own importing French furniture. David feels it is a risk. 'All very well in summer,' he says. 'Don't fancy all those crossings in December.' Martha agrees. 'And what happens when French furniture is no longer fashionable?' 'French furniture,' David says, 'will always be fashionable.' And they both laugh as if it's a private joke (which it isn't quite, but the pretence is comfortable none the less).

Last Sunday he had picked her up at her flat before their walk in a local suburban park ('Our rus in urbe,' he said, which *was* a private joke, a casual nod to their life before). He liked the colour scheme. It had all changed since he was last there. Martha's taste shifts in relation to fashion every two years or so and the most recent overhaul (from cluttered 'Victorian House' to minimalist 'Relaxed Home') took place, not uncoincidentally, shortly after she and David split up. To Martha, this tour of her decorative details, this most intimate

191

side of her, was a rite of passage. He walked around, as if valuing it all, struck particularly by an unsigned oil – lilacs in a blue vase – in the bedroom (a bargain at Borough Market). In the bathroom, he loved the painted washstand (a house clearance in Suffolk), but felt the overall look was let down by the functional modern mirror over the sink (B&Q). Martha, still perturbed by the sight of him in her bedroom, was astounded by this observation. She couldn't believe she had let the eyesore through herself. 'I suppose you get used to things; if they hang around for too long, you stop noticing them,' she said. He nodded thoughtfully. 'Hmmm.' And she suspected his mind was on something else.

Now, in the restaurant, he tells her he has 'come across' a Venetian mirror in the Furniture Department that would be just perfect.

'Old or repro?' asks Martha.

'Old.'

Martha inhales sharply. 'Square or oval?'

'Oval. Or rather octangular, if you can imagine it.'

'I can.' Martha closes her eyes. 'With a fleur de lys crown and base?'

'Exactly.' He has his head on one side.

'How much?'

He dips his spoon into his soup and says, 'Tell you later.'

She tuts. She says, 'Oh go on,' and he says, 'No,' and she tuts again, shuddering in frustration like it's a game. When he gets up to go to the lavatory, throwing his big white napkin on the table, not in surrender but in challenge, he casts her a purposefully flirtatious look over his shoulder and narrows his eyes.

Martha knows this isn't just a 'catch up' date with an ex. You don't have four 'catch up' dates with an ex in two weeks. Having run through friends, family, every mutual acquaintance, they have nothing left to catch up *with*. But they are still pretending they might. They are in that grey area of a relationship (though 'grey' is too drab a word, 'pastel' would be better, or, considering their shared interests, *daub*), when two currents are at play – the gentle ebb and flow of just good friends and the vigorous red-flag tug of 'Where is this going?'

On the surface, Martha is lightness and little jokes. She threw back her head when he remembered that weekend with Karen and Keith in Kent ('that *awful* fish and chips they made us eat; that *wonderful* gastropub down the road'). And during their walk they discussed, with maturity and restraint, certain details of their previous relationship (in particular their previous inability to discuss, with maturity and restraint, certain details of their relationship), so the impression is of openness and ease. But it is a sham – more of a sham than plain awkwardness – because underneath she is seething with questions. Why is she here? She has never made a decision to reopen her interest in him, and yet finds herself intrigued none the less. Why is he? Is she a possession that has slipped his grasp? And Maddy Long Legs, what of her? As far as she knows, she is still floating around his life, doing whatever Long Legs do, bumping into light bulbs, catching in people's hair. After her first question at the graveside, after that 'telling' pause, she doesn't know what to ask. Have they split up? But then the suit and 'the Cotswolds'? Could Maddy be involved with those? She feels a sharpening of sexual interest, a keening, when she thinks about David in bed with someone else.

'So the Cotswolds?' she says airily, when he returns from the lavatory. 'What happens there?'

'A lot of picturesque stone cottages.' He sits down, fluttering his napkin again like a matador before a bull. 'Some gently rolling countryside.'

'Ha. Ha. A valuation?'

'No. Um . . .' Their main courses arrive. David gives the waiter an acknowledging nod and then pulls at an eyelash in the corner of one eye. (Evasive action or coincidental itch?) When the waiter has gone, he says, 'A party. Lunchtime drinks.'

'Lunchtime drinks?' Martha says it as if she means, 'Oh, how posh,' but she's thinking, 'Oh, who with?'

'Yes. Lunchtime drinks.' David picks up his knife and fork. 'Quite nice. Some friends of mine have upped sticks and bought a place outside Chipping Campden. Lovely countryside and beautiful house. Bit of a schlep, though.'

Martha, thinking, What friends? New friends? Old friends? Friends of his? Friends of Maddy's? Do I mind? Should I care?, says, 'Oh.'

'Mm. Anyway.'

'Was it fun?'

'Yes. It was. It was nice.'

'Just drinks?'

'Oh, food as well. A sort of barbecue, I suppose. Children around. You know the sort of thing.'

Martha feels a pang of something unfamiliar. 'Have they got kids, these friends?'

'Er, yes, they've got two. Though there were others there as well.' David frowns as if slightly baffled. 'I'm not sure who the rest of them belonged to exactly. You couldn't tell who belonged to whom. Every time you opened a door there was another one. Watching a video or scribbling on the walls or scratching toys across the original flagstone floor. Some of their friends were quite . . . Bohemian, I suppose. Not artistic Bohemian, just sort of a bit tatty? I was talking to one woman and she said she froze her breastmilk. Beautiful house, though, God.'

Martha has put down her knife and fork and is looking at him. There is a pause. There are several things Martha thinks of saying. She wants to ask if he thinks it is possible to have children and keep them tidy; whether actually lots of people don't freeze their breastmilk somewhere along the way; whether he had ever really wanted to have children with her. 'Farmhouse?' she says finally.

David is wiping the remaining gravy on his plate with a mop of bread, clearing a dark unguent puddle into paler gloopy swirls. 'More of a cottage, but a large one. In the middle of the village. Quite low ceilings. But the rooms aren't a bad size. And it's Grade Two listed.'

'Century?'

'Early nineteenth, possibly late eighteenth.'

Martha puts the other things to the back of her mind. 'And have they got good taste?' she says.

David crosses his plate with another piece of bread and pops it into his mouth, both gestures neat and fastidious. The plate is altogether clean now. Dishwasher clean. The hunks of bone David has placed delicately on his side plate.

There are crumbs of bread there, too, and scrapings of left-over butter, but in front of him, there is nothing. A circle of white: a helping of sticky, complicated meat reduced to a polished disc of milky porcelain.

'Oh yes,' he says. 'Their taste is perfect.'

For the first week after the cat moved out, Martha expected to push against him when she opened the flat door, and when she didn't the door would swing wide too fast and bang against the far wall. In bed she would move her feet gingerly for fear of kicking him off, and then, finding emptiness, would scissor them back and forth, tossing the duvet as if shaking some life into it. His absence was almost as strong as a presence, but she has got used to it now. It is nice, for one thing, not to have to keep wiping pawprints off the kitchen worktop. None the less, this evening, when she climbs the stairs, she thinks fondly of her temporary lodger. Funnily enough, she forgot to tell David about him. In all the 'catch up' stories and anecdotes, the cat has somehow slipped the net. The Kitten saga is not something she has shared with her ex.

David had wanted her to come back for coffee. His flat was only a couple of streets away from the restaurant – his lovely, light-filled (up-lighted, down-lighted, over-picture-spotlighted) flat, a draw in itself. But Martha had been adamant. In her head it seemed important to play it cool, or distant, or ambivalent, to send out a message – whatever it was: she couldn't have said for sure.

'Please,' he had said. 'I've got something to show you. To give you. A surprise.' She had shaken her head. 'OK,' he said, always the gentleman. 'At least let me call you a cab.'

But she had set off, with a wave over her shoulder, to the bus stop.

He waited until there was half a block between them and then he called after her. 'Martha!'

'What?' She had turned, expecting more persuasions. The little-boy voice he would adopt to engineer his own way.

'You've got paint on your face!'

'What?'

'Paint. On your face.'

'What?' She rubbed her hands over it. 'You could have told me.'

'I thought it was a style thing,' he shouted, laughing.

Now home, she goes straight to the bathroom and looks at herself in the (functional modern) mirror above the basin. She is poised with a flannel when the phone rings. David, she thinks, checking she got home safely, or Geraldine (who has to break radio silence some time soon). But it is Fred.

'Hellooo,' he says, drawing the end of his greeting into a hum, a habit with him she has noticed.

'Oh hello,' she says. 'You're ringing late.'

'I tried you earlier, but . . . No. Answer.' He says the last two words with import. (Another habit – sometimes there seems to be a rhyme and reason to which words he chooses to emphasise, other times not.)

'I've been out. Out and about. Out on the town. How are you? How's Kitten?'

'Kitten's um . . . well, listen for yourself.' There is a rustle and then the muffled vibration of a cat's purr.

When Martha hears human breathing again, she says, 'I think that's almost as bad as putting your toddler on.'

'I haven't got a toddler.'

'You know what I mean.'

'Oh, er . . . Hang on. Go back to bed. What are you doing?'

There is a clunk and Fred says, 'I'll be back in, er, a second. I've just got to . . . sort out Hazel. Come on. Up.'

Martha sits down on the bed, and rubs her eyes. She has seen Fred several times over the last fortnight. She delivered the cat, by car, in its box, and stayed for a cup of tea and a Sherbet Fountain. And then two days after that, Fred came into the shop and hovered and finally asked her if she would come and value some of his 'odds and ends'. Martha – furious at the weakness that leads her to the Collofs' front door – had said she would, and is currently holding in the basement: a bedroom armchair in need of reupholstering, a wrought-iron antique cot (painted in peach gloss), a couple of leather suitcases with broken catches, and a box of Lesney cars. Lesney, Fred assured her, is the precursor to Matchbox and 'worth a mint'. She told him she knew a man who probably knew a man (Jason always knew a man), and she'd ask him next time he came in.

April, as usual, thinks Martha is a mug. After a couple of hours with the wire wool on the antique cot, she thinks she is a sadistic mug. But for Martha, Fred is a project, a piece of bric-a-brac that only wants the best bringing out. At every visit to the house – he keeps unearthing more things – she has slipped in a hint about changes that could be made to the decor. She has said, 'How about painting the hall white?' She has left the card of a 'Clutter Consultant' she got talking to once at the Ideal Home Exhibition. And she has begged him to let her 'find a good home' for the oil of the horses in the sitting room. 'Don't you like it?' he asked. 'Do you want me to be honest?' she said. 'I hate it.' He said, 'How sad,' but she wasn't sure if he meant his taste or her response to it.

She has the phone to her ear and is holding the cooled flannel across her face, feeling it balloon in and out against her mouth as she breathes. They have talked about other things, too. He asked her more about her father and she told him about the arguments through the wall and the girl in the car. He said, 'Is it hard to let go?' She said, 'I try to think of him as having gone into the next room.'

In exchange for this, in that barter of intimacy, they talked about his wife Lucy; about how she had been so young when she'd got pregnant; how she had always resented not going to university, how he still loves her, but has always felt the pull of her desire to be elsewhere. Her mother, Eileen, eaten up with guilt at her daughter's behaviour, comes round to look after the children when she can. Lucy is on her way back from India at the moment. But, as she is coming via Australia, Fred thinks she may be some time.

On one visit to the house, Martha looked at the children and wondered about their mother leaving them. They are odd, nervy kids. Stan usually has a globule of green snot running from his nose. Hazel is jumpy and unpredictable. She can be sweet and charming, but if you ask her a question, about school, or friends, she might answer properly but she might answer in gobbledy-gook like a baby, or with her mouth stretched so that the words come out drawled and self-conscious. One day she repeated everything Martha said back to her until Martha felt her nerves were stretched to screaming point. She couldn't wait to get out of the house. But if they were yours? That would be different, wouldn't it? There has been the odd moment when she felt that, without even trying, she has connected with them, and that, to her own surprise, they seem to like her. (She is, after all, the woman who brought them the cat and therefore, like some sort of Egyptian goddess, to be worshipped.) Stan got on her lap the day she sorted through the Lesneys, tucking his legs up, and he leant his head back against her arm and she felt the looseness in it, the weight of him, as her hands moved across the table. Another time, Hazel wanted to brush Martha's hair. Her strokes were so slight they hardly reached her scalp. Martha felt that, if she had had time, she would have let Hazel carry on, that the gentle fiddling could have been soothing, but actually, the slightness itself jangled her nerves and she pulled away before she could stop herself. At those moments she has felt a glimmer of what it must be like to love a child and yet feel suffocated by them. Maybe it is not the child but the burden of your own love you need to escape from.

'What are you doing? What's that noise?' Fred is back.

'I'm holding a flannel to my face.'

'Is that a nice thing to do?'

She rolls the flannel up. 'God, I've just remembered, when I was little, and used to stay with my grandmother, I would chew her bath sponge in the bath. It was my favourite thing. I remember her taking one away from me because I'd chewed the last one to threads. She said, "When you're grown up you can buy your own sponges to chew." Of course I don't. But I remember the texture of it, the warm taste of plastic and soap, the water squeezing out between my teeth.' She laughs. 'I wonder what that was about.'

'Perhaps it just . . . felt nice.'

'Yes, you're right.' Martha chucks the flannel across the room and through the doorway of the bathroom. It lands wetly on the floor. She follows after it, picks it up, and hangs it over the basin, wanders back into the bedroom and puts on a CD with the volume low. 'Yes. Yup. You're right. I always try and read things into everything, but you're probably right.'

'Sometimes immediate sensation is all,' he says. 'What's that?'

'What's what?'

'That music.'

'It's an Overture.'

'An Overture to . . . er, what?'

Martha pauses. She answers in the form of a question. 'Lionel Bart's *Oliver*?'

Fred says, 'Great film,' and for a little while after that she can hear him humming.

Martha remembers that she has talked to Jason and that he *does* know a man, and that he will be round to see the Lesneys sooner than you can say 'offshore account'. (Fred thinks selling the Dinkys means Never Working Again.)

201

Fred tells her that might be lucky because he has had a disastrous Sunday. He had got it wrong. He thought he was doing a four-year-old party, but he walked into a room of eight-year-olds. 'Is that the end of the world?' Martha asks. 'So end of the world is it,' he replies, 'that from then on the parents decide it's three friends and a trip to the ice-rink. Anyway, it was awful.' He had brought the wrong tricks with him and they all shouted he was rubbish. 'You need someone there to protect you,' she says, and then Fred says, 'Well you could come one day? Be my lovely assistant.'

It is a question not a suggestion (this is how the conversation is going tonight), but she doesn't answer. It hangs there for a bit. She is not stupid: she knows he is drawn to her. It's not vanity so much as realism. A man in his position with two small children and no looks, or fortune, not even a very nice house to compensate, isn't exactly going to be fussy; all he needs is someone to rumple up his sheets and then help him change them afterwards. Oh, she likes him, that's true enough. Just not in that way. The last time she went round, he was wearing shorts and she had to keep her eyes up, away from his bony knees and the dark hairs on his skinny calves.

So, after a pause, she says, to make her point, 'So why am I seeing David when actually I'm still hung up on Nick? Should I settle? Or should I hold out for perfection?' Fred doesn't say much in return – that's not what he does – but when she tells him that, 'Ex marks the spot,' he laughs vigorously. 'The Ex Files,' she improvises. And he laughs some more. His laugh is low, and fumbling.

She is about to recast Keith's drowning man gag – her

202

past flashing before Fred's eyes – when she hears the shop bell ringing. 'Come with me,' she says. 'In case it's a mad axe murderer.'

'I expect it'll be a cab for someone else,' he says. 'Or a misdirected pizza.'

'That's OK, I'm hungry,' she says. 'I only really had salad.' But she takes the phone down with her anyway, through the shop to the door and, for a moment, she thinks it is a cab for somebody else, because a man is standing there by a black taxi with his engine running. 'Can I help you?' she asks through the glass.

'Delivery,' the man says. 'Delivery for Martha Bone?'

And out of the passenger seat he lugs a big brown package wrapped in string.

'It's half past eleven at night,' she says, opening the door.

But the cab driver just shrugs and hands over the parcel. 'Watch out,' he says. 'It's heavy.'

Martha has the phone under her chin. She says, when she's closed the door, 'I've got a parcel here. Do you think it's safe to open it?'

'It's the middle of the night,' Fred says. 'Who sends a parcel by taxi in the middle of the night?'

Martha isn't listening. She has unwrapped the note. It says 'To Martha, Stuck in Balham, love David'; she can feel herself flushing as she reads it. And now she is pulling at the knots, tearing at the brown paper and pulling it aside, and there in her hands is the most precious, gorgeous, generous, antique Venetian mirror. Octagonal with a fleurs de lys crown and base.

'What is it?' asks Fred. She has forgotten the phone.

'Nothing,' she says. 'Look, I'll ring you in the morning, OK?'

She carries the mirror up to the bathroom – her palms against the pointed edges; her fingers caressing the felt back – and holds it in front of the mirror above the basin. It is the perfect size for the space. The glass is silvery when you look at it straight on, but green from the side, like water. The decorative leaves cast shadows across the surface, little pits of darkness that send sparks of light into the room. It brings everything together. It is perfect. She leans forward to look into the glass and scratches the last streak of paint off her forehead with her nails.

chapter ten

the conservatory

'A conservatory gives life a new dimension.'

Interior Design Solutions
by Ruth Pretty
(Cassell, 1999)

'IN, TWO, THREE. Out. Punch. In, two, three, Out. Punch.'
   The man on the video is lying on his front, lifting his pelvis and squeezing his perineum. Geraldine looks down between the double pendulum of her breasts to her own stomach muscles. Improving? Hard to tell, but she thinks so. She looks back at the television. 'Now for the lower rainbow,' the man says, through his teeth. Hm. This bit's hard. She forces the small of her back into an arch. It is the breathing she's got to crack. It seems to be the opposite of the breathing you're supposed to do for her yoga class. That's more in for four, out for eight. Feeling the air ease

out all the way down to your toes, rather than punching it out from your solar plexus. The one relaxes, the other empowers. Relaxing. Empowering. Punch. She still hasn't worked out if it's all right to do both. The woman at her new health club said it was fine. Dip in and out, she said. But maybe she should dip in there, in a proper class, before dipping out into stage two of the video. It may be called 'Bottoms Up!', but it is her back she is worried about straining.

'Ow!' She feels a dart of exquisite agony – not her back, but the palm of her hand, which has landed on an upturned ridge of hard plastic. 'Ooh.' She scrambles on to her knees and picks it up. It is a yellow piece of Lego. She bends across to pull out the new dedicated-Lego box from the immaculately tidy toy shelf and unclips the lid. A stray piece. A small hard yellow brick, easily overlooked, but essential to the construction of the Sky Ranger Propeller Plane. Lego deserters used to be chucked into a bright pink straw basket (Geraldine's summer handbag until one of the handles frayed away; like many middle-aged residents of suburban London, Geraldine likes the illusion that her weekly shop is really taking place in an open-air French market). But Katrina, on her arrival two weeks ago, has imposed order upon the playroom. Hard boxes with lids that snap shut. Everything has its place now, everything its purpose.

Geraldine doesn't know why she denied herself help for so long. She was always being told, by the kind of mothers who turn up at the school gates in lipstick and trainers, that it was 'the answer', but resisted on the grounds that anything that applied the same criteria to motherhood as mathematics couldn't be right. Also, she wasn't happy with the thought of having a stranger in the house. Now she sees how wrong that was. Do everything yourself, you do nothing *for* yourself. And it doesn't feel like failure, letting Katrina look after the children. It is liberation. Martha can think what she likes. Eliza can do what she likes. If she wants the water-colour of the swans – *if she wants Graham's old slippers* – so be it. Geraldine is keeping the china shepherdess and that's final. Geraldine is her own person now, not pushed around by Other People.

It is extraordinary how not having to empty the dish-washer once a day, how working out instead of cleaning up, has changed her outlook on life. It has made her realise how important it is emotionally to be in shape physically. She looks back at the person she was becoming – squashy and dimpled, her flesh flowing, her responses loose and uncon-trolled. How could she have let herself go?

Geraldine replaces the brick in the compartment of the box dedicated to air travel, clicks the lid back and gives herself an internal slap of satisfaction. Look after the little things and the bigger ones look after themselves. One L-shaped brick of Lego, one gyro-copter ready for take-off. She puts the box, square and solid, back in its place on the shelf and inhales. One tightened perineum, one sex life on the up.

*

On the table in front of Martha are four bell jars, a bunch of watering can roses, a line of shoe lasts and a plastic bottle of tomato ketchup. Her feet are bare because her plimsolls are drying on the radiator. The cat dashes in, shaking with indignation, and rubs itself against her calves. It is raining: one of those sudden, vertical October rains in which the whole world seems to be dissolving and coming apart. In the street outside, drains are overflowing, gutters already blocked with autumn leaves are torrents, and the traffic is at a standstill. But here at the back of the house the rain seems flat and still and it doesn't seem to touch them. Even with the door open, Fred's orange kitchen feels warm and enclosed, like the inside of a car on a long journey.

'So,' says Hazel, who is sitting next to her eating a supper of fishfingers and Cheesy Wotsits. 'We had Painting. And then Reading. And then we were supposed to have outside play, but it was too wet so we had *The Lion King* in the gym.'

'You mean you acted it out?' Martha is studying the bell jars carefully. She is sure she can do something with them. There will be some decorative trick, some conceptual joke. She just has to think. Could she balance them, inverted, in wrought-iron mesh? Fill them with bulbs or attractively bound editions of Sylvia Plath? (Does Faber still do those small gingham hardbacks?)

'No. Silly. We watched it. The video.'

Stan is licking the last orange dust out of his packet. He has got ketchup all around his mouth. 'I hate *The Lion King*.'

'Yeah, because it makes you cry.'

'It doesn't make me cry.'

'Yes it does. You're a cry baby. Cry baby, cry baby.'

Fred, leaning against the back door, stubs his cigarette out on the doorjamb and chucks the end, still glowing, into the garden. It hisses into a lilac bush. 'Hazel,' he warns mildly.

Martha looks up from the jar. 'What's it about then, *The Lion King*?' she asks.

'Don't you know?'

'No. I don't know anything. We didn't have videos in my day. We had *Jackanory* or nothing. Though I do remember going to see *Fantasia* with my dad. Just me and him. That made a change.'

Fred says, 'It's good to remember things like that.'

'Well.' Hazel takes a deep breath and begins to tell her. After a while Stan joins in, and at one point scrambles over to Martha until he's standing right by her. When Hazel explains about the old lion dying, he closes his eyes as if he is trying to block the sound out and has got his senses muddled. Martha nudges him and holds a shoe last in each hand to make them dance. Fred is watching from the other side of the kitchen. He is looking particularly pale and scarecrow-like today. The sleeves of his jacket are even shorter than usual – the knobbles of his wrists show – and there are pink rims under his eyes. He has lit another cigarette and when he inhales, his fingers have a slight shake to them. Martha knows he has had a postcard from his wife. From New Zealand.

He says, 'Er . . . you two. If you've finished, go and get ready for bed.'

'Oh-wa.' Hazel hangs on his leg, then wheedles. 'Can't we watch a video?'

'Sounds like you've watched enough today.' After Martha says this she opens her eyes wide and jerks her head from side to side, as if to say, 'Who said that?'

'Do you think we're all born with those phrases in our head?' says Fred. 'Or are they learned? Anyway, Martha's right. Come on.' He steers them out of the room.

Stan says, 'Can Martha read my stories?'

Fred says, 'I don't think so.'

'I don't mind,' she says.

'It's OK.' He takes the children upstairs. There's the sound of water being run and lots of stomping. Then it goes quiet and he comes back in. 'Drink?' he says. 'A little beer, or a gin and tonic.'

'Oh . . . I'd better go. I'm seeing David. At his flat, too – first time. Very portentous. Oh, all right, just a little one, a very weak one because I'm driving. Have you got any more gin or did we finish it last time?'

'Er . . .' Fred opens the cupboard and produces an empty bottle of gin.

'Looks like we finished it,' he says slowly. Then he wraps it in a tea-towel and, scooping some gel pens and colouring books out of the way, stands it upright in the middle of the table. He leans on it, pushing down, until it seems to be disappearing, and then there's a clunk and Martha bends down and there it is on the floor – except when she bends to pick it up, it's full.

'You're amazing,' she says, holding it to her cheek. 'Can you do it with everything? Must save a fortune on supermarket bills.' She hands him the half-empty ketchup bottle. 'Can you do it with this?'

'Er . . .' Fred makes a face. 'Well I can't, actually.'

'Oh. That's a shame. Do it again.'

'No.' He puts the empty gin bottle back in the cupboard and pours them both a drink from the full one.

'So how did you do it?' Martha is just teasing. She doesn't think he's going to tell her. But he holds out his hand. In it is the top of a gin bottle – a false top.

'It's an, er, illusion. I replaced the empty gin bottle with this, pretended to push it through and then dropped the full bottle on to the floor with my other hand.'

'But when did you swap the empty bottle for the false top?'

'Didn't you see me do it?'

'No. Not at all. And I was watching you the whole time.'

'There you go. That's the magic. Not the end result but the process. Doing things under your eyes without you seeing. Look—'

He points at the fridge and then crosses over and opens it. From inside the door he produces a bottle of tonic, and from the ice box a tray of ice cubes, and brings them back to the table. He pours the tonic on top of the gin in the glasses and then hands her the ice cube tray. Poking out of an empty section is a watch. Her watch! She feels her wrist. It's gone.

'How the hell did you . . .?'

'You didn't notice me doing it?'

'No! But how did it get in the ice box?'

'Well, you didn't feel me slip it off because you were concentrating on the gin bottle, and you didn't see me put it in the ice cube tray just then because you were concentrating on the tonic. It's all about displacing the attention elsewhere.'

He takes a sip from his glass. 'Sleight of hand and misdirection.'

'Oh Dad.' Hazel stands in the doorway to the kitchen in a pair of pink pyjamas. 'Don't tell people how it's done. That's not what a proper magician does. Smarty Arty doesn't even tell people what his real name is.'

'Yes, well.' Fred puts the children's plates in the dishwasher and wipes his hands on a tea-towel. 'There's ordinary magicians and there's . . .' From the cloth he produces a feathery red carnation. 'Mr Magic!' He brandishes it like a rapier, then places the plastic stem between his teeth and, sinking to the floor, skids on one knee across the tiles to Martha's bare feet. 'M'd'm,' he says through the flower.

Hazel is giggling and Martha starts laughing too. 'Mr Magic seems to bring out a different side to you,' she says.

He stands up to tuck the plastic carnation behind Martha's ear. She can smell the gin on his breath. Very slightly, she pulls away.

'Misdirection,' he says. 'And sleight of hand.'

In the car, in stationary traffic, trying to get across Albert Bridge into Chelsea, Martha readjusts the mirror to study her face. She looks flushed (she shouldn't have said yes to the gin and tonic) and her eyes are bright. The carnation, which Fred said she could borrow until the weekend, when he needs it for a try-out at a local brasserie, gives her an eccentric thrift-shop flamenco look. She puts her head on one side and pouts, shrugging up a shoulder. The car behind beeps; she swizzles the mirror back into place and moves up a few places on the bridge.

Fred asked her to stay for supper. He said, 'I've got a whole chicken here, ready glazed and stuffed.' But Martha reminded him she had a date and said, anyway, she never ate anything ready glazed and stuffed. She meant it as a joke, but Fred looked hurt. 'Is it naff and vulgar to buy something ready stuffed? As naff and vulgar as the horse picture and my taste in wristwatches?' Martha had said, 'No, just revolting. JOKE,' because he hadn't laughed.

She had to put her plimsolls back on before she left – warm now but still wet and soggy inside. 'Ugh,' she said, resting her hand on Fred's thin shoulder to balance herself. He seemed to flinch. Hazel was sitting at the top of the stairs. 'She gets in and out of bed all the time,' he said suddenly, the moment with the magic gone. 'She won't go to sleep. I miss my wife.'

The rain hits the roof like static. There is green fractured through the windscreen, clear and then blurred as the windscreen wipers ratchet across. She rolls forward a few places. It dissolves to red. Of course he misses his wife. And those kids need a mother. The light changes again and this time she passes through it, the bulbs on the bridge disappearing through the sodden rear window like a pleasure boat going out to sea.

The traffic frees, as if undammed, as soon as she crosses the river. It doesn't take long after that to get to David's flat. There is nowhere to park outside so she has to leave the car a couple of streets away, hold a newspaper over her head, and run back. She is soaked when she arrives. There is

213

papier mâché all over her shoulders and newsprint on her fingers. Her shoes squelch.

David buzzes her in. Despite its chi-chi Kensington location, the building isn't as grand as it could be. Some of the apartments are peppercorn rents, so no one has bothered to spend money on communal parts. The walls were once white but are now unintentionally rag-rolled with grime, and the carpet is a sticky beige. Some efficient person has organised a post system just inside the door: square wicker baskets below the occupants' names on neat white labels. There is an additional sign above David's box reading 'No Flyers', which has tickled one of the other residents sufficiently to stuff the box with advertisements for pizza deliveries.

David has opened the flat door and is waiting there on the first floor for her. He is wearing jeans and a white shirt with the top two buttons undone. He has hooked his glasses there. (He doesn't wear them very often. Martha is beginning to wonder, with affection, if they are not just a pose.) His sleeves are rolled up and his forearms have the remote blistered look of an old tan. Boat shoes, whitened with salt from a recent sea trip, are on his feet. Resting in his palm is a tiny cup of coffee; two fingers of the other hand crooked through the handle. His knuckles seem huge, his nails white scrubbed crescents.

He smiles. 'You're late. I was worried you weren't coming.'

Something garlicky and delicious wafts out of the open door. Glenn Gould is playing Bach. Martha puts her hand up to smooth her wet hair and, doing that, remembers the carnation. Only then does she realise she must have dropped it in the street.

Greg opens the front door to find the children's bags and school clothes regimented in the hall for the following day and a table laid in the empty kitchen. There is a sweet meaty smell emanating from the oven and a bottle of red wine uncorked on the side.

He hangs up his coat, lines his briefcase up next to the satchels and goes upstairs. It is all quiet. There are no children hollering in the bath, no wet towels strewn over the floor of the landing, no strip of light under the bedroom doors, no murmuring inside. He leans in to see Patrick and Ivor, damply tousled and open-mouthed in their bunks. Next door, Anna is asleep, too, her arm curled around a naked doll, its plastic limbs splayed at an angle. Greg rejoins the doll's legs into a more comfortable position, rearranges the duvet and kisses her hot cheek.

'Geraldine!' He stands on the landing. She doesn't answer. He has news that she will find extremely gratifying. David told him at lunch that he'd been seeing rather a lot of Martha, that Maddy Long Legs has got the chop, that tonight he is hoping . . . But where is she? She isn't in the bedroom, though there are signs of recent habitation – the duvet is dishevelled and shoes and garments are scattered across the floor, a trail from the open wardrobe to the door. It is getting a bit crowded in here, what with Hilly Bone's dressing table and chest of drawers, all the additional nick-nacks. He shuts the wardrobe, puts his hand for a moment on Geraldine's cello that stands gathering dust in the corner beside it, leaves the clothes and goes downstairs.

Someone is in the kitchen, bent down with the oven door open, but it isn't Geraldine, it's Katrina. Her hair is scraped back in a ponytail and her normally whey-faced skin is flushed with the heat. They were lucky to get her at such short notice and she is marvellous, he knows that. But he can't help thinking, God, if you're going to have a twenty-two-year-old living in the house, couldn't she at least be – not very PC this, you couldn't say it in front of the girls at the office – a bit sexier? Bit of a thrill over the old break-fast cereal? A little frisson as you pass on the way to the bathroom? Whatever happened to the Swedish au pair? You never seem to hear about them any more. It's all Czechs and Turks and Poles. What do all those fit, young Swedish girls do instead? Play tennis?

Katrina stands up as she sees him in the doorway. She has a tiny waist but huge thighs. 'Oh.'

'Hello!' he says jovially, coming into the room.

'Hi. Mr Hewitt.'

'Greg. You don't know where Geraldine's put herself, do you? The kids are asleep, I see.'

'Sorry?' Katrina's English is still formative.

'Geraldine? Where is she?' Gregory widens his eyes and stretches out his arms with his hands upwards to illustrate vacancy and bafflement.

'Sorry?'

'GERALDINE?'

'Oh. G-em.'

'Sorry?'

'G-em.' Katrina stamps on the spot, moving her arms back and forth as if marching.

'The gym?'

'Yes.' She nods. 'G-em.'

'Still?'

'Er?'

Katrina points at the clock and the oven and puts her hands on one side again, sadly.

'Right. Oh well, let's eat. I'm starving. Had a bit of a day at the paper and there's nothing like a bit of a day at the paper for building an appetite. There's nothing like a pint of bitter in the pub afterwards, but there you go.'

'Sorry?'

'Only burbling. Let's eat. I'll be OC crockery, you do the honours with the grub.'

He gathers together a couple of plates while Katrina retrieves the dish – containing some sort of stew with dumplings – from the oven. As she slides it on to a mat on the table she catches her wrist on the side and says, 'Ach.'

'Hot?' he says.

She nods. 'Hot.' She enunciates the word clearly, rolling the 'h', drawing out the 't'. For a second Greg remembers Geraldine dabbing the children's fingers against a radiator to warn them. She would say, 'Hot,' just like that. It used to irritate him actually, the way it always irritates one to hear a person one loves speaking in any way unnaturally – to children, or dogs, or foreigners. But the patience that she had with them when they were small was something to behold. She did everything slowly, still does, never a sense of urgency, moving through the house as if underwater. He would come in from work and he'd have to clap his hands to get things moving, to get the children into bed and the supper on. And then there would be the barrage of things hollering for his attention: batteries to be replaced, stabilisers to come on or off, basketball hoops to be fixed, children to take *back* to bed later (and in and out of their bed all night, Geraldine slumbering on), a whole maelstrom of inconsequential nothings.

It is a matter of both gratification and frustration to him that his home life is so metallically separate from his work. 'Good day?' Geraldine will ask when he comes in the door, or – in one of her little reductive jokes, taking a single idea of hers (foreign pages equal distant wars) and turning it into cartoon – 'Back from the battlefield?' What do you say? Where do you start? Because of course that isn't what it's about at all. It's about diplomacy and endless missed deadlines and failed fucking summits and train crashes on the other side of the world, hundreds dead, which you have to fight to get mentioned on the bottom of page two. Oh, he's feeling old and jaded, that's for sure. People used to say Greg Hewitt knows his stuff, but knowing your stuff doesn't add up to much these days. The new guy, straight from features, 'an ideas man', thrusting his ignorance about like a trophy ('Where is Matabeleland when it's at home?'), bullishly confident that he alone knows what the reader really wants.

Greg has served up two helpings and has picked up his knife and fork before he realises Katrina is not sitting down. 'Not hungry?' he says. There is a little performance after that from which he gathers she ate with the children, and then she smiles and nods and leaves him there in the kitchen on his own.

He makes an involuntary snort through his lips which he realises, after he has done it, is a release of tension. The house is quiet. He wonders again where Geraldine is. And to be honest, for all his complaining, it feels a bit flat with the chaps in bed. Because those inconsequential nothings aren't just a frustration, they are a gratification too, a comfort. There is escalating tension in the Middle East, there is the nerve-racking petty intrigue of the office, and there is here, somehow impermeable. He sighs, gets up to fetch the evening paper from his briefcase and settles down to news and stew.

He is still sitting there, his empty plate thrust to one side, when there is a familiar clash and the sound of keys being thrown on the hall radiator and Geraldine bursts into the kitchen clutching handfuls of carrier bags.

'What happened to you?' he says.

'Greg! That is awful! What do you mean, "What happened to you?" Can't you think of anything nicer to say?'

He simply meant to ask where had she been. Now he sees something *has* happened to her. She clearly isn't offended by his tone because she has kissed him on the head and is twirling around the room, stopping only at the oven to inspect herself in the silvery blur of the stainless steel splashback. 'Look,' she says, turning to face him. 'Hair. Make-up. New top. And look . . .' She spins to the doorway where she has left the bunch of bags, and pulls out a pair of pale blue baggy trousers which she holds up against herself.

219

'Maharishis. All for me. Look – embroidery on the calves. Isn't that gorgeous? And –' She stuffs the trousers back and yanks out a blue jacket which she also holds up – 'denim blazer. Earl! You've got to go for quality for an item like that. There was one in Gap but it wasn't a patch on this and Susie persuaded me. And . . .' She bends to rummage in another bag.

'So. Fun at the G-em Summit, then,' Greg says.

'What?'

'The GM summit? The g-em? The gym.'

'Oh, the gym.' Geraldine gives a fleeting smile to signal she has recognised the presence of a joke, but is too absorbed elsewhere to dwell on it. 'Yes it was fab. I had Salsaerobics and a swim. But since then I've been playing truant. It's all right.' She puts out her hand before he says anything. 'I rang Katrina and she was fine about it. She's so brilliant, much better than I am. Did she put my casserole in? Fabby. Was it delish? Don't really fancy it myself. I'm a bit off meat. So anyway, Susie and I nipped into Kingston for late night shopping and they were handing out leaflets for a new salon offering free colour with every cut. And after that, I thought I needed some more make-up and there was a demonstration at the Bobbi Brown counter in Bentalls and – *voilà*!'

She has come up close and this time she is clearly expecting a comment. Now she mentions it he sees her make-up, as well as her hair, is different. How exactly he couldn't quite say, and whether it's *better* . . . He doesn't have an opinion. He's been urging her to spend some money on herself, but now that she has . . . He thought she looked nice before. Is that the sort of thing she wants him to say?

'Gosh,' he says, raising his eyebrows.

'What?' Geraldine sits down next to him, and holds her face up like a child waiting for a flannel. 'What do you think? Be honest.'

And if Greg was in touch with his emotions – which he prides himself on not being – he would acknowledge now that he feels a pang, a twist, as if a small part of him has snagged on something sharp. But his subconscious tells him he is being ridiculous, that it must be to do with the quietness of the house when he got in, with not having had a chance to see the children, with having to eat on his own, or the strain of making conversation with Katrina. Yes, it's probably something to do with Katrina – a sort of empathy; here she is far away from home, not being able to speak the lingo – because Geraldine looks fine. Her hair *was* a mess before, it had got very long and she had to twist it back into a knot all the time, and when they made love it would fall forward into his face, into his eyes, into his mouth . . .

'So?' His wife is staring at him, hard-eyed, her hair sleek and jagged, her cheek and shoulder bones pointed. In this light, she doesn't look soft any more, but all angles.

He turns back to his paper. 'Very nice, old girl,' he says.

David, unusually in a man, understands the importance of an enveloping towel. Stepping out of the shower, Martha wraps herself in something so thick and white she wants to bite it. When she was growing up, you dried yourself in cloth like sandpaper; the moisture she blots on this hardly dents the pile.

She folds it over the bath, twists her hair into a turban and throws on the equally virginal bathrobe that is hanging on the back of the door. At the mirror she inspects her face for damage. She bares her teeth. A bottle of Listerine sits on the shelf above the basin and she swills a capful around her mouth. Next to that is a small vial of aftershave with a French label. Unscrewing the lid, she breathes in the new nutmeg smell of David. She puts it back and is about to leave the room when she notices the bottle of Clarins Body Lotion (*Lait Corps Soyeux*) next to it. The label promises to revitalise your skin with 3.5 per cent 'Plant-Marine Cell Extracts'. She unscrews the lid and dabs some on her hand. It smells sharp and clean like sticky-back plastic. David has always been careful about hygiene, but even he is not the 'plant-marine cell extract' type. She considers this for a moment and then swings open the bathroom cabinet. Inside is toothpaste, floss, anti-dandruff shampoo, a packet of razor blades and a lipstick. 'Barely There' it is called. But *there*.

The brand is expensive, the casing matt-brown, and when she twists it up, she sees that the lipstick itself is half-used, moulded into a particular angle, leaf-veined with the marks of someone else's lips. Whose lips? Maddy's? Maddy's lip-prints. The intimacy of it takes her breath away. She rolls it over her own mouth. When she licks it, it tastes of powder and perfume on old dresses. The colour is like a red wine stain. It makes her look different, her eyes brighter. Has David kissed a mouth wearing this lipstick? Does he still? She is stirred, jealous, curious. Martha and David have not slept together yet. They are not 'back together'. But in his company, the rest of her life, the *past* that seemed so full of

222

possibilities without him, recedes as in the wrong end of a telescope. Recently, Martha has been trying to remember exactly why she split up from him. It wasn't just Geneva or the fish and chips. Faintly, as if catching on the wind the smell of a distant bonfire, she remembers something uneasy and heavy that might have been boredom. But now, with the tingle of another woman's lipstick on her mouth, it seems spoilt, decadent, to have been bored. Not a real reason for leaving someone at all.

She clicks the cupboard shut and, her lips still flaming, goes out into the bedroom. Every piece of furniture in David's flat is a work of art, on display against the white walls and pale carpet. The only thing out of place is her wet clothes, and even these, while she was showering, David has laid neatly over the radiators to dry. The bed is mahogany, shaped like a wave. A king-sized *bateau lit*. The bedside table is walnut. It has a single drawer. Martha hovers. She thinks about opening it to unearth further evidence. But then her eyes focus on the picture above it, a small brilliantly coloured portrait of a woman. It is by a sixteenth-century Venetian artist, and the discovery of it, unattributed, in a house sale in Sussex ten years before, was one of the big moments of David's career. He could have sold it for profit and acclaim, but he had chosen not to. It has been carefully renovated, layers of old-house grime removed, so that the colours spangle. The woman is standing with her right arm held across her body. Her cheeks are red, her eyebrows arched. There is light in her eyes and her mouth angled as if she has just said something, or is just about to. She is wearing an ornate cobalt dress, with jet velvet sleeves, puffed from the elbow – the texture so rich you want to reach out and stroke the fabric. Her white bosom melts above it. But David didn't keep it for any of this. He kept it for the necklace around her neck – a thick gold chain with an extraordinarily elaborate jewel-encrusted pendant on the end. Martha looks at it now and smiles with secret knowledge. You have to search hard for David's passion. Here it is, hidden in a small exquisite detail in a small exquisite picture. Does Maddy know where to look? She doubts it. And in her mind at this moment, a close understanding of someone equates with love. So she doesn't open the drawer of the bedside table after all.

David is sitting in a fine Windsor chair at a small table in what he calls his 'conservatory', a large balcony covered over with Victorian glass panels at the back of the sitting room. When David first inherited the flat from his godfather, five years ago, they went together to buy a jasmine from the local garden centre. It had just been his birthday and while he was paying, Martha slipped secretly to another till and bought him a terracotta pot – cylindrical with ivy engraved up the side – as a present. She sees now that the pot has been replaced. This one is slate and rectangular and more modern. And bigger, which of course was probably the point, because the jasmine is huge now – there are tendrils reaching down from the ceiling. The air is rich with a sweet, invasive smell. The rain hammers on the glass roof. Martha wonders if, now she's clean and in a white bathrobe, they are finally going to have sex.

David says, 'Well, I'm certainly free so that would be nice.'

Martha starts. Then she realises there is a small black phone against his far ear.

'Hang on a moment. Let me put you on to her.' David is holding the phone out. He mouths something, but the word is too long and complicated to read.

Frowning, Martha says, 'Hello?'

'Matt-ski. You dark horse. You're actually there, are you? Having a shower, I hear.'

'Geraldine.'

'Greg's just told me your wonderful news. He has waited all evening. Charming. Men. He had lunch with David. I tried you at home to ask you everything, but no answer, so I thought I'd ring David to grill him and then he said you were there too. In the shower!'

'What wonderful news?' Martha takes the glass of wine David is holding out for her.

'About you two getting back together. Martha, I'm so pleased. I've been longing for this. I knew you should never have split up. It's brilliant. Are you absolutely thrilled? Clever girl.'

'Clever girl . . .'

'So I just asked David if the two of you wanted to come to supper on Saturday week. I thought I'd have a family get-together. Susie's about to fly back to Vancouver and I thought it would be nice to have a little do to wave her off. I've asked Eliza, well I've left a message, so she might grace us with her presence. And Dad'll be over; you knew that, didn't you? Just a short visit. He's got some stuff to organise for the boat. He's staying with Eliza because it's 'in town', as he puts it. Cramped but there you go. So will you come? David says he's free.'

Martha looks down at David sitting in the chair next to her. 'He's free, is he?'

David is nodding and wincing at the same time. 'Well, I'll have to check my diary,' says Martha. 'And anyway, I don't know if you're right.'

'What?'

'About . . . you know.'

'Oh Matt. What are you talking about? David told Greg . . . Oh piddle, am I jumping the gun? Have I got it all wrong?'

David bends down, ducking his head to adjust the feet of the table, as if to give Martha some privacy. It is a small circular occasional table. Four tapered legs. The top is marquetry and boxwood. Circa 1900. It is not dissimilar to the one her mother used to sit at playing patience. Clock patience, or the game David would play with her when she was ill in which you lay the cards in three separate piles. She has an image of his dark head next to her mother's buff-grey one, whispering about diamonds and hearts.

'Martha. What's happening?'

'What do you mean?'

'I mean, are you back together or not? And either way, can you make the do?'

David straightens up and looks at her. He smiles quizzically. She closes her eyes for a moment, a slow blink. When she opens them, he has diverted his attention to her naked leg. She watches as he reaches out his hand to touch it, rotating his thumb and finger on the skin just above her knee, and she stands very still. Their reflections in the conservatory window, his white shirt and her soft, thick gown, are a blur against the streaking rain. Martha's mother used to call a party 'a do'. Martha remembers the 'do' when she introduced David to the family, the expression of almost disbelief on her mother's face that Martha could have found anyone so 'suitable'.

She dabs the tip of one finger along her lipsticked mouth. Geraldine is saying something, but Martha interrupts. 'I think probably we are,' she says.

Geraldine puts down the phone, claps her hands together and then turns them over to admire her new red nails. 'Good,' she says.

Greg looks up from *Newsnight* to nod. She's not sure if he's heard.

'All good. We'll be back where we started before we know it. I wonder if he'll take her skiing again this year?'

'Maybe.'

'You could sound a bit more enthusiastic.'

'Sorry?'

'Turn the vol down if you can't hear me.'

'The volume,' he corrects, still disconcerted by her new look.

'You are the limit,' she says.

chapter eleven

the dining room

'Table, to clean. Marks on a polished table, caused by
hot plates, disappear when rubbed with
camphorated oil.'

Laurie's Household Encyclopaedia,
edited by W. H. Steer
(T. Werner Laurie Ltd, 1931)

MARTHA's customers, like her ghosts, obey a clock of their
own. There is no telling when they will descend. On some
Saturdays her shop is silent but for the sound of her own
breathing. On other Saturdays she can't hear herself think.
Today is one of those days. The whole of Balham appears to
have woken up with nineteenth-century French furniture
at the top of its list of priorities and has charged down to
pick up and put down her sconces, to open and close her
cupboards, to test the springs of her reupholstered Victorian
armchairs, to *fiddle*. A couple of long-nosed women are hot
on the heels of armoires. They have been sent by their friend

Charlotte Fraser. Does Martha remember? She asked them to tell Martha how much she is 'loving' hers and to pass on her good wishes. She hopes Martha is getting over her loss.

Martha smiles and nods, but her eyes dart to the gaggle of children with rudely striped lollies in their hands. Fluorescent drips have begun to run down on to the seagrass flooring. 'Jo-lly good,' she says, intercepting them on their way to the dappled-green velvet-covered chaise longue with its smattering of antique chintz cushions. 'Let's stand over here now, shall we?'

She is prodding them, teeth-gritted, in the direction of the mat when the door swings open and there is Jason, which is odd because he doesn't usually come on a Saturday. Martha hasn't seen him for a few weeks. She has been buying prudently in view of the imminent rent rise, and has been holding off extra expenditure. He has a person with him.

'Mornin' all,' says Jason. He is wearing an Iron Maiden T-shirt and a blue blazer. His friend, who is big and stooped and has thin shoulder-length hair with a small, round bald patch on top like a shiny coin in a patch of long grass, looks at Martha through his front fronds. Jason says, 'I've brought you my Dinky man. Mark. Martha.'

'Oh, your Dinky man. Brilliant. At last. Hello.' Martha smiles and gestures to the back of the shop. 'Sit over there for a sec and I'll just . . .'

She outlines the rarity of that particular type of armoire – 'an armoirette' she calls it – to the two women, but says she will do her best. She writes their names down in her book. She mops up the day-glo puddles of melted lolly. She sells a pair of bell jars (filled, in the end, with moss, compost and hyacinth bulbs, and suspended from picture hooks), and answers questions on the dimensions of a nineteenth-century fruitwood dining table. There are two white over-lapping rings on one end, which, she assures the customer, only add to its 'character'. And then, once she realises that the young couple who are debating the decorative advantages of *this* marble console table over *that* contemporary oak-veneer console table in Heal's are going to be debating for some time, she goes down to the basement for Fred's toy cars and joins the two men at the back of the shop.

Jason's associate, Mark, who is sitting on a child's cot bed, his knees by his chin, cannot conceal his excitement when he catches sight of the box, when he sees that each vehicle has its own little cardboard compartment, a separate garage so to speak. His voice comes out high and strangulated. 'Novelty boxed! Can I . . .?'

'Of course.'

There is a sharp intake of breath from the man. 'Ford Zodiac,' he gulps. 'Lesney series number thirty-three.' And then, 'Lamborghini Marzal, "Matchbox" series twenty, 1969. Oh fuck, Kennel Truck, 1968, "Matchbox" series, number fifty. Oh boy. Oh boy.'

Jason and Martha exchange glances as he burrows. Jason, who is leaning against a chest of drawers, says, 'You're look-ing different. I've never seen you in a suit before.'

'Oh.' Martha smooths her skirt with her hands as if removing invisible creases. 'Yes. Smart, isn't it? It's a present.'

'And heels? You fancy geezer, you,' he says.

Martha waggles one for his benefit. 'Thank you.'

'Very grown up. Designer get up, is it?'

'All right. You don't have to go on.'

'I'm just saying.'

'Yes, all right.'

'I thought you were broke?'

'They were presents.'

'Tights, too. Or are they stockings?'

'I'll give you five thousand for the lot.' The car man's offer comes out in a rush. Martha and Jason look up from her legs.

Jason says, 'Mark's a collector. I preferred how you looked before.'

Martha ignores the last thing. It seemed to have come out by accident. She says to Mark, 'Oh, I see. You're not a dealer?'

'No. Toys. I collect vintage toys. Twentieth century. Vehicles and action figures, mainly. It's been an interesting day for me. I picked up a 1973 Boxed Escape from Colditz Action Man Set at a toy fair in Cheam earlier. Complete with German and British uniforms, all the paperwork, and Sentry Box. Three hundred pounds. There was a tiny tear in the fold of the box, but otherwise perfect.'

'Right. I see. OK. Let me just go and make a quick call to . . . to the proprietor.'

Martha says 'proprietor', rather than 'owner', because she is panicking. She has done some research and £5,000 is considerably more than she was expecting. From her desk, she dials Fred's number. His mother-in-law answers. Fred is washing the car. Martha tells him, when he comes to the phone, that in future he can pay a boy scout to do it. 'Whatever happened to bob a job?' he says.

As soon as she puts the phone down, Martha is accosted by another customer, a woman pushing a buggy who wants cutlery – bone-handled knives, that sort of thing. Martha tells her she rarely stocks it and the woman is about to lug the buggy all the way out again when Martha remembers the Collofs' collection, wrapped in the back of the car, and dashes out to get it. She and the woman are sorting through the bundle and she is trying to work out how much to charge when Fred arrives. She waves him in the direction of Jason and Mark and the three of them sit on the little children's bed at the back, talking in a huddle, as if in some sort of backstreet drug deal. The woman quite likes the cutlery and is holding it up to the light when there is wailing from the buggy, so she takes the baby out and is bobbing it around, choosing spoons over its head. Then the door opens again and this time it is April, blowing in off the street, trailing scarves and shouting for her mobile phone which she says she left here the day before. She is shaking the cushions all around and the shop seems to be full of crashing cars and clinking cutlery, the air twirling with feathers, small babies and separate conversations, when standing in the doorway, a leather suit-bag over his shoulder, his silver hair trendily short, his face tanned, is Martha's father.

Martha drops a fork. 'Neville!' she says.

He hurls the suit-bag on to the chaise longue, knocking the remaining bell jar and spilling some compost on to the marble console. He crosses the room to kiss her, smiling warmly over his shoulder at the puffa woman.

'Hello Matty,' he says, but really to the puffa woman's baby whose fingers he has already caught in his brown hand. 'I know I'm seeing you later but I was passing so I thought I'd pop in, see how things are. How are you, darling?' he says. This time to her.

'I'm fine. Listen, hang on. I won't be a second. We're just finishing off, aren't we?'

The puffa woman says they are and, blushing slightly under the attractively crinkled eye of Martha's father, decides to buy the complete canteen.

Martha is used to the effect her father has on women. In photographs of him as a young man, he is the spit of Eliza: seal-like, sleek and dark (even under his dog-eared Afghan coat). His blue eyes are milkier now and the hair above the high arch of his forehead is grey, but age has, if anything, improved his face: the weightier jowls and the crinkled white ditches of his forehead add interest to the bland, smooth surfaces. Add to all this the benefits of a young French wife – the jeans, the trainers, the general air of fitness and sexual alertness – and it is no surprise that April should sashay over to be introduced. Even the baby has started cooing. 'How old is she?' Neville asks the baby's mother. 'Great age. I've got two little ones myself.'

'Oh, so you're Martha's DAD, are you?' April says, holding her scarf at arm's length on either side of her neck and pulling it back and forth like a towel. 'You're Martha's FATHER! She's kept you hidden! I can't believe you're her FATHER!'

'Yes, OK April.' Martha, processing the puffa woman's payment, feels as if she is the parent in the situation. April has dropped the scarf and is holding out her hand to be shaken. She looks more cheerful today. Her cheeks are flushed and clear and her hair shiny. Neville has picked up April's plump hand and kissed it. And now, with a little whistle, he is explaining the origin of the calluses on the pads of his fingers ('That's what happens when you spend your life messing about on boats'), and this leads on to his yacht at Antibes, and his house in Grasse, *his whole life* in France. April and the woman who has bought the cutlery, and the baby of the woman who has bought the cutlery, listen entranced. 'Honestly,' Martha says.

She turns to the back of the shop where Fred and Jason and the car man are staring at them. She begins to roll her eyes at Fred – at least he won't be taken in by this ridiculous display. But he is frowning at her. His chin is at an angle. And for a split-second she wonders why he looks so odd before she remembers: she told him Neville was dead.

Neville, very much alive, says, 'Don't they, darling?'

She turns back, flustered. 'Sorry?'

'My little girls. Françoise and Odaline. They speak French like natives, don't they?'

'That's probably because they are natives,' she says, motioning frantically for Fred to come over. 'It would be odd if they didn't.'

But Fred is ignoring her. He finishes up with the Dinky obsessive. A cheque is signed and handed over. And then the three men stand, shake hands and come to the front of the shop. Jason puts his hand up at Martha in a businesslike manner as he passes, ducking his head and breathing in through his teeth to show he is in a hurry. He and his friend help the woman with the all-terrain buggy down the steps and then the three of them are gone.

Fred is still standing there. Martha puts her hand out to touch his sleeve. She says, 'Neville. This is a friend of mine. Fred. Fred, this is Neville, my father.' She has her back to her father when she says this and she winces theatrically to show she knows she has some explaining to do. Fred's face is without expression. He says, 'I thought you were dead.'

Neville gives a shout of laughter. 'Dead,' he says. 'Not last time I looked.'

April says, 'Far from it.'

Martha opens her mouth to explain. She puts her hand on the back of her head and cups the other over her eyebrows. She grins at the floor. 'Long story,' she begins.

Neville, noticing the cheque in Fred's hand, says, 'Been doing a bit of business?'

Fred says, 'I've just sold my old toy cars.'

'Toy cars? How interesting. I used to have a lot of toy cars,' says Neville. 'I don't know what happened to them.' He looks at Martha with his eyebrows raised questioningly, then turns back to Fred. 'You know, just having girls. Five girls,' he tells April. 'From forty to four: can you believe it?'

'And you so . . . boyish,' April answers.

'You got children?' Neville asks Fred.

Fred is turning the handle on the door. He says, 'Two.'

'I love children,' Neville continues. 'Particularly when they're little. You off? Nice to have met you.' He clicks together the index finger and thumb of one hand and then shoots the arm out at Fred in a bonding gesture. He looks disappointed for a moment, then continues in the same intimately jovial tone as before. 'But there is nothing like a baby in the house. When are you due, sweetheart?'

Martha, who has gone to the door to shout goodbye after Fred, glances round quickly. Neville is looking at April. April tugs her scarf tightly around her neck. 'Sorry?' she mutters.

'Your baby, darling. When's it due?'

This time April pulls her coat across her middle. The cold is blowing through the open shop door. She mumbles something that sounds like, 'January.'

'I can always tell. Well, best of luck. Got a nice man in the background, have you?'

April, in a low voice says, 'Manchester.'

'Fabulous. Well, I'm sure Martha's looking after you.'

April hasn't met Martha's eyes but now she looks at her and then quickly away.

Martha lets go of the door. It begins to slide closed on its own with a quiet sigh, but at the last minute the wind picks it up and slams it. She says, 'I do my best.'

Geraldine's limpid body glides through the blue water. She reaches and kicks, breathes in, breathes out. There are no windows here – the pool is underground – and the ceiling is low. The water hums when her ear dips through it; another swimmer passes her with a chirrup. But all the sounds of her Saturday morning – the whingeing of small children, the barking of dogs, the thumping of both on the stairs – hit the water and stream away.

In, out. Before, she felt faint pity for the mothers she met with their au pairs and their personal trainers, ready in their Nikes at the school gate. How narrow their minds must be, she had thought; how thin the satisfaction of a sinuous upper arm; how empty their lives. Now she sees that it is not endorphins but the emptiness itself that is the drug. When she is here, or in the gym, concentrating on her body, she feels all other responsibilities peel off and leave her. Later, she will worry about tonight's supper and tomorrow's homework; she will face up to seeing Eliza. Next week, perhaps, she will get the cello out and think about playing again. But for now it's just her and the water – so warm it's like her own blood. And after her fifty lengths, she will shower, and transfer to the beauty clinic where a woman in a pink T-shirt and surgical trousers will talk through the latest 'procedure' on Geraldine's list: plastic surgery without the surgery. Or, for that matter, without the plastic. 'Micro-currents like the smallest currents you can get – an exercise routine for the face,' she will say. 'OK?' There will be an upward lilt in her voice because there are even different rules of intonation here.

Five weeks ago, Geraldine would have laughed at this. Not now. Now she will arch her (already 'threaded') eyebrows with interest at each boast of 'a natural ingredient'. And then, face tingling, she will postpone going home a little longer. (Greg is capable of laying the table; Katrina can handle the kids.) She will find herself on a quick detour to the shops. The new trousers, perfect as they are, will be just a little more perfect with a new top. And the new skirt needs shoes. Each outfit, each 'natural' procedure, keeps leading to the next.

She reaches the bars, turns and kicks away again. In, out. In, out. Once you start, it is almost impossible to stop.

*

Martha inhales the smell of old leather and oil that permeates David's 1960s Jaguar. She rubs the cracks in the beige seat beneath her legs. David turns to smile at her, puts a hand on her knee, on her tights just below her skirt, rolls it around gently like one might palm a trackball on a computer keyboard, and then returns it to the steering wheel. On the car radio, people are discussing a new exhibition of tiaras at the V&A.

The lights of Tooting High Street are stationary on either side of them. Somewhere in the distance a water main has burst. Horns blare and the side streets are jammed with cars squeezed in at angles. The whole world seems to be heading in the same direction tonight, and no one is going anywhere.

Martha stares out of her window and wonders about April. She thinks about her belly growing and stretching without Martha noticing. Next to the car is a shop full of brightly coloured saris. Sheets of blue and pink cloth, sheer and sparkling, stretch from the balletic fingertips of the plastic model to her pointed toes. Rolls of rich, gold-tipped fabric lean against the walls. David inches forward. From the open window of the next shop along, vegetables tumble out on to the pavement like jewels: long, tapered courgettes with orange plumes; heaps of ribbed green okra; mountains of bruised garnet grapes. There are two women chatting as they pick through the glistening red and yellow peppers; a man in a cream shirt watches them from the doorway. On the radio, the presenter says: 'So, on to the Oriental Circlet designed by Prince Albert for Queen Victoria – a noble expression of the jewellery arts or an empty symbol of majesty?'

Martha thinks about April coming in late, her skin grey,

spittle in the corners of her mouth. She remembers the sound of retching in the lavatory. She thinks about her on the phone, her muttered, intense conversations. The mood swings, the pink cheeks, the doughnuts! How can a person not notice something like that happening under their nose? What sort of person doesn't notice? Or what sort of person, working side by side with someone every day, isn't *told*?

April had left with Neville in the end, cadging a lift to the Tube, slinking off under cover of his shadow. She smiled at Martha before she went out, but her eyes darted about. A better person would have rung April straight away, the moment she'd gone, to reassure her. But Martha felt too in need of reassurance herself, too resentful, too overwhelmed by a sense of her own failure. Whose life can she say she is part of if not April's?

When David arrived, she had told him straight away, relieved to have someone to open up to. He had shrugged. He said, 'It's her life.' Martha asked him why he thought April hadn't felt able to tell her. 'Am I so cold?' she said, but David thought she was probably worried about her contract. 'Is maternity leave built in?' he said. Martha said their agreement was verbal and he said, 'There you go.' After a bit, he added, 'Silly girl.'

'At least we're through the lights,' he says now. 'We might not be too late after all.'

'Good.' David's hand rests on the gearstick and she gives it a quick squeeze. 'I hate being late for Geraldine.'

They might have been later, and she might not have minded. Here is something else to worry about. She had left

239

David with a drink in the sitting room and gone to have a bath. With her head tipped forward, feeling the water stream through the soap in her hair, she had willed him to push the door open. But when he didn't, she realised she was relieved. She had wanted to have bathroom sex, not for itself but because it had seemed the sort of thing that *should* happen, like proof, like a vindication.

Sex is embarrassing between them: there are no two ways about it. Without his clothes on, there are stripes across David's arms and legs where his freckled summer tan ends. His white body feels cool like a pillar. There are bits of him, a triangle of delicate, almost translucent skin from his hips to his groin, that Martha feels she knows as well as her own. She loves him, but she keeps her eyes tight shut when she kisses him. There is none of that frantic erotic newness of the first time they slept together eight years ago, jagged limbs and mouths. But the gratifications of the hundredth time are missing, too. At climax, David used to shout, a high, squirming shout, 'Oh fuck, Oh Christ.' There was one weekend in Milan when the thinness of the hotel walls became a matter of hysteria for them. But these days he is quieter and doesn't swear. It is as if a sheen of politeness has come between them and the selfish comfort of familiarity. Martha finds herself fantasising about men she cares less about. She has put aside most of her ghosts (one of these days she is even going to throw out the bin bag of letters), but Nick Martin still lingers. At night when she can't sleep, she finds herself looking through the phone book. Karen says the two of them need to relax, to feel at home with each other again. Martha is working on this.

'I can't tell you how glad I am that you're coming with me,' she says. 'It's terribly brave of you.'

He says, still looking ahead, 'I like your family.'

'It's true, isn't it? You do.' Martha smiles up at him. 'How amazing.'

They reach the dual carriageway and David at last puts his foot down. The houses behind the crash barriers strobe past, one after another, front doors, leaded windows, leylandii, gates, fences; everything upright and straight, lining their road to her sister's house as if in salute.

Geraldine – or someone purporting to be Geraldine – opens the door to Martha and David in what can only be described as 'a new outfit', though this hardly does it justice.

David says, 'Crikey, look at you!'

Martha says, 'God.'

Geraldine is wearing baggy beige trousers with pockets at the knees and a vivid seagreen embroidered dragon crawling up one leg. They are slung low over her hips, and a pouch of white tummy peeps out below a tight turquoise cap-sleeved T-shirt. 'Princess' is emblazoned in silver across her chest.

'What?' she says. She might be flushing under her bronzed cheekbones. Her eyes look like eagle's eyes, or the markings on military planes.

'Your trousers.' Martha opts for the least controversial item on display. 'Are they combats?'

'No. They are Maharishis, thank you very much.'

David says, 'Ah.'

'But if the Maharishi wasn't opposed to violence,' says Martha, 'you could call them . . . All I mean is, they look like combats.'

'Well they are not.' Geraldine slaps her thighs, as if giving her cellulite a quick press. Painted nails flash crimson against the beige. 'Anyway, leave me alone. Look at you, Miss Skirt. And congratulations – late as you are, for once you're not the last. Eliza hasn't yet deigned to turn up. Come and say hello to Daddy.'

David and Martha follow her along the corridor. They pass the playroom. Martha pokes her head in. The children are in their pyjamas watching television and don't look up. The dogs, in their baskets, are chewing their own feet. 'The Boy' is on the wall.

The atmosphere in the kitchen is that of a party waiting to happen rather than one in full swing. Greg is drying glasses at the sink. He is wearing pink sailing trousers and clumpy new trainers which make him look awkward. His cheeks are heavy and there are beads of sweat on his brow. Neville is at the kitchen table. In his dapper dark suit and red tie, with his tanned, raked face, he looks out of place, like a managing director having a cup of coffee in a greasy spoon. When he sees Martha and David, he says, 'Ah! David, dear boy. Darling M!' and half makes to get up. But he ends up just rearranging himself in his chair, giving the fabric of his trousers a little tug. In the space between the fine blue wool and the fashionable laced shoe, there is a glimmer of scarlet sock.

He has been deep in one of his anecdotes. Graham's daughter Susie is sitting next to him. She is wearing the same trousers as Geraldine, only hers are white and have a snake not a dragon. Once Martha has kissed her father and greeted Susie, Neville swills the wine in his glass and gestures to the pale young woman opposite. 'Meet Katrina. The wonderwoman of Kingston.'

'Our au pair,' says Geraldine from the fridge.

'She has struggled across Europe to bring aid and harmony to this house, haven't you, darling?' Neville pats her hand. 'Leaving behind her family, her friends, her fiancé.'

Katrina says, 'I am from Slovakia.'

'Can you believe it? When she arrived, the family she was planning to come to had given the job to someone else. She was homeless, practically destitute. Out of the street, on her ear. Weren't you, Katrina?'

'Sorry?'

'Homeless.'

Geraldine says, 'Dad. Leave the poor girl alone.'

Katrina decides to leave *them* alone. 'A woman with a social life,' sighs Geraldine as she exits.

David and Greg are standing over by a rosewood bookcase that, until a few weeks ago, had displayed Hilly Bone's Everyman editions of Dickens. Now it houses Jocelyn Dimbleby and Delia Smith. Greg is talking about work – something about a new boss. Geraldine is flapping around between the oven and the fridge and the dining room. Neville is trying out his charm on Susie. 'Fascinating country, Canada,' he is saying. 'God, I'd love to go there.' Susie is chopping chives curtly. 'Well you should,' she says. 'While you can.'

Through the window, outside in the garden, Julia and Ian are swaying up and down in formation, like a Scottish reel in slow motion.

'What are they up to?' Martha asks Susie.

'Getting the babies to sleep. Apparently walking up and down helps.'

'Haven't they heard of babysitters?'

Geraldine scoops Susie's chives into a dish. 'You're an angel. They use her mother sometimes.'

Susie puts her head on one side. 'I think, Martha, if you had gone through what they have gone through,' she nods a couple of times as if to confirm Martha's sympathy, 'you would be protective, too. Do you know what I mean? I know it's hard but we've got to try not to judge people.'

'Yes of course.' Martha smiles grimly, thinking not just an angel but a saint.

Geraldine, clattering around with dishes and plates, says, 'Isn't it time ours were in bed?'

Greg doesn't hear her and carries on talking to David. But instead of repeating the question (actually a thinly veiled instruction), Geraldine says, 'Oh all right, oh God, I'll do it,' and flies out of the room. No one else seems to have noticed, but Martha is taken aback. Although she has always assumed that deep down her sister is unhappy, the surface impression in the house is usually relaxed to the point of chaos – family life at its most aesthetically hideous: dog-eaten toys and crayoned walls. Today everything is awkward and jagged. Geraldine won't keep still and Greg looks exhausted. Neville, the magnificently self-regarding guest of honour, is oblivious, but around him there is flitting and jarring.

She gets up and says to Greg, 'Any chance of a drink?'

Greg says, 'Of course. Sorry. What am I thinking?' and slugs out a glass of red wine for her. 'She's given up,' he hisses.

'Who?'

'Ger. She's given up booze and you'll notice she doesn't eat her food at the same time.'

'The same time as what?'

He whispers, one eye on the door, 'She won't eat meat at the same time as potatoes. She has to digest her fruit before she eats her vegetables. It's a bloody nightmare.'

David looks alarmed. 'So what are we eating tonight?'

'Chicken.'

'Ah. Good. She does a good chicken. The usual, I suppose?'

Greg says, 'She'll cook but she won't eat with you. She just sits and stares, like a disapproving dog.'

Susie is looking over at them from the table. She says loudly (not just an angel and a saint, but a lipreader, too), 'Actually it's called trophology and there is a lot of medical evidence to support it.' She turns to Neville. 'I mean, at your age, you really should consider it. Combining the wrong foods, eating proteins with starch, the typical Western diet, causes havoc on the digestive system. It's the major source of fat and cholesterol accumulation in the body. Do you eat hamburgers?'

Neville says, 'Never touch them.'

'OK then, steak and chips?'

'Steak frites, oh yes, of course. With a green salad usually.' Neville looks relieved. He breathes in to show off his slim waist and looks around for approval.

'Well there you go,' says Susie. 'Sticky deposits in your arteries. Your colon lined with mucus. You should do something about it before it's too late.'

She smiles sweetly at Julia and Ian who are coming in

from the garden. Julia is wearing expensive jeans with a crease down the front, but her eyes are tired and she has lipstick on her teeth. There is a scabby rash on Ian's neck. They mouth greetings at Martha and David and, limbs rigid, toes soft, move like moon-walkers with their bundles towards the hall. Ian is just easing through it with his elbows when there is a loud peal and the rattle of the front door and the voice of Eliza coming towards them.

'Sorry we're late, everyone,' she says. 'Burst water main in Wandsworth. Bloody nightmare. Julia! Ian! You've got the babies with you! Again! Oh! Sorry!' Julia's bundle has started crying. Julia looks as if she might be about to, too. She and Ian disappear into the house. Eliza says, 'Oh dear. Never mind. It's about time they used babysitters like the rest of the world. Oh look, Mummy's little rosewood bookcase. Bit wasted for cookery books, wouldn't you say? Hi, Neville. How was your day?'

Neville says, 'We've just been hearing about trophology.'

'What's trophology?' Eliza is kissing everybody. She looks effortlessly relaxed in her faded jeans and white T-shirt. 'Hi, David. Long time no see. Martha, what on earth are you wearing? What's happened here? There's Geraldine over there in her Princess T-shirt and pop-star street clothes. And here's our reliable tomboy in –' She turns Martha round so she can look at the label in the back of her dress – 'Armani. Very nice.'

'It's to do with not eating steak and frites at the same time,' Neville says. 'Fatty deposits, mucus-lined colons.' His suntan seems to have paled a little.

Martha says, 'It was a present from David.'

'Oh, you mean the Hay Diet. Are you on the Hay Diet, Ger?'

Geraldine is handing Denis a pile of cutlery. 'I don't know anything about being on a diet.'

Eliza taps her playfully around the waist. There is a cruel look in her eye. 'Well, don't leave it too long, Princess. Not if you're intent on hipsters.'

Geraldine says, 'I am involved in trophology. It is the science of food. All I am doing, Eliza, is looking after myself. Inside and out.'

But Eliza is pretending not to hear. She has gone over to the table to join Neville. 'Budge up, handsome,' she says, perching on the edge of his chair. 'Well I hope we've got something decent to eat. I'm starving-wharving.' She winks at her father.

Geraldine says, 'Chicken.'

David, comfortable in the thought of himself as Geraldine's favourite, steps forward and puts his arm around her shoulders. 'Sometimes I dream about your chicken,' he says. 'Your world-famous Coronation Chicken.'

'Grilled,' she says.

They don't eat in the kitchen. Geraldine has laid the dining room table for ten and lit the candles, even though it is grilled chicken and salad. Even though it is family. There have always been distinctions in this house between 'kitchen suppers' and 'the dining room'. Greg finds it hard to keep track of the rules. They seem to be laid out more in relation to the importance Geraldine wishes to bestow on an occasion than on any intrinsic formality within it. In the past he has been caught on the hop, about to chuck cutlery on the kitchen table for a takeaway to celebrate a neighbour's birthday, only to discover it has been 'set' elsewhere; or, worse, ushering the editor of his newspaper (coaxed into the suburbs for a repast with one of his longest employees) into a cold, empty room.

Now, for this communal meal, in honour of his father-in-law and his father-in-law's late ex-wife's stepdaughter (what *is* this about? What lengths will his wife go to to manipulate 'The Family'?), they stream into the smartest room of the house (the *only* smart room in the house), forcedly jolly at the corralling. Geraldine flits about at the door, telling people where to sit. 'You can't go there, Denis,' she says, 'that's next to your wife,' and, 'Oops, up you get, Julia; girl, boy, remember.' Everyone obeys her, but they stand by their allotted chairs awkwardly for a moment, too formal to sit down.

All, that is, except Neville. Steered by his eldest daughter to the head of the table, he plonks himself into his seat, flourishes his napkin and says, 'In Grasse no one ever bothers with seating plans. You just chuck some bread, some cheese, some pâté on the table and whoever happens to be there, children, adults, *les voisins*, *le notier*, just help themselves. A plate of food, a glass of wine, the sunset, the love of a beautiful woman . . .' He tips back in his chair with one elbow on the table. But the chairs, mahogany and satin-cushioned, passed down from Greg's mother when she went into the nursing home, are, like their former owner, a little unsteady on their feet, and he buckles for a moment, an

248

expression of surprise on his face, before Susie, who appears to have taken it upon herself to behave like a nurse discreetly attendant on a wealthy if wilful patient, slots him back in.

She says, mildly now, 'Pâté, cheese and bread. You might as well just block your arteries with a shovel.'

Julia, at the other end of the table, says, 'That's quite enough about arteries, thank you very much. You'll put me right off my food.'

Susie says, 'You should listen, if you want to tackle Ian's eczema. Dairy is a known allergen. Smile, but if Dad had paid attention to his diet then maybe he would be with us today. At this meal.'

Martha catches David's eye. He blinks slowly and mouths something she can't read. It might be 'God forbid', although she's not sure. Before, it was always his role – the outsider who sympathised with the sisters but was above prejudice himself – to be nice about Graham. This time round there are subtle adjustments in his attitude towards her relations, like a piano slightly out of tune.

Julia gives a radiant smile. She sets her glass down very carefully on the table; it hardly makes a sound but her shoulder is rigid. 'Yes, well, had you been here visiting him on a daily basis, schlepping up from Surrey, checking that he was eating at all, not to mention keeping an eye on his medication, trying to tempt him to eat anything – in the end he only wanted Fray Bentos – then maybe you would have a point.' She smiles again.

Martha, who has done none of these things, looks down at the table.

Geraldine comes in again with a plate of chicken and misses this. She says, 'Sit,' as if trying out a new jollying tactic on a room of dogs.

Greg and Geraldine's dining room is lined with dark red, gold-crested wallpaper. Martha considers it hideous and old-fashioned. A chandelier dangles dustily in the centre of the ceiling. A pair of silver salt and pepper shakers stand to Lilliputian attention in front of her place setting. She picks one up and studies it. It's familiar: it belonged to her mother and her grandmother before that. She puts it back on the table with a clink. When Geraldine, who is at one end, facing her father, passes the plates, they scrape and clank. Martha watches her elder sister hold a crystal glass up and turn it against the light, to check it for smears. Her mouth is gathered and a tiny frown flits across her forehead as she wipes it on her linen napkin.

Martha turns to Ian, who is next to her, and asks him how he is, and whether he has any news about Chestnut Drive. He tells her they have just received two offers, one from a developer and one from the next door neighbours, the Quinces, who would like to knock the two houses together. 'Though only the ground floor, not all the way up the house,' Ian adds, 'because they wouldn't get a return on that.'

Geraldine says, 'Well, obviously we'll accept the nice neighbours' offer, won't we? We don't want some horrible developer. There's no argument, is there?'

Eliza says, 'Hold your horses.'

Ian says, 'The developer is offering another fifty grand.'

Eliza says, 'See?'

Geraldine jabs two spoons into the platter of grilled chicken and thrusts it to David. 'I cannot believe I'm hearing this,' she says.

'Hearing what?' says Eliza.

Geraldine throws herself back in her chair, her eyes casting around the table. She takes a gulp from her glass, which is holding a cordial of elderflower and ginseng. 'You knew about this already, did you, Eliza? Martha? Did you? You didn't? Well, you agree with me, don't you? You won't let them sell the house, Mummy's house, to the highest bidder?'

Martha rubs her eyes. 'Um,' she says.

But before she can say anything else, David says, 'I suppose selling something to the highest bidder is what is customary in these matters. And when it comes down to it there isn't really room for sentiment.'

'But my mother's house . . .'

'It was my father's house, too. In recent years at least.' Ian hasn't spoken for a while.

'Yes,' says Julia, nodding forcefully at her husband.

Martha, with her head full of the rent rise, says quietly, 'Graham would hate it to be sold to a developer. It was his thing after all. Developers moving in and taking over the area.'

Susie, who is picking through a bowl of salad, says, 'This is barking. Dad would have wanted us to get as much dosh for it as we could. He wanted the best for his children.'

Geraldine says, 'Susie!'

'I'm sorry, Geraldine. But money's money. And frankly, I could do with as much as I can get.'

Martha says, 'We all could.'

Geraldine is looking tearful, her mascara'd eyes like daisies. 'Dad?' she implores.

Neville gives his tie a flick as if shaking water from it. 'Nothing to do with me any more, I'm afraid, sweetie. Sold my say long ago.' He puffs out his cheeks and reapplies himself to unpicking the chives from his portion of potato salad.

'Under the circumstances –' Ian's forehead has flushed red – 'I've instructed the estate agent to go back to Mr and Mrs Quince and give them an opportunity to match the developer's offer. I also believe we need to be in full possession of other information, such as how the capital in each case is being raised. And I would suggest that we reconvene at some point, when the position is clearer, for a final decision. Also, there is the matter of the remortgage . . . Um . . . Over the last year, certain legal pressures have been brought to bear and my father was constrained, at one point, to take out a further loan against the house.'

Eliza says, 'He remortgaged the house? Fuck.'

Martha feels a wedge of anxiety expand in her chest. The sale of the house has been a soft insulation against her own financial worries.

Geraldine says, 'What? What's happened?'

Eliza says, 'We're fucked, that's what.'

Everyone begins talking at once. Greg and David bend back in their chairs and talk practicalities behind Julia. Denis, in his own quiet way, tries to preach patience and understanding. But Neville, more because he is rendered uncomfortable by any subject that touches on his previous marriage than through any altruistic desire to defuse the discussion, slaps his thigh loudly and rests one hand on the top of his head. 'I say,' he says. 'Did anyone else catch that programme last night in which those two rather attractive girls threw away that poor woman's entire wardrobe? Did you? Said none of it fitted "the rules". That she had to buy a whole lot of new clothes. What's all that about? And that was followed by that other programme with that little camp Yorkshireman buggering up people's perfectly nice gardens. This poor elderly couple went away for the weekend and the television company bunged in a hideous Japanese water feature. We flicked over from that and on the other side that Carol Vorderman was doing the same thing to someone's front room. Painting it lilac! An army man, too! What is going on? I come back to England and all the media seems to do is go on about change this, change that, do this to yourself, do that, eat this, don't eat that, steak frites off the menu, wear this, don't wear that.'

Everyone looks at him. Eliza laughs. She says, 'You're right, Neville. Get someone in, get a new garden, a new living room, and a new lifestyle might come too. Find a new look and a new personality to go with it. The makeover artist is the new god. The question is, is it a benevolent god? Or one that makes people feel unhappy as they are?'

Geraldine fingers the outsized purple diamanté cross she is wearing around her neck. She says, 'Eliza, it is not "a religion", buying a few new things to make you feel better about yourself. I saw the programme, too, Daddy, and the woman at the end felt much more confident. She took off the wedding ring she'd worn since her divorce.'

Neville, buttering another hunk of French stick, says,

'Yes, but did you see her two weeks later? She looked just as much of a mess as she had when they started.'

Greg says, 'Spent a fortune in the meantime. Expensive business, new clothes. Expensive business, the old me, me, me. Meanwhile in East Timor—'

Eliza interrupts, 'It's the same as Martha's shop, isn't it? People come into your shop not because they *need* a new bed or sofa – they'd go to a department store for that. They come into your shop because they *want* a new bed or sofa, one that fits into the current "look". One that will make their house "look" different, that will transform the "style" in which they live.'

Martha says simply, 'People find things comforting. Isn't that all it is?'

'But you're educating their eye.' David laughs. 'In a sense at least. It's a style thing, not a value thing.' He turns to Eliza. 'Basically, attractive as a lot of it is, Martha sells tat. Dressed-up tat. Nobody is coming away with anything of any value, of any long-term significance; simply with something that looks pretty, for the moment. It's a sort of con. They are buying a lifestyle. Just like the fashion business. In fact Martha's business *is* the fashion business.'

'Sorry?' Martha looks at him. 'I thought I was in the antique business.'

Eliza puts her head on one side. She and David always used to have a little sparring thing going on. 'But isn't the grown up stuff you do subject to fashion too? I mean, what determines the value of a Regency desk or a pearl necklace? It isn't just their intrinsic value, is it? Rarity counts. Supply and demand, and demand goes up when something is in fashion.'

Martha waits for David to fight back. That's what he would have done in the old days. But he looks down and winces. Julia's knife and fork are clicking against the china. Ian, next to her, is trying to slice more meat off a chicken wing. Her father has picked his up with his fingers and is gnawing at it.

Susie: 'So who are these gods then, Eliza? The people who make the television programmes? Martha with her funny little shop? I don't understand. If it's a tyranny, who are the tyrants?'

Eliza laughs. 'Interesting question. Who determines fashion? Obviously designers, but they are responding as much as anything to what has gone before. Fashion itself creates fashion. But that's not what I'm talking about. I'm interested in this trend for complete re-creation, this culture of transformation. Where does that come from? All these books, telling you how to decorate, all these programmes. I don't know. A new century, a desire for a new beginning? Or a godless society in which people flounder for excuses to change? I don't know. Possessions as the new gods. Household gods!'

That's when Geraldine stands up. Her chair makes a grinding noise on the floor. 'If all this is just a dig at me, Eliza, why don't you say it?'

Eliza says, 'It's not a dig at you.'

'Oh really.'

'Geraldine, it's not a dig at you. It was Neville who brought the subject up. It interests me. But if you want to get personal, it is also intriguing how a good Catholic girl like you can have become so grasping.'

Geraldine swallows. She twists her face into a heavily ironic expression of confusion. 'Sorry? Grasping?'

Eliza laughs again, more lightly. 'I only mean the tea-leafing of Mummy's things. I notice the house is stuffed full.'

'If this is about "The Boy"?'

'Which you have.' Eliza has stopped smiling.

'And you don't have anything, I suppose? What about the Chesterfield and the oak chest?'

The two of them are glaring at each other. Martha can't think of anything to say and, looking round the table at the blank expressions on the other faces, she realises she isn't alone. It's almost a relief to give up. It is as if this argument has been trying to get out all evening. She thinks she might say, 'What about me? I haven't got anything, but I'll settle for the Penwork Tea Caddy.' She picks up her wine and takes a swig for courage. The glass has left a ring on the table.

And then Martha sees Julia start. In the doorway, Ivor is standing in his pyjamas. His face looks startled, his eyes out of focus, as if the light is dazzling him. You would say he had 'bed hair' if he didn't always have bed hair. He mumbles, 'Mum. I need you.'

Geraldine starts clearing away the plates angrily. 'Run up. I'll only be a minute.' But Greg has already scraped back his chair, and so has Neville and so has Denis and he's the closest. There is an undignified scrabble at the door, but Uncle wins out. Ivor looks up at Denis like a supplicant. When Denis scoops Ivor under his arm, Martha sees the wet streaks down her nephew's pyjama legs. Out in the hall, Denis can be heard saying, 'Chase you up there, champ.' And the clatter of the two of them on the stairs sounds like an escape.

*

Lots of people leave and Martha gets drunk. Ian and Julia remember they have a bad night ahead of them. Eliza doesn't bother with an excuse. At the door, she says, 'Well I've taken the salt cellar so she can put that in her pipe and smoke it.'

Geraldine has a weep in the kitchen. Susie comforts her while Martha and Greg clear the table. Neville, passing through, says, 'What are all these tears for, then? Don't like my girls falling out.' David, trying to make a joke, adds, 'It's only a salt cellar.' Geraldine says, 'What salt cellar? You mean she's taken the salt cellar?' and then cries all over again. Martha hustles him into the sitting room, where Neville, shepherded in by Susie and told to 'rest up in here for a bit', takes over occupation of the sofa. He has managed to corral a bottle of wine and he leans forward to top up their glasses. Martha wonders idly whether he's going to drive home to Eliza's or stay over. He sees her looking. 'Bugger arteries,' he says.

It is cosy in here. Geraldine lit a fire earlier and, though it has given the bulk of its performance to an empty room, the embers are still warm. Martha sits in an armchair closest to the grate and nurses her glass. She feels the evening loosen. Conversation, which around the formal dining table had been pinioned, swells and spreads. She can hear Geraldine laughing in the kitchen. Neville and David are sitting opposite her on the sofa. They are both slouched back; they are both supporting one ankle on the other knee. They both seem to be wearing red socks. David laughs at something her father says, and afterwards he gives the collar of his shirt a settling tweak. She realises she is drunk. Her eyes half close and when the room swims, the two men seem to merge for a moment.

She hears her father say, 'Martha seems well, I must say. You must be good for her.' And David nods and looks across at her but then, twisting away, says something she doesn't catch. He turns back and sees her watching. He says, 'Getting your life back in order, aren't I?' and she laughs, curling up her legs and pretending to flick dust off her skirt.

Later, he says, 'Let's get you home, then,' and pulls her out of her chair. Geraldine has gone to bed. In the car, with orange street light on his cheek, David says, 'How about coming down to Chichester with me this weekend? We could leave late Friday and come back early Monday morning and get two full days in. A long walk in the New Forest. A little pootle around Bosham in the boat. Dinner in the Waterman's Arms. An early night. One of Mum's world-famous cooked breakfasts. I know the folks are longing to see you again.'

'What about my "funny little shop"?'

'Can't you close it for one weekend?'

She is not quite drunk enough to forget her responsibilities. She can't keep closing up. She can't ask April to stand in, not now she's pregnant. 'Well . . .' she begins.

David looks at her and smiles expectantly. 'Not really,' she finishes.

David's face stiffens and when he turns the car into her road, the indicator tick-tucks like a sound of disapproval.

*

Shortly after falling asleep, Martha surfaces abruptly, like someone bursting from warm water into cold air, and lies there, next to David, in her Victorian cast-iron bed, wide awake and sober.

At first she thinks it must be the sheets that disturbed her. Drunk and woozy, she had found their love-making infinitely improved. They had undressed each other carefully, and then reached mutual climax with concerted passion. But afterwards, David had nuzzled sleepily into her neck and Martha hadn't liked to ruin the moment by moving him. Now the sheets are damp and cold, and her legs feel sticky. She shifts her buttocks over the bed to a drier patch and scrabbles under the pillow for her nightdress to blot her thighs. But there is something – not April's revelation, which fills her still with confusion, with a kind of murky unhappiness, but something else. She has a sense of discomfort, of being in trouble, of having been caught out, just an unease, but it takes a moment to recall why.

Of course. Fred. It's nothing now she remembers it. In the morning she will go round and explain to Fred how she just happened to end up telling him her father was dead. He is sure to understand. But, for the rest of the night, Martha lies awake in her beautiful bed, next to her perfect boyfriend, in sheets that have dried, smarting with irritation.

chapter twelve

the playroom

'Since, like studies and work-rooms, [playrooms] are
essentially luxury spaces, they can be treated with a
touch of fantasy. So take advantage of the sudden
freedom and play around with the space
without inhibition.'

The Decorating Book
by Mary Gilliatt
(Michael Joseph, 1981)

'WORK?' David says. 'On a Sunday? Can't it wait?' He pulls
Martha towards him. He is sitting at the kitchen table in the
forest-green bathrobe he has unpacked from the small, tight
mock-alligator Mulberry overnight case that arrived with
him. A striped badger shaving brush, an ivory-handled razor
and a wooden pot of lemon-scented soap are already lodged
on the basin, below the Venetian mirror, in the bathroom.
This morning, after her shower, Martha ran the brush across
her cheek. It felt soft and seductive, like a cat's tail.

'OK,' she says, pinioned between his knees. 'I'll do it this afternoon. After our walk.' David likes a walk on a Sunday. It is one of the things he and Martha have in common. They like 'Sunday walks' and 'pub lunches' and 'candlelit dinners', pursuits to be enjoyed in inverted commas, as if ordered by mail order from Blissful Lifestyle Inc. Keith once asked her, years ago, if she and David ever 'just slobbed around'. She had repeated this to David, who had said, 'Slob?', and in his mouth the word sounded indecent. She hasn't seen Karen and Keith for a fortnight now, though she has spoken to them on the phone. Their glimmering disapproval of David – 'her jeweller', as they have started calling him again – engenders new resentment in her. They don't know him like she does.

David releases her and tucks the two edges of his robe into the gap between his legs. 'Now,' he says, 'what about a nice "leisurely breakfast"?'

The flat can't offer much in the line of breakfast, let alone a leisurely one, so Martha throws on some clothes and ventures out for papers and food. Bread, vacuum-packed bacon, orange juice with no bits. The woman in the shop smiles hello at her and Martha thinks, 'Not a single woman in control of my life, but a hunter-gatherer returning to my man.' The concerns about Fred, the need to tidy *that* up, don't seem as pressing in daylight as they did in the sooty shadows of night. She feels cheered up after her orgasm, too (maybe even ready for another one). She will worry about April later. There are piles of crinkled orange leaves in the gutter and she kicks through them cheerfully. Only there are puddles lurking beneath which spray her shoes with muddy water.

When she gets back to the flat, David is dressed and waiting

261

at the kitchen table. While she was out, April had rung, but David tells Martha to ring her back later. In one of his characteristic lurches of impatience, he is keen to get on. They are at Pen Ponds carpark in Richmond Park by noon. David hauls a pair of glossy Hunter wellies out of the boot and takes in a succession of deep breaths, each one followed by a noisy exhalation. 'Fresh air,' he says with satisfaction, as if blowing his own trumpet.

There are dogs and children in the park today. A couple of horses in the distance. Someone is flying a kite in the shape of a cow. David throws his arm around Martha's shoulders. She has forgotten how tiny he could make her feel. When he puts his arm around her like this – which he has always done, out of habit, whenever they walked anywhere – he hunches himself over her so that she slots in beneath him, like a piece in a jigsaw or a pastry cutter within the one the next size up. He is full of good spirits. As they circumnavigate the pond, swollen with fresh rain (as well as Hilly's ashes and Graham's aftershave), he tells her he saw Maddy in the week at a sale of Indian artefacts. She had turned her back on him. 'I feel like such a cad,' he says happily. (Martha finds this revelation and others like it an anti-climax after her month of imagining the girl in his bed.) He has been asked to write a chapter on Cartier for the *Encyclopaedia of World Antiques*. There are rumours that a Middle-Eastern prince is thinking of taking his collection to auction, including a thirty-two-carat pink Agra diamond that might reach a record price. The sky is an insipid blue and the air is still. A tiny plane crosses on the horizon and it takes ages for the miniature roar to reach them. 'Penny for your thoughts?' says David.

When they get back to her flat, she thinks David might have commitments elsewhere, leaving her free to sort her day out, but he doesn't seem to. He digs into the Mulberry bag for his book – a novel, recently shortlisted for a prestigious literary prize, about eighteenth-century settlers in Tanzania – and lies on her Howard sofa in his socks saying things like 'this is the life' and 'what more could one ask?' She makes coffee, cleans the kitchen floor and flicks through the papers. After a while, he gets up, opens a bottle of wine, shuffles through her pile of CDs, chooses Barry Manilow (jesting, 'Ah! Chopin's Prelude in C Minor') and settles back down. Eliza leaves a message on the answer phone wanting to talk about Geraldine. David tweaks Martha's thigh with his toes. 'Go on, give us a massage,' he says. When she goes to the loo, she hears him ringing round trying to get a dinner reservation for eight o'clock. A table for two. She asks him who he's taking. 'You, of course,' he says. 'Who else?'

At four o'clock, the phone goes and she answers for distraction. It's April. She says, 'I'm sorry to keep ringing, but I really wanted to talk to you about the baby and I'm sorry I haven't. It's just been difficult and it was hard to find the right moment.'

Martha takes the phone into the kitchen and sits down at the table. There is a strange dull October light in the room. The weak mauve sky outside the window is full of criss-cross wisps of cloud and aeroplane-trails, as if it doesn't have the strength to fight them off. She says, 'I'm surprised you didn't tell me, that's all.'

April says, 'It's sort of none of your business,' but there's no fight in her voice.

'April. You know, we see each other every day. I thought we were friends.'

'Well – you're my boss.' April says this flatly.

'Just your boss?'

'Come on, don't lay this on me. You're not exactly—' April's voice rises.

'What?'

'Nothing.'

There is a pattern of dirt on the lino by the kitchen table, a half circle of smaller circles. Martha stares at it until she realises it's the mark left on the damp floor by her expensive new trainers. She tries to think of something to say. She doesn't know if she's angry or upset. She feels hollowed out, hopeless.

In the end, she says, 'So, is this chap in Manchester going to stand by you?' and April says, 'Steve's a bit confused' and the name is a surprise to Martha, a shock that she's never heard it. She asks if April loves him, if he's 'the one', and April says, 'whatever that means', sounding years older than she is, years older than Martha. 'I've always wanted to keep it,' she says. 'My mum says I'm too young but I don't care. It's what I want.'

Martha asks where April and the baby are going to live. 'You're going to have to leave the squat,' she says. 'Will you move home?' April laughs again for an answer. 'And what will you do for money? Will Steve be able to support you both?'

This time April is silent. Martha says, 'Of course you can carry on working until the baby comes. I didn't mean that. But after . . .'

April's tone cools again. She says she has to go and hangs up. Martha is left feeling restless and frustrated with herself.

David is still reading his novel – he has a half-smile on his lips. He says, 'Hmm?' when she comes back in, without looking up. She tells him she's going out. She doesn't explain. She simply says she has to see a customer about some toy cars. 'Don't be long,' David says, which she takes to mean he doesn't plan on going anywhere himself.

Fred's pistachio car is parked right outside his house so Martha rattles the letter-box. She is going to say, 'Fred, I am so sorry. There's been a terrible misunderstanding,' and after that they will be friends again and she can ask him what she should do about April. But it isn't Fred who comes to the door; it's a bird-like woman in a velvet shirt and leggings, long grey-blonde hair tied up in a chignon, kingfisher eye-shadow in an arch. The woman, who must be Eileen, Fred's mother-in-law, looks at her without curiosity, then bends and says, 'Don't you dare. In. In.' The cat is trying to make a bolt for the great outdoors.

Martha makes a barrier with her arms and legs and steers him back inside. 'You must be Eileen,' she says. Hazel is hanging on the banisters, and to her, Martha says, 'Hi,' in a high voice.

Eileen smiles half-heartedly. Her lipstick has seeped into the threads of skin above her lips. 'Hello, Martha,' says Hazel. She slides down the stairs to join her grandmother. She has frilly white socks above her sandals. A long strand of pearls dangles from her neck.

Eileen says, 'Can I help you?'

'I'm sorry. I'm Martha, from the antique shop? I just wanted a quick word with Fred if he's in.'

Eileen says, 'I'm afraid –' in the tone of one who isn't – 'he's not here.' There are crinkles of grease where her kirby-grips secure her hair.

'Three-thirty to five,' Hazel says. 'Lucy Kitchener's party. Number fifty-seven. I could have gone, Stan did, only Nan said we could go through Mum's jewellery so I didn't want to. Do you want to see it?' Martha notices there are sparkly paste clip-ons dwarfing Hazel's ears. Her pink T-shirt is too small and the white edging on the collar is grey with over-washing. She is wearing lipstick and rouge too. She looks grotesquely pretty, like one of those American tweenie beauty queens.

Eileen says, 'You could come in and wait if you like.'

'Oh.' Martha looks over her shoulder. The last thing she wants to do is go in to look at Fred's wife's jewellery. 'Maybe I'll just wander down and meet him there. Or actually, maybe I'll come back later.' She backs down the step. 'Thanks.'

'As you like,' says Eileen.

Martha does intend to go home, and maybe not to come back later at all, but she is walking in the direction of number 57 anyway, and as the house gets nearer, her pace slows. When she reaches the house, which has two balloons bobbing disconsolately at the front gate (there were three but one is sagging, wrinkled and deflated, like a used condom), she stops, for curiosity's sake if nothing else. It is a smarter house than average: the paintwork outside is iri-descent white, and the hedge sharply clipped. The curtains in the upstairs windows are swagged. And inside – she can see, as she peers through the privet – there must be enough space to give the front room over to the children. The walls are circus-tented in green and white stripes, the overhead light is an aeroplane in flight. Furniture, which has been pushed to the walls, is elf-sized. Elaborately framed pictures of Babar and Tintin line the walls.

There are no children in evidence. But to one side of the window, perched on a miniature chair with his knees to his chin, is a figure in a flowery shirt and a pinstripe suit. He looks strange because he isn't wearing his glasses. He is leaning forward with his elbows on his knees, in one hand a pot of orange jelly and in the other a cigarette.

Martha goes up the path and leans over the bins to tap on the window. Somehow she hadn't been expecting a costume. Fred looks up. He raises the hand with the cigarette in it, without enthusiasm, like a driver registering automatic thanks to a waiting car. Martha smiles and beckons him over. But he doesn't smile back. In fact he turns away. Stung, she taps again.

'Where are the children?' she says loudly through the glass. 'Have you eaten them?'

He gestures with his head to the back of the house. 'Having tea,' he mouths.

'Fred.' A car goes past. There is a smell of rotting vegetables. 'I want to talk to you.'

'You want to talk to me.'

'Are you going to let me in?'

'What, now?' He's mouthing; she's shouting.

'Yes.'

He frowns and shakes his head. 'Not really a good time, Martha.'

'Fred. Please. I've got to talk to you. I want to say I'm sorry.'

He puts his palms upwards.

'What, you just going to mime at me now?'

He laughs, but not for long. He stands up and comes closer to the window. He says, 'I'm not angry. It doesn't matter. I don't understand you, but er . . . well, that's it. Look, I'm at work here. This is my job.' He takes a last drag on the cigarette and twists it out in the frilly pot of orange jelly.

Martha is right up to the window. She is pressing her fingertips on the cold glass, as if trying to conduct her words through it. 'Please, Fred. Let me explain. About my father, Neville. It just happened. I didn't mean to lie. It wasn't him but my stepfather who died. It was a misunderstanding. A woman was in the shop buying a very expensive armoire and she found out there had been a death and she got the wrong end of the stick and then you came in and . . . it just gathered pace.'

Fred says, 'Why didn't you just tell me? Why did you let me go on thinking it? You had plenty of opportunity.'

'I don't know. I just didn't. It didn't seem worth it.'

He turns away. 'Well, there you go then.'

'No. No. Please . . .' She taps her nails on the window. He is leaning towards her and suddenly he puts his fist against the glass, near her hand. The window rattles in the casement. Martha's hand jumps away.

'Fred. Let me in, Fred. Just for a sec.'

He looks at her and then gets up abruptly, as if impatient. She doesn't know if he is coming or has gone altogether, but a moment later the front door opens. She brushes past the bins. Hullabaloo comes from the house. She says (it is a relief not to have to shout through glass), 'Fred. Fred. I'm so sorry. It was just a misunderstanding.'

'I end up looking stupid,' he says.

Martha smiles. 'I know you do. It's the purple braces that do it.'

Fred pulls back into the house. 'Stop, stop, stop,' she says. 'I'm sorry.' She has her hand on his flowery sleeve. It's a batwing sleeve so he is still several feet away. 'I'm the one who looks stupid. I didn't think it would matter. Everything you said about my father was really helpful. The fact that he was alive not dead stopped mattering. And I didn't think—'

'What?'

'That we'd become friends, I suppose.'

She is still holding on to the sleeve but there is less resistance and she gives it a tug. Fred comes out on to the step. He is standing there, tall and thin and gangly, like a clown on stilts, though he is just a clown in shoes. Big black floppy shoes with black and white striped laces. He seems unfamiliar, someone she's never met before. It is partly the lack of glasses. His eyes look magnified without them. But he is looking at her with grudging sympathy, as if he doesn't want to see her upset.

He says, 'You don't know what you are doing.' His lips, surrounded by chalky make-up, look indecently naked like the lips of someone with a beard. There is a golden fleck of tobacco on one of them. She reaches up to flick it away, and before she knows what she is doing she has stretched up further and put her lips to his mouth. It was supposed to be just a kiss, just an apologetic kiss, a kiss to make him *like her* again, but after a second he starts kissing her back, and his hands are in her hair, and there is rushing in Martha's ears and her stomach turns to liquid, and the kiss goes on much longer than it should do – though not as long as Martha would have let it. Because behind Fred, from out of the kitchen, burbles a stream of small children, chortling and screeching and blowing small trumpets, and here they are tugging at him and jumping up and down, 'Mr Magic, Mr Magic!', and a couple of women have flustered up behind them and are saying, 'Oh, the door, the door.' Fred and Martha separate and he says, 'Come in and wait for me.' And Martha is swept into the house and on to a child-sized chair in the playroom, listening to twenty small children squealing and shouting and screaming at every word Mr Magic utters (or every word he mimes), while inside she is squealing and shouting and screaming herself.

There is only half an hour left. Martha is aware of some juggling and some feather-duster activity and of the hilarity caused when Fred forgets how to clap. She can still taste the nicotine in her mouth. Lucy Kitchener's parents, who are watching from the doorway, are tense with emotions of their own. Fred's routine has holes in it; you can see the wooden rabbit poking out of the bottom of its house when it's sup- posed to have 'gone for a walk'. They are not sure if he has all the children's attention: little Harry there, who is inching his way closer to those 'magic' cooking pots; Sasha, who won't sit still; his own child, sitting separate from the others. But when the children throw themselves sideways on to the floor at any joke that tickles them, Fred looks at Martha across the room and it is as if everything about her has disappeared, apart from the bit of her that looks back at him.

At last, parents arrive, heads cocked, brightly smiling, and the show ends. Somehow Martha is off her chair and nodding politely and helping Fred pass out balloons and cards bearing his details. Then he packs his stuff into his little leather suitcase and his big black magic trolley, and gathers together Stan and his cheque and all his clobber, and the three of them leave the house and start walking down the road.

Stan skips on ahead. He has his hands full of party bag and Ballerina cake. Fred says, 'Were you at least close to your stepfather?'

Martha says, 'No.'

He darts her a look and then shakes his head. To Martha's relief he is smiling very slightly now.

'Um . . . Can I help you with that?'

Fred is having to push his magic trolley thing along with his knees. The bottom shelf keeps slipping off and catching on the pavement. 'I'm fine as I am,' he says.

Stan is way ahead of them now and has disappeared through the front gate of the house. They can hear him at the letter-box, shouting, 'Nan. Twig. They had marshmallow hats!'

Fred says quickly, 'Have you got time for a quick drink?'

Martha says, 'Not really, but OK.'

Fred says, 'I'll just change. Er, clean up. Eileen's here so we can go to the pub. And um . . .' He makes a noise that is like the sound of air being released suddenly through his nostrils.

271

In the hall, he grabs her hand quickly and squeezes. Then he thunders up the stairs and there is his voice and Eileen's voice and, intermingled, high-pitched, complaining, those of Stan and Hazel. After a minute, Fred comes to the top of the landing and calls down. He tells her to wait in the sitting room, that he won't be a moment.

Martha goes in and leans against the back of the marine blue sofa. It doesn't give way softly like feathers, but bows energetically beneath her like foam. She moves away and, clearing some plastic toys (a Barbie with matted hair; a miniature brush with grey bristles), sits down on the edge of the winged armchair.

She tries to breathe properly. She can still feel the pressure of his hand on hers. When she holds it up she expects to see the impression of his thumb on her flesh. A door catches in a draught and slams. She hears the sound of running water overhead. Fred will be in the bathroom, stripping off his magician's outfit, wiping his soft mouth with a flannel. The pipes in the walls crank and gurgle. She imagines him standing in the bathroom, just up those stairs, naked. In the shower, his long, thin, pale body streaming. His bones. The sharp, moving point in his neck. The water stops. She imagines him drying his skin, and dressing. But then, Hazel's T-shirt dashes into her head. With its greying, fraying edges. She remembers the piles of washing that punctuate the stairs. She conjures up (he is not the only magician round here) something drab and holey. Something drab and holey intermingled with children's tatty T-shirts. Y-fronts.

The room feels airless and hot. When she breathes in she has to do so in stages, as if there's an obstruction the air has

272

to get past. In an upstairs room, Hazel is whining. Martha can't hear what she's saying but she can tell from the tone. Nobody has come down. She keeps thinking one of the children is going to burst in, but they don't. She can see the dust on the television screen. On the back of the seat, the imitation-tapestry upholstery is darkened and greasy where someone's head has rubbed. The sides of the sofa are dragged where Kitten must have sharpened its claws. On one corner there is a dent, thick with hair, where he must sleep. There is a stain – ink, felt-tip? – on the carpet by her feet. She pulls the corner of the rug which has flipped over backwards to cover it. The tassels feel matted and grimy.

'No!' Hazel suddenly shouts from upstairs. 'I don't want pizza!'

There is the sound of muttered adult voices. More shrieking.

Martha looks around her at the flesh-pink walls and the huge television; the tat, the toys, the cheap sofa, the cat hairs. Abruptly, she stands up. She makes for the door, and at this point she may only be going to call up, to check that Fred is almost ready, but her eyes fall on the picture on the far wall: the purple horses, the spiked paint, the white-tipped waves crashing on to the shore. Only, in the picture, there doesn't seem to be a shore. It is all choppy and jagged; the horses' feet disappear. There is no still point. And as she stares at it, each brush stroke seems to separate and move until she can't even see the shapes any more, until she can't even see what the picture is. She rubs her eyes and it clears. She can see it now all right. She takes a step back. It is the worst picture she has ever seen in her life. How could

273

anyone like this picture? she thinks. How could anyone *live* with it?

She takes a deep breath. She sees herself from afar, a woman in dryclean-only black trousers (given to her by a handsome, rich, abandoned boyfriend), hanging around in this vile room while a sweet oddbod, an accountant, a *clown*, with whining children and Y-fronts, takes off his baggy trousers. She runs her hands through her hair and smooths it back behind her ears. In the hall, she can hear the sound of a television and small splashes from the bathroom, the staccato sound of a blade in water. Stepping past the bikes and the carrier bags, freeing herself from the snare of hanging coats, Martha Bone opens the front door and closes it behind her.

She walks quickly, then runs past number 57, down the road and around the corner. Her throat hurts with the sudden exertion. She slows. Her stomach clenches with nerves, and dread. Her head is filled with everything she was about to do and everything she has done. She feels sickened. He was right, she thinks: she doesn't know what she is doing.

There are not many phone boxes in this part of residential south London any more, but it happens that Martha is standing by one of the few. It is graffitied and the door is off its hinges. She goes in. Even open, it smells dankly of urine. She has a thought to ring Fred and apologise – *again*; to make another excuse. But the number she dials is Karen's.

Karen answers, sounding harassed. There is the catcall wailing of a tiny baby in the background.

Martha says, 'Karen, do you think I'm just not the mothering type?'

'Er . . .'

'Sorry, is this a bad time?'

'It's not great. Sssh. Sssh.' The catcall has got louder and Karen's voice is jerking up and down.

'I don't know, I . . .'

'Do you want to come round?'

'No. All I mean is . . .'

'Has something happened with David?'

'No! No. Everything's fine.'

'Is this something to do with Nick?' The baby must really be trying Karen's patience because she sounds exasperated.

'Nick? No. I just . . .'

'Look, Matty, can I ring you back? Kit's starving and I can't get my top off when I'm holding the phone.'

'Yes, of course—' Martha's money is running out. They are about to be disconnected anyway. But for a moment she holds the receiver tightly to her ear. It smells of other people's sweat. She can still hear Karen cooing gently to the baby. Gently, of course, because the exasperation isn't directed at Kit but at her. She wants to say something before Karen hangs up, to make it all fine again, but even as she begins to form the words the line has gone dead.

Martha's turmoil lasts until mid-evening. It is only when sitting opposite David in a restaurant by the river in west London, dipping chunks of charred ciabatta into velvety green olive oil, that she begins to put the whole incident into perspective.

David is telling her about a staff reshuffle at his office, while she runs over things in her head. It is not surprising that she and Karen should be distanced from each other. It's just a stage. April *is* a silly girl not to have told her. And as for Fred – she considers the sequence of events carefully and concludes she was the victim of inappropriate emotions: guilt, pity and hysteria. She had over-reacted to the kiss – which was just a kiss, after all – and leapt to certain conclusions regarding Fred's motives, which were, undoubtedly, wildly inaccurate. She had imagined that the drink would lead to some sort of declaration, whereas in truth he probably wanted to sort out the father thing, apologise for over-reacting about that himself, maybe even reopen negotiations with regard to the ongoing clear-out of his attic. In the morning, or maybe later in the week (after all, she convinces herself, there is no hurry – no hurry at all), she will phone him to apologise and explain. She will say something about the lateness, her realisation that his children needed him, about David waiting at home, etc, etc, remind him that he was in the bathroom and she hadn't liked to, well, burst in on him, and that he can bring his bric-a-brac round any time.

Establishing this in her mind, she smiles warmly across the table at David. He puts his hand on hers. He says, 'So what do you think? Are you up for it? Do you think it's a good idea?'

She shakes her head slightly. 'Sorry?'

'Shall I put a word in for you at South Ken? I know they

want fresh, uncynical eyes. Obviously you're not trained in any sense of the word, and we may have to blur your lack of qualifications, but you are very experienced and you can learn on the job.'

'The job?'

'The one I've just been talking about. In Garden Statuary.'

'Oh.' Now he mentions it, various phrases from his conversation parachute into her brain, late but intact. 'Business-getter', 'Recent opening', 'An eye for', 'Angels and urns'.

'Oh, I see,' she says.

'Because honestly, I don't know.' He shakes his head, still smiling. 'It's a dodgy business, isn't it, the old shop? The landlord's clearly being a complete pig. And even if you restructure somehow – get rid of April once she sprogs – you're only going to cover your overheads. And all those odd characters who wander in and out. I don't really like to think of you there on your own, prey to whatever.'

'Don't you?'

He stops smiling and gazes into her eyes. He puts out a finger and traces a line from her forehead over her nose to her mouth. Martha tries to bite it. He still looks serious. 'No. I don't,' he says.

'You are very kind to me,' she says.

He shakes his head. 'No. I'm not.'

He takes the wine out of the silver cooler and tops up her glass and his. Then he wipes his hand – a little wet, probably from the bottle – on his stiff white napkin, and returns it with a clumsy flourish to his knee. And after he has done that, he tells Martha that he loves her, that he

277

realises how much happier he has been since they have been reunited, and that he has been thinking recently how nice it would be if she gave up her bolthole in Balham and came to live with him in his flat in Kensington. He doesn't want to hurry her, but they could reopen negotiations with regard to marriage, maybe even think about starting a family. It would be good, wouldn't it? he says, to get things on an even keel. After all, neither of them is getting any younger and, you know – he gives her a sweet smile – 'Important Clocks' ticking.

Martha hides behind her fringe. She doesn't even look up when he makes this little joke. She can hear the nervousness in his voice. She tears the warm olive bread on her side plate into tiny crumbs. She builds the crumbs into castles. She demolishes the castles with her thumb. There is a piece of loose skin in the corner of her lower lip which she is ripping with her teeth. She wants him to stop talking, but she knows, if he does, she will have to answer. She wants to run out of the restaurant, but she knows, if she does, she'll never see him again. Anyway, what kind of person runs out on two people in one day? What kind of person runs out on people *all the time*? She still has to yank her mind back from Fred. Fred with his washing and the 'I don't want pizza' and the hassle. She realises that David provides her with a structure. He grounds her within her own family. And now he's talking again about starting one of their own. Her heart tightens. Is this how she could start again? In the two years in which they were apart, she was adrift. She has an image of her basement, filled with three-legged tables, chairs with the stuffing spilling out: messy, chaotic, frightening, full of potential, but unfinished. Unfinished business.

So what is holding her back? The images fade and all that's left is the eighteen-year-old Nick Martin. Nick Martin, whom she has forgotten in all this. She lets herself wallow in a moment of sentiment. Nick Martin, her first love, the embodiment of her hopes for the future and dreams of the past, whom she is probably never going to see again.

'So?' David must have sat back because his voice sounds further away than it did. She is going to have to say something. She pushes her fringe aside and glances up and, in doing so, catches the expression on his face. His mouth is smiling, but the rest of his face is still, as if he has to keep it like that or it might crack altogether. And with the tenderness in her that this evokes, it all suddenly seems so simple that she can't imagine what she has been worrying about. The piece of tangled thread that is her life tightens and straightens. The chafing anxieties about the shop, about Fred, about Nick, about April, fall away. With the side of her hand she sweeps the breadcrumbs into a neat line, and says yes.

chapter thirteen

the garage

'Tools become decorative items in their own
right when hung up on the wall.'

Junk Style
by Melanie Molesworth
(Ryland Peters & Small, 1998)

MARTHA peels back the clingfilm and takes in a deep, suspi-
cious sniff. The smell is pungent. It makes her nose tingle. On
the phone, Greg had said he didn't know the recipe himself but
he was sure there was curry powder and raisins and he could
visualise Geraldine wrestling the chicken pieces out of their
skin – using the same arm movements that you need to pull a
child out of its wetsuit – but other than that Martha's guess was
as good as his. You'll have to wing it, he said. 'Ha, ha.' Geraldine
wouldn't be back until the following day. 'She's on retreat,' he
added manfully (or maybe simply loudly to be heard above the
family battle cries around him). 'With her yogi.'

Martha grapples the clingfilm back into place and returns the dish to the satisfyingly bare fridge. She dries the spoon she used for stirring and lodges it in the top of the only remaining open crate on the floor. The bin bag she has used for the last bits of rubbish, she ties up and leaves by the door to take down later. The other bin bag, the one that has lived in her kitchen all autumn, is still under the table. She eyes it guiltily. It looks so huge and cumbersome and heavy, she doesn't know what to do with it. She decides once again to leave it where it is and goes into the bedroom to change. There are two outfits laid on the bed: a simple pale pink sheath dress for the evening (a moving-in present from David), and jeans and T-shirt for the following day. Everything else is in the suitcases lined up on the floor.

The dress is halfway over her head when the phone rings. It is David, who has only been gone a couple of hours, but sounds anxious.

'Everything's fine,' she says.

'And are you sure you don't want to come over here later? Or me to come to you?'

'David, I am sure, honestly. I'd like to spend one more night here on my own.'

The dress has little pearl buttons down one side and she does them up while they are on the phone, pushing each fragile disc into place, one by one, each exquisite, brittle shell representative of David's love and concern, until the fabric is secure and tight around her.

'And you'll be OK at this thing?'

'Yes. I'll be OK.'

'See you tomorrow then. I'll pick you up around midday. I can't wait.'

'I can't wait either,' echoes Martha.

It is a month since David asked her to move in with him and it has taken until now to get herself packed and organised. There seem to have been a hundred and one things to do. There was the job at the auction house to be prepared and interviewed for, David's 'folks' in Sussex to re-meet and re-charm, wealthy clients to impress (mainly at the opera, which is convenient as the education of Martha's musical tastes is one of David's ongoing projects), weekends away to be negotiated. Lots of women, Martha suspects, would pinch themselves if their lover started thrusting City Break brochures at them over the cornflakes, would leap into comparative studies of Vienna v Venice with delight and abandon. She says things like, 'Could we talk about this later?' It seems she had forgotten how pressing David's life could be, how easily squashed her own. Oh, she realises the sense of it – her market friends and auction connections, her feuding sisters, her Sunday routines with Keith and Karen (long fallen by the way-side), so scrappy in comparison to the many engagements with David's godparents, the regular meetings with his colleagues and university crowd, the tickets, the advance bookings. And she knows that his enthusiasm to involve her is evidence only of his commitment. But it still de-mands effort to work out where her own stand should be. She doesn't want to be overpowered, but still less does she want to demonstrate the intransigence that, in Greg's words, 'buggered them up last time'. She just wishes she could clear her head to see what would be best *now* without feeling the pressure of *before*.

And then there is the shop. Two days ago, she received a phone call from Garden Statuary, announcing how charmed and impressed they had been by her knowledge of decorative stone lions and how they would like to offer her the job. She asked to have until Monday to think about it. She has intended to talk it over with David (of course, he will tell her it makes sense: who wants to schlepp from Kensington to Balham every day?), but until now she has put this off.

She should discuss it with April, too, although really it is no longer any of April's business. April has begrudgingly agreed to sublet the flat until the baby is born, at which point she will move in with her mother in north London. Martha has made it clear that from January, professionally it is all up for grabs. An antique shop is no place for a small child. And anyway, in David's phrase, April needs to get her life in order. April seems to concur. An uneasy truce has been established between them. Martha has kept up a ready stream of café doughnuts and kept down demands for painting. She would like them to be friends. (Secretly, she has plans that somewhere along the way, between now and a summer crabbing on a Cornish beach, the two of them will push prams *together* in the park.) But April is increasingly distant. Martha knows it is ridiculous, but she has a strange feeling of abandonment, as if forces outside her are making the decision for her.

The shop, too, seems to know something is up. Martha has done her best to make the existing stock look inviting, but the bulb in a table light at the back keeps flickering, even though she's changed it, and the dried hops that were garlanded across the ceiling have begun unexpectedly to moult: dusty, empty, dried-up seeds scatter the floor as fast as she can clear them. Spaces have begun to materialise: the pile of Welsh blankets is getting low; hooks look jagged with nothing on them. When she closes the door behind her tonight, with the bag of rubbish in one hand, even the bell sounds rusty, as if it is tinkling in reproach.

It is early in November now, the first Saturday after Guy Fawkes Night, and there is a damp, woody smell of bonfire in the air, the smell of old canvas and charred leather. Distant unseen rockets explode like machinegun fire. Karen looks jumpy when she comes to the door. Her face is blotchy and her red hair is pulled back in an untidy ponytail. She is wearing trousers with a drawstring waist and trainers, and carrying a plate of cheese. She greets Martha tensely and then shouts back into the house for Keith: 'Controlled crying. Don't forget. Don't give in.'

Martha, wondering how you regulate a child's crying, says, 'That sounds a bit violent.'

'Desperation,' says Karen through gritted teeth. She puts the cheese into the back seat of the car and gets into the front. 'Why am I letting you do this to me?' she says to Martha.

'Because it will be fun?'

Karen's expression doesn't change.

'OK,' Martha says. 'Interesting.'

'I thought you were done with this nostalgia thing.'

'I know, but they asked. Ages ago. It would be rude not to

go now. And I am intrigued. Aren't you? Don't you have any curiosity about how people have turned out?'

Karen is putting on some lipstick in the overhead mirror. 'Not really,' she says curtly, smacking her lips together. 'Well. Maybe a little bit. But you and I are in different life zones. I don't have the time to think about it. My head is full of the next feed and the next appointment at the clinic and how much Kit has slipped off her growth centile and when I'm next going to get a full night's sleep and whether Keith and I are ever going to have sex again and how I'm going to get rid of this –' aggressively, she grabs the fold of skin above the drawstring – 'and what it'll be like going back to work and is the woman I interviewed yesterday a better childminder than the woman I'm seeing tomorrow?'

Martha has put the moment in the phone box out of her mind. But it comes back to her now with a stab.

Karen catches Martha's expression. In the same sharp tone as before, she says, 'We haven't seen you for weeks.'

Martha says, 'I know, I've been . . .'

'David keeping you busy?'

'Yes. I . . .' What should she say? Should she say something now? Martha flails for words, but they all seem too dangerous. Words seem to break things. Isn't it better just to leave things as they are, to let them mend on their own? Haven't they been friends long enough to allow resentments to flow past unspoken?

'Well, drop in sometime. It's not easy having a small baby, you know. It's pretty bloody lonely.'

There is a pause. Martha says, 'I'm sorry.'

'It's OK.' Karen dabs on some blusher, her face at an angle.

She hesitates for a moment and then says, 'You're right. This do will be fascinating. You look smart, by the way. We'll have a laugh.'

So Martha turns the key in the ignition and drives them to Jane Pritchet's house in Wimbledon. 'Jane Pritchet, now a midwife at St George's,' she explains, putting lots of jolliness in her voice to clear the air. 'She used to play goal attack, straight blonde hair, flat chest – you remember.' Martha parks in a road of semi-detached mock Tudors. 'She married Phil Dunston from the boys' school.'

'And Phil: remind me?'

'He was the one who rang and booked cabs for members of staff that time. There was a row of black taxis outside and cross drivers saying, "Car for Mr Beasley. School to the VD Clinic," and Mr Beasley had to be called out of a science lesson to sort it out.'

'Oh yes.' Karen snaps the mascara brush back into its tube and tries out a lipsticked smile in the rear-view mirror. 'And now what?'

'I don't know. We'll find out.'

One press on the doorbell causes a cascade of bells, and they wait, clutching their bowls like votive offerings, until the door opens to reveal a thin girl with blonde hair and regular features who looks like Jane, but who is only about seven. 'In there,' she utters with contempt, gesturing them to the back of the house before throwing herself into a room to the left of the door where she is eating Hula Hoops and watching *Baywatch*.

Karen and Martha look at each other. Karen makes a snorting noise. The hall, all brass wall-lights and concealed radiators, smells of heat and garlic. There is chatter and the occasional shriek over Ian Dury.

Martha says, '"New Boots And Panties"?'

'Sounds like,' Karen answers, and Martha realises it's going to be all right between them after all.

Karen pushes Martha slightly ahead of her. She has her fingers at her back like a gun.

The pine-clad kitchen is packed with people. Everyone seems outsize, not ghosts at all, but solid, fleshy, larger even than they should be. Martha stands at the door, with Karen just behind her. She sees features that are shockingly familiar to her: the hump-bridge of a nose, a dewy rosebud mouth, a harshly sloping chin. At first it seems as if these encumbrances have been kidnapped by strangers, by cartoon characters, but slowly her eye adjusts to the new shape of their owners – thinner, or fatter, more hair, less hair, greying, dyed; male eyebrows hedging, female eyebrows plucked – and their names tumble like a rollcall into her brain. Each name seems hilarious, a comedy routine in itself. Amy Blanche, Mark Leonard, Susan Painter, Danielle Lawrence, Jane Pritchet. She recognises her emailer, Susan Doughty (*Sasha* Doughty now) by the unco-ordinated enthusiasm of her movements – clicking and jerking her fingers to 'Hit Me With Your Rhythm Stick'. She is talking to someone who might be Phil Dunston, only his face is plumper and rounder as if the years have slowly inflated him. She sees the glistening bald head of first boyfriend Simon Fletcher in the distance. He throws it back as he laughs, his airline pate hitting the light, and she moves sideways so as to be off radar.

Jane Pritchet, at the breakfast bar tearing clingfilm off similar bowls to theirs, looks up. Her blonde hair is mahogany and determinedly short, with a jagged fringe. She is wearing a school tie and a gymslip over long school socks. Her face lights up when she sees them, but artificially so, in the manner of a Christmas tree in an overdecorated room. 'Hiya!' she calls. 'Look, everyone – Martha and Karen are here!'

Everyone is busy elsewhere, but Martha hears herself say, 'Hiya!' back.

Karen eyes the gymslip and says, 'Well, Jane, you're certainly in the spirit of things.'

They hand her the Coronation Chicken and the cheese. 'Fantastic!' says Jane. 'Yum. Yumm. How perfect. What a spread!' Her front teeth have been capped since school. It makes her seem artificial, like a doll of herself. She is jerking her shoulders back and forth enthusiastically, acting up, allowing no pause for embarrassment. They are a reproach to their scornful young selves. Jane says, conspiratorially, 'Isn't this mad? Isn't this wild? What are we doing here?' Karen begins to back out of the door, elbows braced for escape. The three of them laugh. Jane narrows her eyes. 'Let's just nick some food and run.' Even if you've put on school uniform, even if you've organised the whole thing, it seems it is important to stand back from this. Martha wonders if the whole room is doing the same, as if they are all pretending it is someone else's school reunion they are gate-crashing. They are all here by default. Jane dips her finger in the chicken and adds, 'Hm. Spicy!'

Sasha Doughty spots them then and comes straight over. She greets them warmly, sings, 'Hit me! Hit me! Hit me!'

along with the music and then puts her head on one side, joke-accusingly, at Martha and says, 'That lunch, huh? What happened?' Martha says, 'Oh I know. Sorry.' And Sasha says, 'Next time: you, me and a cheesy quiche – it's a date.' And Martha says, 'You bet.'

Karen says, 'So what happened to Susan?'

'Well, I just always hated being Susan and one day I woke up and said to myself, "Susan, you can be anything you like, anything in the world." So here I am. I'm much happier. If people don't like it they know where they can stuff it. HIT ME!' She wiggles her shoulders.

Karen laughs. Martha is glad because she finds she likes Sasha, too. 'Good for you.'

Martha goes to get them a drink. Phil Dunston, who has short brown hair, cut in a fringe high across his brow like a scull-cap, and one of those faces that starts off bold and disappears, a big forehead and a little chin, is officiating at the bowl of punch. There is a suspiciously large range of spirit bottles by his side. He says, after he has kissed her with an enthusiastic, loud smack, 'School cup all right for you?'

'You mean . . .?'

'Yep. It seemed important to be authentic.'

'We'll all be puking in the lavs.'

'As I said, it seemed important to be authentic.'

'Oh all right then. But mainly cherries and orange segments. I'm driving.'

'Bit of a top up, Ange?' Jane calls over to her from the other side of the room.

Phil remembers Martha – 'little shy thing, weren't you?' – but wants mainly to hear about her sisters, especially Eliza.

Everyone always wants to hear about Eliza. She fills him in on Eliza's job. 'Cor, yes,' he says when Martha tells him Eliza whips financial institutions into shape, 'I bet she does.'

She is hearing about his job as an engineer for British Telecom when there is a small commotion at the door and Tracey Richards spirals into the room, wearing a tight pencil skirt and fishnets, and clutching a tub of supermarket houmus. 'I've parked over a drive,' she shrieks. 'Does it matter? Bloody nightmare, parking round here! And anyway where *are* we? *Sutton?* Darling, move!'

Phil says, 'Who the hell is that?' and Martha tells him it is Tracey Richards and he says, 'What, mousy Tracey Richards?' and she says yes, probably that's true, but that the mousy Tracey Richards has long been swallowed up and that she has her own PR agency now. He sighs and says, 'God, her too? So everyone's in PR, are they?' Martha smiles, studying the brown streaks on his teeth. Then there is a tap on her shoulder and she turns to see Amy Blanche from her French set. Amy and Martha were never particularly friendly, but Amy, who has a flat, colourless face and almost no chin (and an unforgettable habit of talking French with her mouth puckered up like a cat's bottom), paws at her as if they had been bosom buddies. 'I see you noticed Tracey Richards's big entrance,' she says, rolling her eyes. 'Who didn't?' She steers herself round so that her back is to Tracey and says, 'Look at the length of her skirt. You can practically see her knickers.' Martha still smiles. Amy adds conspiratorially, 'Single and childless at thirty-eight. Sad, isn't it? She always was desperate for a man.'

Martha says, 'I don't know about that.'

Phil says, 'Nice legs, actually.'

Amy ignores this and sings, 'Clock ticking.'

Martha says, 'Important Clocks.'

Amy says, 'Anyway, what about you? Sash tells me you work with the homeless – what a good person you must be – and that you've got a tiny baby. Aren't tiny babies to die for? You just wait till they grow up. Mine are such a handful. I'm in catering. Well, freezer meals mainly. Shepherd's pies. Toads in the hole. Family meals, for the busy working mum. Ironic, huh? There I am slogging my guts out to make things easier for others.'

Martha says, 'No, that's the other one. That's Karen. I'm Martha, and I don't have a baby and I'm not a good person and I run a shop.' Then, over Amy's shoulder, she calls, 'Tracey, how lovely to see you.'

Tracey, who has been enthusing all this time to Jane about the house ('So retro-fashionable, mock Tudor'), says, 'Martha!' and crosses over to kiss her on both cheeks.

Martha says, 'Save me,' in her ear and, without missing a beat, Tracey says, 'Oh my God: John! Martha, look, it's John. Come and say hello to John with me.' And, with her ringed hand on Martha's elbow (and whispering, 'What are we doing here?' in her ear), she whisks her over to the other side of the room where a solitary man in a button-down shirt tucked so tightly into his jeans it looks gathered is closely investigating a bowl of Pringles. 'John!' Tracey cries.

The man straightens up. There are crisp crumbs on his lower lip. Brushing the tips of his fingers against each other, he says, 'It's Mervyn, actually.'

'Of course. Mervyn! It's been . . .'

Over by the school cup, Amy and Phil are still staring at them.

Tracey says, 'Years. Years at least.'

Martha says, 'Gosh, yes. Mervyn.' She is racking her brains. 'We were in the school play together, weren't we?'

Tracey says, 'Mercutio. You played Mercutio.'

'No. It was Lysander. He was Lysander. Weren't you the history master's son?'

Mervyn clears his throat. 'Er. I don't think I've ever met either of you before,' he says. 'I went to school in Worcestershire. I'm only here because I'm married to Amy.'

Amy, who has materialised at their side, takes a sip of punch from a polystyrene cup and says, 'Have you met my husband? I know no one else has brought theirs, but I hate driving at night. We are a bit in the wilds of Oxfordshire. And we always get a babysitter on Saturdays, and it seemed a shame to waste her. It's so important to have time on your own when you have children. You'll find that, both of you, if you ever . . .'

Martha and Tracey exchange glances and move gently away towards the door to the garden. It is open and outside in the dark, on the patch of leaf-strewn lawn, by the climbing frame, is a gang of smokers. They are definitely a gang. The smokers in their school always were. Martha sees Zach Wilson and Kath Wren. There are swirling haloes above their heads. She can't be sure but she thinks Zach (expelled, if she remembers rightly, for harder offences) puckers his mouth and blows a smoke ring. She asks Tracey if she thinks really cool people go to school reunions and Tracey says, 'Darling, we're here, aren't we?' and gives her a kiss on the cheek.

A man on the outskirts of this group appears to be staring at Martha. He narrows his eyes when she notices him and puts his head on one side. He is wearing jeans and a green T-shirt. She smiles questioningly and he makes his way over. 'I know you,' he says. He is good-looking, with nice eyes, but with that bullet-marked skin that comes after bad acne. Tracey digs a fingernail into the top of Martha's leg.

'Do you? I don't . . .'

'Yeah. I do. Um . . . I think you went out with a friend of mine?'

'Did I?' Martha thinks she might be going red. 'Were you at the boys' school?' Now she comes to look closely, he does seem familiar.

'Yeah, I was. I stayed down a year. But Nick? Nick Martin?'

Nick Martin. The room goes still. 'Yes I did.'

'I lived next door. I remember you coming round a lot. You had much longer hair and you used to flick it all the time.'

Tracey says, 'The elusive Nick Martin.'

Nick's next door neighbour turns to her now and says, 'So did you go out with someone I knew, too?' and Tracey says, 'Wouldn't you have remembered if I had?' and he laughs. When he stops, she says, 'Actually I had specs then and late-onset braces so you probably wouldn't.'

They introduce themselves. He is called Andrew Young and he is a fashion photographer.

Martha says, 'So, um, do you . . . ever see him?'

'Who?'

Tracey says for her, 'The elusive Nick Martin.'

Andrew Young feels in his back pocket for a box of matches and lights up. He nods as he inhales. Then he lets the smoke out slowly and says, 'When he's in the country.'

Martha's throat feels dry. 'When he's in the country?' she repeats.

'Yeah. You know he's an economic advisor? After his Ph.D. at the LSE, he went into local government. Now he advises goverments all over the place. For a long time he was in America. I'm not sure where he is now.'

Martha says casually, 'And is he married and settled down? A string of kids behind him?'

'Not last time I heard. Still single. Still looking for Ms Right.' He gives Martha a beady look. 'Maybe you broke his heart.'

Tracey says, 'And do you have a number for him? That's what we really want.'

'Er.' Andrew feels in his pocket, brings out a battered wallet and flicks through the cards in one of the slots. 'Er . . . no, not on me. But I can get one.'

'That would be nice,' Martha says.

Food: that's what she needs. And there does seem to be a bustle at the breakfast bar. People are breaking from their groups, their cliques, and have begun to mill in that direction. Karen, who is standing in a makeshift queue behind Simon Fletcher, is gesticulating at her to come over. Martha leaves Tracey and Andrew, who appear to have discovered a whole slew of mutual acquaintances, and joins her. She has to exchange a few words with Simon (she asks politely after his wife and kids; he tells her Carol has had a new coil fitted and little Ali has just got her BAGA grade 4, which is a little more than Martha wanted to know). But then he is coaxed away by a circular platter of dips and she says softly in Karen's ear, 'That man over there, who is called Andrew, still sees Nick Martin.'

'Really?' Karen spins round. There are two wet circles on her shirt.

'Yes. What's that?'

'What?'

'That? Have you spilt your drink?'

Karen looks down. 'Oh bugger. I'm leaking.'

'You're leaking?'

'Milk.'

Martha pulls off her cardigan and wraps it gently around Karen's shoulders.

Karen says, 'It's all this telling everyone about the baby. I start lactating.'

Martha, who is still adjusting the cardigan, says quietly, 'Do you love her that much? I mean, is it just extraordinary how much you love her?'

And Karen looks at her for a moment and says that yes, it is, that you can't imagine what it's like, and smiles at her.

But they have reached the front of the queue and become temporarily separated on the conveyor belt of choice and exclamation ('Lethal garlic bread!' says Jane. 'Don't go kissing anyone tonight!'), before joining the flow towards the sitting room. On the stairs, Jane and Phil's daughter is having an altercation with her father. She says, 'Oh, do I have to go to bed? That is so, like, uncool.'

Tracey and Andrew pass, with their coats over their arms. Martha asks them where they're going and Tracey says, 'Pub. We just need something a bit stronger, or actually something a bit less strong. We'll be back in a while. Come. If. You. Want.' She widens her eyes and fixes them on Martha, as if to say, Make. Sure. You. Don't.

Andrew says, 'Hey, about that number. I'll dig it out and pass it on to Jane and Phil.'

Martha, casually, says, 'Sure.'

The sitting room is full of chairs and floor cushions, but all are taken except for an empty place on one of the two sofas. Karen heads purposefully in this direction and perches on the arm next to the empty place which she leaves for Martha. But on the other side of it, thigh to thigh like an engaged couple in their first meeting with the vicar, are Amy and Mervyn. Martha winces at Karen and diverts just in time. Instead, she finds a little corner on the floor between some chairs where she sits and eats happily for a while, listening to the scraps of conversation around her. In the kitchen it was do-you-remember-so-and-so? and reminiscences about lesbian games teachers and Seventies bomb scares, pranks, bunkings off, sexual and chemical experiments. Now those memories appear to have been exhausted. On one sofa a man and a woman, who may twenty years before have put their tongues in each other's mouths during 'Nights in White Satin', are discussing bedwetting in the under-fives. On cushions by the fireplace it is the price of houses in south Wimbledon. And on the far sofa, Karen, Amy and Merv are deep into the pros and cons of speed bumps.

Martha is chasing the last chilled grain of rice salad around her paper plate when she hears someone say, 'Budge up,' and Sasha sits down next to her. Sasha says, 'Trust you to skulk in a corner, spying on everybody! You dark horse, you,' and then launches into how Karen had told her all about Martha being reunited with her ex and how absolutely romantic that is. After that she provides a whispered running commentary on all the people Martha can't remember. 'That's Hilary Blount on the settee, who used to run the bridge club. She's talking to Philip Merant – he used to have a Mohican which is why you probably don't recognise him. Oh, coming in now and sitting next to Karen is Phil – you know him. He and Jane have been married for yonks and yonks. I'm surprised you weren't at the wedding. What a lovely do that was. You've never seen such a wonderful finger buffet.

'Oh and look, there's – sshh. She's coming this way.' She breaks off.

Martha looks up. Standing above them in a frilly cream shirt is a woman with hair tucked behind her ears and the expression of someone who is waiting for something to happen, or for something to be brought to them. Martha says, 'Hello,' politely, and then, with delayed recognition, 'Oh, Tessa!' And Tessa (who used to sit next to her in history and draw pictures of her gerbils in the margins of her First World War workbooks) squeezes down on to the floor and says, 'I'm not hungry, but it is wonderful to be here, to see all these old faces and to know that people are settled and happy in their own lives.'

'Speak for yourself,' says Martha.

Tessa clasps her skirt around her knees and says, 'I am. I have Jesus.'

It is quite loud in the sitting room now. Phil has put more music on the stereo. Martha says, 'You have Jesus?'

'Yes. I do. I am in God's church.'

297

Martha says, 'God's church. That's nice.'

Sasha, leaning across and only half hearing over the lyrics of a Madness song, says, 'Oh, are you? Active in the church, I mean. Yes, we are too. Or rather I am. I find it very hard to get my husband out of bed in the morning. It was the primary school that got me into it first. You have to "attend" or at least show your face once in a while to get your child in, bloody nightmare at first, but you know, actually, I find it helpful. It gives me a framework for life in general. There I am pootling along and I think, what would God do now? Hm . . . he'd let that green mini in at the lights, that's for sure. And he'd give hubby the cup of tea in the nice mug while keeping the chipped one with too much milk in for himself. That's the terrible thing about marriage. When you start off you always give your other half the nicest helping – the biggest plate of shepherd's pie or the one with the crispiest portion of cheesy topping. But after a bit, you start thinking, Hm, maybe I'll have that one and he can have the slightly smaller helping with the burnt bits. Human nature, I suppose. Anyway,' she smiles brightly, casting around, 'what were we talking about? Oh yes. The Church.' She smiles at Martha. 'Well, you know me, I'm anyone's for a coffee morning.'

Martha laughs. Tessa says, 'I've converted to Catholicism, but it isn't enough for me. There isn't enough Bible study. The Catholic church is bread and water and I need meat.'

Sasha says, 'One of the lovely things about where we live is the organic farmshops. I don't know where I'd be on Sundays after all that holiness without my organic lamb shoulders.'

298

Martha is beginning to enjoy herself, but Karen is trying to catch her eye. She is standing with Phil by the door now. She calls, 'Martha. Phil's got something to show us. Come over here quickly.'

Sasha says, 'Ooh. Interesting. Wonder what that is!' Martha squeezes her hand, tells her she'll be right back, and steps across a trail of plates and legs to Phil and Karen.

Karen says, 'I thought you might need saving. I've already had the meat and veg treatment. There's only so much a soul can take.'

'Oh I see. I'm all right.'

Karen says, 'Phil has got something special to show us in his garage.'

'Oh really?'

'Yep,' says Phil.

'I asked him if he had any secret passions and he said this.'

'Passion,' says Phil, 'is an understatement.'

They follow him back into the kitchen and to a door at the side. Jane, who is eating with a group at the table, says, 'Oh no, Phil. You're not!'

'I am,' he says.

'Oh, Phil.' Jane tuts loudly and dramatically, a woman with no time for her husband's foolishness. She rolls her eyes at the people she is with, as if to announce that others may be taken in by him, but not her. Martha finds this moment infinitely touching: a gesture that looks like contempt, but is actually love.

Phil has unlocked the door, pushed it open and stretched his arm in to turn on a switch. He stands aside for Karen and Martha to go in first. 'Da-la,' he says.

The garage is as clinically clean and organised as a pathology lab. There are rows of shelves for boxed implements and ointments and lines of jars filled with nuts and bolts. The walls are painted white and the floor is pristine concrete. But in the middle of it, where you might expect a body to be, is a big pink car.

Karen says, 'It's a car! You've got a car in here. A garage with a car in it, how amazing. You devil, you.'

'This —' says Phil, running his hands over the shiny chrome strip along the side — 'is no ordinary car. This is a 1956 Ford Crown Victoria. 312V8. In sunset coral and colonial white. Fully automatic. Power steering, power brakes.'

Karen laughs. 'It's just a car,' she says. 'A big old American car.'

'You may say that,' Phil spits on his finger and rubs a tiny mark on the wing, 'but you would be wrong. This is an extremely rare, valuable classic motor. In prime working order. There are people who would kill to get their hands on this car. You could take this car out of the garage right now and drive it anywhere you wanted and it would get you there in style, comfort and without a hitch. It could drive from Albuquerque to Oklahoma City, from Baltimore to Philadelphia . . .'

Karen remarks that she doesn't think Baltimore to Philadelphia is very far.

Martha says, 'But would it get Mr Beasley from School to the VD Clinic?'

'Anyway,' Karen says, 'you told me you never took it anywhere.'

Phil runs a hand over the wing where the mark was.

'That's true. It is my little piece of perfection. My little slice of history. I want to keep it safe. Five minutes out there in the real world and it'd be scrap iron. You'd have some wanker run a key down the side or bash into the back in a parking space. No.' He shakes his head and makes a satisfied clicking noise with his tongue. 'My little baby's staying here.'

Karen, solemnly, says, 'She's very lovely. You should be very proud.'

Phil is gazing at the car as if he could do so all night. 'I mean, look at those fins.'

Martha shakes her head. 'Fins ain't what they used to be.'

Karen, says, 'It's the fin end of the wedge.'

Martha says, 'These foolish fins . . .'

Karen throws her arms out. 'Remind me of you.'

Phil doesn't seem to hear them. 'One day,' he says, 'if we move to a house with a bigger garage, I'm going to get a 1949 Buick Roadmaster.'

He turns to go back to the kitchen, with Karen, still grinning, behind. But Martha doesn't follow immediately. She stares at the car for a moment longer. It looks ridiculous in this small, neat garage, like a beached blancmange or a huge pink balloon that has floated away from a carnival float and become entangled in the chimney of a factory. She is reminded for a moment of the man Jason brought along to the shop and his passion for Lesneys.

Karen says, 'Are you coming?'

Martha says yes. But she looks over her shoulder one more time and she can't help thinking there is something marvellous about it, too. This isn't an object that has been imbued with sentimental value like her mother's furniture or 'The Boy', it's not a memento or an antique like the ones that layer up her own life, that shore up her sense of self. It is just a hobby, something kept alongside but separate from Phil's life: a piece of 1950s America behind a garage door; a sunset coral and colonial white vehicle of stationary dreams; a glorious piece of nostalgia kept safely in a box.

On the way home, lounging in the passenger seat of Martha's Volvo, Karen says that she had a marvellous time and that she is delighted she went. She is full of chat: at how extraordinary that formerly gerbil-loving, now Jesus-loving Tessa has become; how hilarious she found Sasha, though she remembered Susan, the previous incarnation, as being a pain. The dullness of Phil – the beer gut on him. The cleavage on Tracey. The new hair on Jane. Isn't it amazing, she says, how people have changed?

Martha laughs and agrees, but privately she doubts if it's true. She wonders if they haven't just become more of the same, if they all haven't just plodded along some predestined path. The cool ones were still the cool ones, the geeks the geeks, the ones somewhere in the middle still, like Martha and Karen, somewhere in the middle.

And hadn't Martha sat watching everyone as she always had? There are people who have definite outlines and others who seem porous, temporary. Phil had said Martha was shy, Sasha had called her aloof, and for a moment, with both of those people, that is how she saw herself. And then, just before they left, she had been collared by Amy who wanted to wish Martha luck 'in her new life'. She made a club-secret joke about storks and 'elderly primigravidas' and a canny card-passing reference to future freezer meals. Martha said, 'News travels fast,' and was left with a scratchy, uncomfortable feeling, like she was wearing a coat that was too tight under the arms.

They have been driving along quiet, dark, empty residential streets, but she turns now into Wimbledon High Street where there are lights and pubs closing and Saturday night revellers idling on pavements. She stops at a pedestrian crossing, to let some people cross, the gearstick round and definite beneath her hand.

Karen has sagged back in her seat, her eyes half-closed, but with a leap of animation, lunges forward and cranks down the window, letting in a shaft of night air, of burnt leaves and sulphur. There is the crackle of fireworks in the distance. 'Cooeeee,' she calls, leaning out. She must be drunk. Goodness knows how many school cups she has sunk.

The lights change. Martha puts the car into gear and starts driving off. 'Careful,' she says.

Karen swings back into the car, breathless from the sudden chill or activity. 'Did you see them?' she says. 'Look. They're still there. Behind us.'

Martha briefly turns round. In the sky, a firework shatters. Beneath it, on the pavement, Tracey and Andrew stand hip to hip, their surprised faces turned in the direction of Karen's shout.

Martha says, 'Oh.'

Karen yanks up the window, sealing the air inside. 'I love a happy ending,' she says.

As it turns out, Martha doesn't spend 'one last night' in her flat. When she draws up outside her friends' house, Karen flounders around in her pockets, says she has forgotten her keys and decides it's all right to rouse Keith.

He comes to the door looking tousled and bemused in bare feet and a towelling bathrobe. He doesn't seem annoyed. He smiles affectionately when he sees Karen leaning against the doorframe and says to Martha, 'Don't go. Come in and tell me everything.' They sit in the kitchen for an hour or so, with Karen saying things like, 'I love all those people. I think we should see them all the time. Martha, why don't we see them all the time? Jane and I think we should have a reunion every month. The next one's here. What do you say? And then after that, yours! And then after that, here again! Lots of lovely lovely reunions.' Martha says to Keith, 'There was punch called school cup. It was very authentic.' To Karen, she says gently, 'There's usually a reason why you stop seeing people. Remember?'

Karen lolls back in her chair. 'You're one to talk. Ms Meet My New Ex.'

Martha laughs but doesn't say anything. Karen moves on to Tracey and Andrew, how they had seen them kissing from the car and how wonderful it was that the reunion had been the trigger for romance.

Keith says, 'Old flames reignited over the school cup?'

Karen nods gaily, but Martha adds, 'Except they weren't old flames. In fact this was the first time they'd met.'

Keith says, 'Oh I see. New love from out of the ashes then. The school reunion as blind date.'

It is warm and cosy in Karen and Keith's kitchen, and even the sound of the baby wailing in the distance doesn't ruin it. Martha is initiated into 'controlled crying' – making one or two of the ten-minute checks herself – and with it, into a different sphere of understanding. The constancy of her friends comes as a surprise to her – a surprise that they are still here, adapting, despite her neglect. The strength of her feelings takes her aback. Karen says, when it's Keith's turn to go upstairs, 'So do you think you and David might start a family?' and Martha, who has picked a muslin off the back of the chair and has folded it neatly into squares, breathing in the smell of talcum powder and milk, says yes she thinks they will. 'What about Nick Martin?' says Karen, and Martha laughs. She says she has put him out of her mind. A little later, Karen, who is beginning to fade, asks if she wants to spend the night. There is no real reason to – it is a short drive from Putney to Balham and Martha has only drunk a couple of orange segments – but the offer is held out like an olive branch and suddenly her flat, the floor a shifting sea of suitcases and boxes, seems an unattractive prospect, and she grabs it.

In the night, as she lies on the sofa in her friends' house – this work in progress – she realises she lied to Karen. Nick Martin is all over her head. He is, finally, only two phone calls away. She is moving in with David the following day. There is a future unfolding before her involving muslins of her own and Cornish beaches. The light springing off wooden floors. White linen on a mahogany bed. Surely, she tells herself, it is wrong to think of her and Nick as somehow linked, that she only got back with David when she gave up hope. Until a month or so ago she hadn't thought about him for years. She remembers the constriction she felt when Amy welcomed her into the bosom of convention. It must be something to do with that. She must resist it. She tries to concentrate on David. She remembers him quizzical at Geraldine's wedding, intrigued by her 'aloofness' (but aloof himself: talking down to her as if she were a child), and on holiday together, the weekend he 'showed' her Rome. It was spring and the plane trees that lined the streets were spraying out seeds; it was like confetti, but Martha's eyes streamed. Christmas with his parents. There was a fire and sherry and cards hanging on ribbons on the back of every door. Martha, edgy with the need to be helpful, cut the carrots not into batons but coins. David's mother breathed in sharply. 'I'm sure they'll taste just the same,' she said.

Will they go there this Christmas? No, they will spend it 'at home'. They will pull a tree, tall enough to reach the ceiling, back through snowy streets. They will strew his flat with garlands of ivy and fir cone, cinnamon stick and gilt. They will stab oranges with cloves. The decorative possibilities are endless. Martha falls asleep with thick, buttery church candles flickering in her head.

chapter fourteen

the doorstep

'The door is both the first thing a visitor sees on entering your home and the last thing on leaving . . . Yet most of us seem to take no notice of them.'

Contemporary Details
by Nonie Niesewand
(Mitchell Beazley, 1992)

THE SHOP feels cold when Martha, wearing her pink sheath dress and carrying a plate of devastated Coronation Chicken, opens the door early the following morning. It is drizzling, but lightly, so that the rain doesn't so much fall as buzz irritatingly around your head like midges. Behind her the street is empty, but has a sordid lived-in air. There are pieces of market debris – squashed fruit, rotten vegetables – in the gutter. Someone has left an empty carton on the pavement by the step and it has dissolved into soggy grey crumbs. Martha wants to shut it outside, but when she closes the door, the smell of mildew drifts in with her, seeps into the joints of the furniture.

Her flat, in its state of suspension, doesn't welcome her either. She takes off her pink dress, has an unsatisfactory shower (too late she realises she has packed her new Lime Blossom soap), puts on her jeans and chooses some music to cheer herself up. Reluctantly, she passes over Andrew Lloyd Webber's *Aspects of Love* in favour of *The Puccini Experience*, a CD she has bought in honour of David. She potters about the flat, stripping the bed, cleaning drawers, scrubbing the bathroom.

She doesn't hear the bell at first. Or if she does her ear tells her brain it is part of *Madame Butterfly*. But after a while, the ringing peels away from the music and she realises that it must have been going on for a while. She clatters down the stairs, assuming it is David, come to roll up his sleeves. But outside the front door is her nephew Ivor, in shorts and a T-shirt and no coat.

'Hello,' she says. The sight of him is both normal and unexpected, like the discovery of a pair of shoes on the pavement or a child's soft toy on a railing. 'What are you doing here? Where's everyone else?'

He mutters something.

She looks up the road. It's empty. 'What did you say?'

'At home,' he says.

Martha's confusion rubs against something rough, creating a little spark of panic. Nothing is in the right place this morning. 'What do you mean, "at home"? Who are you with?'

Ivor kicks at the dissolved carton on the pavement. He says truculently, 'Nobody.'

Martha grabs his shoulder. 'God, you're soaked,' she says.

'What's the matter? What's happened? Who knows you're here?'

He mutters something else.

She pulls him into her shop and bends down. She puts her other hand on his other shoulder to make him face her. 'What?'

'No one.'

'What do you mean?'

'I've run away.'

'Fucking hell.' Martha stands up and heads for the shop phone.

Ivor looks up at this. 'NO, DON'T.'

She pauses, her hand on the receiver. 'Don't be ridiculous.' She feels a bolt of irritation towards him. 'They'll be going out of their minds with worry.'

Ivor kicks his shoe backwards against the door. 'They won't even have noticed,' he says. 'They think I'm at football.'

'Well, I'm going to ring them anyway.' She starts dialling. There is the sound of the door. Ivor is halfway out. 'Come back right now.'

Ivor pauses, his hand on the handle. His teeth are gritted. 'If you ring them I'm going.'

Martha has a moment of indecision. She could still ring them and physically make him stay. He is only a child after all. A weak one at that. But she sees him rub his eyes, leaving a smear of dirt across one cheek. On his feet are football boots. She thinks of him hobbling all the way here, and softens. 'OK. Look. Come upstairs. Let's get you warm. Are you hungry?'

She continues to fire questions at him as they climb the stairs. Greg had left him at football – a drop-in club at the local park – but he had slunk off before the coach noticed him. He caught a train at Kingston – 'no one looks at your ticket on Sundays' – and had meant to go to Victoria but the guard was coming so he jumped out at Clapham Junction. He got through the barriers by sticking close to a couple with suitcases. And then he walked. He remembered the way from the time they visited that playground on the Common. The rubbish one that doesn't have swings.

Martha says, 'You walked all the way here from Clapham Junction?'

'Yes.' He still looks defiant, but also as if he might be about to cry.

'You must be exhausted.'

Martha strips Ivor of his sopping clothes, puts them in the tumble-dryer and runs him a bath. It must be hotter than he is used to, because when he first gets in – lowering his thin, pale limbs – for a few minutes he sits very still, with an expression of concentration on his face. She leaves him and goes downstairs to use the phone in the shop.

'Hello yes?'

'Katrina. It's Martha, Geraldine's sister. I've got Ivor here. Is Geraldine or Greg there?'

'Ivor is at football?'

'No. No. Katrina. Can you get me Geraldine? Or Greg?'

'No one is here now.'

'OK. Katrina. Listen carefully. This is important. Can you understand me? Tell me if you don't.'

'OK.'

'Ivor. Is. Here. With. Me. He is at Martha's. Not football.'

'Ivor is not at football?'

'No. So don't go and get him. And tell Greg or Geraldine the moment they come in. Ivor's fine. He's at Martha's. Tell them that, too. But I'll keep trying.'

Martha thinks Katrina understands. With any luck Martha will be able to persuade Ivor into the car and drive him home before Greg or Geraldine get in.

In the flat she hears abrupt splashings and slurpings and when she goes back into the bathroom he has tipped on to his stomach and, head down, is shooting himself from one end of the bath to the other, like a snorkler or a human submarine. She lifts him out, wraps him in a clean towel from one of her suitcases, and puts him on the sofa in front of the television. It is 10.10 a.m. She asks him if he is hungry and he says he is starving. She asks him what he would like.

Ivor doesn't look up from the Powerpuff Girls. She has to repeat the question several times. Finally, she gets him to answer. He says, 'What have you got?'

'I haven't got anything. But I can get something. What would you like if you could have anything?'

'A Sausage and Egg McMuffin.'

'From McDonald's?'

'Yeah. But hold the egg. And can I have Coke with it?'

'Coke for breakfast?'

'They let you. It's in the price.'

'OK. I'll be five minutes.'

She thinks she should lock the door in case he should take it into his head to wander off again, and she is sorting through the keys when the phone rings. She runs to pick it up, but it's only Tracey, her voice smoke-bound and tired. Martha says she can't really talk, but Tracey, who had left Andrew's flat that morning with bristle-marks on her chin, has a phone number to give her. 'Nick Martin,' she says. 'The love of your life. Ready and waiting in Stockwell.'

Martha writes the number on a piece of newspaper that is sticking out of a crate in the kitchen. She tells Tracey she is glad she had a nice time. 'Far too young for me, darling,' Tracey says before hanging up. 'But fun while it lasted.'

Outside McDonald's is a woman with a tray of poppies. It is Remembrance Sunday. Martha had forgotten. When she gets home, with a poppy in her button hole and the McBreakfast in a small paper bag (it feels so light and insubstantial, she can't imagine it is enough to sustain him), Ivor is still huddled in his towel, staring at the television. She tells him he has to eat in the kitchen but the look he gives her is so abject, she says, 'Oh, OK, just this once.'

She sits next to him as he opens his parcel. When he brings his hands out, the towel falls away from his shoulders and she tucks it around his body. It wraps round several times. His upper arms are so skinny they look like they might snap. The tips of his ears are pink. She feels her heart twist. He devours his hash brown slither in its paper sachet quickly, with small, quick bites. It smells of nothing, or of the air you get in McDonald's – fried grease and paper and air conditioning. When Ivor reaches his muffin, he says, 'Oh-wa. I said no egg.'

Martha peers over, concerned. 'Oh, sorry. I forgot. Can you take it out, or has it dripped over everything?' But it hasn't. It is a symmetrical white floppy disc – no sign of

312

yolk, dripping or otherwise – and it slips out without leaving a trace. She sits back, watching him. She worries about the ketchup on the raw skin below his mouth. Once she dabs it with a paper napkin and he darts his head away as if stung. 'Sorry,' she says.

She waits until the cartoon has ended (it keeps stopping and starting; she thinks it will go on for ever) and then switches off the television.

'OK,' she says, when he has given up complaining. 'What's going on? Why have you run away?'

Ivor takes a long time sucking up some Coke and then he says, 'I dunno.'

'Ivor, you must know. No one runs away without a reason. Is it something at home?'

'No.'

'At school? Is anyone being horrible to you?'

'No.'

Martha tries to remember what troubled her when she was six. 'Are Mum and Dad arguing?' She thinks back to the tension between Geraldine and Greg at the dinner party. 'Is it that that's upsetting you?'

'No. Not really.'

Martha asks him if there are problems with Patrick, if he is ever bullied, if there are any teachers he feels uncomfortable with. She says if there is anything that's worrying him that he feels he can't for whatever reason tell people, to tell her now.

Ivor looks increasingly sulky. He says, 'Can't I watch *Hollyoaks*?' But she says she wants to sort out what is bothering him first, and finally his answer comes out in a rush.

He pushes his cup of Coke away from him. 'I hate football and Dad knows I hate football and he still made me go.'

Martha looks at him in surprise. She wants to laugh with relief. 'But that's what dads are like,' she says. 'You just have to tell him. He probably thinks you want to go. We'll tell him today.'

'But I have told him. It doesn't make any difference . . . Mum doesn't make me go. She lets me stay at home, or go with her to watch Patrick at tae kwon do.'

Martha has picked up the television remote control ready to hand to him. 'At least you've got one parent on your side. That's all that matters.'

'But Mum's not there. It's always Katrina. The other day she made me have her bath water and it was oily and had bits floating in it.'

'She's just at this yoga thing. She'll be back later today.'

Ivor stares at the dark television screen. 'She's not like my mum any more. She looks different, her hair is all funny, and she smells different.'

Martha puts the remote control down. 'Of course she's your mum.' She strokes his hair, because it seems like the sort of thing she should do, and as she does so she feels a pull of love, not really for Ivor, although he is implicated, but more, surprisingly, for Geraldine. 'She's always going to be your mum.'

Ivor doesn't say anything. He seems suddenly very interested in the McDonald's bag on the table.

'The thing is, you can't always expect people to stay the same. That would be boring, wouldn't it? I think her new hair's great, though I haven't told her that.' Martha puts her finger to her mouth and adds conspiratorially, 'I mean, that's the thing about sisters, sometimes you keep that sort of thing to yourself.' Ivor looks at her then. Encouraged, Martha carries on: 'I know she seems busy at the moment with this yoga thing, and you might think you have less of her than before, but you don't, you know. You really don't. Because I know your mum very, very well and I know how much she loves you. And that, even when she isn't doing all the things she does all the time, like cooking your meals and getting your clothes ready for school and making your bed and tidying your toys, she is thinking about you. Even when you're not there, she's thinking about you.' Ivor is still staring at her. His face is blank and pinched, but his mouth is moving very slightly.

He says, 'Not me. Anna and Patrick. Not me.'

Martha thinks how fortunate it is that she is here to answer him. 'She does think about you too, Ivor. She loves you just as much as them. And your dad does. Maybe differently. But just as much. You just feel as if they don't because you're in the middle.' She puts her finger under his chin so she can look at him. 'But it's great being the middle child. You don't have to be anything you don't want to be. You don't have to be "the grown up one" or "the baby one". You can be anything you want. You're the free one. The freest of all.' There is an obstruction in Martha's throat. She swallows to clear it. 'And the thing about families is they are often all mixed up, and fathers and mothers and brothers and sisters can sometimes be awful and bossy and horrible to each other, and not even like each other very much some of the time. No one's family is perfect.' She takes Ivor's hand

315

and squeezes it. 'And, goodness, you're lucky because yours is still quite tidy, with a mum and dad and a brother and a sister. I've got half-sisters and stepbrothers and a stepmother young enough to be my sister. But families can be like that. And you know something, poppet?' – this poppet just slipped out – 'They never go away. They'll always be there. I mean—' Martha breaks off as she realises something momentous and touching. 'You came to me, didn't you? I'm your family, too.'

Ivor doesn't answer.

She says, 'Was it the Harry Potter wand?'

Ivor has been eyeing the television remote, but he flicks her a look. 'I'd've got to Denis and Eliza's,' he says. 'If that conductor hadn't come.'

As it happens, Martha doesn't get to drop Ivor home into the bosom of his family. She doesn't get the chance. Because the bosom of his family comes to pick him up instead.

She has dialled Geraldine and Greg several times again, with no answer, and she and Ivor are watching the service at the Cenotaph on the BBC when a car pulls up outside and she hears the jangle of familiar voices in the street. Throwing open the window, she sees Greg and Geraldine already on the pavement, white-lipped, loose-cheeked with anxiety, and Patrick and Anna clambering out of the back seat. Anna is carrying a pink balloon and it bobs on the end of the string. There are shouts of, 'No. Bradley. Back. Monty. Stay,' but it is too late: the dogs, frantic as everyone else, have bounded out, too.

316

Martha calls down, her voice as calming as she can make it, 'It's OK. He's fine. He's fine.'

Geraldine looks up, her eyes squinted against the drizzle. She is wearing loose drawstring trousers and a pink sweat-shirt – no make-up. She says, 'Thank God.'

A few minutes later the flat is full of damp people and wet animals. Monty, Bradley and the two new children are in and out of doorways, getting tangled in legs. Anna's balloon, which she says was her special one but she's brought it for Ivor, bumps against the ceiling. And Geraldine and Greg sit on either side of Ivor on the sofa, talking in low, steady voices, telling him how much they love him and how he must never, ever, ever do anything like that ever, ever again. Martha stands listening to them in the doorway – she doesn't have a role any more.

'I was out of my mind with worry,' Geraldine says.

Greg says, 'You didn't even know he was missing until he was found.'

Geraldine glares at him. 'That's enough from you. You big bully. If it hadn't been for you—' She stops. 'Anyway, darling, if you don't want to go to football, you don't have to.'

Greg tucks Ivor's head under his arm, as you might do with the ball in a game of rugby, and gives it an affec-tionate squeeze. 'Maybe when you're a bit older, old man,' he says.

Ivor's face has already lost its pinched look, but at this a patch of colour appears in his cheeks. He bashes his squashed head against his father's chest and says, 'Help!' But he is grinning. Greg frees him and runs both hands through his own hair. He says, across the room to Martha, 'Walked

317

from Clapham Junction, did he?' Then, with a small note of admiration in his voice, 'Little tyke.'

But Ivor hasn't heard this. Extracting himself from his mother's arms and trailing his towel like a train, he has careered off to join his siblings who are up to something in the bathroom. There is yelping and splashing in there as if it is the dogs who are having a bath now. (Maybe because it is the dogs who are having a bath now.)

Geraldine gives a great trembling sigh. 'I keep imagining what might have happened.'

Greg says, 'Well it didn't, did it?'

'Yes. But . . . OK,' Geraldine begins forcefully, but she grabs Greg's hand and kisses it impulsively instead. He puts his other arm around her. 'Our kidlets,' she says.

'I know.' Greg shakes his head, as if to stop her saying anything else.

He has taken his arm from Geraldine's shoulder and the two of them are holding each other's hands now – not romantically, but tightly in a fist, half raised like team members. Geraldine is resting her forehead in her other palm, away from him, and Greg bends so that he can see her eyes. He says, 'Come on, old girl. It's OK. Nothing's happened.' And Geraldine nods very slightly.

Geraldine spots Martha watching them. She sighs again while raising her eyes to the ceiling, simultaneously an expression of her own anxiousness and exasperation at her own anxiousness. She says heavily, 'After all that, I could kill a coff.'

Martha smiles. She thinks: they are happy after all. All along she had thought they weren't, but they are.

She says, 'I thought you'd given up?'

Geraldine stands. She runs her fingers across the top of Greg's head, and lightly combs a tweak of hair behind his ear. 'Well, I sneak the odd one in here and there. Got to have some pleasures in life.'

'Let's see what I can do.'

Martha goes into the kitchen, puts on the kettle and rummages around in a box for her coffee plunger and the bone china mugs. She has to get the Le Creuset saucepans out, and the Magimix: it lies scattered across the floor like the pieces of some medieval instrument of torture. Geraldine follows her in. 'Got any milch?' she says.

Martha hasn't (no milk, no Coffee Mate). She asks Geraldine whether it is permissible to combine caffeine with dairy. Geraldine narrows her eyes and goes into the sitting room to send Greg for some. 'Off you go, Gregorian,' Martha hears her say. 'And take the dogs. And your coat. It's a bit cold out. A bit chill on the will.'

When she comes back, she stands in the doorway, surveying the boxes. 'So today's the day,' she says.

'Yep. Looks like.'

Geraldine steps over the Magimix attachments. 'Ivor was the last thing you needed, then. Thanks for being so brilliant.'

Martha is warming her hands on the heating kettle. 'I didn't do anything. I was just here. All I did was be in.'

'You did more than that. You calmed him down, which is quite an achievement. Particularly Ivor. He's such a touchy little chap. Anyway, being in – it's a greatly under-rated virtue.'

Martha laughs. She knows she didn't do much, but she is still aware of a shift somewhere in her sense of herself. She *managed* something. Maybe she isn't as hopeless as she has always believed. And with that thought her friends and family seem to open up to her – to be full of possibilities. There are all those children to get to know. Patrick and Anna. The twins! And it's so obvious she can't believe she hasn't thought of it before: she could look after Kit one Sunday night, if they'll let her, and send Karen and Keith out to the cinema on their own. She spoons coffee into the cafetière; dark, heaped grains. 'Sorry about your yoga,' she says.

Geraldine leans against the counter, her back to the window. Her new haircut is beginning to grow out. It is curling over her eyes, frizzing at the back. 'God. It was awful. There I was, in a position called the Downward Facing Dog, when my mobile went off. Strictly forbidden to bring mobiles in. There was the room, silent but for the occasional squeak of foot on mat, the odd low-level om, and suddenly it's ringing with a tinkling rendition of "The Ride of the Valkyries". You should have seen the glares. I've burnt my boats now. I can't imagine my yogi will have me back. He doesn't think much of worldly concerns being brought into his inner sanctum, let alone Wagner.'

'And his inner sanctum is . . .?'

'A scout hut in Collier's Wood. The end of the Northern Line. Yeah, yeah, I've heard all the jokes from Greg. Leaving the outside world behind; end of the line, etcetera. Actually, it was quite cold in there and I've caught a verruca. And anyway, I should have been at Mass. Or with the children.

I've let everything slip. I'm a terrible Catholic and a terrible mother. I've let things deteriorate with Eliza. All I've been thinking about is myself – my yoga, my diet, my new clothes. I haven't been thinking about the children at all. It's as if once I started – getting Katrina to pick them up from school; not being there at teatime; leaving them for Greg to sort out at weekends – I couldn't stop. It seems to be all or nothing. It was such a relief not to have to worry about them at all, to know that someone else was in charge of all that. It seemed so easy once I'd started. I mean, this thing with Ivor, I've just let them slip away from me.'

The kettle has boiled. Martha pours steaming water over the coffee grains, watching them dance and sift. 'I'm sure that's not true.'

'No. It is. I lost touch with him, with all of them.'

Martha carries the cafetière and the cups over to the table and sits down. The plunger is still too stiff to push. She says, 'It could be worse. This magician I know, his wife has just buggered off. The children haven't seen her for months. I don't know how someone could do that.'

'You start leaving them by degrees.'

Martha looks up. Geraldine is still leaning against the counter. She hasn't moved. But her lips are tight and her eyes are bright.

Martha says awkwardly, 'Well, I'm sure you're being too hard on yourself. I'm sure you're allowed some things, some time, that's just for you. Look at Eliza, she's never there at all in the week. No one says she's a bad mother. And she isn't a bad mother. It's just a different way of doing things. Anyway,

Ger. It could have been worse. It was only a weekend yoga retreat in Collier's Wood.'

Geraldine doesn't smile. One of the laces of her trainers is undone, and with the other foot she is rubbing it back and forth along the floor so that a section of it is flattened, not white any more but grey. 'Then why did he run away?'

'Isn't that just the sort of thing kids do?'

'Not really, Martha.'

Martha slowly, carefully, pushes the plunger into the coffee. This time it moves down smoothly. She says, 'Could it be something as simple as the hair? He seemed a bit obsessed that you were different.'

'Did he?' Geraldine scrapes back a chair and sits down next to her. 'Kids hate change. There's nothing worse for them. They like routine and . . . things to carry on exactly as they were yesterday and the day before.'

There is a silence. It is suspiciously quiet in the bathroom. Martha lowers her brow and rolls her eyes from side to side in an exaggerated demonstration of listening. Geraldine sighs and says, 'A camp. They'll be making a camp. They're obsessed with camps.'

Martha pours the coffee into the cups and passes one to her sister. 'Well you have to show them that nothing ever stays the same. Show them that change is a good thing. How boring life would be if we always knew where we were. If we were always looking back . . .'

'Here you go, girls. Milko.' Greg crashes into the kitchen with a bottle of milk and an armful of papers. The dogs, unleashed, snuffle excitedly towards the bathroom. Greg has bought them all poppies. He pins one on to his wife's sweatshirt, leaves Martha's on the table when he realises she already has one, and then gestures to the sitting room with his copy of *The Observer*. 'We'd better be shoving off soon, but I'll leave you two girls for a minute, shall I?'

Martha says, 'We're putting the world to rights.'

Greg says, mock conspiratorially as he bumbles out, 'Get her to start playing the cello again, won't you?'

Geraldine gets out a tissue and blows her nose. Then she says, 'He's right. That's what I should be doing with my extra time. Not preening.'

'She's letting her talent go to waste,' shouts Greg from the sofa. 'Nothing sexier than a woman with a large instrument between her legs.'

'Greg.' Geraldine frowns, but looks pleased. Martha laughs.

For a while after this, Geraldine and Martha chat companionably about where Geraldine might take her cello-playing now the children are at school: local orchestras, teaching, guest appearances. And then they start talking about Martha and David's plans. Martha doesn't mention the job in Garden Statuary, but she refers to possible changes in the balance of her life. She says, 'If it works, of course. I mean, I am getting on. I am thirty-eight.' Geraldine says, 'Can you give yourself maternity leave? I don't suppose you can.' Her tone is bright and breezy, but it strikes Martha that she had expected more from her sister, that Martha had brought the subject up to make her happy, that Geraldine, emotional as she is, should be *moved* at the thought of Martha and David conceiving. She says, to nudge her along, 'You would lend me all your old baby stuff, wouldn't you?' But Geraldine only gives a small smile and says something about it being a bit tatty.

Martha says, 'Don't you think we'll make good parents?'

Geraldine says, 'Of course I do, Matt. You'll make lovely parents.'

But then there is a silence. Geraldine pushes her chair back and looks out of the window. She says, 'It seems to be lightening up.' Martha stares at the piece of newspaper with Nick Martin's telephone number on. And then Geraldine turns back, and says, 'Are you sure you're doing the right thing?'

'What?' For a moment, Martha is confused.

'You moving in with David. Is it what you really, really want?'

'What do you mean?' Martha takes a sip of her coffee. There is a bitter taste on the tip of her tongue. 'It'll be nice.'

'Exactly. Nice? I may be speaking out of turn, but it's as if you're both pretending, playing a part with each other. I feel terribly guilty because I pushed you together, but when you came to supper you seemed so stiff. And seeing you now, well I just would expect you to seem more excited. It's as if you're trying to please me, not yourself. And what's happened to the shop? Your wonderful shop? It's so empty.'

'My wonderful shop . . . I thought you liked David.'

'I do. I really do. He's the sort of man I go for. You know, in many ways, he's just like Greg. They are both organised and tidy and . . . everything I'm not. It's why I love David. It's why Greg and I rub along so well. I know I exasperate him and he drives me mad . . .'

'And that's a good thing?'

324

'If you let each other be different, you can see each other's virtues and vices without them being muddled up with your own. You don't get fire without friction; you don't get passion. What do I mean? What do I know? If you're happy, Matts, then I am too. But, maybe, I was just worried that what we were just saying applies to you, too. About always looking to the past, sticking with the familiar and—'

'I thought you wanted me to get back with David?'

'I do, but . . .'

'What are you saying?'

'Don't do anything you don't want to do.'

Martha puts her cup down on the table. Coffee jerks over the rim. She stares at the drops, but she can't tell if it's a drip or a flood, if it's going to spread and stain and engulf the tablecloth, or whether it's nothing. She knows she is sitting on a chair, but she feels disembodied for an instant: she can't feel her feet; the air is full of particles of noise. There are Magimix blades all over the floor. Her voice comes high and twisted. 'I don't know what I want.'

Geraldine gets a cloth and mops at the spillage. She doesn't look at Martha. 'You think too much. You don't do anything. You don't show anything. You never have. You overanalyse things. Like your house, everything dinky-do and in place and don't touch this and don't sit on that. I can't imagine you having a baby because babies are messy, Martha, they aren't neat and tidy and predictable. You are so uptight and . . . well, snobbish. You never, you never have, just done what you feel.'

When Geraldine uses 'Martha' as punctuation, her tone reasonable, judgemental, superior, Martha feels a cold heat, like an ice burn, start at her toes and work its way up. It's a relief. It gives her something to concentrate on. 'It's always got to be personal with you, hasn't it?' she says. 'If you don't cry at the drop of a hat, then you're not up to Geraldine's standards. '

'That's not what I'm saying.'

'Well what are you saying?'

'I just mean that if it doesn't feel right, don't do it. It doesn't matter how it looks. You don't have to hold it up to the light and inspect it. It doesn't have to look right. It just has to *feel* right.'

A minute ago, Martha felt warm and affectionately protective towards her sister. Now she wants to destroy her. She says, 'I'm going to vote for the developers. If it comes down to it and there's a vote I think "Mummy's house", "the parental home", should go to the highest bidder. Bugger sentiment.'

Geraldine puts the cloth back in the sink. 'I agree,' she says.

'What?'

'I agree. There's a place for sentiment, which is in relationships. And there are other aspects of life where it has no place at all: houses, property, objects.'

'So what about "The Boy"?' Martha throws this out like a challenge.

'I'm giving it to Eliza.'

'Really? When did you decide this?'

'Just now.' Geraldine sits down at the table. 'Today. It makes me realise how silly I've been, falling out with Eliza over an object. I know our mother's dead. She's not in the house. Or in "The Boy" . . .'

'No. I'll tell you where our mother is. She's sitting oppo-site me now.' Martha is still furious, but even as she says this she feels a laugh growing inside her.

Geraldine blinks slowly. 'It's just bricks and mortar. She is not in the things she loved. They are just things. And things, like clothes and make-up, aren't what matter. They're dis-tractions.'

'Yes. But things . . .'

The noise in the flat, the timpani of children and dogs against the percussion of running water and the rattling drone of the pipes, has been getting louder through this argument. The sisters have had to shout to hear themselves. But as Martha flails now, her ear hooks on Ivor's voice, the loudest of all, a Tarzan cry above his siblings. It's a voice on the move, and in the drama in the bathroom the others hush as Ivor attempts whatever he's about to attempt. He yodels with all the daring, unbridled enthusiasm of a naked six-year-old. And then there is a resounding rip. A thump, a clattering crash, and then a splinteringly loud, gloriously thrilling, monumental crash. A split second of shocked silence follows. Then one of the dogs starts barking and Patrick says, 'Sssh. Sssh.' Ivor yells, 'Hide. Someone's coming.' Greg says, 'Fuck.' But in the kitchen, Martha and Geraldine haven't moved. They are too busy laughing.

In the ensuing kerfuffle Martha misses the arrival of David. Someone has switched off the television, hurled *The Puccini Experience* to one side, and put on *The A–Z of British TV*

Themes. The dogs are tied to chair legs, but keep tangling themselves up and yapping, and the kids are in the bedroom, playing 'a nice quiet shopping game' ('Fat chance,' says Greg) involving Martha's bed, a box of her price tags and the contents of her suitcases. Martha and Geraldine 'deal with the worst' in the bathroom. The camp – an elaborate construction centring on the bathmat, the shower curtain and several towels – has imploded in the bath. The loo seat is askew and the bottle of scented bath oil is on its side in the sink, leaking a blue trail across the porcelain. And all over the floor are silvery green fragments of Venetian glass. The felted back is intact and there are gashes of etched mirror still affixed to it, like old teeth, but the rest has shattered into glinting splinters. Martha wonders for a fleeting moment whether to preserve the separate pieces, to collect them together carefully, but it's a headachey, scratchy thought, and in the end, when she sweeps the whole lot up – so carelessly she cuts her finger on a tiny shard (the drop of blood tastes warm and salty like sweat) – she feels nothing but relief.

She is on her way to the kitchen with a loaded dustpan when she comes across David looking shell-shocked in the sitting room.

'I've just been hearing about Ivor's escapade,' he says loudly over the theme tune to *The Avengers*. He is wearing pale grey chinos and a white shirt with parallel ironing lines on each side of his chest. 'I could have been here earlier if you'd rung.' His hand is over one of the dogs' muzzles – trying to stop him from burrowing in his crotch.

'Bradley!' Greg says, yanking on a lead. 'Stop rogering David!'

'Oh, how sweet of you,' Martha says. It occurs to her for the first time that it had not even crossed her mind to ring him. 'Isn't it awful. But at least he's all right. And hasn't he been brave?'

When Martha bends down to kiss him, David whispers in her ear, 'I've got a little welcome lunch, a rack of lamb, waiting for us at home.'

She says, 'I don't think we can get away just yet.'

But Greg has heard this and, once Ivor's clothes have been retrieved, starts rounding up his troops. Patrick and Ivor jostle on the stairs and Anna is whining because, if Ivor has had a McDonald's Breakfast, she wants a Happy Meal, and Greg shouts, 'Order, you lot,' so the events of the morning appear already to have been swept up. Geraldine comes down behind them, with a handful of crumpled newspaper and glass. She says, 'Sorry about the mess.'

Martha takes the rubbish from her and says it doesn't matter, and at the door of the shop, Geraldine hugs her and says, 'Thanks M. For "being in",' and Martha says it was nothing, and Geraldine says, 'I just want you to be happy; do whatever you think is right,' and unexpectedly, Martha feels something prick behind her eyes. She squeezes Ivor's shoulder before he gets in the car and then stands back to wave them off. It is her role in life to wave off families from her step. Geraldine has let Patrick sit in the front and has got into the back herself, and wraps her arms around Anna and Ivor on each side of her. But she bends her head so she can see her sister. The two of them look at each other as Greg turns round in the road, and Martha makes a face which isn't quite a smile, though it is closer to that than anything.

Martha puts the paper-wrapped glass in the bin and, alone in the shop, she takes a moment to sweep up some of the moulted hops. She straightens a pair of *toile de jouy* cushions on a mid-nineteenth-century neo-rococo chaise longue. There is a footstool beside it, which she had left with its original needlepoint seat. It strikes her that it would be more attractive with some bright, modern Ian Mankin checks. It hadn't occurred to her until now. And along the tapered treads of the fruit-picking ladder, which she had always considered so delicately decorative, she could hang linen tea-towels, give it a *use*. And as for that old rocking horse, she must get it working properly. What's the point of a rocking horse that won't rock? She will get Jason on the case, maybe even respray it (bugger authenticity), and give it to April, for the baby. Is this furniture really so vulnerable? Isn't it the fear of something breaking rather than the breakage itself that ties you? Would a child be so much in the way? Looking around her now, at this room full of *stuff*, it all seems so adaptable, so robust.

David is still sitting back on the sofa, with one leg crossed up high on his thigh, when she gets upstairs. He makes a noise like a horse blowing through its lips as he sees her standing in the door. 'Chaos!' he says. 'Have you seen what they've done in your bedroom? And the bathroom! I don't believe it. Shattered. Bloody chaos.'

Martha still doesn't move. 'You match my sofa,' she says.

'You're going to have to pack all over again, you poor love.'

'Different fabric, obviously. Though haven't you got some summery linen ones that match exactly? A suit?'

'Er . . .?' David laughs. There are bristles on his cheek – his only-on-a-Sunday beard.

'It doesn't matter.'

Martha goes into the bedroom, which is in an extraordinary mess. The dogs have chewed the pashmina throw; the children have been in the suitcases; the floor is a sea of clothes and sheets and bits of paper. She picks something up. It's one of the labels they used for their game. 'A delightful brass bed with unusual barley twist posts' it reads. David calls, 'Are you talking about my Paul Smith?'

'Maybe,' she says.

Under the pashmina she finds a pair of wet orange-red underpants with a picture of a racing car on the front.

'Look,' she says, taking them into the sitting room. 'Ivor forgot his knickers.' She puts them on her head and does a stupid dance. She hums 'The Ride of the Valkyries'. She smiles at David, camouflaged against her Howard sofa. David watches her guardedly.

'Come on,' he says. 'Let's get you sorted, shall we?' He makes as if to stand up, but frowns and leans down. Under his foot is a white rubber object which he picks up by one corner and holds out. 'Oh God,' he says mournfully, sitting back down. 'Now what's this?'

Martha takes the underpants off her head and lays them across one of her scallop-edged cushions. She considers them, with her head on one side (the colour goes well, actually). Then she sits down next to David, takes the object from him and says, 'It's the egg from a McMuffin.'

'Bloody hell.'

They sit side by side in silence for a moment. The flat

331

seems very quiet now everyone has gone. She says, 'What a morning.'

'God. I know. And I wasn't even here.'

'I'm so sorry about your mirror.'

'It's not my mirror. It's yours. I'll find you another one.'

'You are very sweet. But please don't.' His eyes meet hers. There is a blackhead in an odd place just below the smile lines under his eyes. 'It was a beautiful mirror, but I won't miss it. Sometimes I think you buy me things, you load me up with possessions, to possess me, to make me something I'm not.'

'Don't be ridiculous.' David cups her face and kisses her – a warm, dry kiss on the mouth. He darts the egg, still in her hand, an anxious look. He says, 'I buy things for both of us. We're a couple. We're an item.'

Martha says, 'An item. "A delightful twenty-first-century couple, French".'

David laughs. He holds his hands flat between his knees and twitches his legs. 'Shall we get going?'

He starts to lever himself up. Martha doesn't move. She says, 'You make me feel vindicated. Like a proper grown up person. David, I do love you. When I'm with you, I feel like a delightful couple. We match. We blend, like your trousers on my sofa. And I know that our life together will be just fine.'

David says, 'Good.'

'But . . .'

'What?'

'I'm not going to give up the shop. I love it. I'm good at it. It's something I've built up myself. I know you think it's naff and tacky and . . .'

332

'Martha, that's OK. I can drop you here in the mornings, you can get a Tube pass, like normal people. You can drive. We could find you a site nearer home.'

'And April . . .'

'Whatever,' David says, impatient now, getting up. He marches, a man of action, into the bedroom where he starts repacking suitcases. Martha still has the egg in her hand. She gets up, walks into the kitchen and, levering the bin open with her foot, drops it in. She realises after she has done it that there's no bin bag there; that the egg has fallen to the bottom and bounced on the metal. She makes to pick it up, but then stands there not moving.

David follows her in. 'What's going on?' he says.

She doesn't turn around.

'Shall we get this place re-sorted and go?'

She doesn't answer. She stares at the wall behind the bin where she notices for the first time some misaimed teabags have left brown smears.

'Are you coming with me or not?'

'Oh David,' she says, still not turning round.

'Martha, history is not going to repeat itself. You are not going to do this to me again.'

'David, I'm sorry,' she says.

There is a silence. She hears the street cleaner going past downstairs. Finally she says, 'We are too similar, David. I thought that was a good thing, actually I thought it was essential, but it isn't. You bring out the side of me that is too tidy. As you told my dad, you want to put my life "in order". But I've begun to think a bit of mess, a bit of disorder, the occasional McMuffin wrapper, you know, the odd splash of

333

orange in an interior, is a good thing. You are a terribly nice person. I just think you can't always stick with what you know, that sometimes you – I – have to take a punt on the unknown.' He is so quiet she thinks he must be just staring at her in horror. She can hear a slight squeaking noise, like a finger on paintwork, and for a moment she imagines him rubbing at a mark on the wall, but when she turns round it is Anna's balloon that is making the sound, still bumping quietly against the ceiling, and she sees that the door is open and David has gone.

The piece of newspaper with Nick Martin's phone number on it is sticking out of one of the boxes in the kitchen. Martha has tidying up and unpacking to do, April's accommodation to sort out, other phone calls to make, but her eyes keep finding their way back to it. She takes the paper out and stares at it. The numbers dance like hieroglyphics. Carefully, she begins to tear around the number, but the paper jags so she folds it instead.

She isn't going to ring him. She has known that all along. She finds when she thinks about him, when she tries to summon him up, nothing comes. All the memories that had seemed so perfect, so perfectly preserved, elude her. The ghosts have gone. It strikes her that memory is actually the biggest spin of all. When she took that taxi ride through Hyde Park and she felt as if the past had been 'unlocked', when she wondered at the selection of memories that bombarded her and concluded it was something to do with the past moment itself – some special quality in it which put her outside herself – she couldn't have been more wrong. It had nothing to do with the nature of the remembered experience and all to do with the state of mind she was in when she remembered it. She picks up the spare poppy on the table and twirls it between her fingers. And what a waste of memory, she thinks, to spend it on yourself.

The big black garbage sack still sits, heavy and unwieldy, in the middle of the floor. She pokes the piece of newspaper into the top of it. And then she decides. There is nothing in here she needs. Only false corners and dead-ends. You carry people around with you in your character; all the people you have been close to have made you a little bit of what you are. That is how the past is kept alive, not through reunions or self-indulgent reveries or catch-up drinks in lonely bars in Victoria. She bends, screwing the plastic into a handle, ready to heave it over her shoulder, to lug it down, banging against her knees, to the car and to the dump. But when she picks it up, it comes off the ground easily and she realises that it is much lighter than she was expecting, that actually it is no weight at all.

The Nightingale Triangle shines as Martha walks towards it later that afternoon. The thick dark clouds have cleared, sucked up into billowing factory-white cumulus, and there are chinks of cold blue sky reflected in the windows of some of the houses. Droplets of water gleam on car roofs, and every other paving stone – the hard pink squares among the porous grey slabs – glistens. Martha found one of April's stripy scarves on the back of a Victorian chair and she grabbed it as she left, wrapping it around her neck like someone spinning sugar, and now she keeps catching fragments of herself in car windows and wing-mirrors, not braced, but open, her pale, white face peering out of a knitted rainbow.

She turns into Fred's road. Every house looks different to her today. The elaborate cheeseplant standing watch at the window of number 17; the lemony plaster lions poking their heads above the parapet at number 19; the windchimes at number 21; the Chinese lantern at 23; the doors, moss-green and canary-yellow and peach; doorknockers shaped like hands or urns; the curtains, velvet and floral and polka-dotted, ruched or folded or slatted; and the snatch of alcove she can just see beyond, filled with photographs or books or mirrors or paintings. And rather than sad, it seems vital to her suddenly that not all the houses should have railings; how varied the run of hedge and picket fence and red-brick wall. How dull if they all looked the same.

And here she is at number 35. She hasn't felt nervous until now. The notion to come hadn't arrived like a bolt of lightning. It had crept up on her all afternoon until it just seemed like the thing to do. But now, when she stops walking, the excitement tightens. The bin-lids are off again and the weeds in the front are still strangling the railings. Someone – Hazel, of course – has left her Barbie bike out front, thrown undignified on its side, and it is smattered with magnifying drops of water. In the upstairs windows, Martha can see small squares and circles randomly dotted at a certain level, which she guesses are Stan's stickers. She starts walking towards the mauve front door. But at the last minute she hesitates, and bends to pick up the bike. And as she straightens, she looks in at the window. Perhaps she had always intended to do this. Perhaps she hopes to catch Fred for an instant, his face unguarded, before he sees her.

And she does catch him. She is fortunate because he might have been in the kitchen, or the garden, or upstairs in the bathroom. She sees him on this end of the sofa, his long legs drawn up sideways as if there was nowhere else to put them, his big black glasses perched on the end of his nose, with Kitten curled up like a fossil on his knee. And on the other side of him is Hazel – in some sort of silk garment, a sari? – and beyond her, Stan. She can only just see Stan's head because taking up the floor in front of all three of them, gesticulating, bangles glinting on her arms, is a woman. And it takes a second for Martha to register this, but it's the woman from the photograph on the fridge, with the gums and the open smile and the shoulder-length blonde hair (though it's longer now, halfway down her arms in fact, and darker on the top). Hazel and Stan's mother, Fred's wife. Back? Back for good? Or back to finish it? Martha looks at Fred again. She has an impression, like a photographic negative, of the expression on his face a second ago, guarded and doubtful, not open and longing as when he gazes at her, and she looks back at him to be sure, but he has bent to stroke the cat now and she can't see his face.

Martha crosses to the doorstep and stays there a moment, her heart thudding. Her instinct is to turn and run, to leave again. But, standing there, she can see through the paler sections of stained glass to the jumble of coats and bags, to Stan's Fireman Sam bike, to the piles of washing in the hall. Through her green triangle, she can make out the shape of Fred's magic box at the bottom of the stairs. Then the sun comes out behind her and the panel flattens. In the green pane now, all she can see is the reflection of the house opposite and she has to put her face right up close to the glass to see behind it into the dark hall.

having it
AND
eating it

SABINE DURRANT

Claire Masterson was the girl at school that Maggie Owen always wanted to be. Confident, good-looking, she was the first to know the facts of life, the first to Sun-In her hair, the first, easily the first, to go all the way. And when Maggie bumps into her twenty years later, it is as if nothing has changed: Claire's life is one of career moves to New York and great sex with married men; Maggie's is one of bringing up her children and never seeing her partner Jake, whose ever-demanding job has become his 'other woman'.

Or has it? Jake is consistently working late, working weekends, taking working trips abroad . . . and when Claire talks a little *too* knowledgeably about his movements, Maggie starts thinking the unthinkable. Her friends think she should confront them, but Maggie's got a better idea: she's going to have her cake and eat it too.

Having It and Eating It is a comic, acutely intelligent novel about motherhood, infidelity, losing yourself and having it all.